Cold Dawn

Steve K. Peacock

ONE

The first dawn in a decade, and she had the perfect view. Nestled at the top of the mast, she had been watching the thick, insistent darkness start to grudgingly relent, turning a deep purple and now into a pleasant navy blue.

It wouldn't be long now, another few minutes and she'd see colour again. Not much, admittedly, but when you live on an ice planet you can't really be picky, can you? Ice is ice is ice, but a bit of blue and yellow in the sky would go a long way towards making a difference.

She felt the ropes shift underneath her and looked down into the face of Thorsten Wolfe, the ship's navigator. He was wearing two pairs of goggles, one over his eyes and the other holding back his hair like a headband.

'You could have done some work before you climbed all the way up here, Wendy,' he said, positioning himself next to her. 'It's not as if you can miss the sunrise.'

'Lighten up, Thor,' she said and giggled. 'See, I made a joke.'

'You can't tell under all these goggles, but I'm doing my serious face at you.'

Wendy rolled her eyes. 'Oh come on, just this once. The beacons can wait another ten minutes, right? I've already primed them; Lucille can spike them without me there if it's completely necessary.'

'How old were you at dusk, kiddo?'

She frowned. 'Ten or something? I don't do birthdays.'

'No wonder you're so excited then.'

'I'm perfectly composed and everything, Thor. Don't go playing the old man with me, just because your job will be obsolete when people can see where they are actually going again.'

Thorsten slammed a hand over his heart and reeled back, nearly falling from his perch. 'Oh, woe is me! A blade in my heart! Forsooth, my life is done. Brat.'

'Fogey.'

'Yes, well, this old man of *thirty-five* came up here with a reason beyond nagging you, I'll have you know.' He took off one of the pairs of goggles and handed them to her. 'Unless you want your eyes to burn out of your head.'

'What, really?' She said, snatching them out of his hand. 'That wasn't in any of the records!'

He smiled, and it made him look pleasant. As pleasant as a man made of sinew and hair could look at any rate. 'I'm an old man, remember. This isn't my first dawn, brat.'

She blew the air out of her nose as a gesture of something, she didn't know what, and put the goggles on. Even in the dark, they had told her, it was still possible to get snow-blind. The ships all had huge lights attached, and the ice was treacherous enough to bounce them right back into your face if you weren't careful, but she had hoped that she could see the sun crest those mountains just once with the naked eye.

She felt Thorsten settle in beside her, silent and reverent. For all his bluster, he was as excited as she was. The rest of the crew were older and this wasn't a true event to them, though the sound from the razors that carried the ship across the ice seemed somewhat muted.

Maybe it was the altitude – she rarely had cause to climb up this high while the ship was in motion – or perhaps the old sods had a sense of occasion after all.

The navy blue was starting to bleed away now, a small arc of a lighter hue was expanding quite rapidly, pushing it away. The goggles dimmed it a little, but she was surprised at how much they still let through, especially once the redness started to bloom through the blue.

Beautiful.

Thorsten put his arm around her, softly but insistently pulling her close for a hug. She let him, folding herself up against his chest and using it to block out what little noise of the razors made it up to her.

As the barest sliver of the sun crept over the mountain of ice in front of them, she couldn't help but smile. It seemed so foolish to be excited about something that seemed so effortless, and yet she didn't care. Ten years of light, ten years of darkness, that was the way of things. Why not make an event of it?

The pair of them sat in silence until the sun pulled itself free of the distant peak, and then in unison they flinched as their radios squawked.

'Right, youth, you've had your little dream date. Back to work,' a guttural voice growled over the feedback.

Thorsten keyed his radio. 'Aye aye, boss.'

'Sir,' Wendy replied.

They climbed down quickly and were met on the deck by a tall man in a heavy coat and heavier boots. Once Wendy would have described him as having a shock of black hair, but as it had started to grey it had graduated to a fright, giving him the appearance of being the only man that would delight in finally going bald one day.

'I hate to impose upon you two, especially you young Milton,' he said, graciously tipping his head towards Wendy. 'However, considering how much I'm paying you I would appreciate you do a little work today, if possible.'

'I already prepared the beacons, sir,' Wendy said. 'I put

a little sign on them and everything, step by step instructions. Lucille should have no problems –'

'Humour me, Milton,' he said. 'The last time we let Lucille spike one on her own she collapsed half of the Lawrence-Kadan line. I'd prefer to avoid another bollocking, if we can. Besides, I need a word with young Wolfe here, and can't have you just sitting about making the forecastle look untidy.'

'Aye sir.'

He nodded towards the back of the deck, to a door haphazardly clanking against the jamb in time with the bob of the ship. As if she needed directions to her own workshop.

In truth, it was Lucille's workshop. She was the ranking engineer, but not through choice. The poor woman had been subject to a battlefield promotion, or so Wendy had been told at length, after her predecessor had thrown himself into the razors one night and Lucille had been the only one willing to unjam them.

At the moment Wendy entered, Lucille was angrily hammering on a rack of beacons.

'I hate these things,' she muttered to herself, twirling a large wrench in one hand. 'They're overly complicated and fiddly. It's like they are designed to break.'

Wendy politely pushed the other woman aside and surveyed the various screens and readouts. 'They weren't designed for rational minds, Lu. Some terrible nerd in a lab somewhere didn't realise that the people who actually have to install this stuff might not know wiggly equations and stuff.'

'And yet you do.'

'It's my job,' she said, tapping her temple in an odd sort of salute.

To be fair to Lucille, the beacons were top-tier technology. From her understanding, it had taken fifty years to build the very first one, and another ten to work out a way of replicating the things in the numbers they needed. Sure, at their core they were just a sort of spruced-up Wi-Fi relay, but they had to survive in the ice for a long time without maintenance.

It wasn't really a surprise that the user experience hadn't been foremost in the mind of the designers.

Wendy gave the racks a once over while Lucille watched, just to be safe. Everything appeared to be in order. She turned to her left, towards the large wrought iron contraption that had been bolted into the only patch of floor into which it would fit.

'Did you get around to calibrating this, Lu?' she said.

Lucille grunted. 'Nah. I tried to follow the instructions you left, but the screen kept flashing at me and then something in the depths of the thing went crunch. Figured I'd leave it for your giant brain.'

'Oh, they do that. Apparently. You need to press *this* button here to reset the torsion spring and then –'

'Wendy, I really don't care. I can just about manage the turbines, and that's only because they have two states – going around and not going around. This is all your business. I'll just stand here quietly until you need me to plug in the payload.'

'As you wish.'

Her radio squealed again, the captain's voice punching through. 'We'll be at the site in five minutes. I'd like to be moving on in six. Three beacons to spike today, children. Bonus pay out if we get to four.'

Easy. The hardest part of the whole procedure was calibrating the thumper – the machine that would fire the beacons into the ground and, hopefully, several feet below the surface – so that the device would get maximum protection and signal strength. Pretty much everything else, except turning the beacons on in the first place, was fool proof.

She had it down to a fine art. The thumper looked complicated, though in a much more rugged and old-fashioned way to its sleek ammunition. It was a big, chunky, imposing device that made you work for its co-operation: twisting knobs and pulling levers and spooling *things*. The very first calibration could take up to twenty minutes while you unlearned that most consumer of fears, the belief that treating it too harshly might break it.

But the thumper was a work horse. A big, industrial goliath. If anything was going to break from your harsh treatment of the thing, it was going to make sure it was you. As a result, Wendy could have it calibrated in about thirty seconds if she rushed, or two minutes at normal pace.

A few moments after the last ratchet clicked into place, the razors whirred to a halt. The sound rang through the air for a second or two afterwards, tainting the silence that replaced it. As a general hum, the razors sounded fine, but the shut down and start up gave them a macabre edge.

'Okay, Lu, load the top one if you wouldn't mind.'

The woman nodded and gripped the beacon, sliding it free of its rack. Thick, ropey muscles bulged under the surface of her exposed arms as she tried to find her balance, though there was little exertion on her face. Once her balance was secure, she deftly moved the device around and loaded it into the thumper like a chrome torpedo.

'They're awkward buggers to shift, Wendy,' she said.

'I know. Don't forget to check the straps on the others.'

'They've never worked themselves loose yet, but I'll check just for you.'

Wendy keyed her radio. 'Ready on your order, sir.'

'Just checking the location, Milton,' came the reply. 'Can't be too careful.'

She risked a glance at Lucille. The woman hid her sheepishness well, but her hands had found the wrench again and her knuckles were white from the grip.

A green light blinked into life behind a pile of spare parts somewhere on the far side of the room.

'Sir?'

'You have a go, Milton. Spike the thing.'

Wendy punched the button as hard as she could. The beauty of the thumper was that it was more mechanic that electronic, but it also meant that the various moving parts needed a bit of force to get going.

But once they were.

There are some noises the human brain can adapt to from prolonged exposure, but not this. The sound of the beacon being driven into the ice by the enormous piston was so severe that it triggered the survival instinct. That wasn't a machine, your brain would say, it was some ancient and ferocious beast.

Although, on the plus side, it was so loud that it invariably drowned out Wendy's startled yelp. That was something.

Ordinarily, that was the end of it. A loud bang, a small whooshing sound, and then a few moments of her eardrums knitting back together after such a terrible kicking. That there was a second loud bang was unusual.

That it heralded a ground quake was even more so.

There wasn't time to speak, only to grab onto something. Wendy wrapped her arms around the chunkiest parts of the thumper, and saw Lucille almost tie herself into the beacon racks as the ship bucked violently for a moment. Tools rattled against their hooks on the walls, a few breaking free but, largely, the ship knew what to do. It was built well all those years ago, and reasonably well kept. They just needed to ride it out.

A second, smaller quake dragged the ship in another direction, catching both the women unprepared. Wendy first, they slammed into the outer wall, grabbing for anything that could save them from a return trip any second.

There was chatter on the radio, but Wendy couldn't make it out. Except for the swearing. That was universal, and no amount of feedback or static was going to conceal that. It died away as the quakes did, and once the ship settled the radio grew silent too.

Wendy and Lucille pulled themselves to their feet slowly, making sure they hadn't broken something important. They looked up as the captain cautiously stepped through the door.

'A word, ladies.'

Lucille was too busy holding her neck to properly lock gaze with him. 'This isn't our fault, Josh. Your wunderkind did everything the way she always does it.'

'Oh, is that so? Is that why *half the damn ship is encased in ice*? Is it?' he said and slammed a fist into the door frame. 'Ow.'

'The beacon must have hit something, a sediment deposit or something,' Wendy said. 'Maybe the ice wasn't as thick as we thought?'

'Aliens,' said Thorsten as his face peered around the door from outside. 'It's *aliens*.'

The captain shoved him back out of view. 'Grow up. It's not aliens, it has never been aliens, and it will *never be* aliens. This is laziness or incompetence or something of that ilk, should never have trusted this job to –'

Lucille punched him before he could finish the sentence, a jaw-cracking uppercut that drove his teeth into his tongue. He staggered for a moment before righting himself, his eyes burning and twitching with wrath.

'There is no way you could have ended that sentence which wouldn't warrant that smack, Josh,' she said, casually slipping into something Wendy would have dubbed a boxer's stance.

The captain pursed his lips, moving his tongue around behind them. Then, with a very noticeable force of will, he pried his frown apart and the rage left his gaze.

'A... fair point,' he said. 'Let's all just take a breath, okay? I can still give you a bollocking when we've calmed down.'

Lucille dropped out of her stance and turned her back

on him, taking up a position over by the thumper. He waited until she wasn't looking before he started massaging his jaw.

'I think we should revisit the alien hypothesis,' came Thorsten's voice.

'We never visited it to begin with, Wolfe.'

'You might want to rethink that, boss.'

The captain rolled his eyes so violently that the momentum threw his head back. He turned and stormed out onto the deck. 'For the last time –'

He stopped mid-sentence, interrupting himself and going completely silent. Then his hand snaked through the door and made a gesture for Wendy and Lucille to follow him.

As she stepped out into the sunlight, the first thing Wendy saw was the damage to the ship. It wasn't as bad as it should have been, she thought, though the fact that one of the razors had punched its way halfway through the deck was somewhat sobering. The masts were cracked, one seemingly held in place entirely by the rigging alone, but for the most part the damage was superficial or to minor bits of equipment.

It took her a moment to look beyond the ship.

There was something hanging in the air, like a fine mist or fog, shimmering away just off the port side. It made the sunlight dance, but aside from looking utterly enchanting it didn't seem to be really doing anything. Thorsten, Lucille and the captain were staring at it in wonder, however.

She joined them at the side of the deck, following the mist down to the ice below. The ice was further up the hull than it should have been by a large margin, the ship had clearly dropped into a ditch of some kind when the beacon had shattered the surface layer, but the cracks didn't extend far from where they were currently lodged. It looked more like the ground had swallowed them than been blasted loose by the spiking.

Something was twinkling down there, though. Was it

glass? An emitter, maybe? That might explain the beautiful dancing fog. She would have to go down there and take a look. Flicking the switch on her belt, she hooked her harness to the nearby balustrade and gingerly lowered herself over the side of the ship.

'Milton,' the captain called after her. 'What the hell are you doing?'

'Science, sir,' she said, slamming her shoes against the thin coating of ice that lined the hull, hoping to gain some traction. 'I need to see just how badly entrenched we are.'

Thorsten's face appeared over the railing. 'But what about the aliens?'

'It's not aliens,' the captain said. 'It's some sort of natural phenomenon. We hit a gas pocket or something.'

'Whatever it is,' Wendy said. 'We're not going anywhere until I get all science-kid on this rut, right captain?'

'You've got a point,' he said. 'But do be careful. I'll send Lucille down to help you.'

'Oh no you bloody won't,' Lucille said.

Wendy took a step down. She didn't slip, which was a good sign. The spikes woven into the soles of her boots were doing their job well. 'If I need help I'll give you a shout, sir. Probably safer I go down alone until I see how stable the ice is down here. I'm the lightest member of the crew, after all.'

'There's a bloody great ship perched on that ice, I don't think Lucille is going to make much of a difference, but if you're sure...'

Another step, failed to slip again. Good. 'I'm sure.'

'Good luck.'

She nodded and started to descend in earnest, as if she knew what she was doing. It wasn't much of a lie, saying that she had to determine how badly entrenched they were. She *did* need to do that, but that could probably have been done from the ship itself. They had sensors and machines that went ping, lots of useful gizmos for keeping track of the ship and its surroundings. That was kind of the point.

But she was curious, like a good little scientist should be. And why not? This situation was perfect for curiosity. It was the sort of thing curiosity was *made* for.

The mist made the climb down a bit more treacherous than she had expected. All of her climbing training had been done in the dark, so doing it in daylight should have made it considerably easier, but the way the mist was disrupting the light that passed through was confusing her. At least it wasn't much of a climb. Having to deal with things like hand holds with this weird lighting would have been awkward.

When she reached the ice, the effect of the mist was greatly reduced. Looking up, what she could see of the sky was covered with it now, a beautiful painting in the air itself. The tail of light was much more visible from underneath too, a faint cone emanating from that glass lens she had seen from above. So, definitely a projection then.

Carefully, she crossed the ice to the lens. The ice creaked under her weight, but it seemed sturdy enough, which made sense once she reached the projector. Most of it was buried, but there were signs that it was considerably larger than the lens itself, with a pitted metal housing vanishing below the ice.

Dropping to her knees, she swept away what loose ice there was, uncovering more of the metal and a few more broken lenses. Not just a projector, but an entire array. Fascinating.

She keyed her radio. 'It's not aliens, sir. Sorry to disappoint Thor.'

'Well obviously,' the captain replied. 'What is it then?'

'Some sort of broken holographic projection thing. I'm willing to bet it's pretty huge, judging from the resolution.'

There was silence for a moment. 'If I ask you what you mean by that, am I going to end up with a very long and boring explanation.'

'I wouldn't say *boring* –'

'You can explain it later. For now, what's our situation look like?'

She walked to the nearest stretch of hull and ran her hand over it and kicked at the ice touching it. 'The ice is pretty strong, I think. If we can get the razors working, we should be able to just drive out, no problem.'

'Oh, it's that easy, is it?' Lucille chimed in. 'I'll get right on shoving that enormous metal blade back through the entire ship and back into its housing, shall I?'

'If you wouldn't mind, it would be a big help,' Wendy said, stifling a giggle.

'What about the beacon,' the captain said. 'Did we at least get that into position?'

'Let me check,' Wendy said, running to the rear of the ship. 'There's, um, *bits* of the beacon still here. I think.'

'How many bits? Can it be repaired?'

'Not really.'

She had missed the impact zone on the way down because the projection had been the focus of her interest. It wasn't really wreckage at this point, the pressure of the thumper didn't allow for that. It either pierced the entire planet or it reduced the payload to sparkly dust. It had done the latter here. It was a moderately frightening display of force for a machine.

'Well, that's *unfortunate,*' he said. 'You better get back up here and prepare another beacon. If we don't spike one here, we don't get paid.'

'Sir, if we spike another one here, it's going to slam into the projection array and make a lot of noise and pretty lights. It's not going to install.'

'Then we'll keep firing them until one does.'

'We don't even know how many it would take to pierce this thing! If I could study it maybe –'

'No, Milton,' he said, and his voice was more stern than it had been. 'We're contractors, not a science ship. If you wanted to study things, you should have stayed on the crawler.'

Thorsten spoke, but not on his own radio. He must have been stood next to the captain. 'If it's not aliens, boss, it's definitely some kind of tech. Old tech maybe? Don't they pay a premium for that back home?'

'*If* it works. *If* they can verify it,' the captain said. 'Spiking beacons is definite, honest, reliable pay.'

'But old tech, boss,' Thorsten said. 'That's a fortune. Worth at least a small look, right? Come on!'

Wendy wanted to join in. Thorsten might have been playing the mercenary card to get the captain on board – and he wasn't wrong either, old tech was worth a hell of a lot of money – but she knew that tone. He was just as intrigued by it as she was. He *had to know*.

If she had ridden to his aid in that argument, however, the captain would have dug in his heels and that would be that. She had seen him do it before, though never over something as potentially momentous as this. The waiting was torturous, however.

'I suppose,' he said at last. 'It might take a while to get the razors working again. If the pair of you want to give this thing a *cursory glance,* then I can allow that. But no wandering off, and nothing that might make this situation any sodding worse, agreed?'

'I promise,' Wendy shot back a little too quickly.

She didn't hear Thorsten's reply, but she inferred his agreement from the sight of him climbing over the railing above her. He practically abseiled down to her, his feet barely touching the hull.

'The captain has a great way with words, doesn't he?' he said as his feet hit the ground. 'This is going to be the best school trip ever!'

'Yay!' Wendy replied, high-fiving him.

'So, where do we begin?'

She shrugged. 'I guess we try and remove some more of the ice?'

Without tools, there was only so much ice they could shift. The going was easiest near the already exposed lens, but even after an hour's work they only managed to liberate a small area. More lenses, all equidistant from each other, more blank metal, rivets, nothing particularly exciting.

'What do you suppose it is?' Thorsten asked.

'It must be something pretty special, right?' she said. 'It's not like projectors are common, and having an array this big...'

Thorsten knocked on the metal with his fist, the sound echoing deep inside. 'It's hollow, we should take a look inside.'

'Happen to have a plasma torch in that belt then, Thor?'

He smiled and cracked his neck, letting his hair fall over his eyes for effect. 'I thought I'd just kick my way through!'

And, to his credit, he tried. He targeted one of the seams where the rivets looked a little more corroded than the rest, driving his boot down hard. The spikes in the soles left small scratches, and he managed to dent the steel a little, but there wasn't much in the way of give. The noise continued to roll around inside, however, building like a maelstrom of sound into some great crescendo. When he finally stopped the echo remained for a good ten seconds.

Then a knocking sound.

Like the ticking of some vast clock, it drummed through the steel in perfect intervals, kicking a few of the other lenses to life. There was a whirring as they aligned with the one that had already been active, enhancing whatever it was projecting.

'Captain,' Wendy shouted into the radio. 'Has, um, anything changed up there?'

'I think I can safely say that machine of yours works, Milton,' he said. 'Get back up here, we've got a fortune to discuss.'

TWO

As the pilot of the Strider, Rostrum Barley was, in essence, a king. The civvies had a council and elected officials and all that nonsense, true, but he was the final word. The city needed a pilot to guide it out of the worst of the weather, and he had been raised from birth to do that job.

It was difficult, painfully so. Thousands of people lived in the belly of the strider and other mobile cities like it, and all those lives were his responsibility.

And he *loved* it.

There were things he didn't like. The meetings for one thing. They were far too frequent, and *far* too boring. But at the end of each one he would go right back to the cockpit and just stare out at the wide world and lose himself.

Only another forty-five minutes to endure.

They had been talking about route planning for fifteen minutes now, twenty old men arguing over a map. He had been content to sit back and watch as, one by one, they suggested more and more dangerous treks merely to outdo their opponents.

But now he was bored.

'Esteemed gentlemen, there will not be any course changes at this time,' he said, closing his eyes and leaning back in his chair.

'But, pilot –' one of them attempted to say. He wasn't sure which one, they all had that same nasal whine to them.

'I need data on every single route, not posturing. The current path might not be resource-rich, but it is well travelled and safe. We've got enough reserves to hold out until we hit the Barret's Point, and research suggests –'

'Research we haven't seen.'

'Research you are not *entitled* to see, councillor,' he said, opening his eyes and fixing them on the speaker. 'Every course change is a risk versus reward scenario, and in this case the rewards do not justify the very real danger that we might encounter the weather. End of discussion.'

Councillor Moses was the only one at the table currently with the backbone to stand up for what he believed in, which Rostrum respected. It was infuriating, but at least the man took his own job as seriously as the pilot did. That was commendable, even if he was usually wrong.

'Pilot,' Moses said. 'If we run out of fuel –'

'Yes, I know. I am well aware. Our big stompy legs don't run on ice water, which is a terrible shame as there is so much around. Let me worry about that, you gentlemen can worry yourselves about the communications project if you like, or the wandering citizens. How are they doing, by the way?'

Moses took a breath and pushed his fingers through his beard. He was waiting for one of the other councillors to speak, but they were always hesitant to engage the pilot. 'We've got twenty galleons out spiking beacons right now, and as of the last clear call there was another fifteen from the crawler and twelve from the roller. The network is coming together; clear call coverage is increasing every day.'

'There you are, see? Dig your teeth into that if you need something to do.'

'We've lost eighteen galleons total since we all started this initiative, Pilot.'

'To what?'

Moses produced a small, chunky tablet from a pocket and tapped at the screen. 'Most of them ran afoul of the weather, some from collapses caused by inexpert beacon spiking, and some have just vanished without trace.'

And still, Rostrum thought, they don't accept the dangers of the weather. Of course the little galleons would get swallowed up by the constant clashing storms, they would think, but the strider is enormous, it could stand tall.

And maybe, *maybe*, they were actually right, but Rostrum was in no rush to test that theory. Safety first, especially if the records were correct about some of the older cities.

'How many dead?' he said quietly.

Moses squinted. 'No way of telling for sure, they're not keen on records, galleon captains. At a guess, I'd say anything from a crew of four to twelve per ship.'

'That... is more than I expected.'

'Indeed.'

'I'll talk to the other pilots at the next clear call. Maybe we can try doubling up for safety. Any news on the other cities?'

Moses tapped his tablet again. 'Outside of the roller and the crawler we've heard nothing. The meteorologists believe they've been cut off behind a storm front, one they're calling Hurricane Bacchus.'

'They're rather poetic down there, aren't they?'

'They claim it's the only way to put up with the utter bleakness of their job. I think they're taking the piss, personally.'

Rostrum laughed. This was better, controlling the flow of conversation, like a proper king of old, holding court.

Hell, most of the people in the room were likely plotting his death at that very moment, just to lend a bit more legitimacy to the analogy.

But, if he was a king...

He stood up. 'Right, I'm done. You gentlemen talk amongst yourselves.'

'The meeting isn't over yet, pilot.'

'It is for me. I have complete faith in you to handle all the things that I don't have to deal with, I'm going to go back to driving one of the last bastions of mankind.'

He had never tried that before, just walking out. It felt good, but probably not something to do regularly. He needed a breather, though. Eighteen galleons; at the worst case that was two hundred and sixteen people lost to the cold. The actual number of people living in the strider was not something he had chosen to memorise – the specifics were unimportant, just the knowledge that the unknown number was vast would do – but time like this had him question that.

Every lost life diminished the city in an immeasurable way. Keeping the numbers nebulous helped to disguise this fact, simplify it. Specifics made it too real.

The corridor to the cockpit was empty, as expected. Most of the people he would have run into were already ensconced in the meeting room, and those that hadn't or couldn't attend would be seeing to their own knitting while they too were free of the spectre of an official visit. He reached the door, placed his eye against the retinal scanner and waited for the lift that would deliver him to the cockpit.

It had used to be called the bridge, back when the city had entrusted the ambulatory authority to a committee rather than a single man, but one of Rostrum's predecessors had renamed it. A window twenty feet across and ten feet high was the main source of light now the sun had risen, the familiar interior lighting having deactivated to save power. Various consoles and computers lay open, bleeding wires that had been fed into a portable terminal that had been bolted to the floor in front of what had been the captain's chair.

The entire deck had been cannibalised to set up a single control point, but it had been that way for so long that Rostrum found it hard to imagine it any other way. Once it had been staffed by a group of maybe seven people, judging from the amount of computers. How did they ever get anything done? His job was so uniquely skilled that he was untouchable, no-one could replace him except for his randomly chosen successor. With a crew of six others, all able to drive the city, it would be madness.

Some of the other cities did it differently too, he understood, but he would never have been able to hack it under their systems either. As he sat in his chair and flicked on the monitors, it was the same familiar quiet that greeted him. At this height you couldn't even hear the giant feet as they tromped their way over the ice.

Peace.

Reports starting scrolling onto his screen. Some from automated sensors, filling him in on what he couldn't see from the cockpit, others from manned departments who were tasked with keeping him updated on various other things. A small storm five clicks to the east could become a hurricane twenty clicks down the road if they weren't careful. Today, thankfully, the reports were largely benign.

He flicked down to his folder of personal correspondence. Most of the pilots swapped messages when they had clear call – when they had a decent gap in the weather for radio transmissions to work – they needed to collaborate to keep one another safe.

It was the crawler files he was looking for today. Their pilot was new, the third alternate replacement for their previous pilot who had died of old age.

> Pilot strider, this is pilot crawler. Roger if you read me, over.

>> I roger that, pilot crawler. This is pilot strider, over.

> Do we always have to be so formal? I had a look through Radek's logs and things seemed very relaxed. Over.

>> Nah, outside of using the *official names* in case anyone else ever hears this, you're good. You don't even need to say over if you don't want to. Over.

> This is a lot to learn.

>> Trust me, kid, it's only going to get worse.

> Great. Anything I should know ahead of time?

>> Probably, but I'm losing clear call here.

> No problem, I'll have a chat with pilot roller if I can. God, it will be so nice when the worker ants get the network up, eh?

>> I can't wait. Might be worth pushing them a little harder, get it done sooner.

> Not a bad idea, pilot strider. I'll convey your suggestion to pilot roller.

>> Thanks. I'll check in when I get clear call again, should be in about –

Signal Lost

How many galleons had the crawler sent? Fifteen? What about the losses?

The terminal stuttered for a moment as it called up the report on the losses. Four losses from the crawler which, on the face of things, wasn't too bad. He could avoid the emotional weight of guilt at having advised her, then. That was nice.

Something beeped beside his console, a warning light telling him one of the joints in the left leg had started to freeze. A call to maintenance would sort that out.

Another report, this time about stockpiles, popped up in the corner of his screen and he dismissed it. It was an automated one, but he was well aware of the trends. The councillors might not have had any real clue, but they were more on the money than he had cared to admit to them. Fuel was fine, basic material for components was fine, but they were starting to run low on spare parts, and the manufactories were grinding themselves to pieces trying to restock the reserve.

The fact of the matter was that the city was *old*, older than anyone could really comprehend. Rostrum had logs dating back several hundred years, but that was a length of time so big that it had no meaning. It was indistinguishable from *always* at this point.

But old machines break, and they break more often the older they are. Having machines make machines, even the spare parts for them, complicated things, as *these* machines could also break. It was a losing battle against entropy, and reading the updates did nothing but upset him. There was always the chance he could beg for parts from one of the other cities, if it came down to that, but they'd make sure the price was high.

Nothing was ever free.

There had been some good progress with the communications network at least. He had found himself habitually pinging the network every day since it had been commissioned. Not that he doubted the accuracy of any reports he was subjected to reading in this regard, but it felt like a pro-active thing to do. It was nice watching something grow, for a change.

There were still gaps, places where the weather managed to interfere with transmission somehow, but the web of redundancy circuits was growing as fast as the reach of the main trunk. On a good day, there was a five-minute window every six hours or so when he could be guaranteed to reach one of the other pilots.

Not right now though. His pings showed no other connections, he was completely alone. This allowed him to indulge in a hobby – the strider didn't need his hand to be constantly on the tiller.

He unfolded a piece of paper he had kept stashed in the gap between his headrest and his chair and smoothed it out against the side of his screen. What had the last node been? #742-C? A crawler node, of course.

> admin access node 743-C
Working...
Connection Established
> new file\document\Chapter17

...

Galveston screamed as the branch gave way and he fell, spiralling, through the thick canopy to the grass below. His gun exploded from the impact, the loaded shell burying itself in his left thigh and leave him writhing in agony.

The woman stepped out of the shadows. She was wearing a dress of spiders now, a million tiny legs crawling over her flesh, revealing her ghastly beauty at random. Her breasts hung down as she leaned over him, and even this close to death he couldn't help but stare.

'Big G, darling,' she said in her sultry crawler-town brogue. 'You shouldn't oughta come after me. Some secrets gotta stay hidden.'

> save
File Saved

Someday, the network would be open to the general public, what there was of them. Yes, for the foreseeable future it was earmarked to pilots and select governmental officials, but it was the start of something. A new world. A smaller world. Maybe they would remember the names of the people who had spearheaded the initiative, assuming they survived long enough, but he wanted more than that.

It was schlocky and trite and heavily riddled with cliché, but it was also ground breaking. An entire novel, hidden in the depths of the network. Electronic archaeology, a legacy for the future to remember him by. It might take decades for people to even *begin* looking, but that was what made it even sweeter. A time capsule. A recognition bomb. He could be long dead, forgotten for years, and then suddenly he would be back.

>> Assistance?

The query interrupted his flow, catching his brain between thoughts and causing him to stall for a moment.

>> Help?

The system didn't send queries like this. It was the

wrong format, but his screen didn't show any other connections.

>> /help??

> Who are you?

>> List all local vessels

> You're not talking to a computer here. Do you even know what you are doing?

>> Exit

> No. You don't get out of this that easily. Who are you? Galleon crew are expressly forbidden from accessing the network.

It was a guess, but it wasn't much of one. It was almost a certainty. There was no-one else who had the equipment outside of a pilot's cockpit, and he was sure this wasn't one of them. For a start, they would know what they were doing.

>> Sorry about that. My technologically adept crew members are indisposed. I'll do the typing now. Captain Joshua Klaus of the crawler-galleon The Ship.

> You named your ship "The Ship"?

>> I wanted something I wouldn't forget.

> What are you doing on this network? You are jeopardising the entire system, it's not calibrated for unexpected bandwidth.

>> We have found something here.

> Found what?

>> Old technology, we believe. Navigation Officer Thorsten Wolfe and Technician Wendigo Milton are investigating, but preliminary examination indicated some degree of operability.

Rostrum blinked.

This was impossible.

He called up a map of the proposed network and searched until he found node 743-C. Spiked today at the frontier of the main trunk, outriding from the crawler. Whatever they were talking about had to be near that location, they needed to connect to the beacon locally.

Survey maps, geological and topological, anything. His terminal spluttered as he tried to open several large files at once, filling the screen with complicated data of which he had only a passing understanding at best. But they were annotated, he had ensured they were labelled where needed, and the areas around that beacon was blank.

Had they missed it? How? The route of the main trunk was chosen because it was the most traversed by the majority of cities – all their paths took them across huge stretches of it regularly, and it was the least hit by weather. Surely one of them would have noticed an irregularity, some sensor or overly vigilant researcher or something.

> Standby.

Even a quick search of the logs with other pilots held no mention of anything like this. It was too good to be true, too perfect.

> I cannot corroborate your alleged find with any research, Captain Klaus.

>> Well, with respect, whoever you are, if we had had research telling us there was something down here, we wouldn't have spiked the beacon here. We're beached and could really do with some assistance.

>> And, not to mention, the reward for this salvage. Assuming you are someone who can pay that.

> I'm the pilot of the strider, captain. If your claims are true, I can pay you.

Rostrum couldn't help thinking that this was some sort of trap. There was a general sense of camaraderie – no, fraternity – amongst all the cities seeing as they were all that was out there in the cold wide world, but that didn't mean they always got on. Families fight from time to time, brothers tease and prank each other, and the pilots and their cities were no different.

But this? This would have been a cruel prank.

But if this was real, why not contact the crawler directly instead of an open call? Or an alleged open call, perhaps they knew he was listening. The crawler wasn't currently on the network, but if they were outriders then it couldn't be too far out of coverage. Their course might even take them directly over the site.

>> How can we prove to you we are on the level.

> Describe, in detail, your find.

>> Standby

The computer blinked without reply for several minutes. It gave Rostrum time to study the maps a little closer.

If there was indeed something buried at that particular node, it was a very good location. Weather charts indicated it had gone largely untouched by the more serious storms for months, and those that did brush past rarely lingered. Current patterns predicted they had three days before a storm troubled them.

They were a day's travel away, half if a nearby squall changed direction. Very, very tempting.

>> hi sorry the boss made me climb back up to talk to you im wendy

> Wendy? Captain Klaus never mentioned you.

>> wendigo milton but please dont use my full name im not a fan

> Understandable. So, tell me what you've found.

>> a big metal thing covered in what I reckon are projectors a few of them still work but more seem to be broken but we only have access to a small segment of the surface and its impossible to tell how big it actually is

> Any distinguishing marks?

>> nothing on the metal but the projectors that work are putting out a strange design ive not seen before

> I don't suppose you have a camera with you?

>> not standard equipment but I do have one yes

>> one sec

File Uploaded

He opened the file and waited for the grainy image to coalesce, line by line, on his screen. When it finally did, he wasn't sure what he was seeing. It was only part of a picture; he could tell that much. There were what seemed to be letters against a colourful backdrop, although the resolution rendered them unreadable. Whether that was the fault of the camera or the image itself, he wasn't sure.

File Uploaded

The second one was tighter on the projection, enough to be certain that it *was* a projection. Through the projection he could make out the landscape, though it was distorted, and there were breaks where the odd snowflake had interrupted a particular beam of light.

> How many projectors are working right now?

>> maybe five?

> And broken?

>> eleven that we can see but probably more under the ice

It sounded legitimate, he had to concede that. The photos especially, while not amazing quality, were enough to pique his curiosity and get his hopes to start rising. Whatever that machine was, it would have parts that hadn't broken when it had. There had to be something they could use in there, or repurpose.

But worth the detour? This would be doing exactly what he had told the councillors he would not do. Then again, such a large reward for so minor a risk...

He hammered in the new heading and wrenched the stick to the side, grabbing the side of his chair with his spare hand while the strider turned. It wasn't intended for sharp course corrections, making the turn uncomfortable though not dangerous. Once on the new heading, a torrent of notifications appeared on screen, no doubt complaints from angry citizens and councillors. They'd keep.

> Okay, Wendy. Tell your captain that I'm heading your way. ETA is about a day, you're safe from the weather for now so just hole up and don't break that prize.

>> k

> And, word of warning, it would be inadvisable to try to sell that to any other city. I've got first rights, and I'll be

mighty cross if you renege on this deal.

>> ill pass that along to the captain

> Okay. See you soon.

He pinged the network one more time to make sure none of the other cities had connected during that exchange – they hadn't – and cranked the throttle.

THREE

By the time she had climbed back down, Thorsten was on his knees by the seam, trying to wedge something between the plates.

'Careful! If you break it they won't pay us a ridiculous sum when they get here,' she said.

He grunted and released the pressure. 'There's a buyer already?'

'Evidently,' she said, sitting next to him. 'The strider seems pretty interested. Have you made any progress?'

Thorsten growled and kicked at his pry bar which, Wendy noticed, was just a piece of metal shorn off the hull as a result of their predicament. 'It's starting to give, I reckon. Pretty sure I can get the rivets to pop with a bit more effort. Give me a hand?'

He got back into position and waved her over. Shifting onto her knees, she lent her weight to the makeshift crowbar. 'Just tell me when.'

'No time like the present. Push!'

The pair of them put everything they had into it, making the metal groan against itself and bulge slightly, but the rivets held. Something about this spurred on Thorsten, however, and he roared as he threw yet more weight onto the bar, forcing more of it into the seam.

'Go on, you bastard! Give!'

The metal's groan rose in pitch, angling for a squeal but not quite managing it. Maybe Thorsten was onto something. Wendy threw in her reserves and felt the metal start to give, slowly but very definitely.

When the first rivet finally gave, it did so so suddenly that the pair of them slammed their fingers down hard, trapped between the steel and the bar. They took a moment to paint the air purple, then turned their attention to the hole they had created.

'It's not much, but it's a good start,' Thorsten said, trying to peer into the dark crack he had opened in the seam. 'You got a torch on that belt?'

She unhooked her belt-light and passed it to him. 'Can you see anything?'

Thorsten angled the blue light into the crack. 'Wires. Not very surprising. We'll need to make the opening wider for a closer look. Have you not got something in that workshop of yours that would help?'

'Probably,' she said. 'But nothing the captain would let us use. I know he wasn't particularly enamoured with the thing, but it's his prize now. Got to keep his baby safe.'

'Then I suppose it's up to me.'

With the first rivet broken, Thorsten found it easier to pop a couple more. The more he opened the seam, the more pressure he could put on the join, and before too long he had managed to pry open a space he could fit his head and one arm into at the same time.

'Oh, this is cool,' he said, his voice echoing from inside.

'What's cool?'

'There's actually quite a bit of space back here,' he said, awkwardly pulling himself out of the hole. 'Once you get past the wiring. Take a look.'

It was a looser fit for her than Thorsten, one of the benefits of her slight build. She managed to get both arms in, and she felt his hands close around her ankles, holding her in place.

Moving the light around she could see he wasn't wrong. The wiring lined the walls, but it wasn't very dense and could be moved aside easily. On the other side was what looked like a catwalk, wide enough for two people to stand abreast, with a roof that could accommodate people pushing six feet. The far wall, however, looked more imposing than the one they had breached. Angry-looking pitted steel with fist-sized rivets, not the fingernail-sized ones on the outside, and signs of welding.

She gave a signal and Thorsten pulled her out. 'We have got to go in there and have a nose about.'

'Hold on there, kiddo,' he said. 'I'm all for broadening my horizons, but there could be anything in there.'

'Exactly,' she said, grabbing her radio. 'Captain, we're going to explore the wreckage.'

There was a beat of silence. 'Why?'

'Just because.'

'That is not a good enough reason. I've read books, this is how people get themselves eaten by ice wraiths.'

'Sir –'

'You'll wait until the buyers get here and then take your share of the profit and go and live a wealthy, safe, life on the city of your choice. Get back up here.'

'If I may,' Thorsten said, taking the radio from Wendy's hand. 'If we know more about the wreck, boss, it would put us in a better bargaining position.'

'I am aware of that,' the captain said. 'But not if you fall off a corroded walkway and get trapped in there.'

'The girl's pretty light, boss. If we squish her in there, I doubt she's got enough heft to break something and fall to her death. Plus, she knows what she's doing.'

Another prolonged silence. 'Fine. But I want actionable results. Find me something that can crank up the price, and do it without dying, if you please, Milton.'

'Yes sir,' she said, snatching back the radio.

She didn't wait for him to change his mind, snapping

the radio and the light back onto her belt and practically diving into the crack. Thorsten's hands seized her ankles again, slowing her down and lowering her in in a more controlled manner.

Getting all the way in was tricky. The wreck was clearly on its side, which meant using the inner wall as a floor. That in itself wasn't so bad, but there wasn't much headroom with it this way, and it would mean crawling. First she had to manoeuvre herself down to that wall without injuring herself or getting stuck. With Thorsten lowering her, however, it was more arduous than dangerous.

The inner wall was cold and, she noticed, looked somehow more impregnable than the outer shell. It was difficult to say how she knew, but from looking at it there was the expectation that each plate would be up to a foot thick. Perhaps they reminded her of the bulkheads in the crawler, it was hard to tell in this light.

She started to move, slowly at first while she assessed the sturdiness of the wall. There was no give in it, and it wasn't long before she was moving at a comfortable pace, although it was easy to convince herself that she wasn't moving at all. The surroundings barely changed, with the only variations being points where the metal had been damaged by something – huge dents the size of her head pockmarked the plates on occasion, usually paired with a similar fissure in the outer wall exposing the ice. Some sort of cannon fire?

The further she went, the frequency of this damage increased until she found one pit that had pierced the inner wall too. She crawled up to it and, peering in, flashed the light down into it.

'Thorsten,' she said into her radio. 'I think I've found a way into the centre of the wreckage. Looks like it's been in a serious fire fight though, I'm not sure what sort of a state it's going to be in.'

The reply was riddled with static, but still legible. 'The

captain's not going to like that. Can you get yourself in deeper without hurting yourself, brat?'

She shuffled around the breach a little, looking for something she could attach her belt rope too. Abseiling down the side of the ship was no different than this, in theory, provided she could find a good anchor point. 'I'll be fine.'

'You better be.'

Looping the rope around the bundles of wiring, she gave it a tug to check it would hold and started to lower herself into the breach. Her choice of anchor made the descent a little springier than she liked and set her on edge, but she reached the floor – or another wall, in this case – without incident.

'Can you still hear me, Thor?'

'Just about.' The static was a little better. 'Did you find anything?'

She shone her light around the room for a moment. The wall she was standing on was cluttered with loose debris and furniture that had surrendered to gravity when the wreck had collapsed. It had mostly sorted itself into piles, in the way unattended detritus seems to do, though nothing she couldn't traverse.

Further up, on the floor now serving as a wall, there was an array of consoles and desks that had been firmly secured to the ground when the thing had gone down. A couple had started to come loose, hanging towards her weirdly cocked, and more still showed signs of something large having obliterated great chunks of them. The largest console, smack in the centre of the room, was untouched though.

'I think this might be a control room or something,' she said, beginning to pace. 'Lots of computers and stuff.'

'Here's a long shot for you: do any of them work?'

'Ha, you're a funny guy, Thor.'

'You're the one that wanted to get all curious and nosy, brat,' he said. 'There might be logs on there, or diaries.

Lots of lovely readables that can tell us what happened to this thing. Or, hell, what it *is*.'

'Good point. I'll try and find out.'

With great care, she managed to swing her rope around the side of the main console and climb up to it. It housed several greenish screens, each with their own keyboard and trackball, and a variety of other slots and sockets that she didn't recognise. Several unilluminated LEDs sat next to big chunky switches to the right of the nearest monitor, with one larger bulb squatting over a circular button.

'There's a lot of potential power buttons here, Thor,' she said.

'I'm sure you can science your way through. Carefully.'

She shifted her weight a little, hoping that the rope wouldn't slip, and swung her way across the desk a little so she could reach the switches and buttons. Starting with the switches, she flicked or pressed them one by one to no result. Now and then there would be the sound of a spring failing somewhere in the depths of the machine, or an ancient capacitor spitting out its last bit of wattage, making an LED flicker for a second, but nothing substantial. Even the ever so promising button yielded nothing.

As she was ready to accept that the machine was broken, she spotted something she had missed. Before she had swung across her view of it had been obscured, but buried in a little nook was one last switch, even chunkier than the others and painted red. No, not a switch, a lever.

If her studies had taught her anything it was that *this* was what a power supply looked like. She grabbed it at pulled. It was rusty and had seized, but she felt it give just a little. Lifting her legs up, she planted them on either side and pulled with all her might.

The lever cracked and a small rain of rust trickled into the air as it started to move, then slammed open completely with such a force that Wendy was not expecting it. She lost her grip, the momentum pushing her free of the console, swinging her out wide and causing her rope to slide free also, sending her tumbling to the floor hard.

She landed on a pile with an almighty crash, the sound of bones breaking, and she was certain that was it for her – that was her neck, internally severed from one bit of misadventure. Laying there, she looked up at the console as it clunked and clicked and sputtered into life. Green text on green screens, scrolling past at a thousand lines a second while the various computers ran through their boot up protocols, all while the little LEDs blinked and danced at her.

The pain started to dull as the room lightning winked on. It was a sickly, halogen yellow, but better than her torch. Gingerly, she tested her limbs to see where the break was. Feet were fine, same for the legs, hips were sore but serviceable, lower back equally so, shoulders and arms throbbing, hands responsive, neck...

She knew moving a suspected broken neck was stupid. If it was broken, moving would likely kill her, but no-one else was getting down to her any time soon and she couldn't handle not knowing for that long. If she moved and died, at least she knew. If she moved and didn't die, then that was even better.

She moved.

And didn't die.

What she did do was turn her head directly towards the real source of the bone-breaking sound: a pile of skeletons onto which she had fallen.

In the dark they had looked like any of the other debris piles, but in the halogen light she could see them for what they were.

'Christ!' she screamed and scampered back across the room, trying to disentangle herself from a ribcage.

'Wendy,' Thorsten shouted over the radio. 'Wendy! Are you okay?'

'I'm not sure okay is the word I'd use, Thor,' she said, breathlessly. 'I'm alive and unhurt though. I found the crew.'

'Yeah? Dead, I'm guessing?'

'So dead.'

'Anything on the computers?'

'Hold on a second.'

She took the second climb a little more seriously. Looping the rope around the console again wasn't ideal, but it had held before she had overexerted herself, it would hold now. The trick was making sure she kept herself in check. It made the climb slower, too, but she wasn't in a rush.

The computer was running an operating system she didn't recognise. Back at the crawler, the jury-rigged machines that she had used for most of her studies ran whatever they had always used. There wasn't much call for new software when there were more practical professions. If it worked, then it could be left alone while they fixed something else.

That said, the crawler had so many different operating systems to deal with, Wendy had gained a knack for picking up the eccentricities of a new one fairly quickly. This one was seemingly entirely command line based, which meant the difficulty lay in the syntax and not the interface, which was easily the worst.

'This is going to be a right pain in the arse, Thor,' she said, rapidly typing in random words from all the command line interfaces she knew. 'Some of the keys are broken off, which means – ow, shit – jamming my finger into these rubbery holes to try and type them.'

'Not the first time you've –'

'Finish that sentence and I'm going to come back up there and eat you.'

Thor's laugh sent the radio into a hectic squeal of feedback and static. 'You need to work on your threats, brat.'

'Dangers of being brought up properly, old man. Now shut up and let me work.'

It didn't take her long to suss out enough of the language to make the computer work, in a manner of speaking. There was a lot of data stuffed into the memory banks, according to the file list, and nothing that stood out to her as actually being written in English. Almost every folder was named in some sort of weird code that had some meaning she couldn't deduce. She had to resort to opening them at random.

'The boss is getting impatient, Wendy,' Thorsten said.

'Well, tough. This computer isn't co-operating. They don't even have a massive document file that details their entire mission handily pinned to the top of their archive. Inconsiderate...'

'Well, I hate to rush you, but –'

She tried another folder and the screen changed. 'Woah, wait, hold on. I've got something here.'

Still, she couldn't read it. Whatever this data was was apparently in the same code as the folder names, but she recognised the formatting. *This* was the log. Every log she had ever seen had the same basic formatting. There was a treasure trove of information buried inside this thing, if only she knew how to read it.

But, that wasn't her job now, was it? Her job was to make sure the thing was worth a fortune, and she had ascertained that quite satisfactorily.

And yet.

She searched the console for any concealed storage spaces. A couple stood out when subjected to more than a cursory survey, which told her that they weren't actually concealed at all, more than she had been inattentive. They were all empty except for one, which held what she was looking for.

At least, she assumed it was what she was looking for. It looked enough like one of the memory discs back on the crawler that she was pretty certain that it fulfilled the same function, although it was almost as big as a sheet of paper, and barely any thicker. She found a slot for it and slid it in, hoping she could work out how to transfer something onto it. She declined to consider how she would get the information off of it later.

After transferring what she could, she started the climb back out.

'Thor, I couldn't get much from the computer, it was all in code or something, but it works and it is *packed* with pre-freeze goodies.'

'How packed are we talking?'

She looked at the disc and slid it into the back of her shirt, the only place she could ably hide it. 'Big enough for it to demand a high price. The tech alone is rare enough, the files are just a nice bonus.'

'Have you already started spending your new wealth then, brat?'

She laughed and it echoed throughout the depths of the wreckage. 'I've been spending that money from the moment I was born, I think. It's not even money at this point, just a lifestyle. I reckon I'll take one of those luxury penthouses on the roller.'

'As if they'd have room for you,' he said. 'Besides, those are hereditary, they won't just give them out to the likes of you.'

'Oh yeah? Then what are you going to do with your share?'

'Buy a galleon, sail off into the big white, see if I can't find something that isn't snow.'

'So, you're going to crash into a massive storm and explode? That's what you're going to do with your riches?'

'Pretty much.'

The breach she had entered through wasn't hard to find, and it was much easier to climb out than it had be to climb in. She sent her arms through first, and Thorsten hauled her out without issue. He looked her up and down once she was back in the sunlight.

'Dusty down there, is it?' he said.

She looked. There was a lot of dust, that was true, but

most of what he had seen was from the bones she had landed on, an off-white residue that crept around her sides like a horrifying hand trying to grab her. A lovely reminder of an image she didn't really want hiding behind her eyes, thanks very much.

'I need a shower.'

'You're not wrong, but you better have a word with the boss first.'

Wendy nodded. Telling him the good news over the radio would have been unsatisfying though, she needed to see the light in his face when she reported back. And then, when that was out the way, she could hose herself down and get to secretly trying to undermine the whole deal accidentally by being nosy and building something that could read the disc.

What a brilliant idea.

Thorsten led the ascent back onto the ship, largely because Wendy had to clip herself back onto the harness. By the time she reached the top, he had already spoiled most of the story.

'– and it's functional,' she heard him saying as she hoisted herself over the railing.

'Bullshit,' said Lucille. 'How is it even holding a charge down there after all this time? Where's the power coming from.'

Wendy unclipped her harness and dropped off the railing onto the deck. 'Residual batteries maybe, or a nuclear engine deeper down. I didn't want to explore too far on my own.'

The captain snapped his fingers. 'Get the rad-box, Wolfe. If Milton has been exposed, best to know now.'

'I'm fine, captain,' she said.

'Yes, well, no harm in checking. Now, tell me exactly what you did see.'

She sat herself down as Thorsten wandered off as ordered. 'I don't really know, to be honest with you captain. It's been in the wars, that much I do know. Lots

38

of what looks like cannon damage.'

'Plasma?'

'I don't know. I didn't find any scorching or melting or anything though. Mostly impact damage I think. But then, the computer room was pretty well preserved, all things considered.'

Lucille scratched her face. 'What sort of impact damage? Any spent ammunition lying around or was it through and through?'

'I didn't see any ammo, but there were a lot of dents. Maybe the loose slugs rolled away deeper into the wreck, I don't know.'

'Hmm,' Lucille said. 'I might actually have an idea about what happened here, you know.'

The captain choked. 'Seriously?'

'I do know things too, Josh. I've got an area of expertise just like the rest of you. Just because I can't work all this computer shit doesn't mean I'm thick, all right?'

Lucille's face was going red, prompting Wendy to step between them. 'What do you think, Lu?'

Her right eye twitched as she broke eye contact with the captain. 'A couple of years back, when I was working crawler security, keeping all the snow-mad crazies from making homes in the suspension pins, a galleon captain found himself a small bit of salvage. Do you remember him? Aubrey Jackdaw.'

'I don't think so,' said Wendy.

'I do,' the captain said. 'Crashed his ship into a galleon graveyard while scouting for metals, right? Brought the co-ordinates back home and made a modest profit.'

'Pretty much,' Lucille said, barely looking at him. 'But what you might not have heard, because we never bothered to tell anyone outside of security, was that one of those dead galleons was military. Proper military, from a few generations back when we actually did proper fighting.'

'No way,' Wendy shrieked. 'A gunboat?! That's so

cool.'

'Hardly,' Lucille said. 'It had taken some pretty epic damage from whatever conflict in had been in, and was essentially just scrap metal. But it had one remaining bit of ordnance. A single shell. Proper fiddly old tech that would have been very helpful to the crawler if we could dismantle it safely. Which we couldn't.'

'What happened?'

Lucille took a breath and closed her eyes. 'Apparently they call them sunbombs, or they do nowadays anyway. They're like giant cannon balls, but they explode when they pierce the hull, flushing whatever is on the other side with a burst of heat so potent that it vaporises tissue.'

'That's... nasty.'

'A relatively clean weapon though,' the captain said. 'Kills the crew, mostly leaves the ship intact to be repurposed or dismantled later. Brutally efficient.'

'Anyway,' Lucille interrupted. 'If you've got decent armour, a sunbomb is pretty useless. But I reckon with the sort of damage you described down there. I don't know. I might be over thinking it. Might just have been your usual old style skirmish with regular weapons and I'm just trying to add a mystery to the situation.'

'Maybe, but it would explain the skeletons,' Wendy said.

'Skeletons?'

'There was a pile of them that I had the good fortune to fall into. Most likely the crew. I mean, they could have decomposed naturally, but it was really cold in there, so...'

The captain ran a hand through his hair. 'Doesn't matter. Makes for a lovely story to tell when we get home, sure, but it's not relevant to our pay day. What does matter is that we've got working tech to sell.'

Wendy looked at him and frowned. 'You really suck the fun out of things sometimes, captain.'

'You can complain about that all you like from atop your massive pile of money, Milton. Now sit still while

Wolfe checks if you're dying horribly.'

She hadn't seen him return, but the moment the captain mentioned him she spotted Thorsten lurking about a few feet away. He was cradling a small rusty box a few inches in size, all sides emblazoned with warning symbols.

'If you are dying,' Thorsten said. 'I get your share.'

Opening the box, he pulled out a syringe and needle the length of his forearm.

FOUR

He could hear them hammering on the door, but they didn't have a chance of getting in.

'Pilot! We demand an explanation!'

'I'm sure you do, councillor, but I'm not inclined to provide one at this time.'

That they would complain about the course change wasn't unseen. They had been lobbying for one for a while now, and that he had done so without giving them the victory was getting on their wick. There wasn't even a legitimate reason not to discuss it with them, he knew, but bullheadedness was driving him right now. He could pass it off as a wish for secrecy – the councillors were notorious gossips – but ultimately he just didn't want to talk to them.

Since laying in the new course, both the crawler and the roller had connected to the network and he had been watching their signals closely. Neither of them seemed to be aware of the prize, judging by their movements, which was good. The crawler was closer, but it was moving slowly, saving fuel no doubt. The roller was more than double the strider's distance from the wreck, but it could move fastest of all three cities if it got a heads up.

It was oddly exhilarating, knowing something the other

pilots didn't know. Granted, he knew a lot of things they didn't – specifics of his city and that sort of thing – but they wouldn't benefit from knowing those sorts of things. But this, it felt like a heist from one of the old books, almost. If he was careful, they'd never even know he'd taken it.

He'd had a bit of time to research what it could be now, and it had only made him more excited. There was a whole catalogue of cities and vessels that had gone missing over the years, and though most of them were galleons there was a few properly interesting things buried out there, by all accounts. It had been a long time since any of the cities had possessed an entourage, losing them to petty wars and encounters with the weather. In a best case scenario, one where he could get this thing operational with minimal cannibalising for the strider, what a feat that would be.

Galveston clung to the antennae with one hand and stared out from the top of the walker. Three days ago it had been buried at the bottom of a forest, entangled in tree roots and mulch, and now it was leading the vanguard of his robot army. The woman didn't stand a chance.

Getting ahead of himself a little, but there wasn't much else to do on the journey. He'd shunted what power he could into the ambulation system, but there wasn't much to spare.

Traffic was picking up on the network, the roller and the crawler were talking to each other. The usual pleasantries, most likely. They had tried them on him when they had connected, but he had ignored them. He didn't want to let anything slip.

But then, what if they had heard? What if they were talking about the wreckage right now?

He logged into their chat.

> Hello you two, pilot strider here.

>> Wotcha, strider, this is roller.

>>> Crawler here, hello buddy.

> Things going okay for you two?

>>> Shit is breaking all over my city, was just asking roller if he had any spare supplies.

>> I've got most of what the lady needs, but not all of it. You got anything to spare, strider?

> Depends what she's after.

There was a list, almost all of it things that were difficult to machine. Nothing he could spare.

> Sorry, we're running low over here too.

>>> I understand, don't worry about it. I need to go and talk with the mechanics and see what can be done to keep us running. TTYL.

** A user has left the conference **

>> She's a lovely girl, but she's running that city into the ground.

> ?

>> I get a call every day about how close her city is to collapse. The crawler has always been temperamental, but never this unreliable. The girl is a joke.

> And you weren't when you got handed the stick the first time?

>> I learned, she is steadfastly refusing to do so. We should give her a crucible.

> That sounds unpleasant. What are you proposing exactly?

>> We wait her out. Give her a taste of rationing what she has so she doesn't come to us all the time for all the little things. A large amount of this job is making do with what you have, after all.

> Maybe.

>> Well, I'm going to do that. You apparently don't have the spares for her, so it doesn't matter. How are things over there?

> We're surviving, for the moment. Nothing worth reporting.

A message slid up from the bottom corner of his screen, he was leaving the network catchment area.

> Going to lose signal. Good luck out there, pilot roller.

>> You too, pilot strider. Check in next clear call.

** Signal lost **

For a moment, he considered giving the wreckage to the crawler. The roller's pilot wasn't exactly wrong about her, she had come across as if she was taking the other cities for granted, but they were a family. You took your family for granted by default, that's what they were for, especially when there were a few family members out of contact for such an extended period. And maybe it was the noble thing to do to let her have the thing, rebuild her reserves and get her back on an equal footing.

But then something seized in the rightmost leg and a thousand different sirens started blaring in the cockpit.

The strider screeched to a halt, the weight of the beast causing it to rock precariously for a moment as the legs tried to find their balance. It had been designed with three legs for just such an event, so while the motion was unsettling Rostrum never felt in danger. The jolt of the thing did throw him from his seat, however.

By the time he righted himself, his console was plastered with a thousand requests for reports and updates. He flicked through them quickly, discarding anything that wasn't information. A message from maintenance was all that seemed relevant, something about the frozen joint he had dispatched them to fix.

He couldn't do any good up here.

A flick of a switch set the strider on lock down, and he heard the enormous metal bolts slide into the hips of the city, keeping the legs locked in their current position. He stormed out of the cockpit and past the confused gaggle of councillors, straight to the nearest elevator.

He watched through the grating as he descended to the drive decks. There was a lot of panic, but that was to be expected. More than a few of the older citizens, people in their late thirties through to their sixties, were trying to calm people down. A great mob of rationality, making no small progress. By the time he reached his destination, over a hundred storeys down, the citizens he was zipping by were less vocal, more restrained.

They were used to things breaking and the resulting calamities, but this had been theatrical almost. The usual breakage was usually so remote that only the people who worked in that area knew, and then by the time the news travelled out to the masses it had already been fixed. Not the legs though, it was hard to keep that contained.

The elevator plunged into the lower levels, away from residential, and things changed quite rapidly. Things were bursting and metal was squealing from the outset, wires were sparking and causing small fires, and worried looking men in protective clothing were doing their best to extinguish them. Utter chaos.

Still, there was enough control over the situation to have one of the superintendents meet him straight off the lift.

'Not going to lie, it's pretty bad,' the man said. He clearly had a talent for understatement. A grimy badge on his chest identified him as Rickman.

'Tell me everything, not just what's in the report.'

Rickman signalled for Rostrum to follow him, leading him through a steam filled corridor into a cavernous filled with enormous machines. The beating heart of the drive train.

He started barking instructions to red-faced men covered in sweat, then turned to Rostrum. 'We sent a couple of men to keep the ice out of the mechanism, as ordered, but they said they found something lodged deep in there. One of them tried to remove it and, boom, this.'

'Boom?'

'Literally, boom,' Rickman said, miming a little explosion with his hands. 'Exploded as soon as they moved it, fused the entire joint. Seized the entire system, which is just leading to this mess. Frankly, if we don't cut power to the entire system, the internals are going to grind themselves into dust trying to move that locked knee.'

'Kill it. Shut down everything you have to.'

'Aye sir,' he said and threw a gesture at someone on a far catwalk. They echoed it to the next, and so on until somewhere in the depths a lever was thrown and the machine noise died away. 'Couldn't do it without your say so, sir.'

'No, I know. Judging from the damage I saw on the way down, I might have to amend that policy in the future.'

'If there is a future.'

'Excuse me?'

Rickman winced and pinched the bridge of his nose. Then he pulled a pipe from his pocket and lit it up. He took a few puffs and offered it to Rostrum, who declined. 'This is a big job, sir. Complete immobilisation. At an absolute push, we can rig it up so you can use the other two legs to move, but I wouldn't recommend it. Ideally, we need to get that knee moving again and patch up whatever damage resulted from that. Best estimate is a week, if we work absolutely round the clock *and* have all the spare parts.'

'Which we almost certainly won't.'

'Aye.'

Rostrum took a breath. 'Is this sabotage?'

'Sir, I wouldn't –'

'You said there was something jammed in the joint. Tell me, honestly, is there a less malevolent explanation for that being there?'

He took a long puff on his pipe. 'Given that it bleeding exploded when my boys moved it... Not likely.'

'Send me the names of everyone with access to that area. Work details, general clearances, whatever. Send it straight to the cockpit. Then get this fixed. If you can.'

'I can fix this, sir,' Rickman said, narrowing his eyes with determination. 'If you believe anything, believe that.'

Rostrum nodded and the engineer vanished into the steam, shouting instructions the whole time.

The damage certainly looked severe. Pilots were expected to have extensive knowledge of the inner workings of their city, both mechanical and personnel. Looking at it now, he could see where every system that fed into the movement of the seized appendage had started to suffer, way back through the chain. As each one failed, it passed the stress backwards like some great continuum of vandalism, wrecking each of them in turn.

It had the look of sabotage about it, whether one included the alleged bomb or not. Messy, conspicuous, contemptuous, all the hallmarks. It was as much for show as it was for effect.

Yet, there had been no warning.

And sabotage at this time? What an amazing coincidence.

He started to think that perhaps he was part of a larger game, one he couldn't see yet. Perhaps there was no wreckage at all and it was just bait to lure him off course, maroon the whole city off the beaten path. Although, all things considered, he couldn't work out the logic.

Whoever the saboteur was, he was clearly skilled enough to sneak in and out undetected. The bomb could have been planted whenever he liked, so why now? Stopping the strider on its planned route was just as good as wherever they were now, the weather would catch them either way. He was missing something.

The engineers bustled around him as he was lost in thought, and after a few jostles he withdrew back to the cockpit, avoiding any idle glances at the other citizens on the way back up. More data was needed before he could tell them anything, and the pleading faces would hang heavy on him if he actually saw them.

He felt safe in the cockpit. It was a place he could catch his breath and plan properly, no distractions. Take his time, think it through, act accordingly. No rushing, no being swayed by pained faces or nagging councillors. Build a solution from the facts at hand.

His legs went out from underneath him. All part of the process. Panic. Fear. The body was just another machine; this was just the decision engine spooling up to maximum efficiency. The power had to come from somewhere, just ease through it.

So much. So much to sort and worry about. Thousands of lives. Weather. Parts. Damage. Mobility. Succession. Pare it down. Prioritise. Focus.

His composure returned quickly once he had purged that vast wave of trepidation. Full system restart, shifting into diagnostic mode, that's all it was. Couldn't have any unnecessary data clogging up his runtime.

First order of business was always the meteorological map. Things could have been worse, all considered. Another twenty minutes on this heading would have had them passing between two vicious storms, the second of which would slam right into them within the hour if they had broken down in that corridor. As it was, they had a couple of hours before an entirely different storm smashed them.

Not enough time for repairs, but it was *time*.

The logical course was to call for aid from the other cities. One of them was probably close enough to at least send some galleons, evacuate some of the citizens before the storm hit, maybe even spare some engineers to hurry the repairs along. But then, what if...

No, he wouldn't even entertain that thought. They were the last humans; this sort of attack was beyond unconscionable.

> SOS. Pilot strider calling SOS.

It was a voice in the darkness. He wasn't even connected to the network at his current location, and clear call was impossible with the proximity of those storms. Sending out a galleon back to the network was feasible, but what if they had been sabotaged too? They'd need to be thoroughly checked first, and that was time they didn't have.

A few dark thoughts had him expecting some sort of reply. That would have made things easier, wouldn't it, if the attacker had been inside the system, lurking? Some malevolent data ghost, waiting for him to call for help and then revealing itself.

But the cursor blinked in silence, no reply was forthcoming. Of course not, far too easy to know there was an enemy out there. Then he would know for a fact exactly how careful to be. There was comfort in certainty.

With a few button presses, he gave the order: a galleon in each cardinal direction, all to try and reach one of the other cities. Tap into the network if they could, but otherwise ride out and search for clear call.

Skeleton crews. No need to have people thinking this was an evacuation. The strider didn't have any life boats and not even a tenth of the population would fit onto the galleons, even at a squeeze.

He exhaled as each of the confirmations blinked onto the screen, followed by the notification of each galleon unclamping. They were visible from the cockpit, the razors carving distinct tracks in the ice far below. What to do now?

Wait? That was the smart move. He had to trust in his people to either fix the strider in time or bring help. Hovering over them would slow them down. Pestering them would slow them down. These were trained people, skilled, knowledgeable in their fields. Just let them work.

It was the ones that had no skills that would be the problem. They'd be knocking on his door again soon, hammering it down with questions and demands. The politicians. Perhaps he could prepare for that instead. They would have to be told.

So much to do, so quickly. It didn't feel real.

Rubbing at the headache rapidly forming behind his eyes, he made for the conference room. Better he meet the politicians in an arena they all understood than they have this conversation in a hallway where the niceties of politics could be easily forgotten.

Evidently they had had the same idea.

Moses was at the front again, talking louder than all the others. 'Of course there will be accountability but now is not the time... Ah, pilot, there you are.'

'Councillor,' Rostrum said with a polite nod. '*Councillors*.'

'The quorum wants an update on what's going on down in ambulation. We've all noticed that we're stationary, and the citizens are coming to us –'

'Yes, well, you'd think they would have heard the explosion.'

There was some uncomfortable shuffling from the group. 'They did. Hence the concern.'

'Trust you push for transparency at a time like this. If we don't regulate what we say –'

'There will be panic,' Moses interrupted. 'I know. For once I agree with you, pilot. That's what I've been trying to tell the others. If we tell the people that this was sabotage, we'll have a witch hunt on our hands. Best to fix the situation quietly and *then* tell them the truth. Just this once.'

'That's not good enough,' another councillor said, pushing her way to the front of the group. 'The people have a right to know.'

Rostrum held up a hand. 'And they will, I promise, when we have all the facts. Right now, we have more important things to deal with than democracy. Namely, trying to keep us all from getting ripped to shreds by the weather.'

He could see the fear in their eyes now, though they tried to hide it behind anger and disgust. *Now* the weather scared them, he realised, and that was good. For all their bluster, they could see the danger now, and they would listen.

If they were to get out of this, they would need to.

FIVE

Wendy had spent twenty minutes trying to manufacture some sort of disc reader for the thing she had pulled out of the computer in the wreckage, but the pain in her arm had made the work considerably harder. Thorsten had done his best to be gentle, but with a needle that big there wasn't much he could do to cushion the blow. The entirety of her left forearm was burning and itching just beneath the skin, and she couldn't help but scratch.

It didn't improve her situation.

At least she hadn't been irradiated. That was nice.

The galleon didn't have anything that could natively read the disc, but it did have a lot of lasers and magnetic heads from more modern readers. It shouldn't have been hard to build something that could manage it. And yet it was proving tricky.

She'd run a couple of tests trying to load the disc by hand, scanning the surface with these lasers and mag-heads slowly just to see if anything would pop up on screen. When that didn't work – as she had known it wouldn't – she had to build something to rotate the disc at varying speeds. She had tried all the standards, none of them worked.

She was losing patience, and the pain was doing nothing to make it easier. As the disc whirred and beeped, refusing to read yet again, it took all her self-control not to smash the thing into a thousand pieces out of sheer frustration.

To be fair, it was mostly Thorsten's appearance that stopped her. He strode in, a big smile on his face and a well-used tube of cream in his hand. 'Thought you might benefit from a little of this.'

'What is it?' she said, shoving the disc-reader out of reach and under some other discarded tech.

'Anaesthetic gel. Turns out the medkits aren't quite as depleted as we thought. This little beauty had fallen out during the crash. Found it lodged between Lu's spare boots and her underwear drawer.'

Wendy rolled up her sleeve and winced as he started to apply the gel to the puncture mark. 'You went through her underwear drawer?'

'It was next to the drawer, tiny pervert. I didn't have to do any snooping.' He rolled his eyes. '*Honestly*. Besides, I get the feeling you're going to want that arm back in working order sooner rather than later.'

'What do you mean?'

He finished applying the gel, flipped the tube in his hand and tucked it away in a pocket. 'Let's not dance around this, brat. You're going to go right back in there as soon as the boss isn't looking, and you're going to persuade me to go with you. Again. And, hell, this time I even *want* you to.'

'You're going to take all the fun out of being naughty if you condone it, you know.'

He smiled. 'There's nothing naughty about having a bit of a looksie around an ancient wreck, right? The boss is going to sell it off, we know that, but there's history in this thing. I'm, I don't know, *interested.*'

'Look at you,' she said, scratching her arm still. 'You're all curious!'

'Something like that.'

In truth, she hadn't really planned to go back to the wreckage. At least, not properly. It was always an option, to sneak down there whilst the rest were killing time or something, but she had wanted access to the disc first.

'Well let's see how things go, old man. Keep an eye out for an opening, then maybe we'll go back down there.'

'Right you are, brat. Get well soon.'

He got up slowly and shot her a look, one she didn't recognise. Joy? No, there was something sad about it. He was a weird one.

When he was gone, she went back to work on the reader, to greater success as the pain in her arm started to dull. She couldn't get at the whole file, but there were bits of it that almost punched their way through the limitations of the equipment, whole documents that clawed their way to the surface.

She pulled up the one with the earliest timestamp, and the device clanked and whirred as it tried to rip the details from the disc. The screen filled with artefacts and broken code for a second, then somehow managed to parse the data into something readable.

>>> *Log Entry* <<<

>*Username: L.Enzo//Command*

>*Date of Entry: I don't fucking know*

>*Marcus died today. That leaves me and Francesca, and she's not got long left. Can't imagine I do either. Been fading in and out of consciousness so much lately that I've lost all track of time. Maybe it's been a week since the last entry? Hard to tell.*

>*I've tried to get the ambulation matrix back online, when I've been conscious. It didn't take too hard a hit in the attack. It should be possible to turn the damn thing back on, but I don't know what I'm doing. Francesca has been trying to talk me through it, but I'm not a patch on her when it comes to engineering. Can't help but thinking we'd be mobile by now if she was on her feet.*

>*Dangerous thoughts to have, I know. Worry about what is, not what isn't. Find a way to make do. And we've been trying. I don't*

know if I'm making any progress though. Francesca insists that if I'm following her directions then I am, but I don't know.

>This job was much more fun when all I had to do was shout at people and they did it all for me.

>Still don't know why they attacked us. Suppose it doesn't matter now. All that matters is getting this thing moving again so that maybe we don't all die here.

>I know the company will find us eventually. I also know that this log is probably being read by some company loss adjuster right now, I'm a realist. It's not your job, but I need to ask something of you, just in case we do all die here.

>There are two other files attached to this one. One of them, well, consider it our wills. Final statements, things we'd like done after we're gone. It's a young crew, we didn't bother sorting this out beforehand. Pretty self-explanatory.

>The other, that's my attempt to detail what Francesca has had me doing. I know that the company will be of a mind to write this off, claim on the insurance. That's the cheaper, most sensible option from a business standpoint. I get it, believe me.

>Thing is, I like this bloody thing. It's kept us safe, until now, and it's a truly fantastic feat of engineering. Don't let them scrap her. Just scrape out our corpses and switch her back on. Give us one last hurrah.

>Or don't. Whatever. We'll be dead. It's not like we'll care.

>>> End of Entry <<<

With the file names corrupted, trying to find these attached files was tricky. But, Wendy considered, even a corrupt name was going to sort of follow a pattern, right? If you work for someone that demands regular officer's logs, you're going to be the sort of company that is really anal about naming conventions. Even corrupted, they should be recognisable as using the same convention, right? Garbled nonsense, yes, but maybe the same length? Something?

No, obviously, that probably wasn't how computers worked. Without a better plan though, her best option was to sift the data for something that looked out of place.

Surprisingly, this worked. A quick scan found two files, again with unreadable names but still unique in the corrupted database. Much smaller names, for one.

She tried both, but one of them was damaged beyond recovery. The second worked though and, thankfully, it was the list of attempted repairs. After a moment of forced reflection on being thankful that the last wills and testaments of the crew had been rendered unreadable and what exactly that meant for her soul, she pored over the document.

In the space of five minutes she learned more about the construction of the wreckage than her entire sojourn through its innards. She'd never left the command deck, judging from these notes. A lot of effort had been put into clearing internal pathways, re-routing conduits, all to feed what seemed to be a sort of processor in the heart of the machine. The ambulation matrix, she supposed.

Frankly, even without knowing how the machine worked properly, this was an inelegant and amateurish attempt at repair. Not that that was an insult – she made those all the time, and they tended to be the ones that worked best – but she was a professional acting amateurishly, that meant she actually knew what she was doing. Even under the guidance of their engineer, this Enzo hadn't a clue.

Wendy couldn't be sure, not without seeing it for herself, but the notes seemed to describe the pair working to crossed purposes. One of them was inept, that much was clear. Some of Enzo's repairs were solid, but others undid them in weird ways. Two steps forward, one back. By the time they had written this document, progress had pretty much ground to a halt.

Obviously she would now *have* to go back down there. If there was a chance she could repair the thing before the boss sold it off? He'd understand, surely. If anything, having it in near enough working order would raise the bounty. He couldn't possibly be angry.

She popped the disc out of the makeshift reader and tucked it into a pocket. Then she did a circuit of the room, grabbing what tools she could. What did she really need, what was worth the extra weight on the line? A couple of different multi-tools maybe, a spool of easily compatible wiring, she was packing with purpose in mind this time.

Pockets loaded, she skulked out of her workshop and right into the beaming smile of Thorsten Wolfe.

'Made up your mind then, have we?'

Every instinct told her to slow down, take a breath, hell, even jump at the suddenness of his appearance. She should have been startled, but she was in the grip of *potential* now, she was far too busy for that. 'I think I can fix it, Thor. I might actually be able to get it working.'

'Are you serious?'

Jesus, were her hands shaking? 'Maybe. I don't know. I think so. I really think so.'

'We should tell the boss; he'll want to hear this.'

'No!' she said, louder than she had meant to. 'I'm still not sure. No sense in getting his hopes up, right?'

'Okay, sure,' he said. 'But this does sound a little shady. Not that I'm against a bit of shade, just want to make sure you know what you're doing.'

He wasn't incorrect, this did sort of feel wrong to Wendy. She'd disobeyed orders before, of course, but that had always been a sort of childish pushing of boundaries when you got down to it. There were orders the boss expected to be ignored by her, and those he was adamant she not flout. It was a dynamic that they had struck pretty quickly once they had started working together.

This felt very much like she was breaking the latter of the two orders, but for once she didn't care. That was new.

'Where are the others anyway?'

Thor shrugged. 'Captain's cabin I expect. There'll be a lot of negotiating needs doing to secure the best price for that wreck. Lu is pretty shrewd when it comes to haggling.'

'So we can sneak out right now then?'

'When I said I'd look for an opening, I didn't mean right this second, brat.'

'Come on,' she said, putting on her best puppy dog eyes. 'Why wait?'

'The two words that always get me into trouble,' he said. 'Fine, but I'm blaming you when we get shouted at. You're like a witch or something.'

'Come on!'

Taking him by the arm, Wendy dragged him to the side of the ship and clipped the pair of them to their lines. One last check to make sure they weren't being watched, and she threw herself over the side, letting the harness slow her decent automatically this time. Uncharacteristically reckless of her, but she was properly excited now.

Her legs slipped on the ice as she landed slightly too fast for her cleats to account for, sending her sprawling onto her bottom. That knocked a little of the reverie out of her, but by the time Thor touched down next to her it was back again.

Thor helped her up and led her over to the opening, lowering her in again gently. Knowing what she was in for this time, she landed daintily and tried to catch her bearings. Soundlessly, Thor dropped down beside her again.

'This is the command deck,' she said. 'All the controls and stuff are up here, but the real meat is down below, right?'

'You sure?'

She frowned and scratched the back of her neck. 'Basic design philosophy sort of says it has to be the lower decks. You want your engines close to your propulsion, right? Plus, there's something primal about being above your engines, makes you feel more in control. We go deep enough, we'll find it I bet.'

'Fair enough,' Thor said. 'But how are we going to get down there exactly?'

'I'm sure we'll find something.'

Find her way to the control room again was easy enough, and this time she even managed to climb in without falling into a pile of skeletons. Things were looking up!

The control room was the heart. She could find her way below decks from here. There was an unspoken language of design when it came to vessels, one she had always known. She could read bulkheads if she tried, map out thing she had yet to see. If she had one good look at the exterior, she could extrapolate the interior. Useless with people, amazing with machines, that's what her parents had always said.

It had been meant nicely, she was sure.

Right, so, a number of different exits, not even counting the one caused by the cannon fire. She'd come in through a side entrance, that was for maintenance and general faffing about. With time it would get her where she needed to be – maintenance always did – but it was inexact. The main corridor, that was the way.

It hadn't really registered with her the first time, mostly because she hadn't been looking for it. The doors were sealed and, because of how the wreck was lying, at an odd angle, partially obscured by debris. They were double doors though, inlaid into the wall in a way that made them obvious, unlike the maintenance exits that she suspected were designed to close flush and vanish into the walls. She navigated her way down and lay next to the panel on what should have been a wall.

She pulled a small contraption from her kit. 'So I think you should stay up here, Thor.'

'Oh you do, do you?'

'Yeah,' she said, clipping wires from the contraption to the door panel. 'If I get things running, you'll need to pilot it all from up here. I probably won't be able to boot the computers and run command diagnostics from down there.'

'Excuse me?'

She tapped a button. A light came on inside the panel. 'I'm plugging it in, but I need you to press the on button.'

'Okay, that I can do.'

'Good,' she said with a smile. 'You might want to move over a little.'

He did, and she tapped another button on her contraption. It sparked a little, then the panel sparked a lot, and the doors jolted apart just a little. There was a whoosh of ancient air, and Wendy let it pass before she jammed one of her tools into the crack and levered the doors further apart.

'That's a long way down,' Thor said. 'So I guess that means it's the right way.'

There was a loud noise as Wendy affixed another line to the floor, letting it unspool into the darkness. She snapped a couple of small glow lamps to the rope and let them fall too, surveying what they illuminated on the way. Didn't seem to be damaged, at least no loose supports or anything that were liable to shake their way free on her own descent.

She snapped her harness onto this new line. 'If I'm right, it shouldn't take me long to find. Stay on the radio, yeah?'

'As if I'd cut contact in the big scary ghost ship.'

They bumped fists and she lowered herself into the opening. She took it slow at first – lesson learned above – checking every foothold as she made her way down. It was remarkably sturdy, all things considered, and after a few minutes of slow descent she felt more comfortable speeding up. It caused a slight problem when she had to change tack to keep on track with where she believed she needed to be, but she put that down to exuberance rather than the wreck itself.

All told, it took her maybe ten minutes to find her way to what seemed to be the engineering hub. An enormous mechanism stood proud in the centre of the room, its innards exposed as a piece of thick metal panelling hung limply open.

Across the rest of the room, rotten fabric had been strung from bulkhead to bulkhead like a series of canopies. Rusted tools and parts were strewn about the canopies, giving the illusion that the things could still hold some weight. Wendy decided not to put this to the test.

Following the path of the topmost canopy, she positioned herself by the mechanism, the more central position giving her a better view of the room itself. It was vast and empty. There were a number of small bins secured to the walls, recessed within in fact, that she was certain would contain tools and spare part similar to those on the canopies. It seemed this hub was devoted almost entirely to servicing this one mechanism.

'Thor, you copy?'

There was a little static on the line, but he was still coming through clearly. 'Yup, I'm here. You find it?'

'I think so,' she said, leaning in for a closer look. 'Looks like I've found the central drive shaft. Makes sense, you'd have to take the matrix offline if this had been dinged.'

'Why?'

Wrinkling her nose in concentration, she set about preliminary repairs. 'If I'm right, the ambulation matrix is like a computer that helps maintain a complicated drive system. The Strider has something similar. Thing is, they're super dim, or really focused. They can't recognise flaws they're not programmed for and can get all jammed up if something goes wrong.'

'That sounds like a pretty massive problem, design-wise,' Thor said. The static was getting worse.

'It is. It really, really, is,' she said. Something sheered off inside the mechanism at her urging, clanking its way down the inside and into the depths. 'They're easy to reprogramme though, if you've read the manual. If you haven't, it's just as easy to turn it off. They're not exactly a necessity, they just make the ride smoother.'

'I think I understand.'

'Good, because I don't think I explained it too well. Give me a second, this is a bit tricky.'

'Understood.'

All the technology they used these days, older than living memory. With the exception of the beacons it was her job to spike, nothing new had really been built in decades, just old tech repurposed or repaired forever. So it shouldn't have been so exciting to work on this, but it was.

The drive shaft was old tech too, but it was *pure*. She'd seen things like it before in galleons and in the cities, but that had been tainted by generations of use and techno-cannibalism. They were pale shadows of what they had been, of the elegant machines that once were. There was something so beautiful about a machine in its original configuration, with study purpose-built parts. It was almost religious.

It was an easy fix, mechanically, but a hard one spiritually.

The attack had knocked a few of the gears out of their internal housing. Without their bearings keeping the motion smooth, they had seized. Dull, boring, a pedestrian problem. Not even a problem really, an inconvenience. If she'd set about the machine with a hammer she would have fixed the issue long before anything broke. Yet still it made her smile.

She fixed it with more finesse than a simple hammering. The gears practically reinserted themselves. That Enzo had had such a hard time fixing the machine seemed inconceivable. But then, perhaps Wendy had walked in at the end of a long procedure. It didn't really match up with all the notes she had read, but there were any number of reasons to sugar-coat the truth on a machine you were trying to keep clear of the scrapheap.

Still, it was curious.

Sealing the panel, she swung her way around the room, trying to find the activation switch for the ambulation matrix. She'd expected it to have a big sign, considering what it did, but nothing.

'Thor, can you do me a favour?'

'Probably,' he said. 'What do you need?'

'Can you have a look at the terminals up there, see if you can find one that turns the matrix back online?'

There was a sound of physical exertion. No-one should be subjected to that right inside their ear. 'Excuse me? Are you saying that the thing you needed to fix is actually up here?'

'No...' she said. 'Maybe. A bit. A little bit of it is. I would still have had to come down here anyway!'

'Yeah, sure. Maybe you should start taking in your surroundings a little before you start climbing into dark pits?'

'Whatever, *dad*, just find the terminal.'

'Oi, watch your mouth, young lady,' he said between grunts. It was taking him longer to reach the cluster of terminals than it did her, but then maybe he wouldn't fall off and nearly kill himself. 'Okay, I think I've got it.'

'It should be nice and simple. Just hit the on switch.'

There was a rumble that permeated the entire wreck. The canopies began to sway, dropping some of their rusty contents as they did so, as the various cogs and whatnot inside the drive shaft started to crunch back to life. It wasn't long before the machine was happily ticking over. Amazing.

In lieu of anyone to high five, Wendy slapped her palm against a wall. The sound echoed louder than the engine noise, which in and of itself was a miracle. They really knew how to build them, way back when.

And, it seemed, she knew how to fix them.

'Did it work?' Thor asked.

She swung her way back to the way she had come in. 'I think so, yeah! We might have just quadrupled the bounty on this thing, Thor.'

'Provided the boss doesn't shout us to death, you mean.'

'He'll be pleased, right?' she said, already halfway back to the command room. It was a much simpler journey to do in reverse, once you already knew the route.

'I hope so,' Thor said. The static had ramped up again and it was making him difficult to hear. 'Oh, shit!'

'What?'

'Standby.'

She broke into a run. Standby indeed! As if she was likely to do that in a creepy ghost ship. Pounding over the unhelpfully angled floor caused her to nearly trip a number of times – her feet catching support beams from when it had been rightly oriented as a wall – but it wasn't too far to go at this point. A couple of twists and she was back at the bottom of her line.

She clipped on and started to climb, fast as she could, an automated ascender boosting her significantly. All the while she was calling to Thorsten, getting nothing but static back in return. Why had she ignored it? Because she was inside a giant tin can? She knew better than that. They all did.

Faster, faster, faster. She had to climb faster. She had to make up for the wilful disregard she – they – had both shown. By the time she crested the doorway at the top of her climb, she was flushed and breathless. Thor was above her, strapped into a harness and hammering away at a terminal. The light from the screen hit all the angles on his face, making him look older, angrier. She didn't like it.

'What's wrong?' she asked. Stupid question, she already knew.

'Storm,' he said. 'I don't know how we missed it.'

'We're supposed to have a few hours yet!'

He ripped off his radio earpiece. 'Well, apparently we don't. The static should have been a clue. I thought –'

'I know, me too. Rule one: radio interference is always the weather. We're idiots.'

'I've tried signalling the ship just in case,' he said, looking down at her. 'Can't get through. Maybe they'll have moved. That would be for the best.'

'Leaving us here doesn't sound like the captain. Besides, the ship is too damaged to move.'

'He'd only wait if he knows we've gone. You don't do a headcount in situations like this. And as for the damage, you of everyone should know that you limp away from the damn storms if you can, you can usually coax *something* out.'

Wendy was trying to move too fast, too panicked. Trying to untangle herself from her line was taking too long, and it was getting longer the more she tried to speed up. She forced herself to stop, take a breath. 'Should we go back up there?'

He was hammering keys again. 'No. Wait – Yes! The storm's too close now, if they've waited for us then they'll never outrun it. But if we get them down here –'

'Maybe. I mean, it's survived the weather so far!'

'You go. I'll blunder around the system, maybe find something that can help.'

She didn't need telling twice. It was autopilot now, there was no thought involved. Once she hit the maintenance tunnels, she could feel the storm. This was the very edge of it, vicious winds thrumming along the exposed steel, reverberating down the corridors. It like a vast ghostly cry, washing over her.

By the time she reached the exit, she could feel it. Stinging, burning cold, howling through the opening they had made. Climbing back out, it lashed at her hands, slapped her face, scratched at her eyes.

She'd never seen the weather up close. The entire purpose of the cities was to avoid it as long as possible, even being able to see it on the horizon was considered a close call or a failure of leadership. Galleon crews got closer than others, sure, but they gave it as wide a berth as they could.

Once. She had seen a storm once, when she was a teenager. Her first date with a girl from her class, out on one of the observation platforms in the middle of the night. It was terrifying to see, such a powerful force of nature way off in the distance. It looked like the end of the world. And yet, she had thought it romantic at the time. That had been the backdrop to her first kiss.

As she poked out her head, she saw the power, but not the romance. The ship was still there, and above it a malignant cloud loomed heavy, dark, the source of this meteorological tantrum. Somewhere up there, the captain and Lu were screaming, she knew it. She couldn't hear it, not over the wind, but she *knew*.

Hauling herself free was hard. The wind was constantly shifting direction, throwing her off balance and, she was sure, intent on shoving her back inside the wreck. But she persevered and finally got to her feet on the surface, trudging to the line and slowly climbing the side of the galleon.

At the top, ship no longer blocking the view, she got to see the storm in all its majesty. For the first time, she saw clouds set against sunlight – the sky strangled by the purpling clouds as the sun strained to break through. All the anger of a neglected world, condensed into a weapon.

The captain and Lu weren't on deck – which wasn't a surprise – but Wendy was hesitant to unbuckle herself from the line to search for them. Staying upright was hard enough as it was, and she was worried that she had only maintained her footing because she had the support of her harness. But then, they'd never hear her over the squall, and the only way to get them to safety would be to have them come with her.

The voice of treason started to speak up in her head. It was a putrid, angular thing, a lurker that picked its moments well. It liked desperation, the grim moments where she could afford to discount nothing out of hand. It whispered to her – because if it had needed to raise its voice then it had not chosen its moment carefully enough – and it told her to leave them.

They'd never know. If they survived they most certainly wouldn't have expected her to come this far. Thorsten would understand that the weather defeated her. Not one of them would know how she hadn't exhausted all options before she gave up.

With a howl, the wind shifted again, whipping against her face and opening a small gash on her cheek. It caught the blood and sprayed a couple of drops up into her eyes. She hissed and swore. It had been hard enough to keep her eyes open as it was, and this was making it worse. No, this was as far as she could go.

Another lash of wind and another cut opened, forcing her to shield her face from the onslaught. It was getting worse. She had to make a decision.

That treasonous voice was saying all the right, rational things. She couldn't dispute that. If she thought about it, everything was telling her to turn back, hide, take shelter. Leave them, they'll probably be fine, and if they die then it's hardly her fault.

Clearly this wasn't a time for thinking, not if it was leading her down that path.

Defiantly, she unhooked her harness.

SIX

The weather maps were wrong, but Rostrum wasn't exactly sure why.

Nothing was more important that keeping the city clear of the weather patterns, and so he took great pains to memorise the daily updates. If he needed to change the route, then he wanted to make those changes as early as possible. Less risk of a mistake if you do it that way.

The storms had always been capricious. They'd been outrunning this particular storm front for months now, and in all that time it had never quite behaved exactly as expected. Numerous course corrections – little ones, minute shifts in bearing that would serve to keep that maelstrom at their backs – had been necessary, but there had never been any real danger. He had *planned* for catastrophic breakdowns, that was his job.

But that plan was all wrong, apparently. The storm was moving in much quicker than it should have done, buoyed by some unseen force.

He had opted not to tell the council this.

His meeting with them following the breakdown had not gone well. Even with his most ardent opponent on side for once, the others had been more prone to panicked posturing than anything constructive. They had acknowledged – at last – that the weather was a real threat that took precedence, but they still insisted that this was all somehow his fault.

He'd sent them home. He could sort this out without their help.

Reports from the drive section had not been encouraging. Even before the storm had sped up, it would have been touch and go as to whether the Strider could have been moving again. Now it seemed they would have to work through the storm, and that would cause more problems than it would fix. He'd made the call for them to focus on weathering the storm rather than avoiding it.

The logs were open on his main console. Every time a city opted to batten down the hatches and brave a storm, those logs were specially marked. With the deal toll.

If you're going to repeat history, you had bloody well better know exactly what you're getting into.

Rostrum had been looking for something, anything, that he could do to make the Strider secure. He'd skimmed maybe fifteen logs so far, and even the ones with the lowest death counts didn't really provide any meaningful explanation as to why. So far, his best option was to trust in his engineering staff to find some way of reinforcing the superstructure.

That was a little annoying. They were good men and women, they knew what they were doing and they could do it a damn sight better without him micromanaging them. But without that occupying him that left him with the saboteur to deal with, and that was something he really didn't want to have to consider.

The comms icon was blinking again. The Strider wasn't getting to clear call any time soon at this rate, but it was still able to connect to the nascent network. He'd had to send out a distress call, that was just good practice, but he hadn't expected anything helpful. They were all too far out, under-supplied or just too self-interested to spare any real support. And that was fine.

He didn't want their pity.

What he did want, was for them to stay connected to the network for as long as possible.

He clicked another icon on his console and typed in a few commands, then opened the comms window.

> Strider here, who's online this time?

>> Wotcha, pilot Strider. Pilot Roller reporting in.

Had he done the Roller yet? No, still at least forty percent to go.

> Nice to hear from you again.

>> I've been trying to put something together to help you, Strider. Got a drive on for volunteers to man galleons to evacuate your populace, deliver supplies, offer mechanical support. Whatever we can do.

> Any luck?

>> A little.

>> No.

>> Not really.

>> People are scared. That storm is very close.

> I know. Unless you have enough room for everyone, a partial evacuation would only make things worse anyway. And, best will in the world, no-one knows the Strider better than its own mechanics. I figure your lot's ideas would just clog up the works.

Seventy percent complete now. Good. Keep him talking.

>> That's what I thought, but I had to tell them. They needed something to do. Our populations mingle a lot, they're concerned. Needed to distract them.

> I understand. Doing the same here. Keep everyone busy, maybe they won't have time to realise how bad things are.

Eighty-three percent.

>> Smart. It's always nice to see we think alike, Strider. You heard anything from Crawler?

> Not much. She's a bit too far out for the network, I

think.

>> Such a fair-weather friend, that one. Calling for help all the time, ignoring you when you truly need it. Bitch.

> She's new. Young. Give her a break.

>> You are far more forgiving than I, Strider. You sweet on her? Been using the network for a little extra-curricular interaction maybe?

> You are disgusting.

>> :)

>> Sorry. I just take this sort of thing quite seriously. I shouldn't have lowered the tone like that.

> It's okay. But chill. My city is the one in trouble, not the Roller.

Ninety-eight percent. Nearly done.

>> I hear you. Anything you want me to chase up? It's unlikely we can get supplies to you before the weather hits, but info or something?

A notification slid into the corner of the screen. One hundred percent.

> Not right now. Keep on the line as long as you can, though. I'll shout if I need something.

> GTG. Pilot business needs my attention.

>> Roger. Good luck, buddy.

He closed the comms window and turned his attention to the program he had been running in the background. A little piece of old-tech software they'd found inside some salvage a year or so back. Useless at the time, but the more the network grew, the more it became useful.

The distress call had been an opportunity. No-one would send any real aid, but they would all make a show of attempting to. There would be open connections to all the nearby cities for much longer than usual, far more regularly, as they dawdled or diverted a little for the sake of solidarity.

This would give him the opening he needed to breach their systems and steal their manifests. He wasn't ready to believe this sabotage was an inside job, and if it was an external one then it meant someone from another city was missing. He'd gone through the Strider's boarding logs and dispatched men to question every recorded foreign citizen aboard, but he doubted he'd find the culprit that way. They'd been too savvy in their attack to get caught out on something so simple.

But maybe, just maybe, there'd be a clue in the other cities' manifests. Some black hole in the personnel assignments, a gap they could use to smuggle out an agent of some sort. Why they would do that, he couldn't say, but it was a better place to start than an internal witch hunt.

The Roller had been the first manifest to download completely. The pilot had been friendly to Rostrum for a long time, so he had maintained the most contact. Of the closest cities, the Roller was the least likely to knowingly try and sabotage the Strider, but Rostrum couldn't rule them out. Could still be a rogue internal faction even if the pilot hadn't sent them.

He fed the Roller's manifest into a program to compare it with his personal one. If there was any correlation there, the machine would find it. He'd do the manual search once that was out the way.

Back to the weather patterns then, to watch his impending doom slowly march across the flickering screen of his console. It would help with his wallowing, let it build to critical mass. He'd already accepted that, to deal with this situation, something was going to have to burst. Fear or anger or disgust, something needed to push trust out of his head so that he could make the hard choices. The feeling growing in him as he watched the storm move closer on his monitor, that was probably what it would be, in the end.

He moved across the cockpit and hit the button for what had been, long ago, the emergency exit. A few generations back, the pilot at the time had realise that there was nowhere to escape to in the event of an emergency, so had set about turning the thing into a sort of balcony. Rostrum has seldom used it, but today he needed the air.

The storm was actually visible now. People would notice soon. That was almost good, gave him yet more motivation to push past whatever barrier was keeping him from doing what needed to be done.

Looking down, he saw the city stretch out beneath him. It didn't really look like anything from this angle, but he could still place every bump and groove to the schematics.

This was how he knew, without checking his console, that it was one of the residential districts that exploded.

The sound never quite travelled up to the balcony, not beyond a dull *whump*. The explosion itself was visible though, a bright lick of flame and a patina of scorched metal sent spiralling to the snow below.

He stormed back inside. Which residential district was it? There were a few clustered around that particular area, stacked atop each other and around the old water tanks. The console didn't even have the report yet; it was still insisting everything was fine.

If that was how things were, he'd find it himself. He called up the power system on his console, looked for circuits that were blown, places without power, and traced them back through the system.

There, that was the one. Engineering Residential B – where all the foremen and managers resided. He should have known.

By the time the confirmation came through on the system, he was already down where the room had been, staring out of a scorched hole into the freezing world beyond. The entire block had been vaporised.

'Smart,' he caught himself saying aloud. 'Very smart.'

'Sir?' someone asked from behind.

He turned. It was Rickman. The man as bloodied and a little singed, but alive. 'Yes?'

'You were muttering to yourself,' the engineer said.

'Humour me,' Rostrum said. 'How were preparations

going for the storm?'

'I just lost my entire senior staff –'

'I know. Answer the question.'

Rickman bristled with rage, his eyes bulging. 'We had a plan. Might not have worked, but might have saved some lives.'

Rostrum sat down, dangling his legs into the void. 'Such curious motives.'

'You're not making any sense.'

'Unfortunately, I am,' Rostrum said and sighed. 'Our saboteur hit the drive systems, beaching us here. Not directly lethal. He did nothing while you were all on repair duty. Then, soon as I move you to survival mode, to keeping us alive, he cuts the head off that effort.'

'You're saying this was a backup plan?'

'I'm saying we need to find this saboteur. Now. Did anyone other than you survive?'

'Not many.'

'Take whoever is left and get back to work. I know it will be slow going and you probably won't be ready in time, but any preparation is better than none.'

'Yes sir.'

Rostrum stood up and mournfully ran his hand over the jagged metal of the door frame. If it was to be war, the other party could have at least had the decency to tell him beforehand.

He needed to talk to Moses, but he didn't really want to move. It would fade if he took his eyes off it. The memory would dim; it wouldn't be so horrific. The human mind was fantastic at this sort of thing, if you let it. It would start to rationalise. This was a small attack really – heinous, but not too crippling. Given time, the dead could be replaced quite easily. A little training course and they could promote from the already quite vast ranks of the engineering crew.

Grim and more than a little mercenary, but that was the reality of things.

But this was two attacks in close proximity. A campaign. It shifted priorities. It wasn't about recovering from the last attack; it was now about stopping the next. You can work around a lone attack, shift solution to deal with the fallout. That's what he had been doing, moving the crews from repairs to reinforcement. That approach didn't work if someone was reacting to those solutions.

He had the advantage right now. Rostrum needed to balance the scales.

Moses arrived eventually, his face ashen and haggard. That was a look Rostrum recognised, the haunted countenance of a man who has had to reassure scared civilians despite knowing nothing himself. You can't manufacture hope, just cede your own to others.

'This is inhuman,' he said. His voice was small, lifeless. 'Why do this?'

'To cripple us,' Rostrum said.

'But why? What purpose does it serve?'

Rostrum stood up, careful not to slip out into the world. 'I don't know. For whatever reason, they want us in this storm.'

'That's madness. Suicide!'

'Yes. We need to find him.'

'Obviously. But he could be anyone.'

'I'm going to activate martial law.'

Moses eyes widened for a moment, then fell. 'Are you sure?'

'We've got no leads, no suspects. He could be literally anyone and we can't allow him the opportunity to subvert the investigation from the inside.'

'The citizens won't like it.'

'I don't care. They'll like getting ripped to shreds by the wind a lot less, I'm sure of that,' Rostrum said. 'Have security usher people back towards secured areas. I'll go back to the cockpit and do what needs to be done.'

'What about the weather?'

'Nothing we can do about that now. We just have to

make sure we're as safe as we can be when we get hit.'

Moses nodded and left. Rostrum allowed him a minute or two before he made for the cockpit again.

Security had already started moving people away from the blast zone, politely herding them towards their own residences and work places, but a couple had slipped through and tried accosting Rostrum for answers. He ignored them, barging through and doing his very best not to hear their pleas as he did so. He took special care to avoid seeing their faces. They weren't his people right now; they couldn't afford to be. They were suspects.

All of them.

They slowed him down a little, but the closer he got to the cockpit the sparser they became. The final march to the elevator was completely deserted, which only made it worse. He wanted the delay. At the top of that elevator was an obligation he so desperately wanted to avoid. A decision he had never wanted to make. Martial law had always meant a failure of leadership as far as he was concerned. Nobody wanted to admit that they were a failure.

Entering the cockpit, he stopped and took a breath. There could be no uncertainty in his voice, nothing that could cast any doubt on this being the right move. This was a matter for a statesman, and that was what he would have to be at that moment.

He sat down, then immediately stood up again. He could pace, he could allow himself that. They wouldn't be able to see.

Reaching over, he tapped at the comms menu until he found the setting for an internal broadcast.

'People of the Strider, this is your pilot,' he began. A good start, nice and authoritative. 'As you may be aware, a mechanical fault has caused us to take a temporary pit stop while we assess the situation and make the necessary repairs. What you may not know, and what I am now obliged to tell you, is that this mechanical fault was not an accident. It was the result of sabotage from a party, or parties, unknown.'

That was good so far, right? No nonsense, truthful without fearmongering, trusting of his populace to do the right thing. They'd need a good charismatic pause to let the information sink in, naturally, but they should still have their critical minds about them.

'Furthermore,' he continued. 'Just moments ago, this saboteur struck again. A bomb of some kind was detonated in the engineering residences, killing an untold amount of people.'

Another pause. There wasn't really a safe way of putting that information. It was pretty grim in even its most objective state, but he needed that narrative.

He tried to slow his pacing. The microphone would pick it up if he wasn't careful. 'At this time, it is clear that whoever this saboteur is, he is invested in stopping any and all preparations to survive the oncoming storm front. I am sure you agree that this cannot be allowed to continue.

'As a result of this, and because we lack the necessary time to suitably screen the populace for this person, I have decided to enact martial law. Please do not interfere in any way with the Green Goddesses in the pursuit of their duties. They are not versed in proportional responses. That will be all.'

There would be complaints all over the internal network soon. His inbox would be clogged with rage and disgust, but this was the only way.

The button for martial law had not only its own table but a plastic shield that could only be opened by means of a keyhole on the far side of the room. He'd never removed the key, it had been firmly wedged into that slot from the moment he became pilot, just as his predecessor had recommended.

Staring at the button now, he knew why. Safeguards were all well and good, but sometimes they could cast doubt on a decision that had to be made. He knew, as he pressed that button, that he would have found it so much harder had he needed to insert that key first.

For a moment, nothing happened. That was always the way, that horrible silence. Then, with a sound like an engine roaring to life, the button and its table receded into the floor, the panels opening up to allow room, belching up a new array of consoles and monitors to replace it. They grew and filled the entire wall on that side of the cockpit, an enormous surveillance bank. Twenty, thirty individual monitors, all with a number of individual windows, displaying cameras.

Every camera was currently fixed on twisted, lumpen metal creations. Automatons, painted green, their arms crossed over their open chest cavities, were slotted into an incalculable number of recesses, colourful LEDs dancing across their various surfaces as they started to draw power.

They really were real. Even knowing that he had to use them, he hadn't realised how much he wanted them to be a lie.

He snapped his fingers and his chair slid across the floor to him. Sitting down, he started to tap at the keys. A single command began the start-up sequence, and he watched on the cameras as entire sections of wall began to recede, revealing the ranks of robots underneath.

One by one, the Green Goddesses – he never knew the origin of the name, that was just how they were called in the logs – began to clank to life and pull themselves free of the walls. The cameras followed them, one per robot, as they stomped forward one step in unison, awaiting further instructions.

The cameras showed him the first signs of discontent at his decision. A group of citizens, anger etched on their faces, were shouting profanities at one group of the Goddesses. They had the look of impending vandalism about them, when fear and anger bubble over. He hoped they were smart enough to keep that in check.

Another few key presses and they were active. An army

of automated workers, designed to substitute for and replace humans in the event of a catastrophe. No humans in the system, no chance for the saboteur to sneak in and wreak havoc. If they could just get through the storm in one peace, then he could worry about rooting out the attacker. No use catching him if everyone was dead.

He pushed away from the surveillance desk, and the chair returned itself and him to its usual position by the pilot's console. Rostrum had little desire to watch the robots at work.

The comms light was blinking. Not much of a surprise. Already people were reporting that a Goddess had brusquely moved them out the way – slapped them aside being more accurate – and injured them somehow. The injuries were probably exaggerated, but there would be more of them to come, until people came to accept they needed to steer clear.

He swiped the messages away into the ether. They'd just foment doubt, and he didn't need that right now. This was the right choice, logically and morally. Fuck the whinging proles.

Still, the comms light was blinking. Another external call, perhaps? The notifications were so overloaded that it made it hard to tell. He clicked into the network interface just to be safe.

> Pilot Strider here. Anyone online?

>> Just me.

>Which "me"?

>> The one that bombed your city.

> That's not a very funny joke.

>> Not a joke. Also, not a bomb. Engineered a power surge in the capacitor clusters lining the engineering residence. Localised explosion. Not great for massive damage, very efficient for contained destruction. Hope you approved.

Could he trace this conversation? Not without the software to do it. Rostrum hadn't a clue about the intricacies of computers – he could only steal the manifests because he had a program that specifically did all that for him – but he had a hard time believing this was coming from inside his own network. This had to be an internal connection. The level of knowledge required...

> Who are you? Someone from the fabrication corps? A foreigner?

>> It wouldn't be prudent to give that information away for free. Not that you can stop me now anyway. Smart move, activating those old robots.

> Last resort. I didn't want to do it.

>> I know. I've read their logs too. A bit bloodthirsty. Or highly strung, I guess you could say. For what it's worth, I'm sorry I made you do that. I'm not mad keen on hurting people, but professional pride demands I do my best.

> So this is all work for hire?

>> Probably wouldn't be unprofessional to admit to that. Besides, I think a little more investigation on your part would reveal how carefully planned this was. You already know I have an agenda, not a stretch to work out that said agenda is not insanity.

Rostrum found himself gripping his armrests tightly, though he only truly noticed because his knuckles were hurting. At least his decisions had drawn the saboteur out. That had to be a good thing.

> You're trying to beach this entire city in the path of a razor storm. Sounds insane to me, especially if you are still on board.

>> Let's be very clear here, I am definitely on board. If I wasn't, I couldn't do this.

All at once, the bank of surveillance monitors blinked off, making the room noticeably darker. Rostrum approached them slowly, carefully tapping at the keyboard when he arrived, using what little skills he had to try and coax them back to life.

After thirty seconds of hammering at keys, they turned

on again, one by one. The cameras had changed now. Instead of following the robots they were inside them, providing a first person perspective of them as they moved.

He went back to his console.

> I admit, that was a little creepy.

>> Nobody really wants to see through someone else's eyes. It's unsettling.

> How did you do that?

>> I'll tell you, but I want you to promise you won't take it as if I'm boasting. I just made sure I was one step ahead of you, which is really easy to do when you understand your target.

> Excuse me?

>> Contingency plans. Disabling the legs was plan A. I suspected that might lead to competent repairmen getting to work, so I prepared for that. Taking them out, as it became necessary, would mean you'd react in kind, so I planned for that too. Fiddling with the cameras was a sign of that.

> ?

>> Keep up, Rostrum. I know you can. I just showed you that I'm in your martial law system. I was in it before you turned it on. It was your next logical move, so I didn't have much of a choice. Think it through.

> If you had that capability, you would have started there.

>> No, I wouldn't. I've got goals, see? If I wanted to just destroy the entire city then maybe I could have started with the robots and just have them punch everyone to death or something, but that's not what I'm after. Besides, we're not actually on the robot plan yet, we're still on plan C.

> I'm guessing plan C is an ultimatum?

>> There's the Rostrum I was waiting for. The smart one. But yes, I have to use the robots as a threat, I'm sorry to say.

> Get it over with.

>> Call off your engineers. Stop trying to repair things. Stop trying to reinforce your city to survive the storm. Let it hit you. Or I'll have the robots see that you do.

> You're bluffing. Besides, letting the storm hit us unprepared is as good as a death sentence anyway.

>> Dramatic. You might survive. Some anyway. I'll kill everyone if I have to turn the robots on you.

> Why is it so important that the storm hit us?

>> Can't tell you that.

> Then I'm going to be smart here, and you're going to listen.

>> If you like.

Rostrum had already gotten more information than he had expected out of this man, how much more could he hope for? Hired gun, a definite agenda that the city not merely fail but that this storm hit it. What did that mean? Why was that important?

And then the one thing he hadn't considered before: the timing.

> This is about that wreck, isn't it?

>> …

> I missed it completely before. There's something there you don't want me to see, or get my hands on, something like that. But everyone knows now, our claim is recorded. The ones who uncovered have given me first crack at it. The Strider is the closest city by far. So, stands to reason, a rival had you disable us so they could reach the prize first.

>> Interesting theory.

> Yup. Which means they don't want us dead in an obvious way. That will make the other cities suspicious of whoever picks up the slack, and that just won't do. A nice tidy accident on the way, much more believable, right?

>> Are you enjoying this? Do you think I'm suddenly going to stand down because you think you've worked something out?

> I'm not finished yet.

>> Yes you are. Take another look at the monitors.

Rostrum looked up. Everything seemed normal at first glance, no horrible bloodbaths being caught on camera or anything. It took him a moment to spot the problem. Ten different robots, in unison side by side, had left their stations and were marching through the upper decks towards him.

Because of course they were. Of course messing with the cameras wasn't the limit of the saboteur's control of the system.

Calmly, Rostrum sat back down.

> What are you doing?

>> Sending your personal army of robots to murder you. They have a bit history of a history of this sort of thing, after all.

Documents started to open automatically, filling his screen. Logs from the previous times the Goddesses had been activated, the casualty reports detailing injuries sustained by people blundering in front of them, the deaths that had come from improper shutdown procedures. Then, finally, a checklist of how, exactly, one should deactivate them.

>> Sorry. Got to set the scene. You were right about one thing; we don't want this looking like anything other than an accident. Oh, and don't try to turn them off. I've messed around with the code so much that I really don't know what it might make them do.

> This is ridiculous!

>> Yes. But the ridiculous jobs are kind of fun when you think about it.

> Not for me!

>> Fair point. On the plus side, they kill you and this is all over. No more danger. Except the storm, obviously. You keep fighting this, things are just going to get more bloody. Ta ta.

Rostrum started to pace again. The robots were

clustering around the bottom of the elevator shaft now, apparently calculating the optimal way in. That bought him time, at least, though he wasn't sure what he could do with it.

Option one: stay and die.

On the plus side, he didn't think the saboteur was lying. If he let the robots gut him, the bastard that sent them wouldn't need to do anything else to ensure the city didn't move. Even if repairs could be made in time, or the city somehow survived the storm thanks to the limited reinforcement, it would be leaderless. It took years of training – both practical and political – to ably steer an entire city through the wastes. Rostrum hadn't even appointed a successor yet.

Option two: fight the robots.

No.

Option three: run.

Run where? There was one way out of the cockpit, and that was down the elevator and right into the waiting metal fists of robo-death. That wouldn't work. Take the emergency exit onto the balcony maybe, climb down several kilometres of frozen metal? Might as well jump and pray the snow is deep enough to break his fall, it would be a better choice.

There was the distant sound of metal tearing as the Goddesses finished their calculations. The lower shaft door wasn't too well secured, but it was still steel. Maybe a minute for them to finish busting through it, judging by their progress on the monitors, maybe five to climb the shaft. The upper door should take longer to breach, especially if he hit the lockdown. The electromagnets would give them some difficulty.

Fifteen minutes, at a generous estimate. Better to say ten. Less, even. That was preferable. It was a day of bad decisions and worse circumstances; so why have this be any different?

First things first. The saboteur might be in the systems,

but he wasn't in the cockpit. Some of the grander, more open systems, he could penetrate those, sure. Not the main foundational ones though. Even if he could get in through some arcane backdoor, they were all centred up in the cockpit. Turn them off, that would starve him of a few things just in case. Housekeeping, easily done.

Rostrum's mind kept turning as he set about this task, each system disabled sparking neurons in his head. He'd once read, perhaps during a brief boredom inspired waltz through the medical database, that simple tasks can jump start the brain. Doing mindless, repetitive things unclogs your brain-tubes or something, gets things flowing better.

He wasn't sure that was exactly right, but it seemed to be doing something. It was giving him ideas.

Given enough time, he could surely come up with some way of fighting the robots. The Strider had never possessed a great armoury, and what weapons it did have were largely reserved for galleon crews, but they had some technical nouse. He could cobble something together – an electrified prod maybe.

Not enough time though. Not up here. He'd need to get out first, then find a place he could hide while he put together a weapon. Or, hell, if he could get out then he could get to the armoury. Go big or go home.

But the only way out was to climb – two thirds of the systems offline now, just external comms and the information suites to do – he'd been over this.

They were in the shaft now, and climbing faster than they had expected. There was no maintenance ladder or anything in there, nothing that could jeopardise the security of the cockpit. They were punching through the steel walls, making their own handholds.

He hit the lockdown and the upper door clunked as the magnets kicked in. Time was running out.

The information suite powered down with a whir. That was it, decision time. First option that popped into his head, that's what he'd have to do.

Bam. Climb.

He burst out onto the balcony and looked down again. The ground hadn't seemed quite so far away before, but then he hadn't been worried about hitting it. It had been just scenery before, like the sky – you never worried about falling at terminal velocity into the clouds.

There had been a theory, amongst those that gave a damn about this sort of thing, that the Strider might have been the oldest surviving city. Or, to be more precise, whatever the Strider had been before it was made into a city was older than whatever constructions had been hollowed out for the other cities. Surely someone must have known once, but that information was buried somewhere deep in the databases.

This theory was based entirely on the fact that, from the outside, the Strider *looked* old. It had an appearance to it that belied a different era of tech from the other cities, purposefully jagged and ugly in a way that the others had only become over time. Heavily modular, easy to swap out parts as if they were expected to break regularly.

Rostrum had never considered whether this lumpen exterior could work as a ladder. He was having to do that now. He threw a foot over the railing and placed it carefully on a metal outcropping. His feet didn't slip, which was good, but he could feel the ice still. He brought the other leg to join the first, hands tight around the railing, and just stood there for a moment.

These were the wrong shoes. He needed his boots with the smart-cleats, not his rubber-soled city shoes. No, what he *needed* to do was to stop coming up with reasons why this wouldn't work. There were plenty of those, but he was going to do it anyway. Now he needed to concentrate on success.

There was another outcrop just off to his left and not too far below him. No railing, but that was fine. He'd only need the railing for the first step, for comfort. Once he was going, it would all be fine. Safe. Easy.

He could hear them at the door as he lowered himself to his knees. The ice soaked through his trousers, and he could feel the cold now. That was good, he hadn't slipped. There was more purchase on watery ice, barely frozen.

Any lie. Any lie that could get him through this.

One foot down, then the other. Belly on the ice. Still secure, if a little damp. Don't get complacent, cocky, but confidence was fine. Confidence was just accepting you could do something; complacency was assuming you couldn't mess it up. Both feet hit the outcrop together, not even the slightest hint of a slip.

He'd need to go faster, but for now he allowed himself a small break for his heart to settle. Yes, he needed to move faster, but he needed his thoughts to move slower. Now he was over the first hurdle, he'd need to be able to think again.

Laying down on his stomach again, Rostrum peered over the edge. The ground was now even further away that it had seemed before, just a white blanket way beneath him, but he thought he could see a pathway down now. Set back a little as the balcony was, the surface of the Strider seemed random and arbitrary in its patterning, but from a position on the surface itself he could get a better look.

The Strider was segmented, like some ancient suit of armour. Every outcrop was a scale in this armour and, as such, there was a rough pattern to it. It had to interlink, it had to overlap, and it seemed it had to cover the *entire* surface. He could actually pick his way down.

He mapped the route in his head and swung his legs down to the next platform. Above him, the robots breached the cockpit in one final roar. From the sound, Rostrum figured that they had just shoved the entire door free of its housing rather than try to deal with the magnets.

A steely green head appeared above him, peering over the rail. The glass lenses set into the surface – pinprick eyes – caught the sun, which didn't help in making the things less terrifying. It hopped the railing before he could find purchase on his new platform and began to climb after him.

He found his footing quickly and scanned for the next step of his journey.

It was at that moment the robot lost its own.

The screech of metal against metal was the only indication that something had gone wrong above him, at least until the Goddess fell past him, arms flailing. Its fingers closed around his wrist as it fell, dragging him down onto his belly yet again, face crashing off the steel platform. For a moment he felt its weight pull him further, towards the edge, towards oblivion, before it lost him and kept falling.

He heard it crash off of three, maybe five, platforms on the way down before it passed out of earshot. By the time he had worked up the courage to look, it was a barely visible speck on the ground.

Rostrum looked up. Three more metal faces were peering at him from above. One reached over the railing and placed its hand on the ice for a moment before removing it. The LEDs on its head blinked for a few seconds, calculating. When they stopped, not one of the robots followed him.

He went back to climbing, keeping an eye on them as he did so. They seemed content to merely watch, and after a few more platforms he stopped paying them heed. It was clear they weren't going to pursue him out here, merely keep him from getting back to the cockpit. Fine, he didn't want to be up there anyway.

Eventually, after twenty minutes of climbing, he hit a platform with no ice at all. A vent port was tucked away at the back, pumping out warm air. He knew a lot about his city, but he'd never bothered to really look at what the world saw. If he survived long enough to take on an apprentice, that was one tradition he would see broken.

He sat in front of the vent for a while, letting the air

dry his damp clothing and fend off the chill that had been forming. Then he peered over the edge again.

This was going to take a long time.

SEVEN

Wendy regretting unbuckling her harness almost instantly. She had a beautiful, vibrant second where the wind allowed her the freedom to move towards the cabin, and then it pounced, as treacherous as it always had been. It lifted her up, throwing her backwards across the deck and into one of the masts.

There was a crack and pain shot through her collarbone and nestled, throbbing, in the back of her skull. Perhaps it might have even knocked her for a loop had the wind not been so insistent on her staying awake. There was a third gash on her face now.

So that was a good plan then. Bravo, Wendigo, you idiot. Now you were going to die from getting flayed to death by a storm, fifty feet from safety. Excellent work. This is what heroes get, remember that for all the drawn out, torturous minutes of searing agony you have left.

Or, you could get up.

The wind had wrapped her around the mast well enough that it had the leverage to keep her in place. The injuries weren't doing her any favours either. But all she had to do was wait for the wind to shift just a little.

It did, and with a scream of pain – thankfully masked

by the squall that had caused it in the first place – she dashed for the cabin. The door opened obligingly, and she slammed it behind her, sliding down it to the floor.

A somewhat wiry Lucille peered at her from underneath a desk. 'Wendy?'

'Excuse my language,' the captain said, popping up from behind her. 'But where the bloody hell have you been?'

Things didn't hurt quite so much now she was out of the wind, but Wendy was sucking air through her teeth to try and drown out what remained. 'Exploring.'

'I did tell you not to go back to that damned wreck,' he said, climbing out from under his shelter. 'I want that clearly on the record for when I bollock you after we survive this.'

She looked up at him. 'Thorsten thought you might have left when you saw the storm coming.'

'He always was an idiot. I don't leave my crew behind, especially not when they have a proper bollocking scheduled. I like my bollockings.'

Lu slapped his calf. 'Stop saying *bollocking*. It's weird.'

'It doesn't matter,' he continued. 'The storm is liable to rip the ship apart anyway.'

Wendy stood up. That was probably a bad idea. 'We think the wreckage is safe enough to hide in. I came back up to tell you to come with us.'

'I don't buy it,' the captain said. 'Surely that thing is corroded all to hell, it's been lying down there for centuries.'

'No, wait,' Lu said, climbing to her feet too. 'That's exactly the point. It's been down there for *centuries,* and it's still there. The ice probably helped shelter it, but it's hardly exposed now. Wendy might have a point.'

He looked at her. 'Are you sure?'

'Josh, I'm sure it'll last better than this ship will. Maybe we'll still get ripped to shreds down there, or frozen, or both, but it'll happen slower than it will up here!'

He looked around at the damage the storm had already caused. Wendy did the same. She hadn't really taken in her surroundings outside, and that had bled over once she was inside, but now she could look. The cabin was crumbling, great rents had been carved out of the walls and ceilings, and the windows were cracking despite the strengthened glass. It had held up well, but it wouldn't survive the storm.

'You're right,' he said. 'Wendy, can you get us down there?'

'It's easy,' she said. 'Got two lines hooked up to the side of the ship still, will take you right down to the entrance. You can't miss it. Well, you can, but don't.'

'Okay, you and Lu go first –'

'No,' Wendy interrupted. 'You two first. There's only two lines and I need a breather before I go back down there. Wait for me just inside and I'll guide you to Thor.'

Lu walked over and hugged her, softly but with love. 'This is absolutely the right idea, but I still think you should go first.'

'Yeah, well, I refuse, so...'

'Fine,' the captain said. He was hiding a smirk very badly. 'You can have your breather, you insubordinate brat. We'll see you down there. Let's go, Lucille.'

Lu took his hand, and all three of them exchanged a look before the pair stepped out into the wind. The door slammed shut behind them.

Wendy sat down again. She wasn't playing the heroine any more, she really did need a rest. In truth, with her new injuries, she wasn't even sure she could get down that line without making something worse. But hey, she was too young to die. She'd get down that line, just once it was certain her invalided blundering wouldn't keep someone trapped on the death ship.

Christ, the wind better not kill her before she had the chance to escape. She really wasn't trying to be a martyr. It would be so embarrassing if the situation decided to make her one.

How long would they need? She tried to peer out of the windows to get a glimpse of them, see if she could try and determine how they were doing, but the wind had cracked the glass too badly. With all the loose bits of ship starting to fly around outside, she couldn't distinguish one source of movement from another.

The walls creaked again, and more cold air rushed in. That had to be long enough. She took a breath and set her feet, then stepped back out onto the deck.

The captain and Lu were gone, so Wendy made straight for the lines. The wind had slowed just a little, apparently more content with juggling the bits of metal it had shaken loose rather than chasing her down. Still, it had enough power in it to buffet her injuries. There were spots on the edges of her vision by the time she reached the lines, all from the pain.

She didn't even look over the edge before she leapt over, harness attached. Again, the harness would slow her fall so that it wasn't dangerous, but this time she couldn't trust herself to descend any other way. It was too likely that *something* was broken, even if she wasn't properly feeling it.

Again, she hit the floor faster than she had meant to, slipping onto her rear for a second time. Not the best way to get a bruised arse, especially when the impact decides to rattle through to your probably-broken bones. She wasn't down long before strong arms hoisted her up.

'All right, flower,' said Lu. 'Where's the entrance?'

Wendy steadied herself. 'It should be really obvious...'

'Well it's not.'

She looked. Had she been turned around? It was hard to tell now; the storm was making it hard to see anything.

A crack or purple lightning slammed into the side of the ship and something inside exploded. She wasn't sure what it could have been, but it didn't have enough force to pierce the hull. It made a hell of a racket though, and the flash from the lightning gave her a moment of visual clarity.

There it was, the entrance, where it had always been. It had iced over, that was the problem. A thin layer of virginal ice had coated the rest of the surface too, it seemed, and had sealed the wreck as part of this invasion.

She ran over to it and drove her boot down onto it. The cleats scored a set of small holes into it, not very deep, and she fell over from the pain.

'Under here,' she said. 'I can't...'

Lu carefully pulled her away and waved her hands frantically into the mist. The captain emerged, carrying a full head of steam, and drove his boot down hard. The ice cracked a little. Lu joined in and, between, them it took only ten stomps to finally get it to yield. Next thing Wendy knew, they were all inside.

'That storm,' the captain said. 'I've never seen one so calm.'

Lu's eyes almost fell out of her head. 'Calm?'

He let that hang for a moment before he answered. 'What I mean is, I've only ever seen them at their prime. I've never seen one spooling up before. I didn't even see it coming. I think we were ground zero.'

'Well, we're out of it now. Right?'

Wendy shifted a little. She'd landed on her face, but apparently her body had forgotten how much that should be hurting right about now. 'We should probably move deeper in, right?'

'Lead on,' the captain said. 'You know this place better than us.'

The wind still rang across the outer shell of the wreck like a bell as they moved, but it was nice to hear it get quieter the deeper then went. By the time they reached the control room, the only reminder that there even was a storm out there was a dull drone way in the distance. That and the massive projection Thorsten had somehow covered the wall with.

'Hi guys,' he said, barely looking at them. 'Have you seen this?'

'Nice to see you too, Wolfe. Glad the weather didn't get you. Oh, yes, we're fine, just a little chilly,' the captain said, wearing that same badly hidden smirk.

Thorsten stopped and looked at them properly. His harness-hammock swayed briefly as he took off his goggles, revealing bloodshot eyes. 'Sorry. Sorry. I got a bit distracted. Wendy was gone long enough that I started to worry, and when I worry I try not to think about things, and then I started playing with the computers –'

'We're fine, Thor,' Wendy said. Then she winced. 'Mostly.'

He squinted at her. 'Hold on, let me take a look at that.'

She opened her mouth to complain, but he had already scuttled back down to ground level like some handsome dreadlocked spider. 'If you insist,' was what she managed.

Ignoring the others, Thorsten started examining her wounds. 'There's a lot of superficial stuff here, that's the stuff that's going to sting. But the collarbone –'

He touched it. Dear god, the pain was transformative. In this case, transforming Wendy from a stoic into a hunched ball of bubbling pain.

'– yeah,' he said. 'That's probably somewhat broken. Not the worst news though.'

'Oh joy,' Wendy said.

'You're soaking. All of you are, actually, but I don't think the other two are going to be in agonising pain when they try to strip off their wet clothes.'

Wendy frowned. She hadn't even noticed. How had that happened? She patted herself down slowly, careful not to anger the malicious collarbone again. Thorsten was right, her clothes were absolutely sodden, as was her hair. Hell, it had even frozen in places.

'I mean,' she said. 'I hadn't noticed so it couldn't be too bad, yeah? It'll dry out down here soon enough.'

'Sure,' Thorsten said. 'That could happen. Just spend a

couple of hours shivering and miserable. Or, and this is much more likely, you'll catch pneumonia and die. If it helps, you'll probably be okay to keep your pants on.'

Lu, who was already midway through stripping off her wet clothes shouted from over his shoulder. 'Oh you're too kind. Dick.'

'Hey, I can't help being the only one in dry clothes,' he shot back with a wink.

'Can't you just cut me out of them?' Wendy said.

The captain was shirtless. Not bad. 'Did you happen to bring your luggage with you? If we can keep your clothes in working order, at least you'll have something to wear in a couple of hours, when it's dry.'

'I know that, it's just... I really don't want to have to go through this pain.'

Thorsten put his hands on either side of her head and locked eyes with her. 'This is going to hurt. Really, really hurt. But it *will* save your life and I promise you it won't last long.'

She swallowed. 'You better be right, Thor. If you're lying, I'm going to hurt you.'

He nodded, and she begrudgingly set about undressing.

It was all a little awkward, but getting her trousers, boots and socks off was pretty painless. Lots of shimmying and a little help from Thor – that was a situation she never thought she would be in – but it didn't take long. The upper body was torture though.

Her coat, fine, not too much trouble. It was oversized and padded so that it could slip off simply anyway. It was her jumper and shirt. She *had* to move her arms for those, and when she did she could feel the bone sliding underneath the skin.

It was moving. *Moving.* That was worse than the pain. Things shouldn't move inside a human body. Everything should be stowed and secured, not gliding all over the place and rubbing up against squishy bits. It was disgusting.

And that was what she tried to focus on as Thor helped her jumper and shirt up over her head. If she could ignore the pain just a little longer, deal with the grosser aspects first, then it would all be over before she had time to care.

That worked. For all of three seconds. Thor was moving it slowly, gingerly, trying to avoid her any pain. Then she screamed, and in one rough movement he yanked her clothes free and she was cold, colder than she had been in a long time.

'Fucking Christ,' she screamed. 'How is this better? Dear fucking god!'

The other three let her finish swearing. There was a lot of swearing to be done, especially for a woman of her size. She needed to turn the air blue, then black. It was medicinal. It was also, judging from the faces of Lu and the captain, terrifying.

Thor apparently found it utterly hilarious.

He waited until she was done. Once the cavalcade of imaginative curses dwindled to a sotto voce stream of mumblings, he piped up again. 'That's the cold you would have been feeling if your brain wasn't a shit. You'll start to warm up now, I promise.'

'That hurt a lot, Thor.'

'You've got a broken clavicle, Wendy. It was always going to hurt.'

'I might just never get dressed again.'

'Please don't say that. It would make my life exceedingly awkward. Anyway, let me take your mind off it with something perplexing. A good mystery will distract you all from the suddenly visible flesh, yes?'

The captain looked extremely uncomfortable, his hands fidgeting about trying to cover himself up. 'Please, yes. Anything.'

Thor beamed and shimmied back up into his web. He strapped himself in front of the terminals again. 'Right, so this is a real time map of the weather, yeah? This baby has good sensors. You can see the area it encompasses here, and this little triangle thing is us.'

He was indicating onto the projection using a laser pointer he had fished from his tool belt.

'It's not very big,' Lu said. 'Is it localised around the ship? That can't be right.'

'That's what I thought too,' Thor said. 'Hang on. Take a closer look.'

A few taps and clicks from the ceiling and the projection zoomed in. Underneath the triangle, a rectangle was visible now, stretching out to the extremities of the storm.

'That's not possible,' the captain said.

'I also thought *that*,' Thor said.

Lu studied the image for a moment. 'I guess that explains why we couldn't see it coming then.'

Wendy rolled her eyes. Something was going unsaid, something obvious, and right now she didn't have the clarity or patience to work it out for herself. 'Why? What? Please stop talking around the point.'

Lu looked at her. 'Wow, when you get grouchy you get *properly* grouchy, don't you, kid?'

'There's a reason I call her brat,' Thor said. 'But okay, condensed version. This storm is exactly the right size to encompass the wreck. It came out of nowhere and formed around us, weirdly at almost exactly the moment you think you fixed the ambulation matrix and possibly got this thing back online.'

'Oh,' Wendy said. 'I see now. You think the wreck is making the storm? Isn't that a bit, I don't know, farfetched?'

'No?'

'Fair enough.'

Lu hunched herself into a ball, trying to hide her shivers. 'Can we stop it?'

'I honestly don't know,' Thor said. 'But, I don't think we have to.'

'I'm pretty sure we do have to,' she said.

'I guess eventually we do, sure,' he said. 'But think of it this way. If that storm is being made by the wreck, then it stands to reason that the wreck is built to survive it. Right? Makes sense?'

The captain was frowning. 'So you think we should just stay down here until, what, this *storm engine* burns itself out? This is another, much bigger, storm front heading our way.'

Another few taps and the projection zoomed out again, further than when it had started. 'That's the thing, look, it's changed course.'

'They don't just change course that drastically. All the simulations –'

'Yes, I know. I'm the one that did the simulations. That storm *should* be heading right for us, but as soon as this little storm kicked up, that one moved. It's doing it slowly, but enough that it won't hit us. We're actually safer here now than we were before, believe it or not.'

'Yeah, I don't believe it,' said Lu. 'This hulk has been down here forever, mouldering. You really think it can survive that bloody hurricane up there?'

'I do,' Wendy said, surprising herself.

'You do?'

'I've seen more of this thing than you, Lu. It's weirdly pristine, all things considered. A fair bit of damage, sure, but not a lot of corrosion. It's made it this far, I think it can weather this.'

She mulled it over for a moment and nodded. The captain exchanged looks with her too, looking a little less satisfied.

He rubbed his hands together idly. 'I still think it would be prudent to find a way to shut this down. Maybe this thing can hold out against what's going on up there, but we need to be able to turn it off. We've got buyers coming in to take this thing off our hands for a start. I don't want them ripped to shreds when they get here.'

Thor nodded. 'I guess that makes sense, boss.'

'You reckon this will up the price, captain?' Wendy asked.

'More than a little,' he said. 'I just hope it doesn't price them out.'

Lu stopped trying to hide that she was shivering. 'Is there a heater or something? I'm turning blue here.'

Thor started cycling through menus on one of the terminals. 'Um, I can have a look. I'm not entirely sure what came back online once Wendy was done tinkering. This system is a bit unwieldy.'

The captain started to hoist himself up towards Thor. 'Let me help. Looks like more than one person was meant to run this joint, might be quicker that way.'

Wendy watched. The ships were called galleons from force of habit, and they had masts and rigging as a redundancy, but no-one had ever used them. If the ice razors broke, you wouldn't have the speed to outrun the storms, so redundancies were more for the sake of doing *something* than as a precaution. The sad thing was, this had denied her a chance to see her captain climb rigging until now.

She had always assumed the captain was sort of above the talents needed by those in his employ. It was the role of a manager, she had always thought, to just sort of *manage*. You paid the people who could actually do things, while you felt big and bossy. Not that this made someone a bad person – the captain had always been fair as far as she was aware – but it did make him a bit useless outside of his bubble.

Because, of course, young people always know exactly how the world works, she found herself thinking as he proved her wrong.

Thor was good at climbing. His job required him to have the ability to shimmy up the rigging to a decent vantage point in case the electronics got all temperamental. He was up and down those ropes every day. The captain made him look like an amateur, practically launching his way into position in a fraction of the time. He barely even touched the ropes, and flat out declined to strap himself in.

Wendy was impressed, and judging from the look on Lu's face she wasn't the only one.

She padded over to Lu and lowered herself down next to her. They huddled together for warmth, which again sent spikes of pain through Wendy, but it was preferable to the cold.

'So how much off-book stuff have you been doing down here, Wendy?' Lu said, nuzzling the younger woman's head into her shoulder.

'I don't know what you mean.'

'I mean that you quite clearly came down here against Josh's orders and faffed around a bit. You must have found something out.'

Wendy blushed a little. 'Not much.'

'But something?'

'I guess. Whatever took this thing down originally didn't kill off the entire crew. A couple survived and were trying to repair it. At least I think they were. When I got down to fixing it, seemed almost like one of them was trying to keep it broken. It was weird.'

'You ever find out what it *is*?'

Wendy shook her head. 'Not yet. The logs were all corrupted, and I haven't had time to look around properly. I don't know, but it doesn't feel military to me. I don't see why someone shot it down.'

'I must admit, it doesn't look very military, as I understand it. Every old tech warship I've scavenged was very big on security,' Lu said. 'It would be odd to find the command centre in this position.'

'Why?'

Lu ruffled her hair, throwing water droplets down onto Wendy's face. 'Too many entrances for one thing, and not nearly armoured enough. Access to the maintenance tunnels is a red flag too, way too easy for boarders to infiltrate your central command.'

'Someone with military-grade weapons took a dislike to them though.'

'Seems that way,' Lu said and shrugged. 'Everything we've learned tells us that sunbombs weren't standard munitions. Although, the way I feel right now, I could do with one detonating in here. Might warm me up a little.'

'That's probably a little drastic, Lu.'

'Is there a medical bay on this tub, you reckon?'

Wendy tried to shrug, but thought better of it. 'I don't know. I didn't see one as I was exploring, but then I wasn't really looking.'

'What did you see?'

'I've only really had a chance to scope out the bits that make it go, and even then I've only seen, like, the central core.'

Lu fidgeted again, making Wendy hiss. 'Sorry. Anyway, once the guys find a way to heat this place up and we can get dressed again, I'll find you a first aid kit or something. I don't know much about medicine, but a wandering collarbone needs setting or something, right?'

'It certainly feels that way at the moment.'

The pair of them watched Thor and the captain fiddle with the consoles for a while longer. In the silence, Wendy started to hear the storm again, lurking out there, drumming on the hull. This time it was soothing though, relaxing. It thrummed in time with her heartbeat, and gave her a kindly distraction from the throbbing pain. It was almost a lullaby.

Eventually, she dozed off, nuzzled into Lu's shoulder. The older woman didn't seem to mind.

Not quite asleep, time began to stretch out. It could have been for a minute, it could have been for an hour, her brain had simply decided she didn't need her internal chronometer for this. So her consciousness floated there, detached from reality and floundering in the soft confines of her own head. Which, she considered, was bloody weird. Then again, she had been through quite a lot in a very short space of time, she probably needed a bit of a soft reboot.

She reconnected with the world at the sound of the heaters clanking to life. A cool breeze washed over her, raising goosebumps on her exposed flesh, and slowly grew warmer over the next minute or so. Distantly, she could hear Thor and the captain cheering.

It didn't take long for the control room to reach a toasty temperature, but the musty smell of the long-dormant heaters whirring to life clung on a little longer. It was enough to finally force her to open her eyes.

There was Lu, on the other side of the room, laying their clothing out in front of one of the vents, right in the path of the hot air. When had she moved? Wendy hadn't felt it. A hand crept idly up to her head, checking what was not serving as her pillow. Thorsten's jacket. She must have been truly asleep to have missed that switch.

'Welcome back to the land of the living,' Thor shouted from the ceiling. Wendy blinked a couple of times and turned to regard him. It was tricky, her entire upper body had decided to seize. 'Before you ask, you've had a couple of hours.'

'Everything hurts,' she said, weakly.

The captain's face slid into view from somewhere behind her right ear. 'Try not to move too much. The adrenaline has probably worn off by now. You'll be getting the pain in full force now, so every little movement is going to hurt like buggery.'

'You know,' she said. 'The thing about buggery –'

'Let's not have this conversation,' the captain interrupted.

Wendy chuckled. He was right, it hurt a lot. It quickly changed from a laugh to a muted scream. 'At least it's warm now.'

Thorsten's harness creaked away above her. 'Sorry it took so long, there's a lot of menus on this thing. You should be able to get dressed pretty soon now.'

Lu snorted. 'The kid can barely move. We need to sort her out some first aid or something before we try and get her dressed. At least some painkillers.'

'Well, yes,' Thorsten said. 'That too.'

Wendy tried to move again. The pain was horrific, but that wasn't what was stopping her. Her body was flat out overruling her now. The pain was a very stern warning that movement was ill-advised, true, but if she tried to ignore it she ran into complete rebellion. Try as she might, she couldn't break down that wall.

She gave up, falling limp. It was only then she noticed their faces. They were staring at her, yes wide.

'What?' she asked through gritted teeth.

Thor's face was ashen. 'You were screaming. Don't you remember?'

'What? When?'

'Like, literally just then. Before you said *what* all chipper and cheerful.'

'I don't... Was I? I don't remember doing that.'

There was a small commotion from across the room. With a face like thunder, Lu was slipping into her somewhat dry clothes. Her boots still squelched loudly as she laced them up. 'Right, that's enough. Girl's going delirious. I'm going to have a look around for some medical supplies or something.'

There was the spectre of disagreement from the captain, as if he might suggest she wait just a little longer. Wendy had thought to make the same objection – at least wait until the clothes were properly dry, she could wait – but Lu's face was not one to question. Wendy had never seen her so focused before.

Neither of them spoke up, not that Wendy had truly wanted to. This feeling had already outstayed its welcome, and even friendly concern for her comrade was rapidly taking a backseat. Besides, Lu could handle it. She could handle anything.

'I haven't been able to call up a full internal schematic,'

Thor said. 'At least not one with the rooms labelled, but your best bet is going to be perhaps one deck down? A couple of big rooms down there, might have something medical-ish down there.'

'Then that's where I'll begin,' Lu said, snapping herself into a harness. And then she was gone, over the edge and down into the same depths Wendy had traversed not so long ago.

The captain cracked his knuckles. 'Well, while she's off playing hero, any update on the storm?'

'Nothing useful,' Thor said. 'It's still there, the other one is still avoiding it. Same old, same old.'

With a thoughtful look, the captain motioned towards Thor, who obligingly threw down his radio. The captain caught it with one hand and keyed it. 'Lu, do you read me?'

There was a hiss. 'What, Josh? I'm still on the bloody rope here.'

'While you're down there, see if you can't find a larder or something. Food and water stores.'

'I'm not sure what good a three-hundred-year old sandwich will do, Josh.'

'If that storm outside doesn't abate, we might have to try. Just in case, keep an eye out.'

There was a moment of silence, followed by a clang from somewhere down the shaft. 'Understood. They might have military rations or something, they last forever. I'll keep a watchful eye out, but medical supplies have priority. Just touched down on the deck, will be in touch.'

Wendy waved to the captain. 'Open comms. I want to hear descriptions.'

'Wendy wants a commentary, Lu,' he said.

'What, why?'

The captain shrugged and handed the radio over to Wendy. 'It'll take my mind off things. And I'm nosy.'

'Yes, yes you are,' Lu said. 'Fine, I'll do my best.'

'Thank you.'

'Okay, so,' Lu said, her voice measured and scientific.

'First things first, no lights here. My voice echoes. Hang on, got to fix my torch. Right, I can see now. Got a lot of doors down here, all with nameplates. Willis, Hart, Enzo –'

'Enzo, they wrote the log,' Wendy said.

'What log?'

'The one that walked me through fixing the matrix. Those other names must be the rest of the crew.'

'Their bunks,' Lu said. 'Good sign. You want to keep the medical bay close to the bunks on a small craft. Saves on needing a ward, you can just send the invalids back to their own beds, keep the med bay just for the drugs.'

'Makes sense, I guess.'

'I don't see a room marked with any sort of medical symbolism. Did the log hint at who the on-staff physician might be?'

'I don't know. I don't think so. I think Enzo was the captain, but they didn't mention anyone by surname anyway.'

'Okay, I'm going to keep moving.' There was silence for a minute or two, other than the tinny sounds of exertion from Lu as she traversed the lower deck. 'We're looking at six cabins here, what I think is a sort of communal rumpus room, shared hygiene facilities. Two of those, one at each end of the corridor. One last door here, no sign, very resistant to opening.'

'What sort of resistance?'

'It doesn't want to open. That sort of resistance.'

Wendy propped herself up on one arm. If her body wanted to object, it forgot to do so. 'Okay, first thing, is it locked or seized?'

'How do I tell?'

'Does it have any movement at all when you try to force it, even the tiniest give?'

Lu grunted, the static on the radio gave it an eldritch quality. 'There's maybe a millimetre of movement there. Snaps right back when I let go.'

'Okay, so it's not seized and it's not a mag-lock. That's

good! Sounds like a bolt-lock though, which is bad. How's your hacking?'

'Abysmal.'

'That's what I thought,' Wendy said. Having a challenge was spiking her adrenaline again, she could feel it. This was pleasant. 'Problem is, bolt-locks have these huge great, well, *bolts* that hold the door in place. That millimetre of movement you feel is the space between the walls of the keep and the bolt itself. That's going to be hard to bust through if you can't hack the system.'

'Well, I can't do that, so I need alternatives.'

Wendy drummed her fingers on the ground for a moment. Even the steel was warm now. 'I can give you three. Kick the door itself in, cut through the frame and then the bolts with an oxy-fuel torch, or hope that you can just force it with enough leverage.'

'This is an interior door, right,' Lu said. 'Interior door on a craft with few crew. A trusted crew. It's not a security door, just a *secure* door.'

'Does that make a difference? A bolt-lock is still pretty sturdy.'

'Well, security doors are designed to keep people out,' Lu said, strain in her voice. 'Secure doors are mostly to give a room some status so it gets treated with respect. You don't go into a secure room without purpose, but no-one going to be overly suspicious that you have.'

'So?'

'So, it may be sealed with a bolt-lock, but it's not going to be a strong one.' There was the sound of metal groaning.

'I get you!'

There was the dull thud of something shearing, followed by the rusty squeak of lazy metal casters. 'Enough leverage and the door pops right open. You can't see this, but I'm currently very happy with myself.'

'I'm impressed either way, Lu. What do you see?'

'Jackpot,' she said. 'Looking at a store room here.

Food, clothing, sundries.'

'Medical supplies?'

'Standby. Yes, a locked cabinet at the back wall. Won't need your help with this one, the glass has been knocked out of its frame, can get what I need through the windows. I'll stock up and be back shortly. We'll get you patched up and you can come explore with me.'

'I mean, I've only saved your life once today. Why stop there?'

'Exactly. Where would I be without my lucky charm? All right, I think I have enough to set the bone and dull the pain, heading back your —'

'What was that, Lu? You cut off.'

'Hold.'

'Lu?'

'There's something moving down here.'

EIGHT

When Rostrum began his descent, he hadn't considered that the storm might hit before he reached the bottom. It hadn't actually done so yet, but it was approaching rapidly. In fact, it still looked closer than the ground did.

He had made it to the third out-take vent, which he guessed was something like fifty storeys down, and it wasn't helping the cold any more. His hands had turned a violent red from the chilled platforms, and while the numbness had made the climb easier for a while he was starting to worry. Blasting them with the warm air from the out-takes brought the stinging sensation back full force, but did little to bring the colour back.

It had taken him hours to get this far. He needed a different solution. The Strider had maintenance hatches riddling its surface, but they were all opened from within, so that wouldn't do. This left him with one unenviable alternative – climbing in through the remains of the residential block.

Rostrum had been watching the smoking crater grow closer and closer with each step downwards he took. It was still maybe twenty storeys down, but it was much more real a goal now than the ground was. Provided the robots weren't waiting for him.

The robots had left him alone on his climb. No more had attempted to follow him after the first, and while he was sure they were still up there watching him, he had long lost sight of the sentinels up on his balcony. He kept expecting to see their fleshless faces peering up at him from the opening he was heading towards, and every platform closer amplified that fear.

When he finally reached the level above the explosion damage, he was too afraid to look. They would be in there, waiting, silently ready to reward him for doing something so daring by ripping him to shreds. The saboteur, always one step ahead of him, would have prepared for this, surely.

But he hadn't.

When Rostrum finally worked up the courage to peek his head into the hole, he found the interior was completely empty. Somehow that was worse.

Swinging his way to safe footing was a gymnastic effort he hadn't thought himself capable of, and perhaps ordinarily he would not have been. He had to climb out onto the twisted metal that remained following the explosion, dig his fingers into the jagged edges, and gain as much momentum on the downswing as he could to clear the gap. The fear of falling a very long way made that quite easy.

Even as he landed on his back, knocking the air from his lungs, lacerating a few fingers on sharp metal seemed worth it. He lay there, panting to refill his lungs, and considered his situation.

He could be reasonably sure, owing to their co-opting by the saboteur, that the Goddesses would be shirking their duties. If they were hunting for him and corralling the citizens, then they wouldn't be in all the inhospitable and cramped parts of the city. So at least he knew where he could hide.

And what would he do while he was hiding? Just stay

there until the storm hit, shredding the city, and hope the robots would piss off once that was over? Even if they survived the storm, he would still need to die to keep the saboteur a secret. So no, he'd have to take the city back before then.

He started laughing. He couldn't help it; the whole situation was so absurd. Not one day ago he had been bored out of his mind, the usual politics and the usual problems driving him to write his crap little detective story into the dark places of the network, just to stay awake. Now he was on the run for his life inside his own city, hunted by the very emergency protocol he had activated.

Perhaps he should take his cues from Galveston. Granted, the grizzled detective wasn't real, but he was still more suited to this sort of situation. But then, if Rostrum had created him, then the capabilities of that man must be inside him somewhere.

You've got a thousand ugly cog-heads hunting you down, kid, Galveston growled inside Rostrum's head. *Baying for blood and sinew like the hounds of old. But they're metal men, with metal thoughts. You've got a V8, supercharged, adrenaline-fuelled supercomputer whirring away in your meat balloon, pal. They don't stand a chance.*

He stood up. It was weird, being on solid ground again. He had forgotten just how much he had needed to be attentive with every step outside. Such a small amount of time in the grand scheme of things, but he had already forgotten how to walk without it being an effort. As this came back to him, finally secure in his footing again, his thighs relaxed, and began to ache.

Perfect.

Scouring his mind, he began searching for useful things on this level. A number of hatches that would get him into the walls – a safe way of moving around the entire city so long as he didn't give the Goddesses reason to search in there. Reaching the armoury was a much more realistic goal now, perhaps even getting down to the docks and escaping as per the original plan.

Yes, that was still the best way. Trying to take back the city alone wouldn't work. There were too many robots to disable, even if he spurred the citizens to action. Even if they somehow managed it, too many people would die. He didn't want to risk that and, weirdly, he felt the saboteur wouldn't want that either.

He found a maintenance hatch nearby and slid into the crawlspace between the interior walls and the hull. Ordinarily the place would be full of low-grade mechanics keeping the basic systems working – or Goddesses doing the same job, during martial law – but Rostrum had been right about the robots keeping to the main corridors.

It would be a much quicker descent from the inside. For a start, there were ladders. Actual ladders, with rungs, not frozen platforms jutting out into the cold. Some of the more coreward areas would even have one-man elevators, letting him skip a number of storeys with ease. It was all but luxurious compared to the outside.

It still took him an hour or so, but it felt like mere minutes compared to how long it would have taken.

The armoury, such as it was, lay in the storey above the galleon dock. It was the closest thing the Strider had to a security checkpoint, and the only route to the galleons routed you straight past it. It had long been held that, were someone to breach the armoury, the rest of the Strider could be taken easily. The counterpoint being that they first had to take the armoury, and anyone who had the firepower to do that wouldn't need the armoury to conquer the city.

Checking the coast was clear, Rostrum emerged from the crawlspace and checked the contents of the armoury. The Goddesses hadn't touched it, which wasn't a surprise. It wasn't as if they needed the weapons. They were weapons in and of themselves, and the best the armoury could offer was a handful of jury-rigged zip guns.

He took a moment to pick out one that looked the

sturdiest and filled his pockets with ammunition. They didn't look as though they would do much damage to the metal forms of the robots, but they had to be better than nothing. It would give him a confidence boost if nothing else.

The gun could only hold two rounds at a time, and Rostrum made sure that the cartridges were fresh. Maintaining the armaments was the lowest of low priorities, and he couldn't be sure how long the bullets in the gun had been sat there. That the thing had been left loaded at all was a bad sign.

Once he was armed, Rostrum began to skulk down towards the galleon docks. There would be Goddesses down here, surely.

He could hear Galveston again.

You've got to stay strong, kid. That little pea-shooter you've got there won't do you much good if you have to pull the trigger. Hell, an asthmatic has a stronger sneeze than that Roscoe you're packing, but the damned cog-heads don't know that. To them, you're death incarnate until you show them otherwise now.

So, Rostrum was losing it. At least he was aware of that, it made it a little more fun.

He saw his first sign of the Goddesses as he approached the customs checkpoint, the final obstacle before the stairs down to the docks proper. There was blood on the walls, a thin smear that dragged all the way across the wall to the top of the stairs. No signs of a struggle though.

The zip gun clicked as he readied it, a green LED illuminating to tell him the small battery was ready. He'd chosen this one for its lack of moving parts – run a small current through the cartridge and it would, in theory, trigger the propellant – as that was less that could go wrong. It suddenly felt very small in his hands, however, now that there was a real chance he might need it.

Rostrum was overly cautious as he crossed to the staircase. The blood was reason enough for a fair bit of caution, but in that moment he felt that one could never be too safe. This was reinforced as he peered down the staircase.

A body lay at the bottom, soaking in a puddle of blood that was so large it bordered on comical. From a distance it may even have elicited a chuckle, but Rostrum was too close. He could see the anguish on the dead face, the wounds.

The stairs were slick with blood too, though the light was dim enough there that it looked more like oil. Not hard to traverse after the crash course in descending a series of frozen platforms, and he reached the body quickly.

He didn't recognise her, but she was dressed like galleon crew. Her jacket was fur-lined, so she wasn't a Strider native. The local fashion was for thick padding rather than a warm lining, which meant she was a foreigner. That made sense. If she hadn't been brought up with the healthy distrust of these robots, he could see her overstepping her bounds and drawing their ire.

She had a command card in her pocket. Rostrum had been hoping for a better gun, but the keys to her galleon would do. Strider and Roller galleons used actual keys, but the Crawler had always had the better tech, and something as needlessly complex as a command card was right up their street. He pocketed it and continued towards the docks.

The robots weren't out in force, but they were a very visible presence. Rostrum had expected them to be on patrol, stomping their way around the many slotted galleons like good little clockwork soldiers. Instead, they were stood sentinel at various points, their heads slowly rotating on their necks. That was the sort of thing you couldn't fail to see.

He needed to reach a galleon, preferably the Crawler-galleon belonging to the corpse he had met on the way in. Retaking the Strider was the obvious end goal here, but he had to talk it through with someone. He needed access to a council, and for that he needed to access the network. Any galleon would have the means to do so, but the higher tech of the Crawler-galleons made them ideal.

Being that she had died where she had, her galleon must have docked recently. That narrowed the search area quite substantially, and it didn't take him long to spot a likely craft a short distance down the docks. Reaching it would require avoiding only one Goddess, which didn't *sound* too hard. There was a pattern to their scanning, after all, should be a simple enough task to stalk through while avoiding the field of vision.

But that was too simple, wasn't it? Far too easy. It was a trap somehow, it had to be. As far as he was aware, the overriding directive of these robots at this time was to find him, specifically, and kill him. Everything they did had to be underpinned by this, which meant that even this simple spectacle had to be designed to catch him. If they suspected he would come down here then they would have some notion as to why. They'd do a better job of keeping him from his target.

Rostrum took another look around.

Nothing else seemed out of place. It was still and silent, save for the dangling ice razors of the many galleons jingling in the wind, not even a creak of something, somewhere, being out of place. But then, it wouldn't be. This trap would be precise, calculated, robotic.

Indecision gripped him. Perhaps this was just paranoia. In all probability, this is *exactly* what it was. He was psyching himself out, too strung out on the fear of what might happen that he hadn't truly thought about whether it was likely. Not that he could do that thinking now, even though he knew he should. It would be tainted and biased by this paranoia.

But then, what if he was right?

Something needed to happen. He couldn't stay there forever, crouched behind a container, just waiting. All that he had to do was accept that there wasn't a choice. Alone he had no plan, but if he could just converse with someone else, that would broaden his options. Whether this was a trap or not, he had to reach a galleon, make that call.

So he moved, slowly. Every step he made was just him moving deeper into the trap, he was convinced. It would spring soon, when he crossed the point of halfway between the container and the galleon. His heart was pumping, one hand gripped tightly to the primed zip gun, the other ready to fumble more ammo from a pocket.

He was still rethinking his plan with every step. Why not just climb into any of the galleons he was passing? Use their network connection. It would work. Hell, that would be even easier. And he had to confess to himself that he didn't have a good answer for that.

Drawing closer to the Crawler-galleon, ready to slip past the sentinel, he told himself that it was actually safer this way. The saboteur had already shown a propensity for subverting Strider technology, who's to say he hadn't rigged up some failsafe to the Strider-galleons? Disabled their connections maybe, installed some sort of back-trace so they could find him instantly the moment the network connection was activated. It was exactly the sort of thing he would do to Galveston. The Crawler-galleon, being from another city, might not be as easy to break as the Strider systems, and probably wasn't even connected when the saboteur made his move.

Well thought out, one step ahead of the saboteur. A completely logical argument for why he should focus entirely on the Crawler-galleon. And bollocks.

All of that may have been true, but it wasn't why he was so focused on the harder objective. He needed this proof. Even if he made contact, the likelihood was that he would need to be the one to go back out there, to brave the Goddesses and enact whatever plan needed enacting. He needed to know he could do more than hide from them – he had to be able to beat them.

There were two fields of vision he needed to avoid. The closest robot was the biggest threat and the most obvious, but there was a second a little way back. He wasn't sure how far they could actually see, and perhaps the distant one wouldn't notice him at all, but that sort of thinking would get him caught. They weren't designed to cover each other's blind spots at least.

For a good portion of their rotations, they did manage to cover each other, but there was a gap. It was small, and it moved so quickly that it would be difficult to exploit silently, but it was there. If he could move at that speed without making noise, just staying in that gap would lead him right to the galleon.

But that was the issue. The decks were thin sheets of corrugated metal atop an industrial plastic, and moving faster than walking pace caused a lot of noise. For the hustle and bustle of normal work conditions, that wasn't a problem. For sneaking about, it was.

He would need to run.

There were ways of running without making a sound. It was all about shifting your weight correctly, he'd read about it in books. He had never been able to replicate it, but there were other ways. Stupid ways. Utterly daft ways. But they might work, and that was all he cared about.

He ducked out of sight again and set about putting his socks on over his shoes. Wherever he had gotten this technique from had long since vanished from his memory, but the idea itself had stayed. He had tried it once before, trying to get some measure of petty vengeance on Moses for a particularly scathing comment, attempting to sneak up behind him outside the council chambers. The socks had little grip, and he found it difficult to move at all, let alone silently, but it seemed otherwise sound.

So long as he didn't slip this time.

Again, he felt like a fool. Did heroes always feel like fools? Was heroism just doing foolish things while believing, *really believing*, that they would work? He was probably getting ahead of himself with that line of thought. Besides, what did it matter if he looked foolish, so long as it worked?

He stood up and tried out his newly muffled feet. A little slippery, but not much worse than the ice had been outside. If he tensed his thighs again, he could probably deal with that. And the footsteps were certainly quieter, if not silent. It shifted the sounds lower, made them dull, much more likely to sink into the background. Now all he needed was his opening.

He watched the heads rotating, glass eyes glinting occasionally as the sun bounced off the snow below and caught them. There was a certain point where they would both glint, that would be his signal to move. If he could stay one step behind the field of view of the closer Goddess, it *should* keep him one step ahead of the more distant one.

Unless he was wrong.

He had better not be wrong.

As the eyes glinted, he moved. Not too far, not too slow, just a steady march between the vision cones until he could reach the galleon. Had he needed to go faster, then the socks might have worked to his detriment, but in this instance they served to keep him on task. Everything in his body was urging him to *go faster*, despite how it would undo the entire plan. The unsteady footing kept him disciplined.

By the time he could slip between the docked galleons, his thighs were burning but the robots were undisturbed. After a moment's rest, he shimmied up the boarding ladder and onto the deck of the galleon, as safe as he could be for now.

It had been a long time since the Crawler had manufactured a galleon, but Rostrum had taken the time over the years to familiarise himself with all the schematics for every city's bigger projects. There was much in the way of co-operation anyway, so most of it was relatively intuitive regardless of this, but it paid to know how to pilot anything one might conceivably need to, one day.

Crawler-galleons had a bridge set into the bow. They liked to be low to the surface, Crawlermen, it was one of their little quirks. If they couldn't feel the razors grinding up the ice right below them, they couldn't settle. Ordinarily, Rostrum found this a bit peculiar, but it suited his purposes perfectly. Out of the way and insulated, my less likely he'd be seen.

He descended the few steps from the deck to the bridge and opened the door with the liberated command key – one key for many locks, a security nightmare but very convenient – closing it behind him. The bridge was stunning, with very little of the mechanical jigsaw aesthetic that was so prevalent in Strider-tech. It was damn near pristine, a relic of the old days, with the exception of a little corner into which was bolted a more recent terminal. Deactivated, of course.

There was a slot on what he suspected was the captain's chair, perfect size for the command key. He inserted it and the bridge came to life. Perhaps he could let himself breathe now.

The conspicuous network terminal was the last screen to blink to life, and the whirring of its internal components drowned out the quiet hum of the more sophisticated – if impossible to replicate – tech around it.

He set about trying to make a connection.

> Pilot Strider calling mayday. Please respond.

>> This is pilot Roller. What's up, bud?

> Serious problem. Martial law subverted by saboteur. Need assistance.

>> Your network address is different.

> Not on my own terminal. Strider network is insecure. Entirely compromised by saboteur.

>> What exactly has happened???

> The saboteur has wrested control of the Green Goddess support robots from me and used them to put

the city on lockdown until the storm hits and probably kills everyone. They want to kill me on sight, and I'm armed with a zip gun that would have a problem shooting a hole through a sheet of paper.

>> Sounds bad.

> YES IT DOES DOESNT IT????

>> Chill. We'll fix it. What do you need from me?

What did he need? Soldiers? The Roller wasn't of a military pedigree, but it had better weapons than the Strider, that wasn't hard. The people wielding them might not be better trained, but they wouldn't need to be. Just having something that could reliably take out the Goddesses from a distance might be enough to carve a route to somewhere they could be reliably shut down.

But that wouldn't help to deal with the saboteur. Rostrum still had no idea who or where that man even was – if he even was a man, just as likely to be a woman – and with him still out there it would be foolish to try and get the Strider mobile again.

> Can you send me the latest weather maps?

>> One sec.

File received

> No time for you to do anything. Storm's too close now.

>> I know. Doesn't mean I wasn't going to offer.

Rostrum's hands curled into fists. It took a lot of effort not to smash them into the terminal. Instead, he channelled that rage into very aggressive typing, slamming each of the keys one by one. Juvenile, but he needed to let it out while he had the privilege of not requiring a level head.

> Nothing much you can do. We just have to weather the storm.

>> You could run?

>Where? What would even be the point?

>> A galleon could outrun the storm. At least that's what my science bods say. We're not so far away. Come

here. I'll see you leave with a few armed men, enough to take back the city.

> Tempting. Who is to say there will even be a city left to retake?

>> Cities have braved the storms before.

> And suffered for it.

>> Endured it.

> Not all of them.

>> No. Not all of them. Not even most of them. But SOME of them. It IS possible. Come here. Let me help.

He typed out an agreement several times, and deleted each of them. It made sense, perfect sense, to go into a brief exile. Come back, retake the city, and he could be assured to survive long enough to pilot that retaken city without incident. Provided it stayed standing.

No-one else had the capability to do his job. He was too important to lose. Fleeing to the Roller while the storm hit made sense.

But yet...

> I can't leave. Maybe there's something I can do here to help.

>> No point arguing this. Right?

> I wish there was.

>> Ok. But I'm not abandoning you. We all survive.

> Appreciate it.

>> As soon as the storm passes, I'll send those men. Watch for them.

> Thank you.

>> You'd do the same for me. Want me to relay things to Crawler? She might be able to send help too?

> Yes.

The chances were that one of them was involved somehow. The saboteur came from somewhere, after all. But Rostrum wasn't about to let that make him paranoid. He didn't know which of them it was – if it even *was* one of them – so better not to burn any bridges.

>> Will do. Are you safe?

> As I can be. How long before the storm front hits?
>> Looks like an hour.
> Great. Wish me luck.
>> Good luck.

Rostrum logged off. Not exactly the most buoying of conversations, but there was a little hope there. If he could just make it through a murderous death-storm, then he might stand a chance of taking back his home. Simple goals were the best goals. At least there was a light at the end of the tunnel.

One hour to prepare. That meant he'd need to try and work out where the most damage would be and steer clear of those areas. Places potentially open to the elements, thinner walls or maintenance hatches. The bridge was one such place, as were most of the council offices, recreation zones and secondary engineering hubs. He could take solace, it least, in those areas having been forcibly evacuated by the Goddesses before the saboteur seized control. That should minimise casualties.

Oh, but there was an area he had forgotten, wasn't there?

The dock.

Of bloody course.

Taking the path of least resistance, the storm would smash its way through the docked galleons, flinging them around and more or less destroying everything for a couple of decks. Galleons were big, heavy, solid things by design, sat atop razors that had one purpose: carving through centuries-old solid ice without hesitation. Interior walls weren't going to do much to stop them, especially if they decided to explode.

He didn't want to be there when it happened, obviously, but he was hesitant to attempt to leave too. The approach had given him the benefit of being able to see what he was dealing with, to spot that blind spot in their surveillance, but he wouldn't have that on the exit. Maybe, if he was careful, he could get a look at one of the

Goddesses, track their vision, but he wouldn't be able to see the other. He'd be flying blind in that regard, and he was just as likely to mess things up and get spotted as to slip back into that perfect void in their vision.

Even if he did, that would still mean the end of the docking level, and that would make it harder for his rescue rangers to come to his aid anyway.

So he would have to close the emergency bulkheads, sealing the dock's entrance. A simple task, provided he was in the cockpit, at his console, without a metal hand trying to squeeze his throat down to the size of a drinking straw.

As he wasn't, it meant crossing to the dock control room, at the very end of the string of moored galleons, and pressing a few buttons.

He pulled the command key from the captain's chair, powering down the galleon once more, and returned to the deck. The cold wind smothered him quickly, and suddenly everything felt a little less hopeful again. The planet had a way of doing that to people, but he could have done without it at that moment.

Looking out over the racks of docked galleons, he counted fifteen between himself and the control room, with three or four Goddesses patrolling the route. Even if he could make it back into the blind spot of the sentinels and use it to skirt around them, he'd never manage it for the few on patrol. They were too unpredictable.

How big was the gap between the galleons? A couple of feet? They were pretty tightly packed when they were hanging for storage and didn't need space to load extra cargo. He could probably jump that, right? Wouldn't even need a run-up. If he never had to touch the ground, that would limit how likely he was for the Goddesses to spot him, surely.

Shuffling over to the side, Rostrum peered at the first galleon in his chain of stepping stones. It was a long way down if he missed – even further if he managed to miss the small boarding gantry too, then he would have nothing but ice to break his fall.

He climbed up onto the edge and gave one last look around. No robots watching. As safe as things were going to be.

Taking a deep breath, he attempted the first jump.

NINE

'What *is* it?' the captain asked, hunched down with his face mere inches from the creature's snout.

'I think it's, like, a cat,' Lu said.

She had brought the thing back up along with a handful of medical supplies, dumping it unceremoniously onto the floor before she set about patching up Wendy. The *thing* had tootled about on the grating for a few moments and then sat down and, apparently, gone to sleep. It hadn't moved for nearly half an hour.

The captain grimaced so hard that his upper lip nearly vanished into his nose. 'Yes, it's *like* a cat, in that it is entirely not at all an actual cat.'

'I mean, it is sort of cat-*ish*,' Wendy said, her face turned away from Lu as she threaded another stitch through a rapidly closing cut.

'Milton, the closest thing this has in common with a cat is that it has legs and what I assume is fur. This... This is just deeply unsettling. We are absolutely not keeping it.'

Wendy flinched as Lu set another stitch.

The captain wasn't entirely wrong about the creature. It was very uncomfortable to look at – its proportions and movements seemed a little off, sort of uncanny, and what passed for fur had matted in some places, rotted in other, over the centuries. That it had survived at all would have been one hell of a surprise, had it not been a machine.

The others hadn't spotted that yet, and she didn't have the energy to tell them while Lu was shoving needles into her face, but she had noticed instantly. The eyes were plastic for a start, betrayed by the dull dry sheen instead of the requisite watery glint present in the biological variety. The movements were uncanny because they were guided by servos, not muscles. And, most telling of all, she could see the metal under the fur, in the places where mange had started to rot it away.

An electric cat *thing*. She hadn't expected to see one of them. Why would she? It sat there, looking at her, its approximated breathing mimicking an animal at rest. What a curious thing to have on a craft such as this.

There was a clattering from above as Thorsten shifted position to another terminal. 'I think I might be making some progress.'

Lu didn't stop stitching. 'You've been up there long enough, so I should hope so.'

'What have you got?' the captain said.

'I've found the program that runs the storm engine.'

'Sounds like progress to me,' the captain said, doing his best to sound stoic. Wendy liked that about him, never let people get their hopes up, but wouldn't crush them either. 'Can you shut it off?'

'Not yet,' Thorsten said. 'Just because I've found what makes the thing run, doesn't mean I understand it. There's a chance, if I just kill the process –'

Wendy lurched, shoving Lu aside. A thousand pinpoints of pain across her body flared up. 'Don't!'

Thorsten turned his gaze on her. 'I wasn't –'

'This system is sophisticated, there must be a web of connections across the entire vessel –'

'– If I kill the process unexpected, it could cause a resonating failure across every connected system, I know.

Give me some credit, Wendy.'

'Oh,' she said. 'Sorry.'

He smiled. 'What I was about to say, captain, was that these systems are so interlinked that I don't trust a hard reset to do anything but make our situation worse. But if I can decipher how this thing works, it *should* be pretty simple to shut down.'

The captain crossed his arms. 'And if not?'

'Then we'll need Wendy on form. I'm sure as hell not doing a hard reset, but I bet the brat could work out a safe way of doing it. Right?'

She mocked a salute. 'Aye aye.'

Lu grumbled and shoved the younger woman back, returning to her stitching. 'Sit still, or this will take much longer. Thor, any sign of the buyers yet?'

'One second,' he said. The ropes creaked as he swung back to the first terminal. 'Something is coming up on the long range scans now I think. It's hard to spot the finer details through what is, at this point, two storms marching comfortably towards third base.'

The captain has turned his attention to the projected map again. 'What's their ETA?'

'I don't know,' Thorsten said. 'They've literally just appeared on the screen, not even remotely enough time to calculate that sort of thing.'

'I just need an estimate –'

'Fine. Approximately *some* minutes. Less than a day, longer than a short wank. What do you want from me? Do you want me to break the storm engine, or do you want me to be a speaking clock? Pick one, I can't do both.'

Naturally, there was a silence. Just a small one.

The captain broke it. 'Thor –'

'No, I'm sorry,' Thorsten said. 'This computer system is getting on my wick. It's just so *old*, it's infuriating. The buys are probably an hour or two away at this point, give or take.'

'I guess that gives you an hour or two to crack the

storm engine, then.'

Thorsten flipped the captain an impolite gesture, but he couldn't help but laugh. 'Did you not hear me bitching about pressure just then?'

'It'll be fine. I trust you.'

'That's as maybe, but it would be easier with Wendy helping me out.'

Lu set another stitch. 'I'm nearly done with the superficial stuff. Then, if she can dress herself, I'll sign off on her helping you out.'

Wendy sat patiently as the last stitch was set. She had tried so hard not to count them, in the hope that it would make it all go quicker. It hadn't worked, but it was nice to know it was nearly done. As Lu snipped the thread, Wendy couldn't help but breathe an actual sigh of relief.

She tried to stand up. The stitches hadn't done much to deal with the internal injuries, but she felt stronger nonetheless.

'What about the bones and stuff?' she asked?

'Nothing seems to be properly broken,' Lu said. 'But we don't have the equipment to deal with the fractures, so you'll have to tough it out. Should be easier now, your skin will hold all your important bits together.'

'I'm not convinced you're a real doctor,' Wendy said. The skin pulled taught against the stitches as she moved to her feet, but she managed it. The pain was a constant, but dulled, sensation now. Manageable.

'I might not be a doctor,' she said. 'But I'm pretty good at sewing.'

'I won't argue that. Can you pass me some clothes or something? I'm suddenly very aware how much of my pants are on show.'

Lu snatched up Wendy's clothes from the floor and tossed them to her. She caught them awkwardly – her arms were still a little sluggish – and they were still a little damp. Better than semi-nakedness however, and probably dry enough to avoid hypothermia now. 'Thanks.'

She set about getting dressed. It was not going to be a quick procedure.

After she was halfway into her trousers, she looked up to see Thorsten frowning extra-hard at his terminal.

'That's... peculiar,' he said. 'Where's *that* coming from?'

'What is it?' Wendy asked, finally negotiating her trousers around her waist.

'There's something running in the background here. It's like a signal, but I don't think it's coming from outside. A recording maybe? Give me a second, I'll try to patch it into the speakers. This place must have some, right?'

There was a hiss as the speakers crackled to life, a violent static assaulting their ears. Then it evened out, mellowed. Still, Wendy had trouble hearing anything at first. There was something in there, hiding in the static, pockets of information, but the hiss was just too much.

Thorsten must have thought the same. Again, his hands became a blur across his keyboard, and the background hiss dissipated even more. The words began to punch through, and Wendy pulled a soggy notepad from a pocket to note them down.

Five, six, nine, twenty-eight, puppet, fourteen, green, ouroboros, quiche.

The voice was robotic, monotonous, and went back to repeating those same words uninterrupted but for a small pause after *quiche*. After a few repetitions, Thorsten turned it off.

'What the hell was that, then?' Wendy asked.

'A code, clearly,' the captain said. 'We all recognise that something so esoteric has to be a code, right?'

'It's not a code,' Lu said. She had a small notebook of her own open.

Thorsten scoffed.' That is *clearly* a code.'

'No,' Lu said. 'It's *trying* to be a code. Whatever it is, it's designed to sound like a coded message without actually fitting any known cipher.'

'That's sort of the point of a code, right?' Thorsten

said.

'The point of a code is to transmit information securely, so that someone can decrypt it at the end. They need to know what sort of cipher it is to do that. The security of the code isn't from not knowing the cipher, it's from not knowing the key. You can encrypt things any number of ways with the same method, but you can't *decrypt* them without the right key.'

'And you're saying this doesn't fit any ciphers?' the captain said.

'Not that I know of,' she said. 'But I concede I am not fully versed in old world weird technology ciphers, so maybe it's just something I can't understand. But it sounds, to me, like something that was meant to sound *like* a code without actually *being* one.'

The captain fell silent for a while. 'Well, we're here, and while Thorsten works on the storm engine, it's not like either of us can do too much to help him. Might as well stay occupied.'

'Sir?'

'Thorsten and Wendy will work on the technical things, the important things, and we'll stay out of their hair working on this alleged code. Keep ourselves busy and active while we wait for the buyers. Sound fair?'

Lu nodded. So did Wendy. She wanted to get back to normal – she'd only been off her feet for an hour or so and already she was bored – and she knew that Lu would cluck around her if there wasn't something to distract the older woman. It wasn't even as if Lu was *that* much older than Wendy, but sometimes a couple of years could feel as much as twenty when she wanted it to.

Thorsten, for his part, was beaming now. That was relief, Wendy knew. Relief that she wasn't as badly hurt as it looked like she was. She had to be wearing the same expression herself, but it was nice to see it reflected in Thor.

'There is one problem,' she said. 'I don't think I'm

going to be able to climb up there in my current state.'

'Not to worry,' Thor said. He pulled out a small tablet from a pocket on his left thigh, followed by a length of thick cable from the matching pocket on his right. Affixing one end of the cable to the cluster of terminals and the other to the tablet, he gently lowered the tablet down into her waiting hands. 'Never liked touchscreen interfaces myself, but should do you fine if you can't climb up here.'

'You had this the whole time?'

'Of course,' he said. 'But it's clunky and awkward to use. Perfect for you, not so much for me.'

'Huh.'

The captain approached and laid a hand on her shoulder. She winced, but he didn't seem to notice. 'Help him get his work done. I won't nag, I won't ask for updates, nothing. Just know that I trust the pair of you can get this done. We'll be over there, trying to decode the mad ramblings of a centuries-old computer.'

'Thanks, captain.'

'If you need us, give us a shout,' he said. Then he took Lu by the arm and led her off to a far wall.

Wendy held the tablet in her bare hands for a moment, letting the feel of technology excite her, reinvigorate her once again. That sense of purpose, it was hard to find a better painkiller.

'Right then, old man,' she said. 'Where do we start?'

'We split the workload,' he said. 'I'll concentrate on the main program, you can sift through all the other nonsense bolted onto the damn thing, see if you can find a way to make the hard reset work and not make everything explode. Sound fair?'

'It'd be easier from down in engineering or something, but I guess I could manage up here with schematics and stuff. Do the theory and all that.'

'I'm not going to tell you how to do your job, you know about this stuff much more than I do. That's why you get the hard job and I get to hit the enter key a lot while hanging from the ceiling in a comfy harness chair.'

'I like the hard jobs,' she said, then caught him sniggering. 'Oh, grow up.'

'Here, I'm pushing you a directory list of all the uncorrupted folders I could find on the system. There's probably schematics or documentation in there you didn't get onto that disk of yours. Might help.'

Her tablet screen lit up. A link to the central data cluster.

'Thanks, I'll give it a skim.'

'Just don't do anything without letting me know first? If I can turn it off safely from up here, I think I'd prefer that.'

'Listen, old man, I'm the mechanic. I know how machines work.'

'I know you do, brat. But I also know you have a habit of getting carried away when you find something interesting. Case in point,' he said and waved his arms, gesturing to the whole vessel. 'See?'

'Point taken.'

'Good girl.'

'I'm going to go off you in a minute, you know.'

There were a lot of files. From what she could tell, a fair few of these folders had been marked as hidden on the database, which meant Thor must have had to crack a few passwords to uncover them. That alone meant there had to be something worthwhile in there.

A good chunk of them seemed to be log files. Diagnostics rather than officer logs, all the background nonsense computers churn out if they're left to their own devices. Not even people who were big into computers could enjoy reading this stuff, and Wendy preferred machines with moving parts larger than electrons. But she was diligent, to a degree, and if nothing else then the error logs would be a good place to start.

It painted a weirdly sterile picture of what was, in truth, a catastrophic attack. The cascade failure of critical systems, all in response to a single blast point. It was peculiar to see how it reverberated through the system, yet important.

She tapped through a few more folders, there was something in particular she needed. Old tech had weird system architecture, it never quite meshed with what they were using these days. You could force connections if you had to, but it was just too alien to properly interlink, and that, she contended, was a result of a fundamental difference in the way people thought about things in each civilisation.

There was a powerful disconnect, a distance of mind that was hard to work around. It required thinking not only counter-intuitively – which was hard enough – but counter-rationally. Electronic forensics was awkward.

Unless you had a Rosetta stone.

The error logs were, in fact, part of this. They showed how problems flowed down-system from the source, which gave her a direction. That wasn't enough though, it was like being able to recognise an engine, not build one.

Thor had mentioned schematics, but Wendy had not been looking for them. It would have been the golden result, sure, but they were never easily accessed if they were even there. She'd seen how modern tech-heads stored their documentation, and she had no reason to believe that this particular facet of the craft had ever changed.

But if she could find that Rosetta stone, build herself a vocabulary, then she wouldn't need that. The architecture itself would tell her where to begin.

It took a while. Cross-referencing error codes with segments of programming was exactly as tedious as it sounded, but it helped her to build a map. A rough, hastily sketched, likely inaccurate map, but close enough to make progress. Over the next hour she was able to identify and separate certain systems into particular strands of code.

It made her feel *alive*.

Climate control had its claws in the timekeeping system, which sort of made sense. But then the on-board alarms were only tangentially linked to the central clock, offering more of a connection with coding hidden in the antivirus scanners in the secondary command consoles. It was a mess, but one she was starting to understand. Given enough time, she could do this.

She was beaming.

A notification slid into view at the top of the tablet. She tapped it. Thor was sending her an instant message.

>> Any luck?

> I'm getting there, Thor.

>> We might have a problem.

> Another one?

>> Don't react. Just look like you're working.

> Why all the cloak and dagger stuff?

>> Don't want people worrying. Might have made a slight mistake.

> What do you mean.

>> Check the power distribution grids. There's a shortcut in the data cluster.

She swiped his message away and tapped through to the grids.

> Well how did you even do that?

>> I genuinely don't know. Was working on trying to work round the problem, create so much system load that it would cannibalise power from elsewhere to keep everything going.

> You were trying to starve the storm engine. That's actually a really good idea.

>> I thought so.

> But this isn't starving it. It's the exact opposite of starving it.

>> Yeah. That shouldn't have happened.

> Redundant turbines for emergencies, I guess. Auxiliaries.

>> Seems whoever built this thing had planned for my

little scheme.

Again, she flipped back to the grids. The auxiliary generators hadn't been obvious on her trip through the engineering deck, but she should have expected them. The cities each had dozens of the things, even a galleon would hold one or two, especially the ones assigned to trailblazing. Stood to reason that this *thing* would have one too.

> I'm not quite seeing the problem, Thor.

>> Well it's making the storm bigger, for one.

> And?

>> And the auxiliaries haven't been ticking over constantly, unlike the main generator.

> Centuries of inactivity, coupled with a sudden massive power drain. Ok, I see the issue. Shit's going to explode.

>> On the plus side, it won't explode until after the buyers are supposed to turn up.

>Yay?

>> Means the deadline is still the deadline. Just now there's also a *dead*line.

>You are rubbish.

Wendy drummed her fingers on the screen for a moment, running some calculations. Nothing to worry about, she was already on track to find what she needed. Probably.

She worked better under pressure anyway. Pile it on, Thor, she could take it.

TEN

Rostrum was exhausted. Jumping from galleon to galleon sounded so easy, but it was rapidly becoming clear just how out of shape he was. The fact that the last jump, which brought him almost to his goal, had caused him to tweak his ankle did nothing to dissuade him of this.

The only saving grace so far was that the robots hadn't seemed to notice his less than graceful journey across decks. They might have had stellar eyesight, but their hearing must have been atrocious.

He pulled himself up to his feet again, gingerly putting pressure on his bad ankle and gauged the next jump. More or less level this time, that was good, for the landing if a little awkward for the run-up. Or hobble-up as it was in this case.

One small jump, one awkward landing, one protesting ankle, and there he was, almost within arm's reach. Yet, the storm had made progress too. Rostrum had taken too long. All those jumps, timed to avoid the gazing eyes of the Goddesses, psyching himself up for each of them, they'd eaten up most of his hour. The wind was picking up, howling through the opening and kicking up the ice and snow from beneath, whipping itself into a vicious squall that hadn't quite the courage to properly enter the docks.

But soon. Already the galleons were starting to sway against their moorings. It was a matter of minutes now before the true storm front hit. And, luckily, only one jump left.

He made the final jump easily, gripping the railing and pulling himself up onto the catwalk and out of sight of the nearby robot prowling the dock below. Rostrum scuttled to the control room and sealed himself inside. The lock was weak, not exactly designed to hold up against steel fists, but it gave him some solace.

The bulkheads could be closed now. It was a single switch, that was all. But would that reveal him to the steel killers waiting for him out there? Almost certainly. There were two places on the Strider where one could close the bulkheads, and they had control of one of them. They'd know *someone* was here if not him, and they'd come.

Yet if he didn't risk it, he'd be giving the storm free access to the literal underbelly of his beached city.

As he laid a hand on the switch, he knew that there had never been a question. He flicked the switch with a grim determination, and the sound of steel on steel filled the deck. Enormous great cogs, hidden in the walls, ground against their housings as they activated for the first time in a long while, sliding the giant bulkheads into place. The rumble dwarfed the wind, and when it finally came to a stop neither could be heard. There was silence.

And darkness.

Rostrum hadn't realised how much light had been coming from the opening, bounced off the snow and up into the Strider. With the bulkhead closed, the docks were nearly pitch black, though a clicking deep in the console told him that some circuit or other was busying itself with attempting to provide replacement light.

He waited, hand clasped tightly around his zip-gun. No noticeable reaction from the Goddesses. That was worst of all. They weren't exactly chatty, but he had hoped he would at least hear their footsteps as they came for him. Considerably less than ideal, but it would give him something to aim for if nothing else. He wanted to know when they were coming, at least.

Another click, then a louder one as a light came on in the distance. Then another, and another, as array after array of powerful daylight bulbs flooded the docks with light.

Empty, not a single Goddess.

Rostrum turned. He knew then. The zip-gun was up and ready before he even finished turning his head, and as his eyes locked on the first of the robots at the door he felt his finger tighten against the trigger before he could properly register it.

There was a line of them, a perfectly sedate queue stretching back along the catwalk, expressionless and silent as the one at the front set about opening the door. Why he had not already breached the room, Rostrum could not say. Perhaps they needed to confirm his identity first? That seemed as likely as anything else, and they had plenty of time to do that as he slowly, steadily, pushed the door off its hinged.

The lock creaked and threatened to give first, but it *was* the hinges that went ultimately. The pins snapping loudly under the Goddess' merciless application of force, sending the door toppling, shattering glass as it landed.

Rostrum fired a shot. The bullet struck the robot in the head, giving it pause, but not even denting it. The glass eyes fixed on him, unblinking – did they even *have* lids? – and it took a step into the room. The queue of robots behind it followed in step, one giant steel worm of doom. Rostrum loaded another shot and fired again, to similar effect. Those eyes, those damnable glass lenses, unflinchingly staring at him as the robot took a second step, then a third.

Enough time for one more shot. Perhaps he'd get

lucky, puncture its power core, cause a cascading explosion that would take them all out. He loaded the third bullet, took aim, and fired. It struck the robot in the eyes, shattering it and punching deep into its head. There was a comical series of light *ping* noises as it bounced around inside, followed by a rattle as it came to a halt.

The robot blinked. They *did* have eyelids after all.

It stopped and regarded Rostrum for a time. Then it cocked its head to one side and opened its mouth, wide. Then wider. Wider still. Even wider again, like a snake, unhinging its jaw, until something fell out and bounced against the floor.

The bullet.

Rostrum wasn't too proud to beg for his life. What did pride get you? Nothing you could use, that was for certain. He sank to his knees and sank back into the corner of the room, hands up, lip trembling, looking for the words, any words, that might save him. All he managed was a stream of incoherent babble. There *were* no words.

The robot reset its jaw and approached him calmly, indifferently, and placed a metal hand around his throat. It began to tighten, and he knew that this was it. This was how he died, with his scream choked out by the emotionless hand of the distant past.

Rostrum stared right into its remaining eye and its blank face as the light faded from his vision.

Then his entire world shook with a thunderous roar, launching him and his killer into the far wall with hellish force, plunging them into darkness once again. Those damned fingers never left his throat.

He sat there, waiting for the squeeze, unable to force himself to resist in any meaningful way. Even as the lights flickered to life again, and he found himself staring once more into that dispassionate face, he did nothing but wait.

And wait.

And wait.

It was a few minutes before he realised that he wasn't

going to die. The metal hand unfurled easily as soon as he worked up the courage to remove it, and he could push the robot away with one hand once that had been achieved. Behind it, he could see the others sent sprawling by the impact. All of them deactivated, some of them broken.

Rostrum stood up, rubbing his neck, and padded over to the control panel again. Green text on a small black screen reinforced his suspicions: the storm was nearly upon him. That jolt must have been a finger reaching out, caressing the Strider before the main bulk of it arrived. A herald.

It wouldn't be long now. More strikes would come soon, vicious forks of lightning dancing over the hull, worse than the last one. But if the first one had taken out the robots somehow...

~Bing Bong~

There was the reverent crackling of an old tape whirring to life somewhere, ready to spout a pre-recorded message into some forgotten microphone somewhere. The citywide broadcast system. It was strange to hear it from this side.

'People,' said the computerised voice in a deliberately posh tone. 'We are in crisis. The installation is in peril, at risk from an external force. Put trust in your superiors, they will lead you to safety. But while they work to liberate you from this situation it would be prudent to seek refuge in the core facilities. They are the most secure, and the most defensible.'

Rostrum scowled and lowered himself down from the control room to the floor. All good advice of course, fantastic advice, had the city not been a *city*. In the centuries the Strider had been walking the ice, the location of that tape had never been documented, it had never been updated. As far as it was concerned, the Strider was still whatever it had been in the old times. It had a crew then, not citizens.

He cursed the saboteur as he made for the exit of the docks. This was always going to happen, but at least if he had been at his post he could have tempered it a little. There would be panic now, an influx of people dashing from where the robots had corralled them and into the strong heart of the city. More people than would fit. It would be chaos.

He found more robots as he went, all of them slumped over or shattered against walls. That settled it, that first jolt must have scrambled their control core. Perhaps the saboteur had always expected that, or not cared. They weren't needed any more, the damage was set to be done regardless.

Back up the stairs, past the body, he found an intercom panel and keyed in his personal code. Things would need co-ordinating now, and though it took a few tries to make a connection, he knew who he needed to talk to.

'Rostrum?' Moses said, his voice tinny through the small speaker. 'Where the bloody hell have you been?'

'On the run from killer robots sent after me by a saboteur.'

'Excuse me?'

'Never mind. I'll elaborate later. I'm down in the docks, I don't have access to my screens. How bad are things?'

There was a pause. 'Bad. The storm has only increased in magnitude as it has gotten closer. Even the very edges of it are pounding us hard. A lot of smaller strikes are hammering against the plating, which is holding, but that big one smashed a hole through an entire computer core.'

'I thought it might have.'

'That's what shut down the Green Goddesses, but it's also shredded meteorological and navigation sensors, the digi-brains that help calculate for the ambulation matrix and the radio triangulation systems.'

'Well that sounds horrible.'

'Means we're crippled, blind, and dumb.'

'Well, at least we weren't planning on going anywhere

anyway. We were already crippled.'

'That's as maybe,' Moses didn't sound impressed. 'Last readings report this is a *big* storm. Bigger than we thought.'

'You heard the broadcast, right?'

'You mean that bloody recording that's going to lead to one hell of a stampede? Everyone heard it.'

'We need to calm people down.'

'How?'

Rostrum tapped a finger, thinking. 'Where did the Goddesses herd everyone?'

'Standard protocol, they ushered everyone back to their homes.'

'Mid-to-outer hull, right?'

'For the most part.'

'Then we've got time,' Rostrum said. 'You can head them off. Catch them before they can get into the core, out where the corridors are still wide enough to accommodate them, and impose some order. Cool them down, let them in at a steady pace so they don't crush themselves to death.'

'On my own?'

'You'll have security, right? What are they for if they can't keep their head in a crisis?'

'Okay, I'll try,' Moses said. 'Listen, about the Green Goddesses –'

'Not now. I can't hear that yet. We've too much to do. Save who we can, that's what's important right now.'

'Understood.'

Rostrum disconnected as another large jolt shook the city. The lights flickered but remained on this time, though he still lost his footing. Then another, and another. The front had reached them now.

He moved further into the city. The docks were pretty central, but exposed even with the bulkheads sealed. Rostrum wasn't one to tempt fate by hanging around just in case. And the further in he went, the louder the sounds of people became. There weren't many residential areas down this low, but it didn't take many to whip up chaos and confusion.

It was like they had been waiting for him as he rounded the corner. Fifty, maybe a full hundred of them, families, milling about in the waiting area, underneath the screens that ordinarily detailed arrivals and departures. All they read now was *error* in big yellow letters, but still the majority of them were looking to it for solace.

The din was all-encompassing, but he didn't need to hear the specifics of what they were saying to know what was going on. Scared fathers, mothers, grandparents, there was a subsection of them who were convinced they could escape this thing. If they could just get to a galleon, they could outrun the weather, it was their only chance, trust them. All of them, pulling at their families, urging them to the docks, while the more level-headed amongst the group pleaded with them to listen to reason.

Already there were fights breaking out, conflicts born of sheer terror. A man the size of a galleon in and of himself, nothing but muscle and frowns, floored by a woman who looked as though harsh language would snap her in half. This was beyond fight or flight.

Rostrum did his best to help, but they weren't willing to listen, not that they could hear him anyway. The sound was riotous, it wasn't even voices anymore, to the point that he couldn't even hear himself speak as he pleaded for them to listen to him. Trying to physically intervene did not good either, earning him a stray punch to the face or an idle elbow to the ribs. He slipped out of the group and retreated back to where he had entered.

Cradling his bruised ribs, he loaded his zip-gun again and aimed it at the ceiling. He took a pained breath and fired it.

It may have been largely useless as a weapon, but it made a hell of a noise. It stopped the fighting dead as, to a person, they all turned their attention to him. Calmly he loaded another round and pocketed the gun, giving the crowd time to actually *see* him.

'I know you're scared,' he said loudly. 'But this isn't the way. Leaving the city might sound smart, but you won't get anywhere. You can't outrun this.'

Another jolt shook the room, sending people sprawling. They were getting more frequent now, and Rostrum was convinced he could hear the plating start to shatter on the outer hull.

A woman stepped forward. Not the one he had seen take down the brute, but she shared the same wild eyes. They all did. 'Cities don't survive storms! Everyone knows that! I'm not going to stay here and do nothing!'

Rostrum held up his hands. 'Listen! Please! It's not a certainty that we're going to die here. Cities have weathered storms before.'

'When?!'

He'd walked into that one, a question he couldn't answer. The best answer he could give, The Drifter over fifty years ago now, wouldn't be sufficient. It survived the storm, true enough, but barely anyone aboard did. That wouldn't calm them down now, and as he stood there floundering while he attempted to answer the woman's question, he could see the crowd turning.

'The weather is dangerous, I won't lie about that to you, but we have known this for hundreds of years. We've prepared for this. Our city is built to survive this; we've seen to it. Galleons are too small to fortify, but this city is not. Please. Just think about it.'

He had to hope they would buy this lie, as close to the truth as it was. They had done everything they could over the many years to strengthen the cities, and the citizens had seen these efforts in action. All the building work, the retrofitting, they had witnessed it all. They hadn't seen the reports about how futile all that work ultimately was, however. It all came down to trust, to how much they *wanted* to believe they were safe.

Rostrum could see in her face that she didn't believe

him. Her eyes shot to the side, to the young boy she had been hiding behind her back. Seven years old? Was that right? It was hard to tell with children, but he was definitely of the right age to force her to the limit. He could respect that, understand that.

She looked back to him. Through him.

'We can't risk it,' she said in a quiet voice, before repeating it louder. 'We can't risk it!'

'She's right,' said a man from deeper in the crowd. 'We've outrun the storms before. That's what we do! We can do it again now!'

Again, an impact shook the room. Rostrum definitely heard the plating shatter this time. It was a one-two punch. He instinctively knew that noise. The storm had started to hammer the hull itself. It wouldn't take long to breach now.

Worse, the crowd knew this too.

The woman turned to look at the crowd. 'Maybe we won't all survive if we run, but I guarantee more of us will than if we stay here!'

There was a murmur of agreement from the crowd, even from the few Rostrum had identified as dissenters beforehand. Panic was like a virus.

'I can't let you,' he said. 'You won't just die, you'll but the rest of the city at risk.'

'I'm sorry,' she said. 'But I can't care about them. None of us can.'

Her hand slipped behind her back, cradling the child behind her. Rostrum did the same, gripping his zip-gun.

'I sealed the docks, you can't get out that way.'

The crowd gasped. The front row of angry, scared people began to march forward as a result. They stopped when he revealed his gun again. It was all reactionary now. There was no room for rationalising here.

'You would all be dead now if I hadn't,' Rostrum continued. 'The storm is here, now, and it would have ripped through the docks if they had been open. If you try to break that seal, you'll die. That's a certainty.'

'Bullshit,' roared someone from the crowd. 'He's just too afraid to do what needs to be done.'

'He's got a gun,' said someone else.

'He won't use it,' said yet another.

The woman stepped forward, dragging her son with her, and started to move towards Rostrum. He stepped back as far as he could, blocking the corridor, and levelled the gun at her. They were right though, there was no way he could use it.

She stepped up to him and placed a hand on his gun, lowering it with barely any effort. Then she leant in and spoke calmly, quietly. 'You're right. We all know it. But we can't sit idle. We can't just let fate decide this. If there's even a chance we can save ourselves, then to hell with the rest of the city. Everyone for themselves.'

The rest of them were falling in behind her now, but all he could do was stare into those sad, scared eyes. Ice blue, pleading, full of unwanted tears waiting to burst free. Of course he could understand that need, the drive to *act* rather than *react*. Especially when it came to safeguarding family.

That was where the dialogue had broken down, he knew. They thought he didn't understand how important family was. He lived alone, isolated, locked away in the cockpit and removed from the rest of society. How could a man with no family possibly grasp the lengths to which someone would go to protect their own? It was wasted effort, that belief was all over their faces.

Rostrum's eyes left hers as she started to walk around him.

He let her get three steps before he shot her in the back.

They had been wrong. He had a family. The largest family of all. He had to save them, even from themselves, and if that meant a hard choice then he would make it. That was his job.

He wasn't about to let this city destroy itself.

ELEVEN

'How likely is this to work, exactly?'

The captain was pacing. Despite his promises, himself and Lu hadn't managed to stay entirely out of Wendy's hair. They'd bashed their heads against the coded message repeatedly and made no progress, so now they were milling about while herself and Thor worked. Not that it mattered much, but the uncertainty in his voice was dampening her confidence a little.

'Can you hear that noise,' she said. The captain's eyes swivelled a little and he nodded. It was hard to miss. 'That is the sound of the auxiliary batteries overloading. The way this is going, if my plan doesn't work, it won't matter. We'll be all manner of exploded before you can complain anyway.'

Thor shifted in the rafters. 'Boss, she knows her stuff.'

'I know,' the captain said and turned back to Wendy. 'I wouldn't have you on my crew if I didn't have faith in you, kid. I'm just making sure you're not rushing this. The buyers will wait for merchandise like this if you need them to.'

She smiled. 'If we had the time, maybe I'd run tests and simulations or something, but I think that this is as far as I can go. I could scour and search this system forever, but I'd just come back to this. It's the only way I can see it working.'

The captain nodded. 'Good enough for me. Get it done, Milton.'

Wendy had already laid the groundwork before she had mentioned the solution to the captain. That was how she knew it would probably work. It was all about arresting the various command lines at key moments, in effect crashing each system individually instead of all at once. A bit like defusing a bomb: you had to cut the wires in the right order.

Still, she held her breath as she killed the last process. The distant hum of the auxiliaries coming to a halt led her to breathe again, but it was the death knell of the storm that finally put them all at ease.

She hadn't realised just how loud the storm had become until it stopped.

Thor was swinging about excitedly in his harness. 'Well, would you take a look at that!'

The silhouette of the storm was shrinking rapidly, dwindling down to a single point somewhere in the middle of the vessel's outline. Then it was gone completely, and that forgotten silence was finally complete.

With barely any effort, Thor climbed down from his perch and dropped down next to her, wrapping his arms around her tightly. It set off the pain from her injuries again, but it was worth it. Not every day you work out how to shut down the most arcane of technology, after all. She wanted a little bit of lauding.

Lu was halfway out the door by the time the hug was over.

'Where are you going?' Wendy asked.

Lu stopped. 'I'm going to make sure we're not buried under a mountain of ice. All well and good we've killed the storm, but there's the effects to consider. Want to come?'

'I *could* do with some fresh air.'

'Survey the results of your efforts, yeah?'

She smiled. 'Exactly.'

The captain laid a hand on her shoulder and handed her a flare with the other. 'You girls have fun. Send this up for the buyers while you're outside though, will you? I'm willing to bet there's not much galleon left for them to home in on.'

'Roger that.'

'Thorsten, you and I will get this wreck ready for the handover. If I know one thing about salvage ops it's that they are going to want to give the records a once over first and foremost.'

Lu and Wendy practically skipped through the corridors as they made their way back to where they had entered the vessel. The storm hadn't gone alone; it had taken a great weight with it. They barely noticed how much they were rushing.

The entrance had iced over anew, they discovered, but it didn't take long for Lu to break through it. *Punch* through it, really. Then she was up and through the hole with a speed that put Thorsten to shame, thrusting a hand back through the gap to help the injured Wendy.

It was brisk outside, but calm. Calmer than Wendy could ever remember. She had spent her life, as everyone had, running from storms. They kept these vicious squalls at their back eternally, barely being able to outpace them, living their lives in that tense atmosphere. Even if you couldn't see a storm, you could feel it coming in the air, sense the pressure variations that heralded it. It was just background noise.

Not here though. The air was dead, slumbering. It made her skin tingle, and conjured a hearty belly laugh that she didn't dare release. She didn't want to spoil the moment with such an outburst.

The ship was gone – thin sheets of wreckage were visible on the ice, scattered as far as the horizon it seemed – and in its place was an unhindered view across the plains.

The wake from their ice razors had been obscured by the storm, it seemed. It had been a big storm on the screen, but that hadn't truly registered until she saw its aftermath with her own eyes.

Lu stalked off to the side. Shielding her eyes from the glare, she was squinting into the sun.

Wendy walked up beside her. 'What are you looking at?'

The older woman pointed into the distance. 'There, can you see them?'

'Who?' Wendy said, and joined in the squinting. 'The buyers?'

'I think so. I don't think anyone else was close enough, right?'

'Think they'll give us a lift home? We're sort of missing transport now.'

Lu crossed her arms. Her voice went flat. 'I hope they do.'

'What's wrong?'

'Nothing. It's just... I never thought this day would come, you know?'

'What do you mean?'

'I didn't get into this line of work to get rich, or find salvage on this scale. I'd done the salvage thing, ripping up old tech security barges for resources was a hard job, I figured this would be easier.'

Wendy laid her head on Lu's shoulder. 'You're scared of being happy?'

'Something like that,' she said. 'It's just... You're always working towards something. As you get closer, your goals shift, you get new ones. You can never actually reach the goalposts, and that's good, means you keep moving forwards. Sometimes, your real goal is to push those posts further and further way. Do you understand?'

'Not really.'

Lu sighed. 'We've jumped right to the finish line, with no time to adapt. When those buyers get here, everything is going to change.'

'But that's a good thing, isn't it?'

'Of course it is,' she said. 'Listen, you okay to send up the flare and see the buyers get here? I should go report back, see if there's anything I can do.'

'Give me a sec, I'll come with you.'

Wendy produced the tube from her pocket, aimed it, and twisted the base. With a small pop, and a loud fizz, the flare launched into the sky and hung there. If the buyers had seen it, she couldn't tell. They didn't seem to change direction, but then they were barely bigger than dots on the horizon anyway.

'There,' Wendy continued. 'All done.'

Lu was staring up at the flare. 'Good.'

'You sure you're okay?'

'Hm? Oh, yes, of course! Don't worry about me. Just don't see clear skies very often. It's a hell of a thing. My emotions are all out of whack, I'll be fine.'

'You sure you don't want to stay up here a little longer? It's not like you need to report this.'

'I've seen enough,' Lu said, snapping her eyes away from the flare. 'But you should stay up here a little longer. Enjoy the calmness. You did this, you should make the most of it. Besides, the fresh air will help your wounds.'

'That doesn't sound like real medicine, you know. Not that I'm arguing. I could enjoy this view for days.'

'Have fun. Doctor's orders. And make sure the entrance doesn't freeze over again, the buyers won't be pleased if they can't see the goods.'

Wendy sat down. The cold spread through her trousers instantly, numbing her buttocks but she didn't care. 'You can count on me.'

Lu smiled and vanished back into the vessel, leaving Wendy with her view.

Everything was golden, which was pretty apt considering the fortune she had coming her way. The sun was so low in the sky that it barely crested the horizon, at the perfect angle to bounce off the ice and snow, making it glare and sparkle.

So that was her share of the fortune spent already. She'd need a place that could replicate this view. For the next ten years, while the sun graced the world with its presence, she wanted to replicate *this* feeling.

And, you know, tinker with all manner of technology under this beautiful sun, of course. She wasn't about to give that up just because she had more money than god.

It took maybe half an hour for the buyers' galleons to draw close enough to identify as something other than indistinct specks on the horizon, and Wendy loved every minute of it. It was another thirty minutes after that when they finally pulled up at the base of the main chunk of debris that had been her ship.

Three men disembarked awkwardly as she made her way over to greet them. They were lean and weather-worn, sporting the dark-ringed eyes of a seasoned galleon crew. Overly cautious too, if their gear was any indication. Far much more than their slight frames could carry easily, and more than they would need by a long shot. It was refreshing to meet people more awkward than her.

The first man off the boat detached himself from his line and strode towards her, hand outstretched. 'You must be one of the people who found the wreck, yes? Casper van Riet, here to take it off your hands.'

Wendy shook his hand. He had a strong grip, despite his thick gloves. 'Wendy Milton, mechanic. Well, I was. Not much of a ship left to work on.'

Van Riet sucked his teeth and looked around at the wreckage. 'Yeah, that was a weird storm. We weren't really expecting to find you guys still alive, all things considered.'

One of the other two crossed his arms. According to a label on his jacket, his name was Johansson. 'We almost turned around but then, poof, it was just gone. Although I'm sure you know that, you were in it after all.'

'Mother nature's had fun with you,' van Riet said,

looking her over. 'You the only survivor?'

She found herself picking at her stitches. 'Not at all. Everyone made it, we hid in the wreck.'

'Huh, fancy that. Get the equipment, boys, looks like we've got a goldmine here,' he said, snapping his fingers. Johansson and the other man grumbled and trudged back towards their ship. 'So your crew is inside then? We're sort of duty bound to deal with only the highest ranking survivor, as charming as you are.'

'Don't worry, I get it. I'm just the welcoming party, I'll lead you down there. You might need to shed some gear though, it's not a big entrance.'

'I'm sure we'll fit.'

'Not like that you won't,' she said and ushered him over to the hole in the hull. 'See?'

Again, van Riet sucked his teeth, then keyed his radio. 'Forget the gear, boys. We'll have to do an old-fashioned survey first.'

Wendy could hear the groans as the men about-faced and stomped their way back over. It didn't take them long to catch up, but they had seemingly spent that short time inventing new ways to stare daggers at van Riet. Clearly these were men that had worked together for a long time. You didn't get that level of animosity if you weren't friends.

They mumbled and grumbled as they each inspected the entrance, unsnapping various bits of gear as they did so. Wendy didn't even recognise half of it, and what she did seemed superfluous to actually carry upon your person, but the sort of people who signed up to work galleons were hardly short of idiosyncrasies. By the time they were done, they'd left a mountain of gear stacked up on the hull and they seemed all but naked in comparison. Despite this, they were still over-prepared.

The muscles tensed visibly in van Riet's jaw as he tried not to shiver. 'There. We should fit now, right?'

'Should do,' Wendy said. 'Follow me, but watch your

step. We think the thing is lying more or less on its side, so walls are floors. You get the idea.'

Every time she wriggled through the hole, it got easier. Even with her injuries, snaking through the gap and the subsequent internal wiring was hardly a chore at all. It wasn't until van Riet and his crew followed her that she was reminded of how tricky it could actually be without practice. It took them a while to negotiate the wires, and when they did they fell flat on their faces, but they managed to laugh it off despite themselves.

One by one, she offered them a hand and helped them up. Not one of them refused it. When they were all back on their feet, she led them through the corridor and towards the bridge.

Van Riet stepped up beside her as they walked. 'Anything you can tell us about this wreck then, Milton?'

'I don't know. What sort of thing do you want to know?'

'Anything that wouldn't have been in the report. For reference, that's basically everything beyond "Hi, we have something old that beeps".'

'I guess I could fill you in on a few things,' she said. 'But we don't really know much. It had a small crew, some sort of exterior projectors, managed to anger a whole lot of people back when it was walking about or however it moved. Lucille, that's our sort of engineer-cum-security person, she says they used sunbombs or something or it?'

'Nasty stuff.'

'That's what she says. You encountered anything like that before?'

Van Riet rubbed at his dark-ringed eyes. 'Nah. We don't tend to do salvage jobs too often, certainly not the big stuff. You know how it is, you get a call for the big jobs and they don't care who it is as long as they are the closest ship out there. Got to stake that claim, right?'

'I guess. This place is super interesting though.'

'How do you mean?'

Wendy slowed down. The hatch to the inner hull was nearby, but it was a little tricky to spot in the dim light. 'It's just so *alien*. We haven't even worked out what it was *for*.'

'You've had a look around then?'

'A little. We were hoping to get it working, thought that might bump up the price a little.'

'It probably would have, to be fair.'

'Yeah. All we managed to do was kick up a massive storm.'

Van Riet's head lolled to one side. 'This thing caused the storm?'

'Sorry, I'm probably saying more than I should!'

'You're right, I didn't mean to push.'

'The captain can probably fill you in better than I can anyway,' she said as her fingers found the hatch. She pulled. 'I'm just –'

She stopped.

On the far side of the room, slumped against the wall, his eyes glassy and lifeless, lay the captain. A pair of bloody bullet wounds in his chest, a third between the eyes.

'Jesus,' one of the men said behind her, she wasn't sure which.

'I don't... What...' Wendy said as she made her way over to the captain, words failing her.

It felt like she had walked into some cosmic joke. This wasn't just unthinkable, it was impossible. Somehow, there was a prank here she wasn't seeing. Surely this couldn't be real?

A thought drummed on the periphery. What was it saying? She couldn't make it out at first. *Wouldn't* make it out. One horrible realisation at a time, please.

What of the others?

'*Jesus*' said the man again. That was van Riet. Probably.

Thorsten was hanging dead in his harness, she already knew. She would have to look to confirm it, but that was a formality. This didn't have the air of a tragic encounter narrowly escaped, this had the atmosphere of a moment of soul-crushing misery. She was going to look up, right into the dead face of her friend. That was going to happen. She *knew* this.

And she did it anyway.

She had thought it would make her scream, or cry. Break down in some way, that was the natural response, wasn't it? That thudding, heavy, emptiness wasn't right. Watching Thorsten swing there, his dead eyes rolled up inside his head, everything else faded away.

There was something pushing through on the edge of her hearing though. Something very insistent. An argument? Who would be arguing? Why?

'– less brutal than this. Getting attached, were we?' van Riet was saying. He sounded more disappointed than angry.

'Come on,' said the other. 'We know the likelihood of me ever getting activated was minimal. That was the whole point. I did my duty.'

'Barely.'

'I did my duty.'

Wendy looked up. The world slammed back in living colour.

Lucille. Van Riet was talking to Lucille. She was still alive.

'I'm not arguing that. I'm just saying that it doesn't look altogether professional.'

'Who cares? No-one's going to see it.'

'That's as maybe, but –'

Lucille locked eyes with Wendy and shoved van Riet aside, stopping him mid-sentence. 'I'm sorry, Wendy.'

Her mouth was dry. 'This was you?'

'Yes.'

'I don't understand.'

There was a click. Van Riet had pulled a gun from somewhere in the folds of his clothing. 'Fortunately, you don't need to. Sorry, kid.'

'Wait!' Lucille said. 'She *is* just a kid. We could at least give her the decency of understanding why this is happening. Right?'

Van Riet's head snapped back towards Lucille, though the gun stayed trained. 'What's the point?'

'The point is that we're not barbarians.'

'Sorry. We don't have the time to waste,' and he steadied his aim.

Not that there was anything to aim at.

Wendy hadn't even thought about it. It was simple, you don't stay still when someone is pointing a gun at you, that was basic common sense. The second his gaze had wavered from her, she was moving, a single sudden burst of energy to take her out of harm's way. And there was only one place she could go.

With a leap, she launched herself forwards and down, into the shaft that led deeper into the vessel, grabbing the line as she fell. She heard van Riet swearing behind her as she fell, Lucille trying to calm him, until she let herself grab the line and slow her decent. It was all over so quickly, yet still she had fallen what seemed to be several levels, and damn near taken the skin off her hands with friction burns.

A face and a gun appeared over the parapet above, aiming down at her. Wendy kicked her legs and swung the rope, using her momentum to slip out of sight and into a dark corridor. With any luck it would be too dark for them to have been able to tell exact which floor she had entered, give her a head start.

'Go after her then,' van Riet said, his voice echoing down the shaft. 'This is your mess to clean up. We've got work to do.'

Lucille was angry, but the rope was already swinging as, Wendy assumed, the other woman lowered herself onto it. 'I know what has to happen, Casper. Don't talk to me like a child.'

'I don't mean to. Just... It has to be you. You need to remind yourself why we do this.'

'I know.'

If Lucille was coming after her, Wendy needed to move. Where she could go, she wasn't sure, but deeper into the darkness couldn't hurt. She snapped a small glow stick and did her best to slip out of sight before Lucille could spot the light.

More than anything else, she wanted to dwell on what she'd just seen. The urge to mourn was overwhelming, and the fact that she had to run for her life first made her taste bile. Not only had Lucille deprived her of her friends – her *family* – but they weren't even cold and she was depriving Wendy of a chance to properly mourn them. That this somehow trumped the fact Lucille was going to kill her as well seemed petty if it was given any thought, but that pettiness was keeping the panic at bay.

Get angry, get away. Get scared, get dead.

That was it, that was the right way to deal. Focus on pithy little sentences, structure the terror, don't think about how someone she had worked with for ages, a friend, just butchered everyone she knew. Don't think about how the buyers were somehow in on it.

Don't let the word *conspiracy* creep into your thoughts.

She didn't run now, she walked. Whatever deck she was on, it was as empty as the others, and her footsteps carried. Lucille's did too, though the echo was too strong to use them as a way of gauging how close the woman was. Stood to reason that the same would be true of Wendy's footsteps too, but she didn't want to test it. Instead she skulked, moving as fast as she dared while keeping sound to a minimum. It wasn't very fast.

It didn't take her long to hit a dead end. The corridor opened up into another one, lined with doors and name plaques. The names of the crew. She was walking in Lucille's footsteps.

On closer inspection, all the doors had been forced, slid back into place afterwards to look sealed. Not one of them would make for a stable hiding place, but perhaps a believable one? The wrenched open the first door and slipped inside, closing it behind her. Then she put an ear to the door and waited.

The distant footsteps faded. She had time to breathe.

Her legs went limp and she pressed her whole face against the chilled metal of the door. At this rate the sound of her heart thundering through her body would give her away, resonate through the door like some great speaker, but she needed the rest. With the immediate danger avoided for at least a couple of minutes, she was already crying.

She rolled over, placing her back to the door and sitting down. Something in one of her pockets clanked against the floor harder than she had expected, and she fished it out. Thorsten's tablet. She still had it.

It dutifully woke itself up in her hands, the white light of the screen dwarfing that of the glow stick. It had remembered the schematics she had been studying, the code she had been sifting through, and her solution to the storm engine conundrum was still loaded into the memory. As was her instant message log with Thorsten as they had puzzled it out together.

With a gesture, the messages were gone. That was a trap she didn't need to get caught in, hopeless nostalgia and denial. She needed to look forward, and that meant she needed to play to her strengths. Wendy couldn't fight her way out, nor sneak. What she was good at was machines, so that would be her salvation. She needed the schematics, and no distractions.

With a grunt, she got up. Her legs resisted, but they'd had their protests now. She needed to work, and for that she needed a network connection. The room needed checking.

It was quite a Spartan room, all things considered, but then most of the belongings had tumbled into one corner as a result of the crash. The bed, set into the wall, had managed to stay still, as had the small end-table that was bolted to it. Everything else had tumbled away from where it had been, serving as a ramp of debris.

If there was a network access point, it was hidden under all that debris, and Wendy didn't want to go searching. The noise, for one, would be hard to hide. But there was the window next to the bed, undoubtedly artificial and electronic. If she could reach that, maybe she could jury-rig some sort of connection. It wouldn't give her access to the main systems, but the base code would be sufficient.

The debris made it easy to reach the bed, and from there it was just a small feat of gymnastics to perch onto the end table and reach the window. The hardest part of the whole ordeal was getting the tablet to interface with the display, but that mostly meant exposing a few wires and fiddling with the cable. At the end of it all, Wendy knew, electronics all want to talk to each other. They're more sociable than humans.

Eventually the schematic started to light up on the screen, indicating it had changed from a cached version to a live update of the power flow once again. The arteries of the machine, laid bare. With a bit of time, she could work out exactly what they were doing.

They were stealing the machine, of course. She hardly needed to be a genius to work that out. Stealing the entire machine and wiping out any witnesses. Your classic pirate behaviour. But knowing *how* they were going to steal it could let her extrapolate the best way to escape. Maybe. It didn't deal with the Lucille problem, but nothing was going to sort that out right now.

Already there was a surge of power heading to the core systems, van Riet had wasted no time. They couldn't get the thing out under its own power, not without properly repairing the ambulation matrix, but access to the diagnostic systems could help speed that up exponentially. It's what she would have done, if not for the storm engine.

So now she had to decide if it was worth trying to stop

them. It was a quick decision: it absolutely was not, at all, worth it. But she was going to try anyway.

Best way to do that? She had to get to engineering again.

She climbed down from her perch and pressed her ear to the door once more. The footsteps were back, but muted and quiet. Lucille couldn't be nearby, more likely a deck above or below Wendy's current location. If she was very careful, Wendy might just be able to slip around behind her and make for engineering.

Jesus, what was she doing? Getting herself killed, that was what. But hey, there were only so many rooms to hide in. She'd get caught eventually, might as well try something stupid and brash.

Those would be some embarrassing last words. Good thing no-one was left to report them.

TWELVE

Rostrum's fingers slackened as soon as he pulled the trigger, but he caught himself before he dropped the gun. As soon as he fired, he was convinced he had made the wrong decision. By the time she hit the floor, he was on the border of sheer panic. They'd lynch him for this, he'd overreacted.

Then she rolled over. She was alive!

He hadn't really aimed when he had shot her, just snap-fired into her back to stop her, and it seemed the bullet had struck her in the shoulder. Painful, but survivable. For them both.

The group had stopped while they drank in the scene. There was no shortage of anger and confusion, but it had stunned them for the moment. They weren't quite sure how to take what he had done, but it wouldn't take them long to decide. If he had killed her outright, that would have been a different matter, but he'd just hurt her. He could still pull this back.

He loaded another round into the gun. How many more was he carrying? Best not to check right now. 'I'm sorry, but you can't endanger –'

The weather cut him off, saying more than he ever could.

Powerful blows started to rock the city from side to

side, throwing everyone off their feet and into the walls. The crowd rolled over itself like a wave of flesh, screams of fear and pain almost drowning out the sounds of the storm battering fatigued metal. Rostrum managed to avoid getting caught in the crowd, but that meant he had no buffer to cushion his blows, and it didn't take long at all for him to get thrown into a stanchion by the impacts.

He lost the grip on his zip-gun and it vanished into the distance somewhere, obscured by the stars flashing before his eyes. Another impact threw him up into the ceiling, then down hard, then up again despite his desperate hands grasping for something, anything to hold him steady.

Then the first wall gave way, taking half the room with it.

And most of the crowd.

The wind roared in to replace them, driving the remaining people back into the far wall, Rostrum included. It got into his eyes, made them sting, and pushed the flesh on his face hard against his skull. This was a flaying wind, he had to get away from it.

Slowly, he dragged himself along the wall. Supports, stanchions, anything he could wrap his fingers around served to pull him along, and when he reached the crowd he began to use them too. Their faces said they were screaming, but he couldn't hear them over the squall. As he climbed over them, in turn, he did his best to signal for them to follow him, like some great conga line. Most were compliant. Those that weren't, he didn't have time to argue with. It was a harsh calculation, but time spent convincing them was time taken away from the others ahead.

After a great deal of effort, a snaking mass of civilians trailing behind him, Rostrum made it to the far side of the room, to a door as yet unclaimed by the weather. Getting himself and his followers through wasn't easy, but as more and more people joined him on solid footing it became easier. When the last one touched down, Rostrum slammed his palm down on a button on the top corner of the frame, sealing the door and blocking out the wind.

Through the small window, Rostrum stared into the wreckage of the room. That was fast. Too fast. Now all he could see was the twisting black and grey anger of nature, the flickers of lightning. It made him feel a little guilty how aptly nature had made his point for him, all things considered, but looking at the survivors he knew that they understood him now.

The woman he had shot was not amongst them. Nor was her son.

Everyone, himself included, took a moment to catch their breath. It let Rostrum count the survivors. Fifteen, from a mob that had numbered at least a hundred.

'We need to keep going,' he said. 'This entire deck is structurally compromised now, we need to get deeper into the city, put more metal between us and the storm.'

'But, the others...' said someone. He had glasses, that's all Rostrum allowed himself to see. 'We can't just –'

A woman shoved him. 'They're dead. Jesus, how could we think –'

Rostrum interrupted. 'It's only a matter of time before the storm carves through this room too. If we're quick, we can put a few more inches of metal between us and the outside, maybe even make it to the core.'

Again the city shook from a number of impacts. It was getting hard to maintain a straight, authoritative face.

'Will this buffeting calm down the deeper in we go?' Glasses asked.

'Yes,' Rostrum lied, dabbing at a fresh wound on his head. Where had that come from? 'The core rooms have impact dampeners that should absorb a fair deal of the kinetic energy.'

Yet another jolt. Glasses nodded his head vigorously. 'Let's go then, can't be worse than here.'

There was a murmur of agreement from the others, and Rostrum awkwardly stepped to the front of the group, using the walls for support against the buffeting. They'd need to move fast and efficiently – no telling how much of their route could disintegrate if they delayed – and avoid the elevators. That meant using service crawl spaces to get to higher decks, which meant retracing his steps.

Easy.

They picked up a few more people on the way, stragglers and injured dug out from underneath the wrecks of the Green Goddesses or collapsed rooms. More than a few dead, too, but Rostrum did his best to ignore them. No time to care about them. Focus.

The climb was the hardest part. The conduits were small by design, heavily cramped even when the city wasn't being bombarded flat by a deathly storm. Constricted by the strain the entire city was under, it was hard going. There were more losses, crushed to death by the city itself, but Rostrum tried to ignore them.

By the time they exited the conduits, all the worse for wear, he had been ignoring them with every ounce of his being. It wasn't making him feel any better.

The core was, despite his conversation with Moses, heaving with people, and it only got worse as he and his group joined the fray. The very centre of the city was mostly devoted to the various systems that kept the city moving, which meant that it wasn't designed for comfort. With all the buffeting launching people around, he could already spot the same tensions forming that had been at the front of his little crowd.

This room in particular was full of rods and pistons that, Rostrum assumed, would have been moving had the city not been crippled. People were using each stationary piston as a sort of nexus, clustering around them in their droves. There was little space between these islands, but enough for people to shove their way through.

A pair of bedraggled security men, barely holding themselves together, came and separated him from his pack. He didn't fight them as they shoved him face first through the writhing mass of terrified people, into a small oasis on the far side. Moses was waiting for him, his eyes red and wide, his back to the largest piston, rising up into a chasm in the ceiling.

'I tried, Rostrum. I honestly tried,' he said. 'But if they stay out there they'll die, I couldn't do that to them.'

'In all likelihood, they'll die in here,' Rostrum said. Then he caught Moses' face. 'But they do stand a better chance in here, and I was stupid to think we had enough pull to stop this. I shouldn't have put that burden on you.'

'What do we do?'

The rocking slackened for a moment, then returned with vengeance. People screamed, pushed and shoved, then returned to their standard level of terror.

'What can we do but wait? Where's the rest of the council?'

'At a guess? Somewhere out there, hugging their families.'

Somewhere above them, an enormous crash indicated that another deck was gone. Debris began to clatter down the shaft behind Moses, and Rostrum took him by the arm to move him a little further away.

'Best estimates, what did the computer say?'

'Huh?'

Rostrum shook him. 'Focus. We're the government, we're supposed to have a handle on this. If we roll double sixes and everything turns out as best as we could hope, how much damage are we looking at?'

Moses blinked and rubbed at his eyes for a moment. 'Catastrophic levels of destruction were present in basically every simulation we had time to run. But... Right, best case scenario was that the storm didn't quite engulf us, that it just slams us from one side as it passes by.'

'And?'

'The Strider is done for, but maybe sixty percent of the people survive.'

'Sixty?'

'That was assuming we were able to control the influx of people into the core. In the sims where we ended up overcrowded like this –'

'I don't need that data. Okay, we need to give these people something to do, right? Keep them busy. Distract them.'

'Are you really sure that's wise?' Moses said. 'There's not even anything *to* do at this point.'

Rostrums nails were biting into his palms. His fists had been balls for what felt like hours now, and he hadn't even noticed really. The dull ache of seizing joints had taken a back seat, as everything was doing. But now his rising blood pressure had reminded him, and staring into the fear in Moses' face was making him realise something.

'*I* need to do something, Moses,' he said. 'I've already seen more people die than I had ever wanted to.'

'You and me both, Rostrum. But I don't think we've seen the last of death today.'

Another hull breach somewhere, closer this time. Not close enough to be a problem for them, but judging by the way it rippled through the crowd it had been close enough for it to be witnessed by the giant snake of refugees.

This, at least, was something Rostrum was becoming accustomed to. He had the measure of the storm now. A few sharp and terrible strikes, then a lull for a minute or so. If he held his breath during the strikes, he could hyperventilate in the breaks. It was probably that others had noticed this loose pattern too.

The lull happened, and he started to breathe again. Then another unexpected jolt caught him, making him choke and splutter. Then another. And another. Getting closer and closer.

'My god,' Moses said, prying himself away from Rostrum and pulling a small terminal out from underneath a railing by the piston. 'It pierced the fuel stores.'

Rostrum coughed air back into his lungs. 'But that's impossible.'

'I know, it should be,' Moses said. 'In even the worst simulations this was an unlikely event. It's set off a chain reaction!'

'To where?'

Moses' fingers raced over the screen, tracing fuel lines and error messages across the various readouts. 'The only place the fuel goes. To the engine. But there are safety interlocks, that'll stop it.'

'Judging from the sound –'

The explosion roared into the room like something from old time mythology. Some monstrous and evil creature of living flame, spreading its wings in spite, before swooping down over the gathered masses. It exploded up and out of the floor, using the channels for each of the pistons as its vector, coalescing above them all before the burning fuel began to rain down on them.

Rostrum and Moses couldn't react, no-one could. It was a terminal panic, all muscle memory and instinct, anything that made a person more than an animal was in hiding. No-one wanted to be behind their own eyes now, at what was certainly the moment of their deaths. Their minds retreated, behind barred gates, and waited out the inevitable.

Some, like Rostrum, looked back, they watched the chaos from afar. And, to a man, they all had the same thought at that very moment.

Not like this.

Rostrum caught the smell of burned flesh almost instantly. He'd never had cause to work with the fuel that kept the Strider running. The secondary systems didn't use it – they had their own, cleaner power sources – but getting a city to walk required monumental amounts of power, and a volatile source of it.

The closest he had ever seen to this were the injuries on the galleon crews he would send out to mine the stuff. Mishandle just a little and you'd suffer. Rostrum had made it a part of his routine to watch these galleons return. It was important he see the sacrifices that kept the city running.

And that meant that now, as it rained from the ceiling, that he knew precisely what fresh hell was destined for everyone in that room.

The scream he let out as the drops hit his skin was lost in all the others.

He never expected to wake up, let alone wake up screaming.

His skin felt tight, and moving gave him the distinct impression that it would crack like old leather. His eyes were blurry, and his breathing was shallow and raspy. The fuel must have hit his face, and it was likely he inhaled some.

As he tried to move, he realised that he was buried under layers of people, enough that he could barely move at all. Clawing his way out was possible, but it would certainly split his skin. Knowing this, he did it anyway, pulling himself free and lying breathless atop the mound.

The buffeting had stopped. How long had he been out? Long enough for the storm to end? Good lord, had he *survived?*

He stretched and rolled over, screaming as more of his flesh split. The entire core was a charnel house now, he saw. The top layer of corpses was little more than pitted and bleached bones, and those underneath were blacked beyond recognition. Perhaps there were other survivors buried deep beneath, as he had been, but they gave no sign of themselves.

With great care, he began to drag himself over the bones. He wasn't really sure where he was going, but he didn't want to stay there, that was for sure. Perhaps if he could get confirmation that the storm had passed he would feel better. Maybe he would find some other survivors – surely not everyone was caught in the explosion.

The dead functioned as a path for him, leading him to one of the core's many exits, and out into what remained of the city proper. The detailed the path of the explosion, with it being decidedly noticeable where the massacre changed from a rain of death to a blast. He preferred those that died from the explosion, it pushed their corpses away from the floor and let him crawl over cool steel instead of warm calcium.

There wasn't far he could crawl. He got his confirmation very quickly – the storm had passed and it had taken a great swathe of the Strider with it. Perhaps it was the first explosion that did it, or the wind, but one side of the city was just gone. He could lie on what remained of the floor and stare out into the mocking blue sky.

Where had this fallen in the simulation hierarchy? Certainly not double sixes, that was damned sure. If there were any other survivors – and he *had* to believe there were – then it would be far short of sixty percent. Snake eyes, almost certainly.

But then, what did he know? A visual inspection told him that half of the city was essentially vaporised, but he was lying on the floor with scorched eyes, trying to make a judgement on a city that could probably be seen from space. Just because what he could see said it was total destruction didn't mean that it was. The city was huge, full of places for people to hide, and the fact that he wasn't lying in snow told him that at least some of these had weathered the storm as well as he had.

He let his face fall to the floor, letting the cold sink into his forehead before rolling down onto his cheeks, each in turn. There was no rush to find out.

His ears were still ringing. He hadn't even noticed. But now the quiet was playing tricks on him, whipping up hallucinations of footsteps echoing through the floor, or voices down distant corridors. Or perhaps they weren't hallucinations, maybe they were real, it didn't matter. After the incessant clattering of the storm, he wasn't ready to let that go yet. Fake sounds or no, they were more welcome than the silence that was waiting for him once his eardrums settled.

Because that silence meant something.

It was time to see if he could stand. Couldn't lie around all day, there was work to be done. Possibly. He didn't want to survive being burned alive only to freeze to death after the fact, or get sepsis in his newly opened rends. The cold was nice after all the heat, but not nice enough to die for.

His legs, it turned out, had barely been burnt at all. A few drops had cut through his trousers, singed his thighs a little, but nothing worth complaining about when compared to the rest of him. Getting upright was manageable, but it took some practice to stay that way. Again, he was going to need to use the wall to keep himself moving.

Rostrum didn't think about where he was going, he just let his legs and the wall guide him. He didn't think about how few bodies he saw as he walked, how he made it to the cockpit elevator so easily, how it still worked. None of that registered. And when the elevator opened at the top, and he stepped out the rapturous applause of the survivors, all of them thankful for what he did to get them through the storm, he continued not to think about it.

Moses stepped forward, hand outstretched. 'By god, Rostrum, you actually did it! You saved us!'

And without thinking, Rostrum shook the man's hand. All animosity was gone, reforged through adversity into something akin to friendship, but stronger. Fire had tempered their metal.

Fire.

There had been fire. He'd been scorched, but his arms were clean and fresh now. He started thinking, and the delusion melted away.

He saw now that he had barely moved, that he was still in that same corridor that looked out over the horizon. There were the corpses, there were death, there was the pain.

More fantasies assailed him as he walked, and he took solace in them for a time. They dulled the pain – both in his heart and from the burns – for a time, and kept him moving. By the time he *did* reach the cockpit elevator, he'd experienced enough hallucinations that he was barely feeling the pain any more. Something had popped behind his eyes and the real world, his body included, was at a distance. Everything was permanently dulled.

There was a pair of dead Green Goddesses at the foot of the elevator, guards most likely. He could see now how they had punched through the door as they had come for him. The upper door had been reinforced, but this one they had simply shredded like paper. They had done the same to the car, ripping through its roof with an apparently bestial fury. It would be quite a climb.

Again, the hallucinations helped. Just reaching the emergency ladder split more skin, but without the pain he could keep going. Once he hauled himself up to the ladder, it was easy going from there. Slow, but easy. He could accrue more and more debt as he climbed, shoving out that pain until he was in a position where it was safe to deal with, and he knew it.

When he finally heaved himself out of the shaft and into the cockpit, over metal bodies and the shattered remains of *this* door, that debt caught up with him. He curled into a ball and cried until the supernova of agony died down. Then he continued, crawling again, to his chair.

'I knew you'd come here eventually, provided you survived,' someone said.

Another hallucination. Rostrum ignored him and kept crawling. His fingers were all but carving their way into the deck with each movement.

'I wanted to look you in the eye once all this way over,' the hallucination said. 'I owed you that much.'

Rostrum reached the back of his chair and wrapped his arm around the base, aiming to drag himself to the front. His fingers closed around fabric, leather, not the polished metal he had expected. Pulling himself around anyway, he got his first look at the hallucination.

He didn't recognise him. The hallucination was dark, tired, with one eye full of blood and the other cold and grey. His hair was long but matted with blood, making it look like dreadlocks, and it meshed with his overly long – though well maintained – facial hair. Whoever he was, he was slumped in Rostrum's chair, and looked like he was in no fit state to go anywhere else.

But, most importantly, he wasn't real.

Slowly, Rostrum clawed his way up the hallucination's legs, up his chest, until he was eye-to-eye with him. 'You're in my chair.'

'I know,' the hallucination said. His grey eye had a split in the iris, but he seemed to be able to see just fine. 'One thing is universal, the injured will always just want to go home. I figured this would count.'

'Move.'

He laughed. It had the same raspy quality to it as Rostrum's breathing. 'I can't. And you're in such a state I'm surprised that you can. You look terrible.'

'I am terrible. Get out of my seat.'

'I'm disappointed you haven't asked who I am.'

'Why would I?' Rostrum said. 'You're not real. Piss off.'

The hallucination lashed out, striking Rostrum across the face and sending him sprawling. 'Not real? How was that for real? I'm trying to be respectful here, you dick. The least you can do is return the favour.'

Rostrum lay on his back and waited for his head to stop spinning. The hallucination hadn't even hit him very hard, but in his current state that didn't matter. He clawed his way back to eye level with the man just the same, though it took even longer this time. 'You're not real.'

The hallucination placed his forehead against Rostrum's. 'I am. I'm the one who did this. Please accept that.'

Not an hallucination then. Rostrum had pictured the

saboteur a hundred times in his head as he had worked to deal with the problems the man had caused, but he'd never pictured him quite like this. There was nothing outlandish or strange about his appearance, it just wasn't one Rostrum had considered, and that was how hallucinations worked, wasn't it? They drew from your imagination, your subconscious, gave things a believable form. He couldn't help but believe that if he *had* hallucinated the saboteur that he would not look like this.

'You're the saboteur?'

'Yes. Sorry about that, but I was hired to do a job.'

'Doesn't look like you've come out of it well.'

The man winced. 'As well as could be expected. I had a long time to study the schematics of the Strider, found as safe a place as I could. Still bloody hurt.'

'Shame it didn't kill you, you murdering shit.'

'If it helps, not everyone died. You little screen here, when it's working, has picked up sporadic movement across various decks.'

'Let me see.'

'Of course.'

The man twisted the screen around to face Rostrum. It was cracked, a big part of it obscured by the growing stain of a damaged LCD, but he could see that the saboteur wasn't lying. It wasn't much, but it was something.

'I should still kill you.'

'And I probably couldn't stop you if you tried, but you've got bigger problems. Look.'

He swivelled the screen back towards him, and Rostrum noticed how much he was favouring his left arm. The man barely moved it, holding it tight against his chest. There was every chance Rostrum could overpower him if he wanted, even in his current state, beat him to death out of sheer survivor's rage. It wouldn't bring back the dead, but he might enjoy it.

The saboteur tapped at the screen a couple of times and turned it back to Rostrum. Now it was showing the communication network, and the various errors indicating that there was no connection.

'See? This is a problem.'

Rostrum squinted. His vision was still blurry. 'It's not as if you could have expected the network interface to survive the storm.'

'That's the thing, I knew it wouldn't. My employer furnished me with a portable connection for just such an eventuality. It's not working.'

'And?'

'And it should be. It *is*, in point of fact. They're just ignoring me.'

Rostrum slouched in closer. 'I don't care. I'm going to try and kill you now.'

'Wait wait wait! Just wait! If they're ignoring me, then that means they've hung me out to try, which means that they are up to something.'

'What?'

'It means this isn't over!'

Rostrum pulled himself up to his full height. It was agony, but it was important. 'Tell me everything. It might just save your life.'

The man took a breath and stood up, again face to face with Rostrum. He looked a bit steadier on his feet than Rostrum, but only barely so. Using his good hand, he peeled some blood-matted hair off his face.

'First things first. I'm Vandal Morley, and I work for the Crawler.'

THIRTEEN

Van Riet had got the intercoms working. The incessant stream of bilge being spouted by that man had Wendy debating the merits of abandoning her current task and pouring her entire will into finding a way to shunt the entire power system through his god damned microphone.

Things were not going well.

Her plan, such as it was, hinged on kicking all manner of shit out of the important bits of the vessel as a distraction, giving her room to move. But that plan was useless if she couldn't reach the damned engineering section.

She knew where she was going, but somehow Lucille had gotten there ahead of her and was busy fiddling with bits of engine instead of, as expected, trying to hunt her down and kill her. It was rude and, quite frankly, incredibly unfair. Lucille had always been the engineer in name only, and had never shown any true aptitude while Wendy had been working with her. Now, after revealing that her true aptitude was in murdering everyone she held dear, she dared to put that to one side to get all up in Wendy's business?

Just *stop it*.

Wendy had taken up refuge just outside the engineering room, but had a pretty decent view inside, and had been watching Lucille work for fifteen minutes now. She hadn't been entirely sure what the other woman had been up to at first, but after van Riet got the intercoms working again she had had more information than she had wanted.

'Casper, you're getting on my nerves,' she heard Lucille say. 'Wendy isn't going to be a problem. I'll smoke her out when I need to, and you're not helping.'

'I'm just informing her that it is in her best interests to stop hiding,' he said.

'Informing her *very loudly and continuously*. There are intercoms in every room of this thing, you've seen the charts. It's *echoing*. A lot. It's distracting.'

'You should be dealing with the final witness.'

'Do you want to come down here and go rooting around inside ancient machinery, Casper? Want to send Renier or the other one –'

'Ivan.'

'– *Ivan* down here to do it instead? Are they trained.'

'You know they're not.'

She kicked something, hard, inside the panel she was working on. 'So just let me do my job. I'll do my other job later.'

'I'm just not comfortable having a potential problem running around in the dark bits of this place while we're working on something so delicate.'

'She's not a problem,' Lucille said. 'Wendy is a damn good mechanic, but she doesn't understand these systems. Not really. She could be a hindrance, but not a true problem. And if we want to stick to the timetable –'

'Let me worry about that,' van Riet interrupted. 'And check what you're saying. If you want to speak freely, eliminate the witness first.'

'I work better in silence anyway.'

Wendy shifted in the darkness. She was sticking steadfast to her doctrine of petty irritations trumping actual, real issues, and being labelled as just a *hindrance* had just shoved its way to the front. Not enough to actually *do* something about it, but then that was the point of the doctrine.

The plan was still to escape, just as it had always been. Hell, if she could just raise the authorities that would be enough. It was the getting rescued more than the escaping that she was actually after. Justice a somewhat close second.

'Right,' Lucille shouted into the intercom, simultaneously entwining her arms in one of the many hammocks that were strewn across the room. 'Try punching it now.'

'You sure? That was awfully quick,' van Riet said.

Lucille sighed. 'The damage was all superficial. Only reason this thing wasn't operational was because someone unplugged a few vital components. I know these systems, so plugging them back in properly was easy.'

'This won't set off the storm engine again? You're sure?'

'Not unless you want it to. I know what I'm doing.'

'Okay. Everyone brace yourselves. Even you, Milton. This is going to be bumpy.'

He didn't give her much time. Less than a second after he finished speaking, everything began to shake. From the engine room, a sound like a heavy stampede rang out, deafening her, and the thumping of the mechanical parts served to increase the vibrations.

Surely, the vessel was going to shake itself apart at this rate. Wendy could hear the cracks forming in the hull from here, could sense how the rivets were going to give way. Even with the first massive lurch, she was expecting everything to end poorly.

Then, as suddenly as it began, the shaking lessened, and she felt the vessel move. It was a slow and ponderous ascent, but that did little to reduce the effect of shifting the entire thing upright again. Wendy watched debris she hadn't even seen start to tumble its way back down the corridor, and it was likely she would have joined the shower if not for her hiding place.

Lucille was swearing from the next room, and her outbursts were increasing in volume and severity as the craft kept shifting its incline. There was a lot of clattering going on, enough to be heard over the tremendous thump of the machinery, which Wendy ascribed to so many tools and spare parts being shaken free after however long. By the time it was all said and done, she would have been surprised if Lucille had avoided a concussion.

The machinery ground down to a pleasant rumble, letting Wendy hear again. She was on her back now, the craft had shifted so much, but it had at least been gradual enough that she hadn't hurt herself. But everything was weird now, she was all turned around. Her entire internal map was forfeit.

'For the first time in centuries, this vessel stands upright,' van Riet said over the intercom again. 'If only it were under better circumstances.'

'Christ,' she heard Lucille say back. 'Have you seen the name of this thing?'

'No. The records only had the reg number, and I can't find the dedication plaque up here.'

'That's because the plaque nearly smacked me in the face just now. It's called The Squib.'

'Seriously? Who named these things?'

Lucille sighed. 'Idiots, I think. I don't particularly care, I just wanted you to stop calling it *the vessel* or something equally grandiose.'

'You're very critical.'

'I just had to kill all my friends. It's cast a bit of a cloud over things, if I'm honest.'

'Not *all* your friends.'

'Right. Yes. Now that we're online, I'll get back to it.'

That was Wendy's cue. She uncoupled herself from the support – difficult, considering how tightly her hands had decided to grip it – and crept down the hall. The lights were working now, more or less, but this only made the newly upright corridors look even more out of place and confusing. That she made her way back to the central column at all felt like an achievement.

The cat-thing was there, resting at the bottom of the shaft in a pile of loose debris. Although it wasn't a shaft any more, it was yet another corridor, the lines they had used to descend it lying limp on the ground. The cat-thing looked at her and then padded off.

Lingering wouldn't be wise – it had been fine when this was a near vertical drop, but now it was just a short stroll to the control centre – but this was her keystone. She could probably find her bearings here, get another way out. The Squib wasn't moving just yet, she had time.

Not much though. Footsteps from somewhere behind her, Lucille's no doubt.

She followed the hallway out and away from the control centre. It had seemed like fathoms when it was a pitch black shaft, but it was only a few steps in the light. It hit a dead end at the inner hull, which is what she had expected. The control room couldn't be the only place with maintenance access to the outer hull.

It wasn't.

She was through the concealed door quickly, and from there it was just a hop, skip and a jump to freedom, provided she could find the breach she had used to enter. Or the one that had killed the Squib in the first place.

That one was easier to find. The wind practically whistled through it, glib and happy, meaning all Wendy had to do was follow it back to the source. If she had explored the inner hull a little more, she would have stumbled right on it.

The breach was huge. It got smaller with each layer it breached though, as it lost speed. Stood to reason, considering how sunbombs were purported to work – wouldn't want it passing all the way through. Still, the initial hole was big enough to peer out of, so Wendy hoisted herself up a little and poked her head out.

She was higher than she expected. From her position, she could see that the Squib was held up by at least two chunky metal legs, with enough points of articulation to make them very versatile. They seemed to connect to the main body somewhere underneath her current position, though the shape of the body meant she couldn't see where. Low enough that it had been buried in the ice, that was certain – some of it still clung to the legs.

Too high to jump though, that was a problem. Maybe if she went back, took one of the lines or ripped enough wires from the wall. Perhaps she could fashion a grappling hook and work her way over to a leg. They were rugged enough that she wouldn't be short of hand holds.

So near and yet so far.

She pulled her head back in time to catch the air shimmer ten feet in front of her. It took her a moment to remember the thing had been lined with emitters – the internals of the thing had been way more interesting – but it was cool to get a better look at them nonetheless. Seeing the Squib from a weird angle before meant she hadn't really *seen* it.

What she had seen of the emitters had been indecipherable nonsense. Too many had been broken to form a coherent picture, but that was on the other side. These ones were skittish, but nearly legible. Trying to read it in reverse was the trickiest part – though having it flicker on and off was a chore too – but she couldn't help herself.

'It says *Just For The Taste of It*, if you're wondering.'

Wendy span around, right into the barrel of a pistol. She hadn't even heard Lucille approach. Damn it!

'How do you know?'

Lucille's eyes were empty on the far side of the weapon. 'I can read Old-World. It's part of the training.'

'I thought it was just backwards.'

'It's that too.'

Despite her words, Wendy had expected to see satisfaction in Lucille's eyes. Someone that could so readily execute her entire crew one after the other had no business looking so sad now. Yes, the eyes were empty, but there was a different between them being empty out of a lack of heart or a desire to hide. Lucille's were by far the latter.

Wendy checked again. Still too far to jump, but was it preferable to a bullet in the face? 'Would I get an answer if I asked why?'

'Probably not a satisfactory one. It's kind of a secret.'

'Oh my god, it *is* a conspiracy.'

'It's not a conspiracy,' Lucille said. The gun quivered a little in her grip, the skin on the back of her hand prickling against the cold. 'It's a calling, one I tried to avoid. That's why I went to work with Josh. I was trying to avoid having to do this, but it's happened now.'

'You're not making sense.'

'Doesn't matter.'

Wendy threw up her hands. 'Wait! You can't just shoot me.'

'I shot them.'

'But you didn't want to!'

The gun lowered a little. 'No, but it's for the greater good.'

Wendy pressed herself back against the breach. 'You keep saying things like that, but it sounds like bullshit to me. What greater good could there possibly be?'

'The one that stops all this happening again. To stop us repeating the mistakes that left us scavenging a frozen shithole.'

'What? No-one even knows what happened back then. You're just talking shit now.'

'We know.'

Wendy let that hang in the air for a moment. 'Excuse me?'

'We, the group I'm a part of, we know. We never forgot. But that knowledge comes with a responsibility, and protecting us from ourselves requires harsh choices. I have to keep this quiet. The survival of all of us is more important than the survival of one of us.'

Wendy wanted to say Lucille was on the verge of tears, but she wasn't. Resignation and regret were all over her face, but there was no conflict there. As much as she might have hated this, there was still nothing in her expression that said she ever doubted it was the right thing to do, which was more than a little disheartening.

Deep down, Wendy had always thought that if it came to it she might be able to talk Lucille out of this. Escape had always been the goal, but talking her down had been the contingency. But she had not seen the conviction in her eyes at the time.

Wendy sighed. 'There's no talking you out of this.'

'No. If news of this find were to get out... People can't be trusted.'

'But news has already gotten out,' she said. 'The captain contacted a city pilot, even had me talk to him. Or are you going to say that was your friends over there?'

'I try not to think about that.'

'Why?'

'Because I don't want to think about the lengths they went to to sterilise that call.'

Wendy crossed her arms and let her voice grow sour. 'Not a fan of the darker side of your little cult?'

'Why do you think I hid from them, Wendy? Of course I'm not a fan. It's a necessary evil, but I don't want to know the details.'

'Well tough, if I have to die here, for this shit conspiracy that I'm not even convinced is real, I *want* you to think about this,' Wendy said, stepping forward. 'You killed the captain, and Thorsten. Our *friends*, and apparently you're going to kill me, now. So you fucking better *think* about this. I want you to know, to the exact number, how many people have died because we found a worthless wreck in the ice. A wreck that isn't even a warship.'

'It's worse.'

'Worse than a warship? Shut up, you're just scraping the barrel for excuses now.'

Lucille's face was red now, her eyes shrunken to pinpricks in her head. 'It's information warfare.'

'Sure, with what sounds like a marketing slogan on the side? A weaponised billboard?'

Lucille went deadpan. 'Yes.'

'Wait,' Wendy said, stumbling over her words. 'What?'

'The Squib is a weaponised billboard. The old times were a lot weirder than you think.'

'How does that even work?'

'You don't need to know that,' Lucille said, and her eyes really were starting to water now. 'And I need to stop talking to you. You're making this too hard.'

'You could *not* shoot me,' Wendy said. 'That's easy.'

'Not as easy as you think,' Lucille said, bringing the gun back up. 'I'm sorry.'

There was a hiss as the intercom sprung to life again. It made both women jump. 'You found Milton yet?'

'I'm just doing it now, Casper,' Lucille snarled. 'Get off my back.'

'Abort, we need her,' van Riet said, audibly grinding his teeth in frustration. 'We can't move.'

'What do you mean we can't move?'

'Your little friend did something to the computers. Oh sure, we can stand the Squib upright again, but now it's asking for security codes that, apparently, I don't have.'

Lucille uncocked the gun. 'And you think she does?'

'I don't know,' van Riet said. 'But they aren't what they're supposed to be, so someone changed them. Bring her back here and we'll see.'

Lucille took a very deep breath and fought off a smile. She gave Wendy a very pointed look. 'I didn't think you'd know how to do that. I'm so glad you're a bloody genius.'

'So am I,' Wendy said, utterly bewildered.

It went without saying – or should have – that she had

no idea the thing even had security codes when it came to piloting it, let alone how to change them. Her entire time inside the code had been devoted to fiddling with whatever was keeping the storm engine running. This wasn't her.

That said, she wasn't about to correct them. Any extra minutes at this point were a gift, one she would happily accept. If she played it cool, dragged her feet, maybe she could stretch things out long enough to get herself another opening.

Ever the optimist, even with a gun in her face.

Lucille led her back to the control centre gently, not even at gunpoint. A short trip, in complete silence, wasn't unexpected but Wendy found it disconcerting all the same. She was an optimist, but keeping your back to someone with a gun, raised or not, was a hard thing to do even with this temporary truce.

Van Riet didn't look pleased to see her. His fake affability had slipped completely now, and his stony face regarded her intently as she was led into the room. His fingers were drumming against something on his belt – probably a weapon, seeing as he was a dick – but he never made a true move for it.

He turned suddenly and slammed his fist down on one of the terminals. 'Fix my ship.'

Wendy scoffed. 'So you can kill me? No thanks.'

'The only reason you're not currently dead is because you're useful. Think it through.'

The captain and Thor were still there. With the ship the right way up, neither man was where she had last seen them, but piled up in a corner along with the bleached bones of the original crew. There were blood trails showing how they had tumbled as the Squib rose to its feet.

She pointed to them. 'You've lost the high ground here.'

There was a click from behind her head. Lucille

readying her gun, most likely.

Van Riet, for his part, barely reacted at all. 'The moral high ground, perhaps. But this is bigger than that. Just fix what you broke and we can discuss clemency.'

'Fine,' she said. 'But it might take some work.'

'Figured as much.'

He beckoned her over and sat her down at one of the terminals. Judging from the blood spatter it was the one Thorsten had died in front of. It felt a bit disrespectful somehow to have not known that before, but seeing as her world had been quite literally turned upside down she didn't reproach herself.

Van Riet or one of his pals had clearly tried to break the system on their own. Evidently Lucille was the only one of them with any technical expertise at all, judging from how poor a job they had done of it. In fact, a cursory glance told her they had tripped yet more security measures and made the job even harder for themselves. That was good for her.

'Whatever you did to try and break the command codes has locked me out of the central data stores,' she said, masking the happiness in her voice. 'First I need to undo *your* attempted hack before I can undo my original one.'

'Get on with it then,' van Riet said. It was more patience than she had expected.

It was harder to do from this terminal than the tablet. The interface was similar, and an actual keyboard was a godsend, but Thorsten had *done things* to the damned machine. He'd moved things around, hidden things, no doubt to streamline the whole thing for his job earlier on, but it made it a pain to work from for anyone else. Everything that wasn't related to dismantling the storm engine's spider web of parasitical systems was locked away behind passwords. A way of avoiding distraction?

All well and good for him, but it made her current job a bit tricky. Now she had to hack some passwords so she had the mean to hack some more passwords to disable a thing stopping her from unhacking a password she had been assumed to have already hacked. She'd barely sat down and already her head was spinning.

Van Riet watched her work for a while before he grew bored. Eventually he wandered off across the room, getting into conversation with Lucille, Johansson and the other man, though she couldn't make out what they were saying. More orders most likely, judging from his gesticulations.

This was good, she worked better when someone wasn't hovering over her shoulder. The captain had understood that.

Johansson had van Riet's attention when she broke the first password. This was good, it meant he missed the influx of data stampeding across her screen, ending in a single text document splashing itself grandly across the whole display. She recognised the style as Thorsten's instantly. Only he would think to hide something and then practically have it launch streamers into the stratosphere when it was discovered.

Brat. As I write this, you're up on the surface, waiting for the buyers. I'm sure they're on the level, but I've got some concerns so I'm writing this to slip to you when no-one's looking. Easier to say things in text, right? Harder to eavesdrop.

Sure, unless you set it to full screen someone's terminal while they are hacking for their life, Thor.

I didn't like the transmission we received. It was an external signal, routed through the internal comms. Only way you can do that is if you knew the wreck and its capabilities ahead of time. It wasn't old. I can't confirm it, but I think the buyers sent it, which means that gobbledegook was intended for one of us.

Bit late to the party there, Thor.

I don't know who, but I know it wasn't either of us. You'd be a shit spy, far too mouthy. But I have a plan now, just in case. We're going to commandeer this wreck.

She smiled. Even beyond the grave, Thorsten had a way of cheering her up.

There's a lot of systems on this tub that I can't identify from the code alone, but I reckon at least one of them has to be some form of security system, right?

I would have done it already if I could, but I think your buddy Enzo pulled the command codes back when things went sour. You reckoned someone was trying to keep this thing offline back then? Without these codes the thing might as well be broken. You can't do shit.

Thing is, I don't think you can wipe them or even change them really. The values are hard-coded into the base code of every single system, subsystem and sub-subsystem. You'd have to go line by line.

But you can make a sort of boot disk, a key. Apparently. There's talk of it in the readme files in any case. That transfers command authority from a person to an object and, by extension, the person in possession of that object. Plug that bastard in, systems online.

I don't know if you'll read this. Hopefully I won't need to send it to you. Hopefully this is all an overreaction. But I didn't make it this long by being reckless. I've got at least one more sunset in me before I've earned that right, and I intend to see it.

If I have sent you this, don't react. I should have put that at the top really, I guess. Anyway, until I'm sure we should keep this between us, just in case. Keep an eye out for the key.

xx

She clicked the text away as soon as she finished reading it. Van Riet and company hadn't noticed her skimming it, and she didn't want them to. A bit of a coincidence that Thor was planning to do the same thing as the men who had him killed, but hardly unlikely. It was the only option available, really – a long shot, but controlling the security system might have helped him repel a force as small as this. At least this gave her a vector.

Everything came down to keys in the end. Passwords and codes were hard to read, sure, but you knew where they were all the time. So long as you knew where the thing that was demanding them was. Physical keys were a pain in the arse and could, in fact, be literally anywhere.

Frankly, it made her want to laugh in despair.

Find some digital keys, that could be anything, in a giant metal walking machine that you don't know or understand. Easy peasy.

Of course, if Thor was right, that meant that there was nothing she could do at this terminal. True, it had been a long shot before, but if the codes were no longer physically in the system then it was all but impossible. Reprogramming the entire thing by hand was a task that would, in all likelihood, take a billion years.

Van Riet was watching her now. It had been too long since she had typed anything. She started hammering keys erratically, pretending to type. He frowned at her from a moment and then looked away. Everything was about buying time.

She put aside her job for a moment and delved deep into the readme files. This was a different skill to poring over technical schematics and documentation, and considerably less fun, but she found what she needed without incident. It confirmed her assumptions.

Thorsten hadn't said directly in his note that only the commanding officer could facilitate the creation of a boot disk, but it had made sense. Now she knew it for sure. Had that been Enzo? They'd certainly sounded in charge in the logs she had read. Did that narrow things down maybe?

Not really. But then, by all accounts it had been a small crew anyway, and people tend to hide things in places where they can watch them. The cabins?

She cleared her throat. 'So, um, I've got some good news and some bad news.'

Van Riet's eyebrows disappeared under his hairline. 'Yes?'

'I think I know how to get the Squib operational again, but I sort of need to go on a scavenger hunt.'

'I don't need to tell you how awfully suspicious that sounds, do I?'

'No,' Wendy said, slumping in her seat. 'But it's the

truth. I need some extra equipment to do the job.'

'Extra equipment you didn't need to do it in the first place?'

Wendy's eyes twinkled. 'Extra equipment I had to stash when I was on the run for my life. It was slowing me down. So, really, this is all your fault.'

Van Riet simmered quietly. She recognised that look, Thor used to have it all the time. He wasn't sure whether to be angry or impressed. Thor had always settled for impressed, but she wasn't as confident with van Riet. 'Fine, but Renier is going with you.'

He nodded to Johansson and he stepped up behind Wendy and pulled her to her feet. This underling wasn't as careful with her as Lucille had been. Clearly van Riet had intended that to send a message. It was understood.

'I'll go too,' Lucille said.

Van Riet shook his head. 'No. Give your gun to Renier, I need you here. I want you to take a look at the computers while Milton is off getting whatever she needs. Not that I don't trust her, but we've got to make sure she hasn't been lying to us, don't we?'

Lucille looked at Wendy, then back to van Riet before handing over her weapon. 'Fair enough.'

Johansson snapped it open and checked the rounds before pocketing it. Another nod to van Riet. He walked over and smiled at Wendy. 'I don't mean to be cruel. We really will discuss things if you do as I've asked. There might be a place for someone as ingenious as you in our group. I know that might sound like an empty promise to butter you up, but it's the truth. Think about it before you try to do anything stupid.'

Johansson placed his arm around her shoulders and gently pushed her forwards. 'Being stupid will get you shot. I'm not a murderer, but I can kill if I have to.'

Wendy's eye twitched. 'You're not the first murderer to say something like that to me today. I'm starting to wonder who you're all really trying to convince.'

He chuckled and shoved her forward slightly harder. 'Come on.'

FOURTEEN

Rostrum had resigned himself to sitting on the floor. As much as he wanted his seat back, Vandal wasn't about to give it up, and Rostrum needed to hear the rest of his story.

'Who on the Crawler hired you?'

Vandal sighed and rubbed at his neck. 'I'm not supposed to know exactly. It was all done digitally through the internal network.'

'You must have at least verified it was legit.'

'Of course. Top encryption, enough hallmarks to let me know it was someone pretty high up. I wasn't about to push, not for a paying job.'

Rostrum let himself fall back, his head resting on the carcass of a robot. 'A paying job? You killed my city for a few coins?'

'In my defence, I wasn't in the best place over on the Crawler,' Vandal said. 'I can't imagine that makes a difference, though.'

'Not really.'

He shifted awkwardly. 'My job was never to kill the city, not exactly. I was hired, as I said, to disable you. They didn't want you beating them somewhere, and they did say that I should limit casualties wherever I could.'

'Awfully nice of them.'

'Look, at least part of the fault lies with you. If you were less efficient then I wouldn't have needed to escalate things. And the robots? I'm going to hold my hands up and say that was a desperation move on both our parts.'

'I'm assuming they didn't want us to get the wreckage that captain contacted us about?'

Vandal shrugged. 'I would guess so. I don't know the specifics on that, they hired me months ago and told me to wait it out here until they sent the activation signal. Gave me plenty of time to plan what I was going to do, scope things out.'

Rostrum sat up again. 'And you did your job.'

'I did my job.'

'Yet now you're telling me everything? Not very loyal.'

'Like I said, it's not over,' Vandal said, pulling himself to his feet. He shuffled over to one of the windows, all broken by the storm, and stared out at the horizon. 'Would have thought I'd be able to see them by now.'

Rostrum raised his voice as far as it would go which, in his current state, wasn't far at all. 'Start making sense.'

'Sorry,' Vandal said. 'The sterilisation teams. When the job was done I was supposed to contact the Crawler for extraction and payment. Like I said, they didn't reply, the network was completely dead despite my swanky gadget they gave me for such a purpose.'

'And?'

'Well, you hear stories, right? People go missing sometimes, whole galleons, and a rumour starts that maybe someone up high wanted something to stay hidden? Maybe they have a secret kill team or two to make sure those things stay secret, yeah?'

Rostrum briefly considered standing up and reclaiming his now empty seat, but rejected that idea. He wasn't up to moving right now. 'I've never heard any stories like that.'

'Maybe it's just something that creeps around on the

Crawler then. Point is, if they're ignoring my extraction request, there has to be a reason.'

'And that reason is, you think, a hardened assassination squad coming to scrub the city clean?'

'No witnesses, maybe?'

Rostrum fell silent. It was a hard thing to accept. There were so few of them left these days, just three confirmed cities left standing. Surely no-one would be so psychotic as to risk the very survival of the human race by culling a third of them out of, what, petty competition? He could maybe see them as far as driving the Strider into the storm, crippling them and causing *some* death for something so insignificant, but to kill off the survivors? That was monstrous.

As monstrous as shooting a scared mother in the back? As ignoring the deaths of however many had fallen on his trek to the core? Things were very suddenly not as cut and dry as they had been mere hours ago.

He could conceive of someone making that call, sending assassins, and labelling it a hard choice. If they had to, if it was *necessary*. He didn't have the luxury of dismissing it outright, not anymore.

'What do the rumours say about these people?' He did stand up this time.

Vandal turned around. 'Fanatics that strike with surgical precision, mostly. Cold, calculating, everything you'd expect from shady psychopaths. They'll clear the city deck by deck until the entire thing is a tomb. As far as anyone else is concerned, the weather will have gutted the city. I should have seen this coming.'

'Plausible deniability.'

'Exactly, and I don't think there'll be time to get salvage teams out here until the next storm cycle. By which point what little evidence they did leave would be lost to the elements.'

'Makes sense,' Rostrum said, finally reclaiming his seat. 'What do we do about it?'

Vandal's head dropped. 'Nothing. There's nothing to be done. I just wanted you to know that it wasn't personal. Gives you a measure of closure, maybe.'

'You're very fatalistic for a murderer.'

'I just know when I'm beaten, that's all.'

Rostrum turned his attention to his computers. Most of them were still deactivated after his daring escape, but as Vandal had showed him, communications was active. Perhaps there was still time to call for help. The Crawler's death squads weren't visible yet, provided they were coming at all, which meant there might still be some time left.

There was always the Roller. They'd offered help before. Maybe...

He began to type slowly, each keystroke an agony as the charred flesh resented being pressed against the plastic.

Vandal approached. 'What are you doing?'

'Sending an SOS.'

'To the Roller I assume?'

'Well I'm not going to go and beg your employer for help, am I?'

A blister popped and Rostrum growled to himself. This was like shouting into the night, but it wasn't as if he had any other option. Wait here and die, or hope to get lucky on the network.

'You do realise,' Vandal said. 'The Crawler will be listening in? Your network isn't very secure.'

'Doesn't matter. I only care about the Roller hearing it. Surely another city headed this way would give the Crawler some pause.'

'You'd think –'

'Besides,' Rostrum said, quickly. 'This isn't my only plan. Help me up.'

'Are you... Are you sure it's safe to touch you?'

'Just help me up.'

Vandal groaned under the strain, but whatever injuries he had clearly weren't enough to weaken him too much.

Holding Rostrum upright seemed harder than it had been to lift him, however, but that was fine. He had hoped that his legs would remember how to work once they were upright again. They'd lasted long enough to get him to his chair, but this was going to take some actual walking.

He took Vandal on a tour of the room, having him escort him from computer to computer while he went through the arduous process of starting them all up again. It wasn't as simple as flipping a switch, it was a lot of coded button presses in precise intervals. Considering the damage, he was surprised any started back up at all.

Rostrum hadn't really seen the damage when he climbed in. He hadn't seen much at all with his scorched eyes, but the longer he stayed in the room the more his eyes were able to focus. Any hope that this meant his eyes weren't as damaged as he first believed was undone by the state of his cockpit.

The storm was always going to hit it hard – big, exposed room surrounded mostly by glass, a prime target – but everything that wasn't bolted down had been obliterated and used to shred half the things that *had* been bolted down. No worse than the rest of the Strider, he supposed, but this was his *home*, his sanctuary. It left a sour taste.

The gentle hum of the computers booting back up helped a little. Half of them obliged, which he hoped would be enough, and he had Vandal escort him back to his seat.

'If there are still people alive here, I owe it to them to give them a way out,' Rostrum said. 'If the damage will let me.'

'What are you thinking?'

'Let me see,' he said and tried to navigate around his various interfaces. He let out an empty laugh. 'The damage report system is damaged.'

'I won't lie, I expected that.'

'I'll just have to go on faith. Shut up a second.'

Vandal held up his hands for a moment and took a step back as Rostrum opened a small panel on the arm of his chair. Inside sat a small lever, which he pulled firmly before shutting the panel once again. Then he took a blackened finger and tapped at the screen. A peal of vicious feedback engulfed the cockpit for a second.

'Christ,' Rostrum said as the noise died down. 'If there's anyone left alive on board, please pay attention. The doors sealing the docking bay have been unsealed, and all command codes for the Strider-registered galleons within have been transmitted. If you can, make your way to the dock and board a galleon of your choice. Make for the Roller if you can. This message will repeat for as long as the systems are able to run it.'

Another peal of feedback signalled the end of the recording. Then, with a single tap at the screen, he pushed it out to all the loudspeakers and intercoms remaining in the city.

'Pretty noble of you, I suppose,' Vandal said.

'Not really. It's my job to keep them safe. The docks probably aren't even there now. I saw a big chunk of that deck just disappear during the storm.'

'So why send them?'

'Just in case.'

Vandal nodded. 'I see.'

'You never know; I might have just done everything I said I did. Maybe the storm didn't get the whole deck, maybe some of the galleons even survived.'

'We could go and look.'

'No.'

'No?'

Rostrum closed his eyes. Nothing split or cracked or burst when he did that, it was completely painless. 'Pretty sure I wouldn't make it down there. If I'm going to die, I'm going to die comfortable and in my home.'

'You're a weird one, Rostrum.'

'I think I'm pretty normal, actually.'

Vandal rocked on his heels for a moment. 'The thing is, and I do hope you won't take this personally, but I don't want to die. Now that I know there might be a way out, I'd be a fool not to take it.'

'Go then,' Rostrum said, his eyes still closed. 'I don't want anyone to die here, even you.'

'Thank you. I'm not sure I deserve this much forgiveness, but you're a better man that I, Rostrum Barley.'

Rostrum counted the man's steps. Was it twenty from the chair to the elevator? Twenty-five maybe. Ten would do. He waited until Vandal had taken ten steps before leaning forward and tapping the screen again.

There was the sound of two thick slabs of metal colliding, followed by a loud curse from Vandal, which in turn was followed by a loud sizzling noise. Rostrum opened his eyes and rotated his chair to face the man.

He was almost to the elevator door – his stride must have been longer than Rostrum thought – and the sudden addition of a wall where the door had been had stunned him into silence.

Vandal looked at him, stuttering. 'W-what the hell?!'

'I lied. You're dying here, Vandal. Not for vengeance, not for justice. Merely for spite.'

'Open the damned door.'

'I can't,' Rostrum said. 'Literally can't. That isn't a door, it's an emergency bulkhead. The Strider, long ago, used to ferry various toxic minerals harvested from the crust of the planet, or so the records say. These bulkheads were the final, last-ditch safety measures in the event of a catastrophic chemical spill. Lock yourself away, wait for rescue. Useless if you ever want to use the Strider again, mind. That sizzling you heard was it welding into place. The cockpit is sealed permanently.'

'Well played.'

'If you're desperate, you can always go out the window. It's a bit of a climb.'

Vandal walked to the balcony and peered over the edge. For a long moment, Rostrum thought he might actually consider it, but then he turned around and came back inside. 'You actually climbed down there?'

'To be fair,' Rostrum said. 'When I did it, there was more city to grab onto.'

The other man spat a hollow laugh. 'Spite it is, then.'

'From hell's heart.'

'I doubt it would have made much difference anyway,' Vandal said, lowering himself to the floor. 'I can see them on the horizon.'

'Where?'

'Just look.'

Rostrum groaned as he turned his head to look at the horizon. In the far distance, glinting against the new sunlight, he spotted a few objects speeding over the ice. It was impossible to identify them, but it could only be them. About an hour away, if their galleons were like the Strider's. Probably sooner.

'We should tell people about this.'

Vandal's voice was muffled as he buries his face in his knees. 'What are you talking about? In fact, shut up, I don't care.'

'People should know the truth about what went on here. If this is the Crawler's doing, then the people of the Roller need to be warned.'

'You can't. Why do you think no-one else had heard of this stuff? It's not like you're their first hit,' Vandal said. He stood up again and turned to stare at the horizon. 'You try to radio, they block it. Try to contact anyone on the network, they'll hijack it.'

'Only because they're watching the communication channels, right? Well I have an alternative.'

'You're just full of plans now, aren't you? Exactly when they don't matter.'

Rostrum hung his head. The skin on the back of his neck felt especially tight compared to the rest, even the other burns. His chin wouldn't even touch his chest now. 'I need your help.'

'You have got to be joking. You've pushed me to the limit of my civility by trapping me up here.'

'You killed everyone in my city!'

'That was the weather, not me!'

The pair locked eyes, Rostrum could tell Vandal didn't believe his own words. 'It was you. But that doesn't have to be your last act. Help me with this, give them a last twist of the knife for betraying you. Think of it as an apology.'

'Fine. Then we can just sit in silence and wait for them to come and kill us?'

'I'll be dead before they get here. You'll get your silence.'

'Morbid bastard. What do you need me to do?'

Rostrum swivelled the screen towards him. 'Type it up, everything you told me. I'd do it myself, but the burns –'

'I get it.'

'I'll do the rest.'

Vandal grimaced as he typed one-handed, the other still plastered to his body. It was slow going, but still faster than Rostrum could have managed. There seemed to be a lot more to say than he had been told – the background details, he supposed – but once Vandal was started he seemed determined to jot down everything he could.

Rostrum's gaze wandered. He didn't want to stare at the bedraggled saboteur right now. He wanted to get one last good look at his home, his sanctuary, and remember it how it had been. It was hard to do now, what with the junked robots and the storm debris, but the longer he stared the more he could look past that.

He was ready for his life to flash before his eyes. The whole thing, all thirty plus years of it. He welcomed it now, in fact. The hallucinations he'd suffered on the way up here were good, but he'd known they weren't real, deep down. But his own memories, he'd know them. Live out his whole life again, one last time. See everyone that had left along the way.

There was no doubt where the flashbacks would start. He'd done very little before he'd been apprenticed to the last pilot, and the moment he had first walked into the cockpit, that had been, in essence, the moment he was born. If he could just hold onto that, trigger that memory...

The damage and the debris began to slip away, and he was there again, walking into the cockpit for the first time behind Everett Naples. Even after they had become friends, Rostrum had always been a little scared of Everett. The man was six and a half foot tall, nearly as wide, and had a beard you could get lost inside. The first time he had led Rostrum inside the cockpit, they were not friends. Rostrum was terrified.

He'd been given the tour, shown all the computers, the view, the chair. It had been so bewildering, but it had never changed. It hadn't changed in generations; it was a constant. Letting him into that room had been inviting him to join a lineage, something greater than himself. It had taken him a long time to realise that, but it had all started that day.

Rostrum hadn't moved anything. All of Everett's keepsakes and decorations were exactly where they had been on that day. The cockpit had, he realised now, been time locked – forever unchanging except in the smallest way. Every pilot left a little of himself in there, and his replacement would absorb that over the years. They never died, not really.

Until now. The memory was hiding the damage from his sight, as he had wanted, but as he walked around on his tour he could see the destruction fading through, like the faintest of shadows. The end of the line.

Everett was talking to him, but he couldn't remember the words. He never remembered the man's words, only his expressions. His voice had been thickly accented, his parents had fled the crash of the Hoverer – he'd nearly forgotten about the days when there had been more than three cities – and they had always been a little hard to follow. It had caused him no end of trouble back then, but it was making him smile now.

He barely even felt his lips splitting.

Rostrum had never added anything to the cockpit. He'd never put his essence into the pool, and never gotten around to picking his replacement for when the time – this time – came. Perhaps the wreckage was his contribution, his grand addition. The full stop at the end of one very long sentence.

Oh god, Galveston. He'd never get to finish that either. All this reliving memories wasn't as fun as he had been led to believe.

His eyes rolled back into his head. Perhaps a little sleep would help. A small power nap, just to keep him going until Vandal was done. It was tiring work, climbing up an entire city while heavily wounded, took it out of you. He could hardly be denied a little rest now, could he?

When Vandal shook him awake, this question was still rattling around his mind. He wanted to be angry but there was nothing left to fuel it, so instead he doubled down on the grogginess. 'What?'

'I've done what you wanted. Consider me atoned.'

'Huh?'

Vandal spoke a little slower. 'You wanted me to tell my story or whatever, I've done it.'

'Oh, right' Rostrum's eyes were blurry again, but not from the corneal damage as before. They were dimmer, darker, like he was looking through a veil. 'That as quick.'

'Quick?' Vandal said with a snort. 'Took me the best part of an hour.'

'Hmm? Of course, yes.'

'Are you all right?'

There was a dull ache behind his eyes, but Rostrum ignored it. 'I'm just dying, nothing major. Show me.'

Vandal swivelled the screen again. 'There.'

'Right, okay,' Rostrum said. He couldn't focus on

anything so precise as letter on the screen, but he flicked his eyes from side to side as if he could. 'That'll do. Now, watch this.'

The benefit of a lifetime sat in front of the same computer day in and day out was that he didn't need to see to do what needed doing. His fingers new the way regardless of his eyes, and even slowed down by the wounds he could manage. He navigated his way through to the node map, as he had done so many times before, and accessed the newest one.

'What are you doing?' Vandal said. 'I already told you that if you try to communicate –'

'If I use the messenger, yes, but they might not think to check this route. No-one has yet.'

There was a chime, the notification that he had admin access to this node. 743-C, the last one he had visited, still stored in his recent destinations file. It was barely any effort at all to add Vandal's file now.

'That's very clever,' Vandal said. 'But hardly a timely way of warning people.'

'I have to hope they have time. Someday, someone will find it.'

'So you're passed spite and onto faith now?'

Rostrum hit the upload button and slumped back in his seat. He could barely see the screen now. 'If you like.'

'So that's it? A message in a bottle?'

'Are they here yet?'

Vandal's voice went flat. 'Yes. They dropped out of view twenty minutes ago. They must have arrived by now.'

'I hope they knock. It's impolite to enter without knocking.'

'Rostrum...'

'It's just the principle. You can't barge in.'

'Rostrum, stop it.'

'It's just... rude...'

Vandal placed a hand on Rostrum's lap. 'Stop it, you're scaring me.'

'Why? Afraid of what you've done? Is it different seeing the corpses to seeing them actually die? Easier to compartmentalise the other way, I guess.'

'I'm sorry.'

Rostrum's hands closed around Vandal's, tight with all his remaining strength. 'I don't care. I guess I didn't move on from spite after all. *Look at me as I die, Vandal.*'

He could feel Vandal try to pull away, but there was no way he would let him. Rostrum had wanted the man dead, and he deserved it, but that was not to be. Nothing to be done about that, but this was better. His last few moments, trapped, with a reminder of the atrocity he committed, that was better. More apt.

With the saboteur clawing at the charred flesh of his hands, Rostrum let out one final deep sigh and waited for death to take him.

FIFTEEN

Johansson had made a concerted effort to be unfriendly. Naturally, Wendy had run into unfriendly types before – she was a young woman pursuing an interest in technology, it was impossible not to run into some horrid mouthbreathers – but they tended to make it look effortless. For them, it was the default setting, just who they were. For Renier Johansson, it became apparent very quickly that it was an affectation.

It was a *good* affectation, he committed to the role completely, but it was still forced. Every time he shoved her onwards a little faster, pointed his gun at her, spat any number of threatening words her way, she spotted the briefest glimpse of remorse in his features. It did little to mitigate things, but it was still nice to see.

The cabins were weird the right way up. When everything was askew they had seemed Spartan, tucking all the personal items into one big pile at the base of the room. Now, things had shifted back the other way, and it made the rooms look much bigger. Considering six of them took up an entire deck near enough, it shouldn't have been a surprise, but her last visit had given her the impression they had been constrictive and tall, not wide and squat.

Wendy started in Enzo's quarters, theorising that they had been the most authoritative of the survivors of the attack. Johansson had watched her dispassionately for a minutes before deigning to help.

He kicked his way through the keepsakes like a child mid-sulk. 'There's a lot of shit here.'

'Yeah, but to be fair I don't think it was all over the floor originally. Besides, I had to keep my stuff hidden, didn't I?'

He snorted. 'Doubt we could have found a thing in here.'

'I'll concede that.'

This succession of poorly thought out plans was starting to take its toll on Wendy. She had gotten down here, sure enough, but now she had to try and search for one thing while ostensibly searching for something else, all while watched by a man with an itchy trigger finger. And the thing she was *supposed* to be looking for didn't even exist. She might as well search for a shovel to dig herself a deeper grave.

It wasn't as if the command key would just be sat on the end table or something. This was just a long and drawn out way of getting caught in a lie. But she'd search anyway, seeing as how she had a track record for getting surprisingly lucky.

Most of Enzo's stuff was boring, or at least expected. Technical manuals, loose jewellery, weird ornaments that Wendy couldn't quite place, a few that she could, and more than a few books. In this configuration it didn't say much about Enzo as a person, but it must have done beforehand.

'Check this out,' Johansson said from the far side of the room. He kicked away at the mess a little and then stooped down to pick up something. 'I think it's a photo.'

He threw it to her and she caught it. It was a digital photo frame, cracked from the fall, with a familiar black blob of leaking liquid crystals obscuring one of the bottom corners. She found the power button on the back and flicked it on.

The woman's face that greeted her was youthful and happy, a brilliant white smile and thin grey eyes. She wore a uniform and was snuggling up with a rather grumpy-looking cat, who in turn was wearing a party hat. Seconds later, the picture changed, a side view of her now, taken by someone else, as she frowned at what looked to be one of the consoles in the control centre. Then another switch, a regal photo of the cat once again.

In all, there seemed to be at least twenty images loaded into the thing, mostly of her or the cat, but some with what Wendy assumed were others members of the crew. They all wore the same uniform, complete with name tags. It was a few pictures in before Wendy could catch the smiling woman's tag – Enzo.

'It's easy to forget that people came before you, sometimes,' Johansson said. 'This isn't my first time salvaging, but I still find I need reminders. Do you mind?'

He held out his hand and she tossed the frame back to him. Without a word, he flipped it over and removed the memory chip before setting about threading it onto his necklace. Wendy hadn't spotted it before, but the blue light from the deprived photo frame helped to light it up as he worked. There were a few small bits of technology attached to it, and the newly applied memory chip fit neatly into a space between two others, both burned out.

Johansson grunted and slipped the necklace back under his shirt.

'Trophies?'

'Technology outlives us all, unfortunately. I like to keep a reminder or two close to my heart, keeps me aware of where it all came from.'

Wendy shook her head. 'You people are so weird.'

'Just find your gear.'

He went back to looking, and she made a show of

doing the same.

She had forgotten that the photo frame would have a memory chip until he removed it, that was embarrassing. Of course it had had to have one, that was where the pictures came from, but it was just so curious that he would remove it. Not shocking so much as unexpected.

But it did get her thinking. She was looking for any sort of data storage device, true enough, but she hadn't been looking beyond the obvious. A spare data chip just lying around perhaps? Labelled *not the command codes*? Hidden away in a secret safe maybe, or just indistinguishable from the other various data chips that worm their way into the life of a crew member on such a vessel.

That was the wrong way of looking at things, though. That was looking at them from the modern perspective, as if she – if indeed it was her that hid them, though this seemed a good starting point to work from – was trying to hide the codes from history. If that had been the case, it wouldn't have been to keep the Squib mired and non-functional. Different motive, different method.

Enzo was hiding those codes from her own crew. Her friends. That meant she needed a way to hide them that *they* wouldn't even think to check.

Working to that model, Wendy would have considered the photo frame an obvious choice now. Digital memory, could store the codes pretty easily if there was enough space for them. Which there most likely wouldn't be. Not that Wendy knew how much space the codes actually took up. No, she needed a better train of thought for this – she had to stick to the psychology not the technology.

Photo frame. Very obviously digital. Not the first place someone would look, but not exactly unlikely that anyone with technical know-how would think to check there once the obvious places had been expended. There was a step on from that.

And then she remembered the cat-thing. Pitted metal peering through mangy fur, a robotic pet. It had to be the same cat that was in the photos, albeit suffering after all this time. There'd be plenty of spare memory hidden away in that thing, and it would take them a fair while to even conceive of looking inside the ship's pet. Hell, they might not have even known it wasn't a real cat – looked real enough in the photos.

'I don't think my stuff's here,' she said.

Johansson didn't look up. 'You said you put it in here. Were you lying?'

'No,' she said quickly. 'But when I left it in here it was before everything got shaken up.'

'Well it's not going to have gone far, is it? No-one's going to have taken it, are they?'

'That's the thing,' she said. 'There is someone else on board the Squib.'

His eyes widened and he thumbed the safety off his gun. His voice went flat. 'What?'

'Woah, chill! I mean that weird robot animal thing!'

His shoulders visibly slackened and he flicked the safety back on. 'Oh, that thing. I don't take it for much of a thief.'

'It wouldn't need to be to steal this stuff,' she said. 'It's not like it's big industrial equipment. You should know, tech gear can be pretty small. It might not even have meant to, just saw it bouncing around in the kerfuffle and took a liking to it.'

'That doesn't sound likely.'

'I don't know what to tell you. My gear isn't here anymore!'

Johansson walked over and took her by the arm. 'Then we go back to the control centre and you get back to work on the computer. We've wasted enough time.'

Wendy shook herself free. 'Listen, dick. It can't be done without my gear. At all. That's sort of the point, right? You want the Squib fully operational, you help me find that weird cat-thing.'

He drummed a hand over the barrel of his gun for a

moment while he mulled it over. His fingernails clicked against the metal like a metronome, and it drew her attention. 'Fine. Let's go.'

She allowed him to see a small, servile smile. If nothing else, he'd need to feel in charge after acquiescing to that, she'd dealt with people like this before. They were in control, but they needed very obvious reminders from time to time. Or maybe that was just what she told herself to make *herself* feel a little more in control.

They went back to the last place Wendy had seen the critter, and started their search there. It had skulked out into the darkness, but she had never seen it move at any great speed. It would make perfect sense for it to take up sprinting now, of course, just as finding it became important. How would you even begin to track a robot?

Eventually, it found them. The noise of something falling over in a distant room led them closer, but they must have walked past it twice before it agreed to step out of the shadows. It looked at them and turned to swagger away, just as a cat should. The servos might have suffered over the years, but the programming had not.

Johansson raised his gun. Wendy slapped her hand over the end of the barrel.

'Hold up,' she said. 'We need it in one piece.'

'Oh do we now? I don't see your gear.'

'Look, my *gear* is all computer programmes. You're not going to see a tiny chip from here, are you? For all I know it could be tangled in its fur.'

'This is sounding more and more farfetched as you go on, kid. If it's that small, why hide it?'

She sighed. 'Think it through. Only reason I'm alive is because you need me to decrypt the computer. If I knew you wanted into the mainframe, why would I just carry the key around with me? I'd hide it so you'd have to cut a deal, right?'

'Hmm,' he scrunched up his face. 'You have an answer for everything, don't you?'

'I try to,' she said. 'Saves on the dilly dallying if I win all the arguments. Now, help me catch this bloody thing.'

Johansson didn't look impressed, but he didn't look violent either, which would do. He lowered his gun and set about stalking up to the cat-thing as quietly as possible. There was a technique to the way he moved – heel to toe, shifting weight only once the foot was flat – that made him look very odd. It did make him suitably silent, however.

The cat-thing continued to trot away, but Johansson was faster. It didn't seem to care about his approach until he grabbed it, then started to buck and weave in his hands. A damaged speaker lodged somewhere inside its throat started to let out what must have once been feline shrieks, but now more resembled some shrill nightmarish beast.

Johansson held it in her direction, arms outstretched as though it might explode. 'A little help?'

Wendy stepped closer and studied the thing for a moment, face mere inches from its whirring metal claws. 'Okay, here we go.'

She flinched a few times, trying to find a gap through the furious rage, her hand trying to dart through to the thing's stomach. Eventually she managed it, suffering only superficial scratches, and flicked what she assumed was the off-switch. The creature went limp instantly.

Johansson relaxed too. 'Thank you.'

'Give it here,' she said. 'I'll see if it ate my stuff or got it trapped in the fur or something.'

He nodded and tossed her the cat-thing. It was heavier than it looked. 'Its fur does seem to have accrued things over the years.'

Wendy had to make a show of the search again, but it was easier on such a small thing. A fair few things had matted into what was left of the fur over the years – filth and grime, loose metal, discarded components from some machine or another – so it was no surprise that the thing weighed more than it should. What she was really looking for, however, was the trigger to eject the memory card nestled in the base of the thing's skull.

The memory port was readily visible, and didn't look as though it had ever been coated with fur. This made sense, she considered, in case you ever needed to make changes to the firmware – part of the appeal of a robot pet, she decided, was that it didn't require actual brain surgery to alter their behaviour. Slicing into the head of a pet to get at its brain defeated the purpose.

She found the release catch inside the ear on the opposite side of the head, and a quick press resulted in the chip popping out of the slot. It looked worn, a little scratched. Admittedly, that could have just been wear and tear from centuries of slogging about in an abandoned wreck, but to Wendy it looked more like it had been removed and reinserted gracelessly during a rush. That felt like a good sign.

'Okay, I think this is it,' she said.

'You think?'

'You know what I mean. Don't start getting pedantic just as you were starting to win me over with your natural charm.'

His lip curled into a snarl. 'I think you are forgetting what sort of situation you are currently in.'

Her face dropped. 'Sorry. You're right. I just default to joking, keeps me going, you know?'

'Just remember where you are,' he said. They dropped into silence for a moment. 'Come on. Let's get you back to the command centre and put your gear to the test, yeah?'

She nodded and he started to lead her back to the heart of the Squib. When they arrived, van Riet and Lucille were deep in conversation, but van Riet cut it short.

'That didn't take long,' he said, leaning on a chair. 'Got everything you need?'

Wendy gripped the card tight in her palm. She hoped so. 'Perhaps. I need some assurances first.'

'That we won't just kill you instantly? Understandable,' he said. 'Look, we're an esoteric, clandestine group. What we do is, well, it's important it stay secret. But that's not to say we don't recruit. If you're useful enough, you're safe. Getting the Squib operation is pretty damn useful.'

'You're talking around the point.'

'Yes, I am,' he said, crossing his arms. 'But I promise I won't kill you *if* you get the Squib operational again. I'll tell you everything you want to know about us, and more. Deal?'

He didn't look like he was lying, but then he hadn't looked deceitful before and look how that had turned out. Still, it wasn't really a choice, as much as he made it look like one. There was the option of doing what he wanted and risking that he was lying, or defying him and definitely getting shot.

Life had been better before every choice had started ending with a gun pointed at her face.

'I'll need my chair,' she said, nodding her head towards Lucille. The other woman stood up and moved. 'And it might take a while.'

Van Riet nodded slowly. 'Take as long as you need, but work as fast as you can.'

She sat down and plugged the chip into the terminal. Though she had half-expected the procedure to be on auto-pilot – drag the codes from the chip thirstily and plug them right back in as was – it was a relief to find that it wasn't that easy. These things should be chunky and require a bit of legwork, some digital red tape. That was how you knew it was legit.

There was a lot of data on the chip, and most of it wasn't the cat-thing's OS. It seemed Enzo had used it as a digital vault long before she thought to hide the command codes in it. She knew it worked, that was why she chose it. If it was good enough for pornography – which, judging from the file directory, it *was* – then it was good enough for the keys to the Squib.

It was also nice to see that the codes were enormous. They managed to take up more space than the actual OS for the cat-thing, which was seriously impressive. Perhaps this was why the thing was so erratic and clearly robotic now – it didn't have the necessary space left to function properly. Or it was just age. Either way, it didn't take her long to find the codes and start the process of reimplementing them to the central data cluster.

The loading bar had milestones. As the progress ticked along, cheerful little speech bubbles informed her of which systems were now back online. It started with something called the *gait identification circuit*, moved quickly onto *vocal personification programme* and *tactile determination* before settling into systems that she understood and made sense. Security came online once the bar hit seventy-five percent, and Wendy surreptitiously flipped to its control page.

She was disappointed. Thorsten's message had her thinking there would be something useful – ceiling turrets, robo-soldiers, the ability to electrify the floors, anything. Instead, what she found was three different levels of internal alarm klaxons, the option to set the eternal image emitters to display a SOS emoticon, and a setting to double-lock all the doors in the residential zone.

Van Riet's shadow slid over her shoulder. 'Sorry, that might have been a bit cruel on our part.'

'Excuse me?' she said, turning to face him.

'The message from your friend, coming at you from beyond the grave. You're not going to like this, but we sort of set you up. As a test.'

'What?'

'Lucille put in a good word for you, but I needed proof. And we really did need the command codes. I thought it might be a good idea to combine the two into one job.'

Wendy's looked to Lucille. The woman couldn't hold eye contact and she looked flush. Wendy felt she looked the same way right about now. 'I don't...'

'Think about it,' van Riet said. 'You wouldn't help us out of the goodness of your heart. Not after what we had to do, so we had to make it look like your idea, like you were getting the drop on us. It was the best way to get what we wanted *and* see how ingenious you are.'

Johansson waved from the other side of the room. 'You really thought I bought your story about the catbot just wandering off with your stuff? I mean, props for trying and everything, and you sold it like a pro, but did you really think that would hold water?'

'I sort of did, actually...'

'To be fair,' van Riet said. 'On someone who wasn't aware? It probably would have. More than half of a good lie is telling it with conviction, and you properly nailed that.'

'This is a lot of effort to go through to have a laugh before you kill me.'

Van Riet threw up his hands. 'No no no! You're not listening. We don't kill if we can help it, we're not psychos or pirates or something. I know it must look that way from your perspective, but that's only because you don't know all the facts. I was sincere in my desire to try and recruit you, at least once I saw your skills.'

'I said you could be useful to the cause,' Lucille said. 'If we told you what was really going on. We need everyone we can get, but the level of secrecy makes it hard to recruit new members. Getting people to see what's really important is both hard and a risk... Casper needed to be sure you were worth the effort.'

'And that was it? Finding some lost codes and plugging them in?'

'Partly,' van Riet said. 'But it was more the method of *how* you found them, thinking around the problem. Our agents have to be able to think on their feet. Add to that your plan to actually turn the system against us? That willingness to try and roll the hard six for your mission? That's what you need to survive as one of us.'

Wendy rubbed at her temple. This was a lot of information very quickly, and it was confusing. They'd gone from friends to enemies and, apparently, back to friends so quickly that it was making her head spin. Did *they* even know what side they were on at this point?

'You killed the captain. You killed Thor. I'm not interested in becoming one of you.'

'I said before how we're trying to save us from ourselves, right?' van Riet said. 'Maybe the full truth will make it easier to understand. What do you know about the ice?'

'It's cold and it's everywhere.'

He laughed. 'Funny. But I should have been clearer. What do you know about where it came from, the reason we spend our lives running from deathly storms in giant mobile cities?'

She thought about it for a moment. 'Not much, not really. I know what everyone else does.'

'Which is?'

'Something happened. There aren't any records of what it was, but it was sudden. The storms came later, there was enough warning to get the cities running.'

'Exactly. That's the broad-strokes history as remembered in the telling. But you're wrong when you say there are no records. Some of the old world survived, and they documented the entire thing. We know exactly what it was that led to this hellish existence, and we know how to reverse it.'

'Bullshit.'

'And,' he continued. 'It's our job to stop people making it worse before we can make it better. The more old world tech the others get their hands on, the more likely it is someone will get it into their head to try and reconfigure something big, and then we're right back to square one.'

'You've said all this before,' Wendy said. 'There's nothing new or insightful in this nonsense.'

Lucille knelt in front of her. 'Then I'll give you the straight facts. According to the records, machines like the Squib froze the world.'

'You are having a laugh.'

'Why do you think they put storm drives on a giant advertising billboard? Because that's what the Squib is, you know. It was designed to walk through a town, provide maximum exposure for a brand.'

Wendy tried to force the full extent of her incredulity onto her face. There was a lot of it to move, however. 'And you said I'm a bad liar.'

'The storm drive,' van Riet said. 'They were supposed to create localised snow storms, that much is true. Small flurries, according to the documentation. Ambience. Whatever they were trying to sell, it was tied to that sort of weather. Something went wrong, supercharged them all. Suddenly it wasn't ambience any more. Millions of storm drives across the planet, all fiddling with the atmosphere. A cascade scenario.'

Wendy frowned. 'But someone tried to destroy this thing and take down the crew.'

'Only way they could see to stop the storms, or so we've read. Didn't work, obviously. By the time they managed it, the storms had become self-sustaining.'

'Dear god,' Wendy said. 'You actually believe all this, don't you?'

'We've seen the evidence,' Lucille said. 'I know it sounds bonkers, I thought so at first too, but it is compelling stuff.'

Van Riet plunged his hands into his pockets. 'You're clearly a smart, inquisitive, capable person, Milton. At least come with us, take a look. If you're still not convinced –'

'You'll shoot me?'

'We have sort of painted ourselves into a corner with that, haven't we? That's why I've let you take a bit of leverage.'

'What?'

He looked over her shoulder at the screen. 'There we go, the transfer is complete. Hello, Computer?'

An artificial voice erupted from the speakers, far too loud for the first few words, before stabilising at a more palatable volume. It sounded like a young woman who had been taught their language phonetically – perfectly comprehensible, but with strange emphases. 'What can I do for you?'

'Can you unlock the navigation systems, please?'

The speakers clicked a couple of times. 'I'm sorry, I can't do that. You do not have the required permissions to make administrative changes.'

'Thank you, Computer,' he said, turning back to Wendy. 'You try.'

'Um... Computer?'

'*Hello*. You've got to say that first. It's just how it's programmed.'

'*Hello*, Computer?' she said.

'What can I do for you?' came the electronic voice again.

'I want to access the navigation systems. Is that possible?'

Click click. 'One moment... Administrator privileges accepted. Welcome, captain *<UNDEFINED>*! Access to all systems has been assigned to you. You may delegate control as you see fit.'

'What the hell?'

Van Riet smiled. 'See? You have complete control of our prize. If you don't name a successor, and we won't compel you to do so, your death would see the entire system shut down yet again. We can't kill you now, not unless we want to spend months reprogramming the entire system from scratch, and we don't.'

'So what's to stop me just walking this thing to the nearest city and selling it off like I was supposed to?'

'There's the danger inherent in our recruitment process,' he said, still smiling. 'We can't stop you doing that. But, and this is the key, I'm hoping you'll at least let us show you the evidence before you do that. We're extending you a level of trust we don't have for the population at large.'

'Awfully nice of you.'

'Lucille recommended you. She doesn't tend to put her neck out for people that don't deserve it, and you've shown yourself to be the sort of person capable of understanding the bigger picture. All I'm asking is that you let us show it to you.'

'And if I still refuse to join you after you've seen it?'

'We'll come to a new arrangement. It, also, will not involve killing you.'

She noted how sinister that sounded. It was hardly as though he was saying she'd be set free unharmed, now was it? Then again, despite his assurances, she wasn't convinced he wouldn't shoot her in the face anyway if she refused to at least hear him out.

And, worst of all, she was interested now.

There was a betrayal and a half. As nonsensical as their story sounded – weaponised billboards flooding the world with artificially induced snow? – even the smallest chance of understanding what had happened all those years ago was worth the risk. She'd climbed into this frozen death trap for less, after all. And it had gotten her friends killed.

She should ignore them out of sheer spite and malice, to hell with the consequences. They don't get to kill off her friends *and* get their prize, and they certainly don't get to worm their way into her head. How could she forgive them that, even if everything they said was true? That would be akin to spitting in Thorsten's face, or even pulling the trigger herself.

But, dammit, she had to know. The Squib was so unusual, there had to be something more going on than she knew about. The writing pulsed out by the emitters had *sounded* like an advert, and despite the damage done to the vessel it clearly wasn't a warship of some kind. Why even invent the storm drive? Too many questions, all easily answered if she just let them show her.

Wendy stared at her feet for a good five minutes and no-one dared to interrupt her. Eventually she looked up, her eyes red and watery from fighting back tears.

Sorry, she thought to herself. *I know you'd understand, Thor. But I have to know.*

Van Riet raised his eyebrows a little. 'Decided what you're going to do?'

'Yes,' she said. 'I need to see this evidence. I'm not saying I believe you, but I have to know for sure.'

Van Riet's face exploded into a bright, gleaming smile. He turned to look at Lucille for a while, her face heavy with relief, and then to Johansson and the other man, both sharing in the glee. Then he reined himself in. 'That's wonderful news. You've made the right decision, I promise you that.'

'So show me.'

'To do that, you've got to come with us somewhere. If you let me have control of navigation, I'll enter the co-ordinates.'

Wendy sniffed. 'Hello, Computer?'

'What can I do for you?' it said.

'I'd like to delegate navigational control to someone.'

Click click click. 'Understood, captain <UNDEFINED>. Please identify your delegate now.'

Wendy pointed at van Riet. 'Um... him.'

Click. 'Delegate assigned. These privileges can be revoked at any time, and stem from the central command authority of captain <UNDEFINED>. Does the delegate understand these conditions?'

'He does,' van Riet said.

'Privileges granted. Would you like to assign an identifier to this delegate?'

'Yes,' van Riet said before Wendy could open her mouth. 'Casper van Riet.'

'Noted. Thank you, navigation officer van Riet.'

'Why do you get a name?' Wendy said.

'Because I told it my name, basically.'

Wendy frowned. 'Computer. I want to set an identifier for myself, can I do that?'

'Yes, captain *<UNDEFINED>*.'

'Wendigo Milton.'

'Thank you, captain Milton.'

Lucille was looking at Wendy. She cocked her head at the older woman. 'It didn't seem proper to use an abbreviation on something so *official*.'

'But you hate your full name,' Lucille said.

'I'm not overly fond of myself right now.'

Van Riet wasn't listening. He had already picked a console and set it to navigation mode. The projected map Thorsten had been using to track the storm was back now, emblazoned on the wall as he tapped in the co-ordinates. Wendy wasn't much of a navigator, but judging from the position on the map, the location was far from the main trunk travelled by the cities, in prime storm territory.

'You may want to find yourself some seats, everyone,' he said. 'I expect this might be a slightly bumpy ride, all things considered.

Wendy sighed and sat down in the nearest seat. The screen attached to it flickered for a moment, before bringing up a command interface. This computer was starting to creep her out a little now.

Lucille and the others found their seats too, though she took the time to secure Thor's and the captain's bodies. She nodded at Wendy, who found herself nodding back. While there was a chance she might forgive herself for betraying Thor and the captain for listening to van Riet, there was none at all she would forgive Lucille for killing them, no matter how respectful she was to the bodies. But she was glad that respect was there. They didn't need to be bouncing around during the journey.

With everyone strapped in, van Riet hit a button on his terminal and Wendy felt the motors spool up. Deep in the bowels of the Squib, ancient moving parts shook themselves free of centuries of rust until, at last, the vessel took its first step in hundreds of years.

SIXTEEN

To begin with, the journey was very uncomfortable. Though she had only caught a glimpse of the great legs that carried the Squib, Wendy's theory was that they were not designed to walk on such thick ice. They had the profile of something that would end in a point, meant for piercing surface frost and reaching the more stable ground beneath.

That wasn't an option these days. The spikes would pierce the surface snow, but the ice underneath would be unyielding. Stable, but slippery. As close to spinning your wheels as you could get without actually having wheels. They made very little progress, and the entire situation was flooded with a general feeling that the Squib was going to fall over and they'd all die.

Eventually, however, the ambulation matrix kicked in properly and began to learn the terrain. It adapted, as she suspected it was designed to, to the new terrain. Pretty quickly, all things considered. It took the best part of an hour, but once it was done the journey was smooth and uneventful. The worst part was hearing the grinding of metal against ice as it got a handle on things.

Once they were set, the Squib moved quickly. Van Riet

kept the map projected on the wall, and the little dot that represented them was bounding across the ice at great speed. It crested drifts taller than itself, though the passengers only knew this because they were listed on the map. The Squib climbed them without effort or indication, keeping the command centre perfectly steady now except for the rarest of thuds.

No-one dared speak during the journey. The noise of the motors wasn't subtle, but it wasn't deafening either. It was insistent, and it was almost as if the passengers were scared of offending it and having the motors grind to a sulking halt. Instead they opted for pointed looks at one another, attempting to convey entire messages through a single glance.

Lucille and Wendy were skilled at this, van Riet also. The other two merely looked continuously bewildered and constipated. They got ignored pretty quickly.

Van Riet's glances were the most interesting, however. He was beside himself with glee, that was obvious, but seemed to maintain a baseline of concern. It wasn't something he was trying to hide though, merely overpower with his unbridled happiness. She couldn't decide if it was a little cute or entirely creepy.

The more they moved, the more she wanted to ask where they were going, why they were striding confidently into the storm belt, why they were all so calm about it, but she knew what the answer would be. They'd tell her to wait, that it would all be explained sufficiently at their destination, as they had before. And perhaps it would be, but if she accepted that then it would stop her thinking about what everything they had already told her actually meant. Then she'd have a lot of spare processing power to worry about *walking face first into the storm belt.*

She had expected to feel the buffering as they passed into the belt, some sort of sign that things were about to get dangerous. Granted, there hadn't been much of that when the storm engine was active, but they had been thoroughly wedged into the ice at the time. Now they were fully exposed, yet the going was completely smooth.

Van Riet caught her questioning gaze and nodded to his console. She frowned and looked at her own. It took her a moment, but nestled deep in the various readouts was the pertinent information: the storm drive was active again, projecting what she assumed would be its own little eye of the storm. She'd not really had the time to consider this application before, what with it being beyond their control and them being on a timetable, but it was giving her ideas now.

A massive storm drive mounted to a city could eliminate the need to keep it mobile. It would make approaching it difficult, but no more so than trying to catch one that was never in the same place twice. The storms would just wash around it, deflected by the city's own guardian storm. Not ideal, but a much better situation.

Except, was it? If what van Riet had said was true, that a whole host of these malfunctioning across the globe had caused the ice and the storms in the first place, running a number of them at that size could have untold effects. But still, it would be worth the risk.

Christ, maybe van Riet and his lot were onto something.

She turned her attention back to the dot on the map. Less thinking, more staring, make the time go quicker. It wasn't as if she needed all the random thinking colouring her already uncertain view of the situation any further.

Eventually they arrived, and the motors spun down to a gentle ticking over. Van Riet stood up and stretched, as did the rest of his team. Wendy watched them for a moment before following suit, surprised at how many muscles decided it was necessary to pop.

'That was much easier than usual,' van Riet said. He had folded one arm over his shoulder and was trying to grab his hand from below with the other. 'Like a hot knife through butter.'

'It's been a long time since I was last here,' Lucille said. 'Will that be a problem.'

Van Riet shook his head. 'I shouldn't think so. Hasn't been any command turnover since you left, that's all that matters.'

Wendy held up a hand. 'Excuse me? Where exactly are we?'

'He wants it to be a surprise,' Lucille said. 'Same way it was when I was recruited. He likes the big reveal.'

Van Riet shrugged. 'I'm a no-thrills sort of guy, allow me this one extravagance.'

Wendy wasn't impressed, but she didn't want to push the issue. Things were getting too friendly, all things considered, and that made her uncomfortable. It was especially daunting how accepting she found herself of them now, mere hours after what they had done. That they were too personable to be evil just made it worse.

'For what it's worth,' Lucille said. 'It is a pretty stunning reveal.'

Wendy sighed. 'Fine, but can we get on with it?'

'That directness will win you a few friends around these parts, Milton,' van Riet said. 'Come on, I'll give you the big reveal.'

'Because that doesn't sound suggestive as hell,' she muttered to herself as, practically skipping, he led her out of the command centre.

They took a short journey down one deck, to a hatch in the hull. Wendy hadn't passed this way before, being that this was deep in the Squib when it had been lying so awkwardly, but it wasn't hard to recognise it as a docking port. The door was a thick steel, heavy with bolts and rivets, hermetically sealed and all other manner of imposing. Even without the hand print scanner, it was a door going to great lengths to look important. Thus, docking port.

'If you'd be so kind,' van Riet said, indicating the

scanner.

Wendy placed her hand on the scanner slowly. The panel glowed momentarily and then, with a hiss, the door unbolted. 'That shouldn't have worked. How does it even know –'

'They weren't very reverent when it came to personal privacy back then,' he said. 'If you've touched anything on this thing, some manner of camera will have scanned your fingerprints. It'll have a whole digital render of you right about now, I should think. Of all of us.'

'That's intensely sinister.'

'On this, I think we are both agreed. They did a lot of things wrong back then.'

'Are we better now?'

'God no. Just different. That's not a judgement though, just an observation.'

When the hissing finally stopped, another couple of bolts popped inside the door and it slowly swung open. On the inside was another door, not nearly as secure, opened by a wheel in the centre. Without waiting for van Riet's recommendation, Wendy gave it a spin and stepped out onto a gantry mounted to the hull.

Lucille hadn't been wrong; it was one hell of a view.

Stretching out below her, orbited by a vicious arrested storm, was an actual city. Not one that walked or drove or hovered, just buildings sprouting up from the ground, hundreds of them, some stretching up towards the sky in ways to rival even the tallest of cities. And on the ground were patches of green and, what looked like... trees.

Van Riet joined her at the railing, resting on his elbows and soaking in the scenery. 'Welcome Home.'

'What?'

'Home. That's what we named this place. It works as both a statement of intent and a handy code when out and about. People don't tend to get suspicious when you start talking about *home*.'

'It's beautiful.'

'Looks better from above, believe me,' he said, pointing down at the city. 'See that greenery? Fake grass to replace the failed attempts to grow the real thing. Those *trees?* Fake too.'

'Still,' she said, eyes glistening. 'I stand by what I said.'

'I'm not trying to tell you otherwise, just keeping your expectations in check. I don't want you dazzled into accepting us, that's hollow. It's got to come intellectually.'

She looked at him. 'I'm perfectly capable of making up my own mind, thanks. I'm not about to be hoodwinked just because your city looks pretty.'

'Good. Enjoy the view though, it'll be a few minutes before they get us down from here.'

She didn't need his permission to do that. It was easy to see why some people might be stunned into acceptance just from seeing the place, despite what she had said before. It wasn't just the greenery – although that was impressive even if it were artificial – but the *space*. The buildings were big and numerous, but there were gaps between them, even courtyards that seemed to serve no purpose other than to merely exude space.

Space was at a premium on the Crawler, and it was the same with the galleon. She had forgotten what it looked like to have a square foot that didn't contain a person. Though, she conceded, from this vantage point she couldn't really make out the people. The Squib was taller than she expected, though hardly giant, but there didn't seem to be much movement on ground level in any case.

The tallest buildings stood in the centre of the city, four or five gleaming towers covered in the dancing reflections of the storms roaring about the boundaries. The other buildings crept out along the floor like roots, smaller but no less sublime in their appearance. She could stare at that sight for hours and still be content if she never actually set foot there.

It took ten minutes, but she'd get her chance nonetheless.

A platform, complete with what seemed to be a cabin of some kind, rose into view so silently that it made her jump. Van Riet grabbed her as she did so and held her still, politely, as it finished latching itself to the gantry. When it was done he released her, and she stuck her head over the side, trying to check underneath the platform for its origin. It sat atop a thick, segmented shaft that stretched down to a base on the ground below, surrounded by a small crew of people dashing around.

There was a whooshing sound as the cabin opened and a woman with short auburn hair and a seemingly permanent smirk popped her head out. 'Welcome Home, Casper. Nicely done.'

He stepped forward and hugged her. 'It's good to be back, Lacey. This is Wendigo –'

Wendy interjected on instinct. 'Wendy.'

'Excuse me. This is *Wendy* Milton, someone who I think could have a place here.'

Lacey's entire face lit up and she clambered out of the cabin and onto the gantry, wrapping her arms around Wendy in a strong hug. 'Oh good! It's lovely to meet new people! I'm Doctor Larissa Charles, but everyone calls me Lacey because Larissa sounds a bit meh, don't you think?'

Wendy didn't return the hug. This was all very odd. 'I guess?'

'Oh, sorry!' Lacey released her. 'I didn't mean to get overly familiar. I've got a bit of a problem with that, but everyone here is a sort of family now. There's not many of us.'

'While I appreciate the warm welcome, I had a family. They were killed very shortly after *Casper* turned up.'

Lacey's friendly demeanour vanished in an instant as she whirled on the man. 'Explanation?'

'The scene had to be sterilised, and our agent on site didn't vouch for them. She did the deed –'

'Grow up and use the proper word, Casper.'

'*Killed* them herself. It had to be done, but this one –'

'Thank you, that's enough I think,' she said and turned back to Wendy. 'Well, you must think we are evil as fuck, huh?'

'The thought had crossed my mind.'

'I'm guessing he's done his best to give you the talk about why that sort of behaviour is necessary, and it didn't really do much to make things better, yeah?'

'Something like that.'

'Then I'll spare you another go at it. Let me show you around instead. I often find context helps.'

She gingerly climbed back up to the cabin and offered Wendy a hand. There was an odd pattern on the skin of her arm, a uniform spackling that Wendy didn't recognise. No matter, she took her hand anyway and let the doctor help in hoisting her up onto the platform. Van Riet followed, quietly, and took up residence in the furthest corner he could manage from the two women.

Lacey pulled a lever and the platform began to descend. 'I'm assuming the rest of your posse are staying on the vessel for the handover?'

Van Riet grumbled. 'Figured it would be best for the kid if she got a more personal introduction. And, like you say, someone has to be around for the handover.'

'Usually the best way,' she said. 'Wendy, I hope you don't feel like I'm talking around you. This isn't the best way to bring people into the fold and it has its quirks, but you're here as an equal.'

'I still don't know where *here* is.'

Lacey shot a disappointed look at van Riet. 'Home is, as best we can tell, the last remnant of an old world city. The only one to survive the ice, at least that we've found. Even then, only barely. There's a storm drive in the central spire, keeps the weather at bay, which is how we're still here, and a fair few of the amenities enjoyed by the old world are still in place here.'

'Your own little paradise?'

She ran her other hand through her hair, scratching the

back of her neck. This one wasn't spackled. 'We certainly like to tell ourselves that, but only to lighten our spirits. This sort of stability comes with a duty to those who live the more nomadic life out there. Our model of survival isn't sustainable to the world at large, but with this freedom we have the luxury of time to look into ways to reverse what the old world did. To cure the planet.'

'Yeah? And how's that going?'

'Slowly,' Lacey said. 'We still don't know all the specifics of what happened, and without that it's a hard thing to reverse.'

'You know more than the rest of us, apparently.'

The cabin lurched as it finished descending, and the doors opened onto a field of the fake grass. Lacey stepped out and signalled for the other two to follow her. 'I'll show you to the technical library, that's where we keep all the documentation that pertains to what happened, originals and translations. I don't expect you'll get much use out of the originals, but you're welcome to re-translate them yourself if you don't trust the authenticity of our versions.'

Most of the people they passed were making a very concerted effort to not be seen staring, but she caught a few heads turning when they thought they were out of view. It should have worried her, she thought, but instead it was just making her self-conscious. The more they stole a stare or two, the more she became aware how under-dressed she was.

Wendy's clothes were functional and well-used – patched and sewn together with whatever was lying around – but these people were pristine. It wasn't even that the clothes were a weird fashion, it was all perfectly recognisable as the same sort of stuff worn in the cities, it just didn't look lived in.

'How many people live here?' she said.

Lacey slowed her pace for a moment. 'Permanent residents, about fifty. Double that if you include the ones we have out there. They don't get back much, it's a bit suspicious if they go missing.'

'But this place is enormous. You barely have anyone living here.'

'The more people we have, the greater the risk something go wrong. And before you mention it, while there is enough room for the people out there to live here, it wouldn't work.'

'Why not?'

'More people, more instability, more energy gets devoted to keeping everything running, less work gets done on fixing the planet. It sounds harsh, but we're playing the long game here.'

'But you want to bring me in.'

'We recruit in small numbers, and only those with skills we can use. Read enough things in here, you should understand why.'

They had arrived at one of the larger buildings on their particular ring. It was a square like the others – a prefab building – but taller if not wider, with fewer windows. A steady trickle of wizened-looking people were going in and out, continuing the tradition of ignoring Wendy until they were out of view.

Lacey led the pair through the queue, garnering a few tuts at first until they recognised her, then it diminished to merely sour glances. A sleepy older gent behind a desk greeted her as they passed, and she directed her full exuberance at him for a moment without slowing down.

A few steps later, they entered the library proper, and Wendy found herself stunned yet again.

Her home, her real one, had never had much of a library. There wasn't the space. Books were digital – much easier to store – for the most part, and the physical ones made their way around the people by the weird magic of social networking. This library, however, was nothing but books, to the point that the floor kept descending, one big round pit, so there could be more walls upon which to mount them.

'So we keep everything from the old world in this place, and that's a lot of stuff,' Lacey said. 'Pretty much everything on this level is the more technical stuff, specifically design documents, manuals, reports on experiments, that sort of thing. The stuff below ground is the tangential stuff – logs and journals and things like that. Personally, I'd recommend you stay on the ground floor for now.'

'This is a lot of stuff.'

Lacey nodded. 'A bit overwhelming? Almost all of it was here when we first started out. We've collected a few books and the like, but mostly we're about reclaiming technology. Honestly, I don't think most of these books have even been read. We keep the most pertinent things, the inspiring stuff, on that table in the centre.'

There *was* a table in the centre, under a slightly brighter light than the rest of the place. A collection of books was stacked atop it, with one in particular leaning against the others, open, as if on a lectern.

'What is it?'

'Contemporary news reports, mostly,' Lacey said. 'The other books are what we use to check on the facts, but that one book is the seed from which all this grew. It was enough for everyone here. We'll wait here if you want to take a look, we don't want to unduly influence you.'

Now Wendy was starting to feel scared again. This was all getting a bit too close to religion for her – a single book that apparently caused epiphanies in all the people in this place seemed unlikely. More likely they were looking for something to believe, something to nicely explain the hardships of the world. It was hardly unheard of for people in the cities to come to religion this way, and she didn't blame them at all.

But she had never been one to take things on faith, and now she was actually walking towards a book that promised it would make her all right with killing. That was what this boiled down to, wasn't it? This was the source of their excuse to take human lives, and that was the most terrifying part of all of this.

Especially if it was right.

She sat down at the desk and began to read.

The book was full of news clippings that had been pasted to the left pages, the translations hand-written on the mirroring right hand one. A long and curious narrative that seemed to support what van Riet and Lacey had told her.

The earlier reports were small stubs, concerned with a breakthrough in how they would power their cities. An increase in solar power, but drawn directly from the sun without the need for solar farms, transmitting that power wirelessly to the grid. Scientists were, the small piece insisted, very excited about the prospects.

The stories continued in this vein for a while, getting larger and more in depth, but all saying the same thing: this would solve our problems. Wendy had to agree, it certainly sounded promising, though she only had a few thousand words of assurance from scientists to go on. It did match up with some things she had read during her education, though. Impossible for them to even conceive of building these days, but a great thought experiment.

Eventually, the articles started to turn. Slowly the message of the pieces moved away from extolling the virtues of this new power source and became much more concerned with the speed at which it was being implemented. The same scientists that had been excited about it were decrying how fast it had been rushed through testing, and the dangers that might bring.

This is an untested technology, one of them was quoted as saying. *While there is a great potential gain from the construction of a Dyson sphere, especially now we actually have the capability to construct one, to launch into that endeavour so soon is foolhardy. From a purely industrial standpoint, the infrastructure isn't there to exploit such a device to its fullest potential just yet, and from a scientific perspective we simply haven't run enough experiments.*

We know that we can harness the sun, that much we have established. We know that we can transmit this power wirelessly. We know that, when this technology is ready, it will end the energy crisis for good. But we don't know what toll this will take on both our society and our planet. To go from small experiments in the laboratory to worldwide implementation is both foolish and profoundly sinister, in my opinion.

He reappeared several times over the next few months, repeating the same warning but being given less and less space each time. Slowly he was silenced by the press, who returned to championing the cause of this Dyson sphere.

None more so than the penultimate entry.

Police clashed with protestors today at the launch site for what has come to be known as the Enlightenment Project. Today, after years of work, the final piece of phase one will be launched, and by the end of the month it will be installed upon the burgeoning station.

While some have maintained a vocal opposition to the project, the Minister for Environment and Energy has recently released a statement labelling such opposition "irresponsible" and "on the wrong side of history", arguing that "now is the time to look to the stars, not remain shackled to the earth".

In response to opposition claims that the project has been rushed due to the astronomical rise in oil prices and the increase in rolling blackouts across many major metropolitan areas, he was also quoted as saying "these people are afraid of change, plain and simple" and that "we have taken all necessary precautions to ensure this is the best route forward for our people".

Several members of the scientific community have refuted this statement, however, though it must be said that in a poll conducted by WePol.gov over eighty percent of people support the Enlightenment Project, putting the naysayers very much in the minority.

While it was interesting, Wendy had to admit she wasn't finding the clarity in these reports that she had expected. An apocalyptic narrative, sure, but nothing that would drive her to such fanatical lengths as the people of Home. She already knew how this story would end, what with having lived it, and it wasn't a shock when she turned the final page to a piece describing how a fleet of marketing walkers were currently plunging the world into a blizzard.

There was nothing here that exonerated them for what they had done. It provided an explanation for the ice, maybe, but a simplistic one at best. A world-shattering catastrophe couldn't happen so easily, surely. There had to be a thousand little nuances to the actual events that brought them to this point. If this alone had brought all of them into the fold, then *that* was the frightening thing. The simple narrative of man dabbling in technology too advanced for them wasn't the whole story, and these people were taking it as damn near gospel.

Wendy scratched her chin and stared at the pages again. She was in trouble. They had tolerated her presence because they believed they would honestly sway her with this document, or at least get her to see why what they did was necessary. They didn't and it hadn't. Now she was in the middle of, essentially, a secret base full of zealots.

Over her shoulder, she could see van Riet and Lacey talking quietly while watching her. They looked so hopeful, almost excited. Was she the final piece in some great puzzle for them? Probably not, that was putting way too much importance on herself, and she knew it. The most important thing about her was her complete and total control of the Squib, and that was only because they had allowed her to take it.

Unless that was all a ruse too.

She was slipping into paranoia now, second guessing everything. It had been all fine and acceptable before, when the evidence was still some nebulous abstract thing that, she could believe, would justify the cold-blooded killing of two of her friends, that would explain how that could happen and those involved remain so affable. That sort of test was difficult to rationalise, but not impossible.

There was still too much she didn't know. The actual mechanics of the thing, the true cause, the possibility for a reversal. First it had been the doorstep pitch, and now the pamphlet. They were trying to drip-feed her into believing while making it look like she was discovering it on her own pace.

Maybe this really was just paranoia, but they had killed the captain and Thor, which justified that more than a little. But what options did she have? Make a scene, push the issue of the Squib, get shot anyway? Humour them, go a little deeper into the rabbit hole, make her inevitable escape attempt harder?

All she had done since this began was make this *inevitable* escape harder. She had to concede now, in the middle of a hidden fortress surrounded by an eternal storm front, that she was not the best at thinking on her feet.

Lacey and van Riet had been joined by a third party now, and their conversation had grown considerably more animated. The good doctor seemed the most involved of the three, that playful exuberance slipping yet again as she quietly but firmly railed on the new man. Van Riet was considerably less involved, it seemed, but his expression was cold.

Wendy closed the book and walked back up to them.

'– wasn't unexpected,' the new man was saying. 'She took a little initiative.'

Lacey spoke slowly, quietly, but with great care. 'While we put her where we did for her initiative, it was with the understanding that things of this magnitude not happen.'

'Larissa, please,' van Riet said. 'She couldn't have known –'

'She is responsible for her choices, Casper. She knew that from the moment she contracted an outsider. We told her, repeatedly to keep it in the family, and she ignored us. Now this?'

He swallowed. 'What do you want us to do? There's still time to call it off.'

'Our hands are tied now,' she said, pinching the bridge of her nose. 'Proceed as usual. When it's done, come back to me and talk me out of doing something drastic with her, okay?'

Van Riet and the other man nodded in unison and turned to leave. The new man tried to start a conversation, but van Riet shut him down promptly. Evidently he was smart enough to know that Lacey clearly didn't want to hear anything as they were leaving. She watched them intently as they left, however.

Wendy waited until they were out of sight. 'What was that all about?'

Lacey looked at her with heavy eyes. 'Another thing that's going to make us look like monsters to you. I'm going to take a guess and say the book didn't convince you?'

'Not entirely.'

'You're kind to sugar the pill like that, but please, speak your mind.'

'I think I see where you are coming from,' Wendy said. 'But it's too reductive. There's more going on that just the technology, even if it *was* the technology that did it. This secretive cabal, stealing and hoarding things because the world at large can't be trusted? I don't see the basis for that. I'm sorry.'

'Don't be. Sometimes I worry that we're too insular here. A closed system. We're just echoing the same thoughts over and over again with no thought to question them. We're all guilty of that, I think. Don't get me wrong, I still think what we're doing is right, but sometimes... Sometimes it feels a hell of a lot like it borders on wrong.'

'What's happened?'

Lacey blinked her watery eyes. 'We might have just destroyed the Strider.'

SEVENTEEN

Wendy listened as Lacey explained the situation. She tried to take it on board and look at it from their side, for no other reason than trying to understand the reasoning, but it was difficult.

They had a number of people inside the cities, of that much she had already been made aware. One of them, apparently, had been placed reasonably high in one city so as to facilitate the more important subterfuges necessary for such a clandestine agenda. All made sense so far.

This agent had, in turn, contracted her own agents, oblivious to the cause, and somehow this agent had managed to wipe out an entire god damn city.

Nope, she wasn't finding an avenue towards understanding here.

'We... *I* always knew that any situation that required her attention could end up this way,' Lacey said. 'They would always involve doing something big, dangerous. But this... Was this too far?'

'Are you genuinely asking me that?' Wendy said. 'Because personally, I think everything I've seen of you people is *too far.*'

'Come with me,' Lacey said, taking her hand. 'Please.'

Wendy allowed herself to be led outside, across the fake grass to a bench under a fake tree. The pair of them sat down and got a good look at the rest of the city in the distance. Another beautiful vista, Wendy could concede that much.

Lacey was staring deeper into the distance. 'I just want to give this to the world. I want to make everyone ready to have things like this, stability and safety. The killing, it was never supposed to be anything more than cutting off frayed edges. Loose ends. Keeping *us* safe so we can make *them* safe.'

'I know; you've told me this before. And, if I'm honest, the frequency at which you keep doing this makes me think you're not really trying to convince me at all.'

'You think I'm trying to convince myself?' Lacey said, still not making eye contact. 'Of course I am. I sign off on killings every day. *Sterilising,* that's what we call it. It's less repellent if you don't call it what it is. So yes, *of course* I'm trying to remind myself that this is the right course of action, and every time we bring in someone new, as rare as that is, they help shore up these beliefs. To a man, they have agreed with the cause after some time in the library.'

'But that book –'

'It's not the book that does it. The people already believe when they get here. They see the city, which is beautiful, and they don't want to leave. Why would they? As soon as they see that this is a place that doesn't move, they feel safe for the first time in their lives. That book could say that the ice was brought by a knock-kneed space ferret with bad breath and a toupee, they'd find meaning in it just to stay here. I'm not so deluded that I don't know that.'

'Is that book even true?'

'Every word,' she said. 'I don't do lying. I don't want people here because they've been tricked. I want them to believe that we can make the world better, and I want them to be people who can do that. You can't trick people that smart, not for prolonged periods. They work you out eventually, and juggling that many lies is doomed to failure anyway. Better they fool themselves. Most of them at least want the full tour before they commit, that's when we know we've got a keeper.'

'But not me.'

'Admittedly, most of our recruits don't get brought straight from the scene of their friends getting killed. That was always going to make you suspicious of us. You'd never see how important what we do is when that's your first impression, right?'

Wendy looked away. Everywhere she looked it was beautiful, it was starting to get annoying. She had begun longing for something ugly to look at to make this easier. 'How are you all so friendly?'

'What do you mean?'

'I had no idea at all that there was anything off about Lucille until she shot my friends. Van Riet and his people levelled threats at me, but they didn't seem to enjoy it, and they still brought me here, to you. He even let me lock him out of the Squib's computer as a show of trust.'

'I don't know,' Lacey said. 'Maybe our priorities have gotten screwed somewhere along the way. But killing off an entire city does make one a bit reflective.'

'I can imagine.'

'You want to leave, don't you?'

'If I say yes are you going to shoot me?'

Lacey closed her eyes and smiled. 'I think, perhaps, there has been enough killing today. But if you leave, you can never come back. There won't even be a question of letting you in, you'd die the second you stepped out of that storm.'

'As if I could make it through there anyway.'

'You'll have something with a storm drive. You've already made it through once.'

'What?'

Lacey finally looked at Wendy. 'Casper's little show of

trust wasn't a trick. He really did let you lock everyone else out of the command system of that walker. We've got a crew on there now trying to break that lock, but you were right in what you told him – that's months of work. We could take you prisoner, or kill you, but we're not those people.'

'Not to tempt fate, but you definitely *are*. Lucille shot my friends for considerably less reason than that.'

'Then maybe I'm just trying to make us better.'

Wendy had a shot all lined up there. *Better at killing thousands of people, maybe,* she thought, but declined to actually say. She could sense that this, finally, was the truth of the matter, and it would be cruel to lay the boot in at this point. There was solace to be taken in knowing that *she* was better than these people, it didn't need flaunting.

Lacey went quiet. Made sense, that level of rampant friendliness fit perfectly with someone on the very cusp of an internal crisis. It had to have been brewing for a long time, and whatever had happened with the Strider had been the final straw. Despite everything, Wendy felt a need to comfort her.

'I agree with some of what you're doing here. How could I not?' she said. 'Thawing the world is a noble goal, but the methods... I would rather see the world frozen solid than support something that saw my friends killed.'

'That's quite short sighted.'

'I don't care.'

'Van Riet was wrong to bring you here.'

'No, I think he was right,' Wendy said. 'No-one will listen to me out there, it's not as if I could fashion an army to come and stop you. Nothing will change. But you've had someone to talk to who isn't on your side. I think that's what you needed.'

'Nothing will change here either,' Lacey said, standing up. 'We all have a *cause* here, and it is important, but I won't jeopardise *all this* either. This is *ours.*'

'I know.'

Lacey began to walk away, and Wendy couldn't find it in her to stop the woman. What would be the point? The argument wasn't going anywhere. This level of, well, sacrifice just wasn't in her, she knew that now. It was time to leave.

The doctor stopped but didn't turn. 'Before you leave, give us one more chance. Walk the streets a little, meet the people. Maybe that will convince you, maybe not, but you should see what you are abandoning before you make your choice.'

Wendy frowned as the woman walked off. *It was time to leave.* And yet...

To come all this way, to see her friends die, and to not at least explore the hidden city it had all led to? This decision was *drowning* in the sunk cost fallacy, but she couldn't pass that up. Could she?

She stood up and started walking. Even as she rose, she had intended to walk away, back towards the Squib, to leave despite herself. But her legs had other ideas, they ignored what she had been thinking and led her inwards, past the library and into the city proper.

It grew eerily empty very quickly. If what Lacey had said was true, that only fifty people lived here full time, then it was to be expected that the place would have huge areas that were just abandoned, but that didn't make it any less spooky. There wasn't even the sound of people nearby – no thundering machines in the distance, no cacophony of voices.

Did people live like this once? In *silence*? Wendy had had to hear the Crawler's turbines droning away from the moment she was born. She didn't really hear it anymore, it was just how the world sounded, it was a *fact*. The hardest part of being out on the galleon had been the nights when they had the luxury of time enough to sit still, to kill the razors and just bask.

That wasn't true silence, not like this, but it was the closest she had been. No machine noise, just the odd creaking of aging steel and the quiet breathing of the crew as they slept. It left her with too much time to think, and yet also somehow suffocated her. It made the world close in on her, felt it press against her skin, made her heart quicken.

Hell, right now she could hear her heartbeat louder than the sentinel storm.

She hadn't turned any corners, and yet she felt lost. From the Squib, the city had looked to be nothing but gleaming white spires, but up close it was a little different. Some buildings were white, true, but far more were covered in huge panes of glass, reflecting the storm in new and interesting ways, sending her eyes spinning.

Wendy took solace under a tree. The path she was walking had been lined with them at regular intervals, sprouting up from circles carved into the paving stones, all uniform in their artificiality. It may have been an approximation of a real tree, but even knowing that didn't make the bark feel any less real.

In the shade of the tree, her heart began to slow, and with the rampant drumbeat gone from her ears she could just about make out a noise on the very edge of her hearing. She began to follow it, tracking it through the streets. It was people, the raucous din of people just being people.

She found them sat outside a building with a sign that said *café*. Fifteen of them perhaps, clustered into various groups across a number of tables, all of them sipping what looked to be warm drinks from sleek white mugs. They didn't care to notice her as she approached.

Van Riet was there, alone at a table, nursing the same white mug as the rest of them, looking deeply pensive. He looked up and spotted her, then nodded and kicked out the chair opposite him. Wendy approached and sat down.

'Fancy seeing you here,' he said, grinning. 'There are a lot of perks of living here, but coffee is probably my favourite.'

'Do you all just get very wistful when you come home?'

He laughed. 'I suppose we do, a little. Those of us that leave, we play a lot of different parts. Home is the only place we can be ourselves, drink our coffee, relax. You know what I mean?'

'Sure.'

'How do you like the place?'

'It's too quiet. A place this big needs more than fifty people living in it.'

Van Riet took a long, loud slurp from his mug. 'You're not wrong. Let me show you something.' He pulled a small tablet from his pocket, unfolded it into something larger, and tapped at the screen. A map flashed up on it. 'A pet project of mine and a few others. Lacey says it's a fantasy, but she has her science and I have mine.'

Wendy leaned over the tablet. 'What am I looking at?'

'The hope is that, eventually, we'll save the world. Then, and only then, we'll open up Home to the bulk of the citizens out there. I figured that they'd need somewhere to call their own. I've been dividing the city into zones for each and every city.'

Wendy squinted at the map. It was detailed work, she had to admit that. The city had been divided into sectors, each devoted to a certain mobile city, then subdivided again for the types of people inside them. From what she could tell, he'd even gone to the trouble of finding ways to allow them to easily intermix socially should they want to, without feeling the pressures of proximity.

'This is very detailed,' she said.

'Thank you,' he replied. 'We've got a fair few people out there, gathering intelligence on your cities. Most of us came from them after all, we know what things are like there.'

'Most of you?'

'Home isn't new, Wendy,' he said. 'We do our fair share of bonking, you know. There are babies born here from time to time.'

'Well, thanks for that information.'

'You asked.'

She shrugged. 'Doesn't look like you've updated this for a while.'

'Excuse me?'

'You've got cities on here that have been gone for decades. The Floater? The Drifter? You've even got the Sailor on here, and that's been gone at least a century.'

His expression shifted. 'Yeah, well, maybe I'm just more optimistic than some.'

He took another long sip of his drink, then sighed and took back his tablet. Wendy leant back in her chair, which creaked against her weight just a little.

'Lacey wanted me to get a look of the city,' she said. 'To see if I could find something here I liked more than the book.'

'That was how she got me, too.'

Wendy frowned. 'But she said –'

'Yeah, she says a lot of things,' he said. 'The book is important. That log of what we as a species did to this planet, we need that final push, but it's a rare person that makes their decision to stay here because of that. That's the past. A past we don't want to repeat, but personally I don't think we can live on that alone. I needed to see the future, and that's what I saw here.'

'Really?'

'Wendy, look at this place,' he said, sweeping a hand around in a large arc. 'These are buildings. *Buildings.* They stand in firm defiance to all the shit going on out there. I never saw my future as nothing but running – from storms, from poverty, all that stuff. But even in my imagination I couldn't conceive of tranquillity like this. This place is sacred.'

'I'm sure you're aware how that sounds?'

'A little overzealous, I know. The cities aren't bad places; we both know that. But they can't last. You said it yourself, we've been losing them one by one for years now. They're treading water, and eventually they'll drown if someone doesn't throw them a rope. When I saw this place, I saw hope.'

'I understand that, I do –'

'That spire in the centre there,' he said, waving a hand towards the tallest building. 'On my first proper day here I went up to the top of that thing and I just stared down at the city. I used to do that before they recruited me, look down at the world from as high up as I could go. I bet you did the same.'

'I did,' she said. 'The Crawler has an observation deck with big windows, great for when you need a little solitude.'

'I know it,' he said. 'But it's not solitude. You're always aware how close you are to another person. On the other side of a wall, mere inches below you to the next deck. You can't stretch out without getting on someone's toes. From that spire, I could. I felt that freedom for the first time, and I realised how precious that is.'

'So you signed on for space?'

'And what it represents, sure,' he said. 'It's an end to fear. We live so closely packed in those mobile cities because we have to, sure, but also because it lets us feel safe. We've always got someone to hold onto, and that's great. That's the enduring human spirit, and I don't mean to knock it in any way. But that's not how we're meant to live. We should get to choose whether we need to hold someone, not be forced into a life of it. That's all.'

'I get the feeling everyone here has some sort of epiphany story like that, am I right?'

He chuckled. 'I expect so. And I expect you think we're all idiots too, as is your right. I mean, there's a guy at that table there, the one in the off-white jacket with the glasses poking out of the breast pocket, I couldn't help but laugh in his face when he told me his tale. But that's devotion, isn't it? Comes from some bloody weird sources.'

'What was his?'

'It was the trees. Something about the texture of the bark. It takes all sorts.'

Wendy looked around. She could see the Squib in the distance, lurking over the smaller buildings, a distant reminder of where she had come from. The other groups nearby were chatting away happily. She was starting to see it now, the homeliness of the place. It wasn't real in the deserted sections, but just add a few people to the mix...

Van Riet downed his drink and slammed the mug down on the table. 'I'd offer to give you a tour, but I can already tell you've made up your mind. I could take you up the tower, show you the storm engine. I could show you where we grow our food, or build our machines, but it wouldn't sway you, would it?'

Seeing it in motion, this living city, she was closer than she had ever been to signing on. But he was right, something wasn't quite gelling with her.

Slowly, Wendy stood up. 'Thank you.'

She began to walk the streets again, moving away from the little island of society in the long-dead city. Her fingers ran along the bark of the trees again as she moved, and she listened to the wind rustle their leaves. Then she found her way to a patch of grass and did the same, just listened to the wind tickle each individual blade.

The city wasn't silent. It had noises of its own, ones she could learn to absorb as she had with the turbines and the people and the rest of the din of everyday life. Perhaps it wouldn't be so bad to stay after all? If they truly wanted to find a way to give this to everyone out there...

Then she looked up from the grass and realised where she was. The outskirts of the city once more, where she had arrived, the Squib looming over her once more.

She took one last long view of the ghost city that was so tempting a place to stay. As a vision of their future, maybe it could stand for something. Where they had been once before and could be again, that beautiful abstract goal. But as a place that existed now it was lesser, a trap. A gorgeous, enticing one, but one nonetheless.

They were running as much as any of the mobile cities out there.

Christ. When did she get so deep?

After that last lingering look, she turned her back on the city and headed back to the Squib. It wasn't a long walk, but she let herself dawdle, to soak up the experience that had kept so many people here, in the city called Home. That fake grass on her feet, leading up towards the spidery vessel in the near-distance, it did feel pretty good.

She hadn't actually *seen* the Squib before, not really. There had been the schematics on the screens inside, those had given her a rough idea of the shape, same with the wiring and programming diagrams. What she had managed to see for herself had been buried under the ice or entirely internal, which wasn't the same thing.

But now it stood on the horizon, in full contrast to the gleaming white city at her back. This tall, angular beast, painted with colours that had once been bright, almost like a logo. Judging from the billboards pumped forth by the emitters, *exactly* like a logo, in fact. The resolution was too fuzzy to make it out exactly, but the reds and whites seemed to flow in the advert as they did on the paintwork.

With the exception of the legs, which were more than a little menacing as a result of their tapering to a point, the Squib looked remarkably non-threatening now it was upright. It had a civil quality to it, especially when compared with the city it was facing. It looked as though it belonged, and she could picture flocks of them just striding around between the buildings, background noise.

And it was *hers.*

This one thing had started all of this, by accident. If they had never spiked the communication beacon right into the hull, this thing would have laid there undisturbed, possibly forever. The captain and Thor would still be alive. And yet, for all intents and purposes, the people that had done all that had just given it away, to her.

That was going to have to mean something, wasn't it? She couldn't just trot it off to another city now, could she? Sell it off for parts and live out her life in luxury. People had died for this, people she knew and liked. Hell, people she *didn't* know. Lacey had never said it, but there was no way it was coincidental that the city who had expressed an interest in buying the Squib had so suddenly been obliterated. That was connected too.

Either way you sliced it, that was an awful lot of responsibility to throw her way, and she had to address that. The people who resided here, they found their meaning there, perhaps she had just done the same. Good thing she had a big stompy robot to help her in that regard, right? Much easier to make your life mean something when you had one of those at your disposal.

By the time she had reached the platform that would take her back up to the Squib, she was all but certain she was going to start some sort of crusade. This had been an awakening, opened her eyes to the reality of things and...

Oh no, this was what had happened to them. No, she'd keep that at bay. This wasn't a cause, it was something else. Merely a responsibility. Different words for the same thing perhaps, but vastly different connotations. If she had to split hairs at this point, she would.

She could hear the work crews before she even entered the Squib. There was a lot of shouting going on, perhaps identifiable as spirited debate if she was feeling charitable. As she wasn't feeling that, it was a row. Several men and woman were engaged in this contretemps, and they weren't interested in stopping to explain things to Wendy.

So she stood in the doorway and watched them. At least the noise would stop her thinking.

In the centre of the din, sat silent and still, she spotted Lucille. She'd pulled out a chair from one of the terminals and was slowly spinning on it, walking herself in a circle and scowling at all the arguments going on around her. For a moment her eternal rotation brought her eye-to-eye with

Wendy, and she stalled briefly. The scowl slackened, and then she went back to spinning slowly.

'Right, that's enough,' Wendy said quietly, her voice drowned out by the shouting. 'Piss off.'

She snaked her way around the various splinter groups of arguing people and made for the closest terminal. A pair of white-coat-clad men were moaning about something on the screen, but they were so engaged in this discussion that she could firmly shove them aside without complaint. Once she had done so, the screen dutifully changed into the same control panel it had before. It even helpfully defaulted to security.

Wendy found it hard not to laugh as she pressed the button for the alarm. It became even harder when she saw the reaction. The noise was ridiculously loud for such a small space, and it hammered off the metal walls indignantly, as if it was actively trying to escape. Instead, it was forced inwards punching people in the head as it did so out of pure, intense vexation.

The arguments ended instantly under such an assault. A dozen or so confused faces turned on her in a flash, jaws agape and eyes wide, as if she had crashed their brains somehow. She let the alarm ring for a couple more seconds, then killed it before the crowd could reboot.

'Out,' she said. 'This is my property and I want you all to bugger off.'

There were murmurings of dissent, but they didn't last. Maybe she was conveying a suitable air of don't-fuck-with-me-right-now to shut them up, or perhaps they just simply didn't have the energy to fight her on this. A number of them looked relieved as they threw up their hands and left the command centre. All except Lucille, who stayed in her chair, slowly rotating.

'You too, Lucille,' Wendy said.

'Nope.'

'Get. Out.'

'I don't want to be here either, Wendy. My reasons are

probably different to yours, but I've no intention of staying here. Pretty obvious you're planning on leaving, and I'm coming with you.'

'After what you've done, I'm not at all concerned with what you *want*. Get out.'

Lucille stood up, kicking the chair back across the room and into the wall. She stormed forward and drew her gun, levelling it at Wendy's face.

Wendy looked past the gun, right at Lucille, who did the same. They said nothing, letting the various unspoken threats hang in the air, mingle with each other, and eventually focus around the drawn weapon. It trembled in the older woman's hands, and Wendy could feel a similar tremor work its way up from the base of her spine.

Then, as suddenly as she had drawn the weapon, Lucille's grip went slack and it rolled forwards onto a single finger. She offered it to Wendy, who carefully retrieved it.

'Three magazines in the lining of my jacket,' she said. 'A knife in my left boot.'

'What are you doing?'

'Surrendering. Anything it will take for you to bring me with you when you leave. Take me to a city, I'll own up to the murders, do my time, whatever.'

'They don't lock people up for murder.'

'Figure of speech. Point being, I'm committed to leaving here with you, and I want to prove it.'

Wendy cautiously removed the items Lucille had mentioned. The knife was a small dagger with a wide base – something that could be braced against the heel of the hand while the blade protruded from between the fingers – and the magazines were well concealed amongst the insulating padding, but they were there and in good nick. The woman had been secretly loaded the entire time.

'Anything else?' Wendy said.

'Not here. Rest of the stuff went up when the ship did.'

'Good, now piss off.'

Lucille suddenly looked very tired. 'I'm not leaving, and you aren't strong enough to physically throw me off of this heap. I've given you the means to kill me, but you won't do that either.'

Wendy looked down at the gun in her hand. She absolutely *could* kill her, couldn't she? After what she'd done? 'No... I won't.'

Lucille nodded and turned away, towards Thor and the captain. 'This has been a right mess, hasn't it?'

'You could say that.'

'What do you plan on doing now?'

Wendy sat down again and looked at the screen. She changed it to the navigation panel. It wasn't as though she had put much thought into her next move, but it had also never been in question. 'I'm going to find the Strider and help the survivors.'

'There won't be any survivors,' Lucille said. 'And if there *are*, there won't be by the time we're through with them. That's how this works.'

'Whatever, I'm going anyway.'

Lucille sighed. 'Then you'll *have* to take me. You don't know where the Strider is or how to find it. I might have an idea.'

'And the price?'

'I just want to leave here.'

'Fine. Tell me how to find it.'

Lucille signalled to the wall. 'Could you bring the map up, please?'

Wendy rolled her eyes but punched it up anyway. It panned over their route for a moment before coming to a halt at where they currently were. Lucille took a few steps over and stared at it. Along the wall, she used her finger to trace various lines.

Wendy crossed her arms. 'Lucille.'

'We've not got many members on the books, we're supposed to keep track of who is where so we can help each other out if we need it. Solidarity. That's a hard habit to break.'

'So?'

'So, I can probably work out where it is by who was in the area. Understand? Here, let me use the computer.'

'Be my guest.'

Lucille wandered over and started typing. A number of small circles appeared on the map all over the place. 'Right, so these are the radii of movement available to the people that could be mobilised to sterilise the Strider at the moment. Most are on cities and would be too conspicuous to activate for this sort of long-term job, right?'

'How many per city?'

'It varies. Doctor Charles likes to move people around from time to time, to make it look like they actually have a life, you know?' She started typing again, and a few of the circles vanished. 'There's still a couple on the cities I wouldn't exactly rule out necessarily, but for ease let's say she'd want something more covert.'

'That's still a frightening number of circles.'

'There's a lot of galleons out building up the network,' she said, deleting more circles. 'But they're sleeper agents like myself, never supposed to go active unless of a big find. So that leaves –'

'Four?'

'Yes. Four galleons crewed entirely by us. One of them is van Riet's, so we can cross that off. That leaves these three here.'

The last three circles had the largest radii, but they didn't intersect at any point. They were reasonably close, however, and seemed to orbit a central point. Judging by their distance from the other cities, Wendy had to guess they were masquerading as survey teams or outriders.

'So that actually leaves us three. Which one would it be?'

Lucille sucked her teeth. 'That's the one advantage of this sort of job. It's *big*. I'd warrant that all three were tasked with it, which means it would have to be within reach of all three of them. So, around here is probably your best bet.'

Another, larger, circle popped up on the map, encompassing a fair chunk of uncharted ice.

'That's nowhere near the main trunk or any of the accepted branch lines,' Wendy said. 'Even on the periphery they'd be taking a chance heading in there.'

'Ice is ice,' Lucille said. 'I'm willing to bet that the pilot of the Strider knew that it's just as dangerous to travel the trunk as it is to go off-piste. Probably worth it for a find such as this.'

'You think he marched the whole city towards the wreck?'

'He did want to verify it personally. Always the chance he'd send a galleon or two to lock things down, but he'd have to take the city there anyway to properly salvage it. He'll have gone off-track.'

'That's still a pretty big area.'

'True, but I can narrow it down even more,' Lucille said. 'If I access Home's meteorological database... There, I can track all the recent storm fronts. To bring down a city so fast, it had to have involved the weather somehow, so if we track it back along its path to where it intercepts this circle...'

'...That's actually not too big an area.'

'So, did I earn my seat?'

Wendy looked at the map. Provided Lucille was correct and this wasn't all just information she had pulled out of her arse, that was a lot of ice she had ruled out. It hardly made up for the murders, but exploiting a murderer for information didn't really ring the morality warning bells either.

'For now,' Wendy said, sliding a fresh magazine into the gun and pocketing the one that had been loaded. 'But I'm keeping these.'

'That's why I gave them to you. If I'd wanted to kill you I wouldn't have recommended you be recruited.'

'So you did want to kill the captain and Thor, huh?'

Lucille went quiet for a moment. 'No.'

'Whatever,' Wendy said. 'If you're staying then go and be useful, make sure that gaggle of wittering nerds have all gotten off the Squib. I don't want to set off and find stowaways.'

Without a word, Lucille acquiesced, leaving the control room. Wendy watched her go and considered sealing the door behind her, but didn't. There was no purpose to Lucille betraying her now and, if she had learned nothing else from these people, they were very keen on there being a purpose for their actions.

It didn't take her long to return, the others having apparently fled rather quickly. She gave Wendy a half-hearted thumbs up and then retrieved her toppled chair. She sat in the centre of the room and went back to slowly rotating, in the opposite direction this time.

Wendy set about programming in the co-ordinates. Van Riet had made it look easy before, pick where you wanted to go and off the Squib trotted. That was, in fact, considerably easier than trying to pilot a galleon, but it was still giving her trouble. It wasn't just tap and go, especially when she had to work out the storm engine as well.

All told, it only took her a couple of minutes, but she was worried that the computer had started to give her a hand at the end. In any case, she felt the welcome lurch as the Squib took its first step, and exhaled happily. It was good to have her own vessel – not as good as serving on the galleon had been – but the freedom that came with it was the next best thing. Back to reality, back to a world where secret cabals don't just swan into your life and ruin it on a whim.

After one last stop, at least.

She activated the storm engine and felt the buffeting shake the Squib a little as it forged a safe path through the natural typhoon. The exit wasn't as graceful as the entrance had been, but neither of the women were thrown from their seats, though Lucille's did slide a little, so Wendy took that as an achievement.

A timer blinked into existence at the bottom of the map, an ETA. It hadn't done that last time, though Wendy had wished it had. Was the computer learning? Adapting itself to make things easier for its new captain? That would be nice, something going well for a change. It had been a while.

Perhaps that was worth investigating. This was her property now, apparently, it would probably be a good idea to understand a bit more how it worked. It wasn't as though she was hard up for time. According to the countdown, she had a few hours to kill anyway.

She also needed to work out what she was even going to do when she hit the Strider, of course. That was arguably more pressing a concern.

I'll wing it, she though. *It's worked out okay for me so far.*

And, she had to admit, that was true. Not so much for those close to her, maybe, but they were all dead now.

Positive thinking.

EIGHTEEN

Rostrum Barley opened his eyes.

He wasn't dead.

For fuck's sake.

As weird as it sounded, he had been hoping he was dead. In those final moments he had been pushing his body to give up, and when he had finally slipped into darkness again it was with the relief that, finally, he was done. But he could hear his heartbeat, the steady thudding of blood pulsing through his head, and it stubbornly refused to cease.

So he opened his eyes, and whatever dark magic had kept the agony at bay for so long was finally broken. What he had been feeling before, all the splits and the burns, that was suddenly as though he had been watching his body through a telescope. Now he was *in* it, and it was hell.

Vandal was curled up on the floor, staring at where the lift shaft had been, muttering to himself. Watching him dulled some of the pain, but not enough.

'Are they here yet?' he managed to say. It was even harder to breathe now.

Vandal's head snapped up towards Rostrum, his eyes wild and bloodshot. 'You're not dead?'

'Not yet. Are they here?'

'I think so,' he said and stood up. He walked to the sealed shaft and placed his ear to the wall. 'I keep thinking I'll be able to hear them.'

'The Strider is huge,' Rostrum said. 'Only way you'll hear them is if they are right outside the door.'

'I know. But still... It feels wrong to know they are out there without being able to hear them, you know?'

Rostrum tried to sit up. His skin wasn't just tight now, it had stuck to the chair. The various oozing juices had formed a sort of paste, damn near gluing his back to the upholstery. It hurt to unstick himself, but then so did everything at this point.

He stood up and shuffled over to the array of terminals that had appeared when he enacted martial law. The bank of monitors was dead, as were the things they were connected to, but he had a small notion. They might not be able to do much up here, but perhaps they could still *see*.

A few keystrokes and a fair portion of the screens blinked to life, the cameras in the eyes of the goddesses. Most didn't work, and those that did were hardly clear pictures, but it was a view of what was left of the Strider, and that was enough.

Vandal peered over his shoulder. 'What are you doing?'

'Won't be able to hear them, but maybe you can see them. You're welcome.'

Rostrum shuffled back to his seat as Vandal stared, completely focused, on the monitors. There seemed to be a decent spread of the city represented in the working cameras, and even a couple who had seemingly been blown free of the Strider were still able to transmit. A fair few were just views of ice and snow, or the sky, but one or two had managed to land so they could see the Strider. From one of these cameras, Rostrum could make out the galleons of their boarders, parked in a neat line a few metres from the wreck. Ropes dangled down from what had once been the dock but was now, as far as he could make out, an orifice of twisted metal. None of the cameras in there had survived, that was certain.

Vandal pointed at a screen. 'There! I think that's them!'

'Where?'

Rostrum followed Vandal's finger to a camera that seemed to be positioned in the remains of engineering. It was a scorched out husk too, just as the core had been, but with fewer people huddled there to experience that level of monstrous death. Now, a trio of sour-faced men with rifles were slowly crunching over the corpses.

Every few steps, one of the men would stoop and check a corpse for signs of life, before sighing and moving on. There was one corpse slumped against the wall, three bullet holes in his chest, but Rostrum couldn't say for sure that it was a result of the men. People do stupid things during a crisis, he had seen that first hand. There were any number of ways that man could have gotten shot.

Though one that was the most likely, admittedly.

They walked out of the room and appeared on another camera, doing the same sweep and clear technique to the bodies in that area. Another team showed up on a third camera doing the same technique – two women and a man, moving quicker than the other group but with no less precision, a few decks up. The cameras only caught the muzzle flashes on the third group, another deck or two above the second.

'You weren't wrong,' Rostrum said. 'Very methodical, aren't they?'

'Just like the rumours said.'

Rostrums console started beeping softly. A message coming through, he recognised that tone. He brought it up. Judging from the protocol used, it was an internal feed.

>>rostrum r u there?

> hi

>> its moses

> youre alive?

>> barely! The fire got me good but I think I got shielded from the worst of it by everyone else

>> I dug myself out and found a few more survivors. We r hiding out in the council offices

> how many of you?

>> thirteen but we think there are more we just havent reached yet, a lot stuck in more exterior rooms

> how do you know?

>> word of mouth from these thirteen and hope mostly

> there are people here to kill us all

>> we know

>> we went down to the docks after your recording, saw the first of them climb in through the doors

>> they opened fire immediately

> you lose anyone?

>> three

> im sorry

>> dont be sorry just tell us how we can fix this

> cant

>> rostrum there are still people alive out here, people to save, thats your job

> maybe but theres nothing to do, we cant stop them

He was, for once in his life, completely out of ideas. It wasn't as though he wanted to roll over and wait for them to kill him – in fact he wanted to roll over and die of his own accord if that was an option – but what could he do?

Vandal caught his eye. The man looked scared, the sort of panic that can only take hold when a controlling personality is robbed of that very same control. He was floundering, splashing about just waiting to drown.

> one sec

'There are thirteen people still alive a couple of decks down,' Rostrum said.

'Not for long.'

'For longer if you help me.'

Vandal threw his head back. 'You just condemned me

to wait out my days locked in this room with you. Why would I help you?'

'Because you didn't want to kill, right?'

'I was prepared to kill. I did kill.'

'But did you *want* to?'

'You know I didn't.'

'Then you'll help. Simple as that.'

'Fine,' Vandal said. 'At least it will give me something to do other than stare at the walls and wait for death. What do you need?'

'I need you to go and get the survivors and bring them back here, to safety.'

Vandal frowned. 'Two problems there, chief. One, they'll breach here eventually, it's not safe. Two, there's no way in or out of here.'

'It's safer than out there. And there is a way in and out of here, I told you about it when I sealed you in.'

'You can't be serious.'

'Out the window, it's only a single deck down. That's barely a climb at all.'

'It's mad is what it is.'

Rostrum tried a comforting smile, but the tightening flesh on his face wouldn't allow him such expression. 'It is, but it might save some lives if you are fast enough.'

'I don't even know where to go. The layout of the council deck wasn't consistent across the schematics.'

'Constantly remodelled. Politicians are very demanding. Take an eye from one of the robots, I'll guide you over the speakers.'

'Won't the killers hear?' Vandal said, but he was already wrenching a glass eye from one of the goddesses.

'Only if they're on that deck, by which point it won't matter.'

With a crunch, an eye came free. 'Will this even work?'

'It has a small battery; it should last long enough to get you there. Just don't dawdle.'

Vandal affixed the eye to his jacket, threading the wire

that protruded from the back of it through button holes to hold it steady. He watched its feed on the monitors. 'I guess it does work. So, what am I doing?'

'Out the window, down one level, try to find a way in. I'll guide you from there.'

'Brilliant.'

Rostrum watched Vandal as he stepped out onto the balcony. He did a remarkable job of not looking absolutely terrified of what he was about to do, even after he peered over the edge. It was easier than it looked, and Rostrum considered telling him as such, but words weren't going to help. Break a leg, don't trip, hold on tight, nothing really seemed appropriate.

Vandal took a few deep breaths, then flipped himself over the balcony and out of sight. Rostrum would have to rely on the camera now.

To his credit, Vandal was moving faster than Rostrum had. The man was either more sprightly than he appeared, or was overcompensating for his fear with sheer speed. In either case, it was working. He hopped gracefully from outcrop to outcrop, carefully placing his landings in the middle of the platforms just in case.

The storm had, unsurprisingly, battered the surface of the Strider, though, and after the first few hops things became more difficult. Vandal had to force himself to slow down, judge his movements more thoughtfully. Huge sections of plating had been pounded flat or ripped clean entirely. It was worse further down, but it still made things slow going even at this level.

On the plus side, it did make it easier for Vandal to gain entrance. One plate had not gone quietly, taking with it the segment of inner wall that it protected. A lovely, spacious hull breach.

Vandal swung himself through and landed awkwardly. The camera didn't give the best view of the surroundings, but it didn't matter. Rostrum knew that deck intimately, he had needed to so as to avoid having to actually talk to the council.

'Head left,' he said, hitting a button on his armrest. 'Look for name plates, that's when you'll know you're in the right place.'

A hand popped into view, giving a thumbs up.

>> rostrum? What r u doing?

> sending help, sit tight

>> help?

> sealed the bridge so if you can get up here it should be a safer place to hold out for a while

>> how do we get up there tho?

> thats why im sending help

Vandal was sprinting down the corridors, checking every door. The council had always demanded more rooms than they had actually needed, but Rostrum hadn't found it quite as annoying as he did now. So many spaces unused that could have been put to a better purpose, all for the ego of the few councillors who wanted to feel as though they were special. It was stupid to feel angry about it now, of course, but who was going to judge him?

There was an odd freedom in being at death's door that he was starting to embrace. Perhaps it was just knowing, with certainty, how this would turn out. Granted, the lives of Moses, Vandal and the others were still very much up in the air, and that wasn't great, but there was only one way this would turn out for him.

He could see how people could give up in moments like this. Hell, he had tried to.

On the screens, the kill teams seemed to have slowed down, at least those he could see. They had moved into areas of the city where the goddesses had not been so fortunate, and a great many of the cameras were offline. Still, despite this, when they did show up on the surveillance, they weren't prowling so much anymore. Instead, they were cataloguing it seemed, writing notes on a small tablet and leaving marks on the walls in pencil. Curious behaviour.

Marking important technology perhaps? There was a lot of incidental technology in the guts of a city like the Strider, all of it tricky to replicate. Stood to reason someone would want to reclaim it once they were done with the witnesses. It would be a waste otherwise. Still, they could have had the decency to wait until they'd cleared the place out. This showed a complete disregard for the survivors, and it was weirdly insulting.

One of the cameras outside went offline, its battery depleted perhaps or the weather interfering with the signal again. He couldn't spy any storms brewing out the window, but at this point nothing would surprise him. He clicked the intercom again.

'Next right, Vandal. You should see the main offices then.'

Another thumbs up and the man swerved as directed. This was a familiar sight, the alleged corridor of power. Getting the gold for the nameplates had been an arduous task, he recalled, but it had been worth it to silence them for a while. Reclaimed gram by gram from damaged and broken tech over the years, finishing each nameplate in turn had swung dissenting voices onto his side. Seemed so pitiful now.

Moses' office was in the centre of them all, and had the most burnished plaque. He'd been the first to get his in gold instead of the traditional dull steel, but it had done little to temper his standoffishness.

'That one.'

A third thumbs up, and Vandal set about trying to pry the door open.

The second kill team popped up on the cameras again, several decks higher than before. They were moving much faster than the team he had spotted cataloguing, it seemed. What did that mean for the unseen third team then? They were already working several decks higher than *this* one, and if they had picked up speed as well...

> moses I need everyone to be ready to go once he

doors open ok?

>> might be hard we have a few injured here but well try

> no choice, theyre moving up fast and I dont know how long we have before they reach your deck

>> understood

>> can hear ur guy at the door, will try to help him

Vandal was having problems, which wasn't a shock. The doors on that level were secure – no-one was more paranoid about their files getting read than a politician – and designed to seal in the event of a power outage, unlike others aboard the Strider. That there was any power on at all was a bit of a miracle, all things considered, so it wasn't unfair to expect that there wouldn't be enough for that particular system.

He tried to find a way to help from his console, but it was a lost cause, a way to keep busy and feel useful.

He could watch the kill teams some more instead, work as overwatch. That was probably the best use of his time, and they kept drawing his eyes anyway.

The first team executed someone on camera. They carried her in from out of view, over the shoulders of one of the men. She was nearly as badly burned as Rostrum had been, and even labelled her as *her* was a bit of a stretch, the few remaining strands of long hair not having succumbed to the fire being the only reason for such a label.

The man set her down gently, leaning her against a wall, and knelt in front of her. He talked and she listened, nodding as best she could. There was a kindness to the whole thing he hadn't expected, and when the man was done he didn't even stand to shoot her, merely drew his gun and put a bullet straight through her head. Then he leant in close and placed his head against hers for a moment.

The other two men were either pretending to ignore the whole thing, or were just very good at focusing on their jobs at hand, because neither deviated from their cataloguing while this went on. It was only once he stood up and wiped her blood from his forehead that they acknowledged him, squeezing his shoulders one after the other in a gesture of understanding.

Rostrum had expected more callousness, and he got that from the second group, though not immediately.

He saw the survivor first. They crawled their way out from under the wreckage of a collapsed section of the city. Small mercies for them, but they had missed any of the firestorms that had roasted most of the people on board, though he was still badly hurt. A few tons of metal crumpling around you isn't about to let you off scot free, after all.

Rostrum had never actually witnessed someone with a concussion, but he assumed that this man was illustrating the effects perfectly. The man moved like he was drunk, but without the sense that he was trying to fight it – as though any control over his motor functions was purely accidental. He tried to stand a couple of times before resigning himself to crawling, and at a decent pace too.

He made it across a few cameras, crawling directly over one in particular, before he juddered viciously as he was riddled with bullets from off-camera. The second group strode in, checked his pulse, and shot him one final time, then moved on with all the grim callousness he had expected from the first group.

Vandal needed to hurry up, and Moses need to up his game. There was no reason to believe the missing third group would be any kinder than the other two.

> are you helping? My guy is having trouble

>> working on it

>> one guy here had a portable gen

>> used it to spring the door to get in and now trying to hook it up on the inside to open it again

>> not easy

> I understand but try

The second group, not content with their execution, were now trying to cut through a hardened bulkhead to access another room. Was that a medical bay? Hard to tell from that angle, but it would explain why they were having trouble getting the door open – another security door.

> they have at least one plasma torch, youre not safe there

>> acutely aware of that thanks rostrum

>> were working as fast as we can

He'd known they'd have plasma torches of some description, and if they hadn't brought them originally they would have acquired them to access the bridge. It wasn't as if the Strider didn't have a stock of the damned things anyway.

It did undermine his plans for keeping this lot safe, though they had never been long-term anyway. Better than doing nothing though, he had to hold onto that. Every moment longer was a victory.

> do you have any weapons?

>> none that work

>> a few of the group r from security but their guns got wrecked during the storm

>> could fashion clubs from debris though?

> anything could help, we need to make the cockpit defensible for when you are up here

>> ok

>> will get the door open first then worry about that

> ok

Vandal had given up trying to pry the door open and was kicking it in a strop. That probably wouldn't work, but it was worth a try. It would be easier to kick the damned things out of their housing, Rostrum considered, than pry them apart with his bare hands.

He worked on the door for a few minutes, but it was steadfast in its resolve. It refused to dent, let alone break from its moorings, and all each kick managed to do was tire out Vandal. Well, that and to illustrate how long it was taking Moses to get the door open from his end.

With one last kick, Vandal slumped to the floor to catch his breath. The door stared at him impassively, mocking him, and then slid open, almost as if it had been waiting for him to finish. It was dark on the other side.

Slowly, Vandal got back to his feet and approached the door. Moses should have already come out to greet him, or at least the man he had tasked with getting the door open, but there was no-one. Peering in, Vandal's hands appeared in front of the camera again.

He swiftly signed *what the fuck* – W-T-Middle finger, to be precise – and stepped into the room. It remained black for a second, then a pair of portable floodlights snapped on. They blinded the camera briefly before they could adapt.

Once they did, Rostrum could see Moses and his group, all stacked haphazardly atop each other, dead. Standing astride them, cutting a pose, were the members of the third kill squad. Two of them had their guns trained on Vandal, the third with a portable terminal in his hand.

>> I lied.

NINETEEN

'What the hell is it?' Lucille asked. She was crouched at the foot of one of the Squib's legs. Crushed between it and the snow was some sort of robot.

'It's some sort of robot,' Wendy said. 'I'm guessing it's not yours?'

'Not as far as I know.'

The pair of them had disembarked the Squib as fast as possible once they had arrived, once Wendy had done what needed doing. The journey had been long and uncomfortable, and they had developed a powerful need to both stretch their legs and not be within arm's reach of each other. They regretted this decision as soon as they stepped outside.

Wendy had been stunned by the state of the Strider. She had seen it from a distance, and in photos, but it didn't resemble itself at all now. Even calling it a wreck would be too generous – all it was now was a pile of twisted metal held upright by a stubborn snowdrift. The huge gashes and puncture marks along the hull, the metal torn like tissue paper and hanging by a thread, all of this had completely disfigured what had once been a striking silhouette.

She hadn't even spotted the robots, that had been

Lucille. Wendy had thought the scattered metal forms were just bits of hull shaken loose by the storm, but the other woman had caused her to give them more attention. They were far more advanced than any she had seen before, and yet somehow also older.

Old tech, naturally. Native to the Strider though? From what she was learning about this weird cabal, that was the only way they could still have access to these robots. At least they were dead now, she wouldn't have to deal with them.

Leaving Lucille to her robot corpse, Wendy trudged closer to the Strider. Three galleons – the ones Lucille had shown on the map no doubt – had parked up perhaps fifty feet from the base of the wrecked city, and she wanted a look in them before she risked entering the city itself.

Lucille's gun hung heavy in Wendy's pocket. The others were here to kill the survivors, she had to remember that. It wasn't as if they'd differentiate between her and a survivor, should they catch her.

This was such a bad idea.

The galleons seemed legitimate enough. They had the expected loadouts – more repeater beacons, mining probes, nothing unexpected – which just made the prospect all the creepier. All indications were that these people just went about their daily lives as normal until they got the call. Just like Lucille. How many people had they betrayed?

Did it even count as betrayal?

There was no need to start getting all poetic about things now. She'd come here to help the survivors if she could, so that was all that mattered. Not the robots, not the motivations of those out to kill said survivors. Find them, run away with them, spend the rest of her life hiding on a giant walking billboard.

Lucille caught up with her and they made their way into the lower levels of the Strider. The ropes placed by the killers were actually pretty welcome, though without ascenders it was murder on Wendy's hands. She couldn't get a decent grip with gloves on, and trying to climb without them left her fingers at the mercy of the spiteful cold. At least she still had her safety clip – trying to force her way up with her rapidly numbing hands led to her losing her grip more than once. By the time they actually entered the dock her hands were bright red, and Lucille's didn't look much better.

It wasn't much of a dock now, just more twisted metal and shattered galleons. Moving through it into the ship proper didn't paint a very hopeful picture. There weren't any bodies, but there also wasn't really anywhere for a body to be, the entire thing was open to the elements now.

'If you let me in on your plan,' Lucille said. 'Maybe I could help.'

'Yes, because you are the most trustworthy and helpful person I know, aren't you?'

'Not to split hairs, but I think I might be now.'

'Yes, because you killed the others.'

Lucille snorted. 'That's a fair point... But I did help you get here.'

'Just shut up,' Wendy said. 'My plan is to find anyone your friends haven't already killed and get them to safety. You know, act like a human?'

Lucille went to respond but stopped herself. There was a silence. 'I don't think many people could have survived this.'

They moved deeper, and the city started to expand a little. The crushed outer sections took the brunt of the damage, it seemed, but that hadn't spared the inner areas. There was still a lot of damage, but most of it had been electronic rather than structural. The corpses were appearing now, blasted with electricity or flash frozen from the storm, pierced by loose shrapnel from the damage outside. Squashed under joists and supports knocked loose.

It wasn't as if Wendy was used to corpses. Before the

Squib, she'd not really had to deal with death. But then she'd fallen into the bones of the Squib crew, and that had been horrifying. Then she'd seen Thor and the captain, which had been equally distressing. Now she was walking through corridors of corpses, and nothing. No reaction.

Perhaps it was the number. There were *many* dead people scattered around as she moved, to the point that they weren't *special*, which felt like a horrible distinction to make. A small number of dead, she reasoned, and you could get caught up in their stories. You could empathise with them, humanise them. They were, or at least had been, actual people that had been up and about once, doing *things*.

These weren't people. These were decorations. Horrible, grotesque, vile decorations, and she knew intellectually that they had been alive once, but it didn't mesh. The stories didn't spring forth, the histories. She couldn't look at the corpses and see the faces, imagine the lives as they had once been. It was too impersonal.

These thoughts made her feel worse than the actual corpses did, and not by a small margin.

They found the first execution several decks up, and while they weren't frequent there were more.

Lucille quickened her pace, pulling in front of Wendy and stopping. 'Okay, you need to listen to me now.'

'Get out the way.'

'Three groups, right?' she said. 'That got here before us. They'll have split up to scour this whole place efficiently and thoroughly. If we're finding corpses now, it already means it is too late. We stay here, they're going to find you and kill you.'

'Maybe, but I'm no letting this all be for nothing. I do have a backup plan.'

'Then tell me what it is, because I'm not going to let you stroll deeper into this bloody mortuary just so you can get shot to death.'

'You're all heart.'

Lucille's face darkened a little. 'I'm more heart than you realise.'

'Look, where do you think we're going?'

'God knows.'

Wendy looked up and traced something on the ceiling with her eyes. 'I know exactly where I'm going. See, look at the wiring.'

Lucille looked up. Thick cables lined the ceiling, where it hadn't been torn free or whatnot from the storm. Following it along, a lone cable would sprout from the central line for each room or device they passed.

'Sure,' Lucille said. 'Wiring.'

'It wasn't like I was going to traipse around an entire city to look for stragglers is it? That would take forever. Let me show you.'

Lucille moved aside and Wendy began to walk again, with more purpose than before. Wherever they were going, it was clearly deeper towards the centre. The bodies were piling up now, and that made the journey harder as they started to cover the floor. Walking over the dead slowed them considerably.

Then they reached an area that had been subjected to some sort of firestorm, and their pace quickened again. Caramelised corpses were stiffer, more solid than the others, made for a decent path.

Eventually the wires led them into a large room, thick with the smell of cooked flesh and dissipating smoke. Again, the floor was nothing but hundreds of dead people, melted together in the throes of death. The machines had survived though – great pistons that disappeared into the floor, each with a scorched computer affixed to them somewhere.

Crunching over to the nearest piston, Wendy pulled Thor's tablet from her pocket and looked for a slot to which to connect it.

'Most people think that if you want to hijack a machine, you need to hit its heart,' Wendy said as she snooped. 'So for things with computer systems, people look for the CPUs and stuff like that. I guess that's a way to do it, but it's the slow path, yeah?'

'Are you seriously giving me a lecture right now, Wendy?'

Wendy ignored her. 'But really you're just looking for a way into the network, or circuit, or whatever. The CPU will sort out all the traffic, and it checks credentials and all that or whatever, but that's not a problem if you're coming from a trusted part of the system. Nowhere will have more trust than wherever all the power meets up. Engineers, we're snotty, having to enter a password every five seconds is going to get right up our nose.'

'I still don't really understand why you're telling me all this. What good is this to us?'

'Well, I'm just basing this on my experience back home, but the best place to hack into a system is always somewhere important. They rely on the physical security, because all the electronic security is designed to stop people breaching these systems from the outside. It's never concerned with breaches *originating* here.'

'fascinating, but –'

'So that means that all I need to do is plug this tablet in here and type a few simple commands, and I can do this...'

She found a suitable socket as she spoke and made the connection. The tablet butted heads with the Strider's internal systems for minute, but she was able to guide it through safely enough. Then she typed those simple commands and a sound like a thousand speakers crashing into each other flooded the room. Feedback, the likes of which she had never imagined, squealed and roared, then echoed itself back through the speakers.

Wendy tapped a button and it fell silent.

Lucille had her fingers in her ears. 'Jesus Christ, Wendy! Well, I guess no-one's going to miss that. Ow!'

'Should get their attention, yeah?' Wendy said.

'Who, exactly?'

'Your pals.'

'Why would you possibly want their attention?'

'Well, like you said,' Wendy said and brought the tablet up to face height. 'They're out there sweeping the Strider. Not going to beat them to any survivors. So we need to get them out of the way.'

Lucille didn't understand. Even the younger woman's lecture, Lucille couldn't map out where she was going. This just made it more fun for Wendy. She would allow that, just this once, because this was a terrible plan. It had been a terrible plan when she had concocted it on the ride over, and it had only gotten worse as she had realised it was her only real option. It was stupid, brash, downright dangerous and almost certainly not going to work.

But because it *had* to work, she needed to believe that it would. She'd had Thorsten for that role before, the person to listen to her spiel when she was working, to nod and smile and look confused in equal measure. To make her feel like a genius.

The least Lucille could do was stand in for him right now.

Smiling, Wendy spoke into the tablet's microphone. 'Hello, I'm Wendigo Milton, and I have a message for the shit-house rats skulking about this city shooting people in the face.'

For her part, Lucille went white as a sheet and hissed. 'No no no, what are you doing?'

'You're here because of me, because of what I found,' Wendy continued. 'And the measures you've taken to keep that secret. Well, I'm here now, with the thing I found. Come and get me.'

She pulled the tablet's connection and pocketed it. Her heart was starting to race now as the adrenaline kicked in again. That was the starting pistol, now she had to run the race.

Lucille was staring at her, jaw unhinged and eyes wide. 'You've actually cracked.'

'All we have to do is stay out of their way. They'll all come looking for me, right? Then they'll decide I've retreated to the Squib and go search that. They'll be out of the way and we can concentrate on the survivors.'

'First of all they'll scour the city though,' Lucille said. 'These are smart people with access to the original schematics of places like this. They'll know all the locations you could have made that broadcast from.'

'Yes, but they're not going to get here instantly, are they? This city is enormous, and they've already done this level. We've got time to hide.'

'This is very risky.'

'It's the only way to search the city without having to look over my shoulder the entire time.'

'… I concede it's not the *worst* plan, but –'

'Frankly I don't care about your opinion,' Wendy said. 'Or you. This is the plan I'm doing.'

Lucille bristled, and Wendy could see her hands reach instinctively for her gun. That was a gesture she had seen before on their travels, long before the woman had revealed her true colours, but she'd never been able to identify it before. An idle jitter of the hand, then back to her usual composed self.

It took longer this time, there was nothing for the fingers to brush. The safety net was gone, and this shone through in her expression. The anger and the uncertainty boiled over ever so briefly, and Wendy herself reached for the gun, worried that she might have pushed Lucille too far.

Then the older woman simmered, calmed, and exhaled. The entire thing had taken no more than a few seconds, but it had really helped spike Wendy's heart rate.

Her blood cooled, Lucille started to look around the room. 'I hope you had a hiding spot in mind. We're a bit obvious here.'

'There are loads of rooms on this level. We'll shelter in one of them. They won't look too closely, right? Not once they realise the Squib is just out there.'

'Lead the way.'

It had sounded like a great idea. At least a good one. An okay one. Not a terrible one. But Wendy did have to concede that she should have picked out the hiding place ahead of time. They'd had the element of surprise, plenty of time to do it, but she'd been doing nothing but winging things since this started and she wanted to play to her strengths.

They found a cabinet a little way down one of the corridors that branched out from the piston room, full of tools and equipment. It was a squeeze, but the pair of them managed to fit themselves into it and close the door. The situation was not at all comfortable, and Wendy doubted either of them would be able to get out without making a scene, but it wasn't an obvious hiding spot either.

They barely had time to shut the doors before they could hear the footsteps approaching, and seconds later they saw figures rush past through the slats in the door. One group of three, then a second group.

'Careful! Careful, careful!' one of them said, and the footsteps slowed. 'This is very likely to be a trap.'

'I know,' said another. 'Either that or this Wendigo customer is suicidal. I mean, has she seen this place?'

'How many other places could she have spliced into the intercoms?'

There was a sound like a piece of paper unrolling, followed by a few dull beeps. 'Any of the engineering nodes would work, I guess. The others have these ones up here covered, these ones have been destroyed or rendered inaccessible.'

'And that one?'

'Main engineering. Still on fire, but she could conceivably manage it. If she was fireproof.'

'For all we know, that bloody thing she found could have had fireproofing technology on it.'

This time, the sound was of paper being rerolled. 'Well

I'm not walking into an inferno.'

'Let me check in with the others, maybe they've found her and we won't need to go firewalking,' he said. There was a short hiss of static indicative of a radio being activated. '3-1, this is 1-1, come in, over.'

'This is 3-1,' came a heavily distorted voice. The signal was weak and the static did its best to garble her words. 'We've got no sighting up here.'

'Balls. You good to check the other places on your level?'

'Already done. Nothing of note. But we're right at the bloody top anyway. If she *is* up here, you lot have been crap at your jobs. Just saying.'

'Don't get lippy with me, Claire.'

'Why? Going to come up here and tell me off, Sean?'

The man seemingly stepped away from his group and closer to Wendy and Lucille. When he spoke again, his voice was considerably quieter. 'People can hear you, you know. Try and be professional, or you *will* be in trouble, missy.'

She giggled. This was getting surreal. 'I'll hold you to that when we get home. But okay, I'll be a good girl for now. We've searched everywhere that makes sense up here, but most of the likely spots are down in your respective zones. We're all boring bureaucratic bullshit up here. Only place left is the bridge, and we were going to check that anyway. Someone has sealed it up tight.'

'Her?'

'Doubt it, not unless she's super dumb. Permanently sealed with some sort of hazmat precaution. Best guess is it's a survivor's holdout. We could leave them, starve them out, but...'

The man sighed. 'Orders are orders. Got to confirm and clear.'

'Sucks, doesn't it?'

'Yup.'

'Think she's run back to her *Squib*? What a stupid

name.'

'Starting to think that's the most likely thing. She could be hiding anywhere on this damned hulk though, so keep your eyes open.'

'Don't I always?'

'Good girl.'

With a click, he silenced the radio and wandered back down towards his group. The one who had been talking to before welcomed him. 'So what's next?'

'We can't go room to room. There's way too much space to try and trap someone who isn't massively injured. She could slip around us easily. So we secure her escape route. We go back down to the docks and secure the Squib.'

'Do we have to call it that?'

'Unfortunately that's its name.'

'Fine.'

'Everyone, grab your gear. We've got to make sure we get down there before she does.'

They were considerably louder on the way out than they had been on the way in. From stationary to sprint in a fraction of a second, gear clattering and feet stomping. It made the group of six sound like a platoon. Or, and this was more likely, Wendy was exaggerating because of how close they had to run past her. That they couldn't hear her heart pounding was a miracle.

When the footsteps were out of earshot, Wendy and Lucille practically fell out of the cabinet.

Wendy got up first, dusting herself off. 'Not graceful, but I think it worked.'

'Didn't get rid of them all,' Lucille said. 'Sounds like there's still up at the top of the city.'

'Yeah, closing in on the survivors. Gives us a place to head though.'

Lucille crossed her arms. 'Give me back my gun, please.'

'Haha, no.'

'Wendy,' Lucille said, slowly. 'I understand that you can't trust me, but I'm not trying to hoodwink you here.'

'Hoodwink?'

'There are still three killers in this city that are going to shoot at us on sight, and you want to run right up to them. Even if you somehow get past them, there's the other six chilling at your escape vehicle. There's going to be a fight.'

'I've got the gun, I'll handle it.'

'Maybe. And maybe you'll be lucky enough to actually succeed. But that's not the best play and you know it. You're the brains, not the brawn. Given time, you could be both, sure, but right now you aren't. Just give me the gun.'

'No.'

Lucille's arm darted forward like a viper, grabbing Wendy by the belt and spinning her round. The other arm slid around her neck, gripping her tightly, as the first searched for the concealed weapon. It gripped it and pulled the gun free as the other arm uncoiled from her neck. A knee came up and shoved the younger woman away. When she turned, it was into the barrel of the gun.

'I could have taken this any time I wanted, Wendy. I asked, *politely*, because I'm trying to show you something.'

'That you're a psycho?'

'That I'm *not* a psycho,' she said. The gun wet limp in her hand again and Wendy snatched it from her. 'I don't need a gun to kill you, and I don't need your permission to take my gun back. I'm only showing you this now so you know exactly what I'm capable of and *why* I'm not doing it.'

Wendy's eyes narrowed. '*Oh I'm so dangerous, look at how dangerous I'm not being?* That's your play?'

'It's not a play. Believe it or not, I just want us to have the best chance of not dying.'

'Unlike, oh I don't know –'

'Stop bringing them up.'

'Stop bringing up the *people you killed?* Oh, sorry if I'm becoming a broken record, but you basically murdered my family. If you didn't want that thrown in your face every five seconds, then maybe you *shouldn't have **fucking** killed them.*'

'I –'

'Shut up,' Wendy said and turned her back on Lucille. 'Either take the gun off me and finish your mission, or shut your mouth and come with me. There's people on the bridge to save.'

Lucille let forth a scowl that could crush a star. 'Wendy, I get the impression we need to talk about this.'

'We could have talked on the journey,' Wendy said. 'You could have talked to us before you murdered Thor and the captain. You could have talked to us at any point from the moment we set out spiking those damned beacons. There was any number of moments where you could have *talked*, and you choose now?'

'I'm trying to make amends here.'

Wendy was moving now, storming through the Strider as though she knew where she was going. Lucille had to make an effort to keep up, but Wendy's rising volume meant she could hear her regardless. 'You can't balance this out. But you're right, I can't exactly get rid of you can I?'

'If you just let me explain –'

'Explain how you're a psycho-killer?'

Lucille grabbed her arm. 'Just *listen*.'

Wendy span and glared at her. Lucille's eyes were sad, haunted even, but her face remained steadfast as always. '*Fine.*'

'Home is a beautiful, seductive idea. There's a reason the internal nomenclature for what I did is *sterilising* and not something more direct. Everyone wants that safety and security, and they aren't concerned how they get it. If word spreads fast enough, from the right people, they'll come for us and wipe out our one last chance at saving the world. That's what Larissa says.'

'This is nothing I haven't heard before.'

'Yes, but you're not listening,' Lucille said. 'With every likeminded person we bring in, the doctrine gets stronger. More people believing the same thing: that we are the last hope for civilisation in the world. The more we believe that, the more we tailor who we recruit to fit that mould, you understand?'

The gun was out again, but Wendy wasn't wielding it like a weapon yet. 'People comfortable carrying shit like this and killing their friends?'

'Yes.'

Wendy placed her hands on her hips and hung her head. She let a lot of things hang in that moment. There was too much anger, she wasn't thinking clearly. She was in the middle of a hostile environment, hunted by gunmen, and she was now dead set on having this argument with Lucille. It was stupid. But it was happening.

She compressed the rage a little, let it simmer. If she was going to do this – and she was going to do it – then it had to be a proper argument, not stupidly childish contrariness. There was no outpunching Lucille, no outshooting her either, but she could outtalk her. Hurt her as badly as she had hurt Wendy, rob her of that perfect justification she treasured so much.

'Maybe I'm giving you too much credit, calling them your friends,' she said. 'The way you work, I don't think it's possible for you to have friends. You're broken.'

Lucille's voice deepened. 'I knew them longer than you did. They were as much my family as yours.'

'Yet you fucked up,' Wendy said. 'You killed off the two people on the crew that probably would have seen the benefit of your crazy cult and left me, the difficult one, to experience it first-hand.'

Another silence. Lucille took a breath, then another, and her shoulders sagged. Almost robotically, she walked past Wendy, deeper into the Strider. 'Yes, I know. Let's go.'

That hurt her, Wendy thought. Not enough pain, but a

good start.

TWENTY

The upper decks seemed hardest hit of all. The city didn't really taper to a point as such, but once you were past the hips, it did start to narrow noticeably. With less metal to absorb the assault, Wendy and Lucille were running into a lot more places open to the elements, and considerably fewer walls.

Wendy had kept the pace slow. She didn't know where the bridge was – other than at the top, because where else would it be? – and didn't want to haplessly blunder into this last group unprepared. Sure, they had *said* they were going to try and bust into the bridge, but that didn't mean it was true. This had been something that, begrudgingly, both her and Lucille had agreed upon.

The tension had not diminished during their travels to the top of the Strider. If anything, the walk had impressed upon Wendy how daft it had been to let her temper boil over like it had. Trying to push through the increasing amount of structural damage was stressful enough without a muscly murderer sulking behind her.

There had been a jump at one point. A huge section of the floor was just gone, a pit several decks deep in its place. It had been a trust exercise loose in the world, just waiting for them, and the worst part was that Wendy found herself trusting Lucille. She let the older woman practically throw her across, giving her the boost she needed to make that jump without issue, and it was only when her feet touched down on the other side that she realised how wrong that moment could have gone.

But then, there *was* something in knowing that Lucille could kill her at any moment if she chose to, a strange clarity in it all. The upper decks started to twist themselves into dark morasses of misshapen metal and darkness, spooky and unwelcoming, but they never quite progressed into putting Wendy on edge.

The environment wasn't scary anymore. There was no fear that something would use the shadows to its advantage, snap her neck and leave her for dead, that instinctual voice silent now. At her back, Wendy had the person who she should have feared would do all that and more, but now she knew that Lucille didn't need those advantages, the wall had come down. Why be afraid of the dark when the monster has outright said it doesn't give a shit about killing you?

But, she conceded, it *had* been scary having the gun taken off of her so easily. It might have made her surroundings less spooky, but Wendy had to admit that it did have some effect much closer to home, knowing now as she did how easily Lucille could have turned the tables had she wanted. She was carrying herself differently now, tenser and with a more paranoid bent. Everything was a little more serious now, and she was nowhere near as secure as she had thought.

Sure, the geography wasn't getting inside her head now, but those fears had found something else to latch onto regardless.

Worst of all, that was probably Lucille's intent. Moreso than getting Wendy to trust her, it was to get her thinking, to respect the situation. Sneaky back-door mentoring – no, that sounded wrong. But it was sneaky nonetheless, and regardless, Wendy kept her hand resting on the gun. If Lucille *was* going to take it again, at least Wendy would know.

She was close to jumping at shadows by the time they caught up with the group. Places so big should not be so quiet, and the noise of the plasma cutter was not the ideal way to bring that to an end. From a distance, before she could identify it, Wendy had started to wonder if it was just an hallucination. The whispers of ghosts, angry at what had happened. At what she had set in motion with her find.

But then it had come into focus, that constant hiss as it began to carve through whatever was in its way. Lucille had urged her to slow down even more, and Wendy had agreed.

Wendy tracked the sound to a corner and peered around it. Two of the group were camped out in the hallway, on either side of the door, plugging canisters into hoses that disappeared into the room behind them. Their guns were on the ground next to them, within arms-reach. Still enough time to ambush them though, if she had to.

'Whoever built this place didn't skimp on the hazmat protocols,' one of them said. 'It shouldn't take this long to cut through.'

The other rolled his eyes. 'You could always take the other route.'

'The one that guy told us about? Yeah, I'm not about to try and climb up the outside of this hunk of scrap without a safety line, thanks.'

'Well if you hadn't killed him, maybe he could have shown us the safest route.'

'That's the job though. I mean, literally, our orders are to kill *everyone*.'

'Yes, but it's the argument of principle over intent, right,' the second said. 'As long as we kill them *eventually*, we're still fulfilling orders. We could have used him to more efficiently mop up the rest, instead of sitting here while we wait for her to carve through several inches of reinforced ultra-steel.'

'You don't know that's what it is –'

'– taking far too long to cut through to be normal metal –'

The first man raised his voice just a little. '– but even if it *is*, that doesn't matter. We hesitate, we waver. Once that starts happening, we put everything in jeopardy.'

'Cold outside, warm in here,' he said, and tapped his chest above his heart.

'Exactly. It might be more efficient to do things your way, but then you remember they are people too and everything gets cloudy. Hence shoot on sight.'

'I know, sorry, I'm just restless.'

'It's cool. I get you.'

Wendy looked around to Lucille, who was utterly expressionless. She took her by the arm and pulled her away from the corner, and back down the corridor a little. The older woman's face didn't change.

'Do you know these two?' Wendy said.

Lucille shook her head. 'No, but I don't know everyone from Home. Left a long time ago, remember? Even then, I didn't know everyone.'

'We need to take them out.'

'I've already told you, there's no *we* in that. I'll take them out.'

'Yeah, no.'

'Look, they find us they'll kill us both. They won't ask me questions, ascertain my identity, just kill us. That's not how we do identification in the field.'

'So how do you do it then? Maybe that's something we can use.'

Lucille squirmed. 'Remember that weird transmission the Squib picked up?'

'Oh of course. Of course it was that.'

'We send them out when we approach a potentially violent situation. Hijack the target's comms if they have them so it looks internal. That's how we do it. It's not a calling card, it won't work on closed operations like this.'

There was a loud clang from around the corner, and the sound of people jumping to their feet. Then a voice with a slight echo, presumably Claire's. 'I'm through!'

'Well we need to do something now,' Wendy said. 'Because in seconds they are going to stroll in there and kill everyone.'

'And if we're not careful, we'll be dead too, and what would that accomplish?'

'At least we would have tried to do the right thing!'

'Jesus...'

Lucille hung her head as Wendy drew the gun. She looked at it for a moment, found the safety, clicked it off, and then produced the knife too. She stalked back up to the corner and took another look. The pair were still detaching the canisters and pulling the pipes free of the doorway, but they were working fast, excited. She had seconds to act.

Don't think, just do. That's what they do, and it works for them. Same motivation, the greater good. Killing had never been her plan, her intent, but it was acceptable to kill a killer, right? Take a life to save a life. It had to be, because this might not have felt good, but it felt right.

Without ceremony, Lucille's arm wrapped around Wendy's throat, locking tight and pulling her backwards. She flailed with the gun, but another strong hand disarmed her for a second time. Foolish, she had left her flank open, even after the warning. She'd forgotten she was *travelling* with a killer. Idiot. Idiot, idiot, *idiot*.

The pair tumbled backwards, and Lucille's legs locked around Wendy's waist as she tightened her grip. 'Shhh, shhh, just let it happen. I'm not going to let you kill yourself. I won't.'

'Why?' Wendy said, breathlessly. Lucille's grip wasn't quite a choke, but she could feel herself flagging anyway. 'Killed Thor... Captain...'

'But not you. Never you,' she said, squeezing harder. 'I had to kill them. They would have agreed. They would have come Home and seen the benefits. They would have stayed. You never would.'

'Don't... Understand...'

'I know, I know. I should have explained it better,' Lucille said, her voice barely above a whisper now. 'But it's hard to talk about. I'm conflicted. Duty first, feelings second. The greater good. I just can't. I'm not strong enough. But then I met you, and you're not special. If it wasn't you, it would have been someone else. There's no shortage of people who would reject what they were shown at Home, but I knew you. I know you.'

'Let... go...'

'I can't. You have to stay safe, get out of here. Ruin Larissa's paradise. I think it needs it. I think you can do that. I couldn't. Now shhhhhh, sleep.'

Try as she might, she couldn't fight it. It wasn't like going to sleep, not really. The world faded out first, like it was draining away, and then her consciousness dimmed with it. Sluggish, scary, but relaxing too. She found she didn't want to fight it. But then she remembered the cold sensation of the knife in her other hand. Lucille hadn't stripped her of that.

With her last ounce of waking thought, she brought it down hard into one of the legs locked about her waist, and instantly the world slammed back into focus. Lucille's arms released her as the woman screamed and clutched at her leg, and Wendy rolled free and tried to crawl away, spluttering.

The group must have heard her. How could they not? That was an animal scream, unexpected and uncontrolled. No missing it.

She turned to look, and she was right. They had heard, and the pair of them had come round the corner at full speed, weapons trained, ready to do their duty. But Lucille had not been idle.

It occurred to Wendy that she had never seen Lucille in action. She had already killed Thor and the captain by the time she found them, and as a crew they had never run into much trouble. There had been a bar fight once, but that had been over pretty quickly – one punch, then she was given a wide berth – and some playful sparring to pass the time. Never fight-for-your-life level stuff.

Until now.

Wendy had gotten her good, and her leg was already soaked with blood. She must have hit an artery. But this wasn't slowing Lucille at all. The knife was still jammed in the muscle, but she was moving as if it wasn't there at all. Ducking, dodging, rolling, striking, it was a sort of fighting that didn't seem real. It was smooth, clean, elegant, when everything she had known about fights was that they were ugly and brutal things.

Not beautiful.

But Lucille made it look divine. The two men were as fast as she was, but they lacked the discipline. They lacked the elegance of Lucille, seemingly recounting specific forms they had been drilled with while she flowed between them and improvised her own. Planning ahead with every movement, so that when they brought the guns into play she was already setting up her movements to knock them off target.

And yet Wendy couldn't help but notice that Lucille wasn't winning. She was outclassing them at every turn, but they were just good enough to dodge any major blows. If she struck at their head, they would dodge. Flip one to prepare for a downwards heel, the other would intervene. The more this happened, the more her form began to falter as the blood loss took its toll.

But then, a lucky break. A flip, a stumble, from one of the men left an opening against the other, and she exploited it to its fullest. Pivoting off her bad leg, she drove the good one deep into his gut, doubling him over, then brought her knee up into his face. His nose exploded across his face, and he went down. The other got up, but Lucille was already spinning towards him, a backhand to the face, stripping his gun as he was rocked, twirling it into her fist.

Bang, that was it for the man on the floor. Bang, the other man too, just as he regained his stable footing.

And just like that, it was over.

Until Claire appeared.

Lucille was not a small woman, but Claire made her look that way. She was a twenty-four-hour gym session away from being legitimately worthy of the term *hulk*, and Wendy was worried that she was going to tear out of her clothes with little effort at all.

Lucille wasn't fazed. What Claire had in muscle, she lacked in speed, even with Lucille's injured leg slowing her down. The larger woman came out swinging, but few of the blows even came close to landing. On the flip side, the ones Lucille landed didn't seem to bother her either.

Where had the gun gone? Wendy had spent the entire fight just watching, breathing, but she could help too. The two men Lucille had already laid out, their guns were on the far side of the fight now, the first casualties of Claire's arrival. But Lucille's gun, the one she had stripped from Wendy in the choke hold, that had to be around somewhere.

It couldn't have gone far. She had heard it bounce, skitter, along the floor when she dropped it. There were only so many places it could have ended up. There was plenty of debris, it had to be under some of that.

Lucille was starting to slow down, her second wind having come to an end, and Claire was exploiting it. One meaty fist caught Lucille in the side of the head, and her bad leg gave out trying to counterbalance the blow. She went down hard, and Claire followed her.

Legs like support beams slammed down on either side of Lucille's chest, pinning her under the rest of the larger woman's weight, and that was all it took for the rain of punches to begin. At first, Lucille did her best to block the blows. Her hands came up, taking the force of the first couple, but she didn't have the energy to keep up her guard. One punch made it through, and the impact sent her arms slack. Once that happened, it was nothing but fists to the face. Lucille had no fight in her.

Wendy was scrabbling, trying in vain to find the gun. It simply couldn't have vanished. It *had* to be under one of the nearby bits of rubble. There was so much of it, but it wasn't as though there was *much* it could actually fit under.

Something cracked in Lucille's face. A cheek bone, her jaw, her nose? Wendy couldn't tell, but whatever it was had caused a lot of blood and bruising already. That was the only sound though, no screaming or pleading from Lucille at all. Either she was the toughest person Wendy had ever met, or she was unconscious.

Judging from the beating, probably both.

Claire would stop soon. Wendy needed a way to protect herself. She *needed* the gun. And then, poking out from some debris, as expected, she found it.

Lucille moved. She waited until Claire started to slow, ripped the blade from her own leg, and thrust it at her assailant's throat. It was lightning fast, a killing blow, but Claire caught it all the same. She wrapped Lucille in her own arms, bringing up a knee to hold them in place, took the knife, and drove it down at Lucille's breast.

Wendy fired twice. Both shots clanged harmlessly off the walls, but the sound caused Claire to pause and notice her, seemingly for the first time. Lucille, her face purple and misshapen, looked to Wendy and shook her head, pleading her not to act.

She knew that was the wrong thing to do. She knew that she needed to shoot Claire either way. There was no reasoning here. Kill or be killed. She *had* to shoot, despite what Lucille said.

But she couldn't. She hesitated for too long, and Claire tackled her.

The fists came up, and she was oddly at peace with that. She had thought she should be screaming, but there was just a calm acceptance to it all, as if *of course this is how it ends. This is all part of an equation: it couldn't end any other way.* Wendy never even thought to try and bring up her guard.

Then another gunshot.

The fists dropped to Claire's sides.

A fourth.

Claire's eyes grew wide.

A fifth.

She slumped over and fell to her side. Dead.

It took a moment for Wendy to tear her eyes from Claire. She had to make sure she was dead, that she wasn't about to get up and pound her face into the floor anyway. Hell, she had to actually accept that *hadn't already happened.* She'd been so ready for it, and now it wasn't happening. It was like waking up to find the sky was plaid. Impossible and somehow daft in equal measure.

Then she looked, right at Lucille, gun in hand. Evidently she had been faster at finding it than Wendy had been. She didn't notice the knife in her chest at first.

'Ow,' was all the older woman managed to say before she slumped back onto the floor.

Wendy scooted over. 'Lu?'

'I'll live. Probably. Jesus Christ, I'd forgotten how much fighting hurts. Especially with a knife in the leg.'

'In my defence,' Wendy said. 'You were trying to choke me to death.'

Lucille tried to laugh, but it turned into a cough. A thin mist of blood sprayed from her mouth. 'Sleeper hold. I wasn't killing you, I was trying to keep you safe. Go on. Go check the survivors.'

'What about you?'

'I'm going to lie here and have a cry, then I'll catch you up. Besides, there are six more people to watch out for.'

'Okay, maybe I can trust you a little.'

Lucille smiled. 'Just don't forgive me.'

TWENTY ONE

If there was one benefit to a scorched cornea, it was that Rostrum could watch them cutting through the bulkhead without going blind. His vision was dim enough already, the searing sparks from the plasma torch wasn't about to make things any worse.

>> I lied.

Rostrum hadn't cleared the chat logs. He was mourning. Not for Vandal Morley, despite sending him to his death, but for what that lie meant. There was no-one left. They were all gone, for certain now. He was the last of the Strider's citizens, unequivocally, definitely. Vandal's death was the death of hope.

It was the most likely result. He had known that from the beginning. But now, well, now it was fact.

They were making good time through the bulkhead. There would be, what, three people on the other side? He'd seen six of them sprint down to the lower decks for some reason, back out into the ice. That meant one group. Three of them. Perhaps he could overpower them.

Ha.

Ha ha.

He couldn't even stand now, let alone fight. Rostrum

had become one with his chair, the blood and pus fusing with the upholstery irrevocably now. But, by Christ, he was going to give them one hell of a foul look when they busted in. They would *know* the level of violent disdain he had for them. Oh yes.

Ha.

The bulkhead fell with a crash as the plasma cutter finished its work. The floor buckled a little under its weight, and the smoke rising from the edges made the resulting hole look much more ominous than it should have. A perfect place to direct the glare though.

He was ready for them. Ready to stare them down, dare them to kill him. He was already dead, he'd already won, he'd robbed them of that. They needed to know it though, to see his victory with their own eyes, and he needed to see their spirits implode with the realisation. All this to, ultimately, kill one corpse that refused to stay still.

The laughter bubbled over. Was he actually delirious now? Probably. Perhaps he had been from the outset, and this was all the fever dream of a man slowly suffocating under a pile of charred corpses. Would that be better? Did it matter? He really wanted to spit in their eyes though. He was liking all this vengeful spite; it was pretty easy to do when you were dying.

They didn't even have the decency to come in, though. The door was as open as it was going to be, it even had a big smouldering welcome mat, but they refused to step through. Rude.

The sounds of conflict didn't echo their way up the shaft at first. Scuffles, gunshots, it was hard to make out really. Fighting for the honour of finishing the job? Oh, how disappointed the winner would be. And after he had put such effort into winning, too. They were putting their all into that scrap, that much he could tell.

He lolled his head over to the screens again. Nothing on the cameras for that level. Of course not, the goddesses hadn't survived on the council deck. He already knew that.

Slipping again. He could see the others out in the snow though, tromping over and away from their galleons. Afraid of his angry stare, no doubt. Cowards. Smart, but cowards nonetheless.

They passed out of view quickly and didn't return. A spirited retreat, running off into the ice like that. Retreating towards their deaths, considerably politer than these bloody uncouth yobs having a fight on his porch.

And then she appeared, stepping through the smoke. This tiny, filthy, thing covered in blood and bandages. Barely more than a child. Had they sent a child to kill him? As if they weren't monstrous enough at this point.

Her face, formerly a stoic and business-like glare, changed when she saw him. Concern, empathy, he hadn't expected that. She rushed over to him.

'Jesus,' she said. 'Are you all right?'

He blinked at her for a moment and then laughed. A proper laugh, a skin-splitting, wound-opening, booming proper laugh. It hurt like hell, but how could he not after a question like that? 'Oh yes, I'm fine.'

'Sorry, clearly a stupid question,' she said. 'I'm, um, I'm Wendy Milton and I'm sort of here to save you?'

'You don't sound very sure of that,' Rostrum said. There was blood in his lungs now, he could feel it pooling. Laughing had been ill-advised.

'Well –'

'Didn't I talk to you on the network? Wendigo?'

'Oh, yes, that was probably me.'

'Hi. I'm the pilot of the Strider. Or I was. Didn't expect them to send you to finish me off. There's a trap I didn't foresee.'

'What? No,' she said. 'I really was coming here to save you, all of you, once I found out what happened.'

'Then you're a little late.'

'I guess...'

'Was there anyone? Did you find anyone at all?'

'No.'

Rostrum nodded and took as deep a breath as his flooding lungs would allow. 'Then I guess this is the end. Sorry, I'm not usually this morbid, but circumstances... You understand.'

She went quiet, and he didn't blame her. He welcomed it, in fact. Speaking was difficult now. Breathing was all but impossible. Drowning was horrible, especially doing it slowly, but even as he was, he didn't want to lose face. He was going to go out strong, as proud as he could, all things considered. It was sort of nice to have an audience for that. Weird how selfish everything became at the end.

But why wouldn't it? He'd spent his life living for others, doing what was best for the good of the city. Every decision, every actions, was weighed against the safety and happiness of thousands of others. It was, ultimately, a selfless life. He deserved a selfish death.

Except...

'I need you to do something for me.'

'Anything,' she said. 'Within reason.'

'Will you read my book?'

'What?'

'It's my legacy, the only thing that will survive this. It's not very good, but I'd like to know at least one person found it. I was trying to be clever, hid it out on the network, but now... Now I just need to know not everything I've done will be forgotten.'

'Sure, okay. I guess.'

He smiled as best he could, and pressed a small device into her hand.

She looked confused, which was to be expected. He'd wanted to tell her to stop this from happening again, bestow upon her some massive undertaking, but he didn't have the authority to do that. And yet something small, a memorial, people asked for those all the time. It left a lot to chance, but who cared? He wouldn't get to find out how it turned out anyway. A small seed of selflessness in his last hurrah of selfishness, that was more than he *had* to give.

Looking into her eyes, he could see the pain there. That was nice. It meant he *would* be remembered, although he had to admit it was more likely to be for his current look than him as a person. It would do. We all want to be remembered, don't we? Nobody wants to fade away, disappear, to have been found expendable.

She would read his book, eventually, and what happened next would be up to her, then. That was enough.

He let out one last, shallow breath and with it went whatever he was still holding onto. All the stress, fear, duty evaporated. He could practically feel his muscles unbinding themselves as he relaxed for what felt like the very first time in his life.

And then, closing his eyes, Rostrum finally died.

TWENTY TWO

The man died, and Wendy wasn't really sure how to take that.

Had this all been for nothing? Well, yes, apparently. She hadn't saved anyone, had barely avoided dying herself so far, and might have actually gotten Lucille killed given her wounds. There wasn't much guilt about that last point, but she would have been remiss to exclude it.

So, she had to rework her plan. Again.

No-one left to save here, that was readily apparent now. Where else could do with a heads up? A city, obviously, but one of those was probably in on this. A fifty fifty shot, if she didn't find a way to check beforehand.

She placed a hand on Rostrum's forehead for a moment. A little reverence couldn't hurt, and he probably deserved it. His flesh was brittle to the touch, and it made her feel uncomfortable, but she gave him a moment of silence.

A few minutes later, she descended the lift shaft and went back to Lucille, who wasn't in a much better state than Rostrum. She wasn't burned beyond recognition, but the fight had taken its toll. Apart from the bruises and the bleeding, her eyes were scarily unfocused. They still

301

managed to lock onto Wendy, but it took a frighteningly long time.

'That was quick,' the older woman said. 'Survivors?'

'Just one. Dead now.'

'I wish I'd known that before the fight,' Lucille said. 'So, what now?'

'I guess we need to tell people what really happened here.'

Lucille frowned. Not an ordinary frown, this one had a distinct message, one Wendy had seen a hundred times as she was growing up. It meant you have no idea or you are so naïve, a vicious and dismissive expression. Wendy had outgrown such judgements, and she made sure her own face reflected this.

In response, Lucille managed to grumble. 'What world do you live in?'

'You could help. You've worked with these people; you can tell everyone about them. That right there would be a mountain of evidence.'

Lucille finally stood up. Her leg wobbled unsteadily under her weight. 'I can do that. I will do that. But you need to ask yourself: why has no-one come forward before?'

'Because –'

'And don't say that something on this scale hasn't happened before, because it has. There were a lot of cities once, and the weather didn't get all of them.'

'Then why?'

'Because,' Lucille said. 'Because without proof, it's just some tall tale from a nobody. You really think people will believe me, the woman who nearly collapsed the Lawrence-Kadan Line? Or you, the baby engineer?'

'We have to try though, maybe someone will listen.'

'We do. We absolutely do, and it's something I've been thinking about for a long time before I even met you, but I want you to accept the reality of things. It almost certainly won't work.'

'Then we bring them back here, show them the truth. They have to believe that.'

Lucille winced. 'Your brand of optimism is infectious.'

'I just... This feels like the right thing to do. Doesn't it?'

'As you've been quick to point out, I don't know right from wrong very well,' Lucille said. 'But yeah, it does.'

'Okay, so, new plan,' Wendy said, as cheerfully as she could muster. 'We make for a city and tell them everything.'

'The Roller.'

'What?'

'The Roller is more likely to believe us. We have an understanding with the Crawler.'

'You lot get around.'

Lucille shrugged. 'You've got a lot more time to scheme when you aren't on the run.'

Wendy offered her a hand, and Lucille took it with little hesitation. There was never a question of forgiving or forgetting, but recent events had shown Wendy that perhaps it was best to reserve judgement for now. In this, they were on the same side, though their history seemed at odds.

'You said something,' Wendy said. 'About Thor and the captain.'

Lucille looked away. 'Yes, I did. I should explain that more, I suppose.'

'Yes, I think you should,' Wendy said.

'They were good people, better than me, but they were optimistic. I didn't know Thorsten too well, but I was very close with Joshua. I knew the kind of man he was and I could see shades of it in Thorsten too.'

'What do you mean?'

'Hopeful,' she said. 'For all their bluster, it wasn't the love of the open snow that kept them going, it was the belief that, one day, all those days on a galleon would pay off, that they'd find something better out there on the ice and could retire. You saw that when we struck the Squib, that joy at having found their payday.'

'So?' Wendy said, shrugging. 'We were all like that. All of us are like that. The world is an unremitting mess; all we have is hope.'

'I know, that's why I went to Home in the first place. It's why, when we tell people about this, we'll find more scorn from those that believe us than those that don't. It's a utopia, we can't compete with that.'

'I saw through it; you seem to have too.'

'It took me a long time. You, not so much. When I realised what was going to happen, that's why I didn't kill you. You're curious, you think about things, even the things you don't think about. Thorsten and Josh, they thought about things too, but there was never a thought to the future, it was only to the now. That's why they would have joined up with us.'

'I feel like you're giving me too much credit here, and it's very weird.'

Lucille chuckled. 'Look at where we are right now, where you want to take us. That's from thinking about the future. Like I've said before, you're not special and there are a lot of people who can think the way you do, but none that have found their way into this position. Home insists upon avoiding people like you.'

'But you were literally just saying my plans are hopeless.'

'And they are,' Lucille said. 'That's the point.'

'I liked you better when you were quiet.'

'Look, point being: I was looking for an out for a long time and never found the courage to take one until I met you. What you're proposing is going to be long and arduous, so you might want to take some of that time to consider what that means.'

Wendy sniffed. Was that a compliment? It sounded like one, but then it also sounded like a really clumsy way to come onto her, and she definitely wasn't about to start thinking about that right now. Or ever.

Hi mum, dad, here's my new girlfriend who murdered a few people for me apparently. Of course, all you care about is the age gap.

But, Wendy conceded, Lucille did have a point. Not once had she really stopped to think about where Wendy was taking the pair of them. Not properly. She was just dragging them through an endless series of right things, and trying to out these killers was just the latest in a long line of good-guy decisions. It was a duty she'd assigned herself, that she could quit at any time, but she knew she wouldn't.

If she had swayed Lucille, then maybe she could sway others too. Maybe, just maybe, her words would be enough to at least get the people of the Roller to consider looking into all this. That would be enough, that would be a victory.

Could Thor and the captain really not have been trusted to think this way? She couldn't believe that. Surely the soul-crushing pressures of the world couldn't have made them so weary.

Then again, maybe she was as bad as them, her hope just pointed in a different direction.

Whatever, there was no choice here. Never had been. For all Lucille had said, she had just wasted time that could be better spent trying to escape the crumbling wreck.

'Can you walk?' she said.

Lucille took a step. She didn't fall. 'Probably.'

'Then let's talk about this later. Over some form of alcohol strong enough to dull my senses so I can actually be bothered to listen. Agreed?'

Lucille nodded, and together they began to retrace their steps.

It had taken them a long time to reach the cockpit of the Strider, and it took even longer to descend back down to the docks. The more they moved the harder it became for Lucille to stay upright, and the paler she became. The wound on her leg wouldn't stop bleeding, and whatever internal injuries she had sustained in the fight were apparently not helping matters. They had to stop halfway to create a makeshift tourniquet, and still she was groggy by the time they actually reached the docks.

The slow pace helped on the lower levels, however. They couldn't take the same route back as they had taken up – too many little jumps that Lucille couldn't make now – so they had to look for alternatives. That meant finding new paths through collapsed ceilings and buckled floors, an endeavour made much safer by a sober pace. Slow going, but safe. At least if one didn't worry too much about the other soldiers.

The longer it took them to reach the docks, the more likely it was that the groups they had distracted would come back. The squib was much smaller than the Strider – it wouldn't take too long for the six of them to run a sweep, mess about with the computers and ultimately discover they couldn't do jack. They'd come back looking for her.

The longer the pair of them took, the more convinced Wendy became that she was about to blunder right into a firing squad.

But she didn't.

Then she was certain that they would be waiting for her outside, at the bottom of the ropes. She couldn't see them, but that hardly ruled it out, did it? The rigmarole of getting herself and Lucille down to the ice gave them plenty of time to line up their shots, and even as her feet hit the ground she was readying herself to dive prone.

But again, she didn't need to.

They had been gone too long. Clearing the Squib shouldn't have taken this long, and a group as apparently astute as those described by Lucille should have shifted their priorities by now.

She placed Lucille down on the ice and stretched. The woman was heavy, and even taking only half her weight was difficult.

'I don't like this,' Wendy said.

'You're wondering where the others are?'

'Yes.'

'Me too,' Lucille said, her head rocking side to side on the ice. 'Has to be an ambush.'

'It's not like they would have gone for a picnic.'

Lucille winced again and growled as she pulled herself back to her feet. Again her balance was off, but there was a grimness in her eyes that told Wendy to leave her be. 'Close quarters. Even with perfect positioning, they can't come at us any more than two at a time, four if they take up a firing phalanx. But they won't.'

'Why not?'

'Because they need you alive long enough to hand over the controls. They should know that by now.'

'And if they don't?'

'They we die when we step through the door. I'll go first.'

'In your state?'

'Even like this I'm a better fighter than you. Let's not have this argument again. Please? I just want to get this done.'

Lucille's eyes were dark hollows now. The sunlight made it worse, letting her brows cast deep shadows over the sockets, letting only the barest glint reach out from the eyes inside. When had she gotten this bad? It hadn't seemed like a gradual thing. First she had looked fine if a little pale, now she was all but a skeleton, at least in her face.

But if Lucille had looked dangerous before the injuries, this only served to make her look even moreso. The muscles and the gait had painted a pretty good picture before, and seeing it in action had cemented it, but now she was beyond that. Maybe her skill would be hampered by her injuries – in fact that was almost certain at this point – but now she was elemental. That look would give people pause, as it was doing to Wendy right now.

As the woman started to shuffle towards the Squib, Wendy skipped up beside her. 'Okay, I won't argue that.'

'Good.'

'But is this really the best way? We know it's probably an ambush, let's not just walk right into it!'

Lucille smiled gently, and again one of her eyes glistened in the darkness. 'It's got to be now, before the damage means adrenaline doesn't do shit to keep me moving. Has to be me.'

'When we get to safety, you're going to have to teach me how to do this stuff, you know.'

'Lesson one then, watch and learn.'

Lucille limped up to the Squib, leaving a trail of blood behind her as she moved, and checked the entrance carefully. With the walker squatting down, it cut an imposing figure but more importantly gave them some shade. Lucille took a moment to let her vision adjust, then stepped inside, Wendy a step or two behind her.

They passed out of the airlock and into the Squib proper, and that was when they sprung the trap. They had two men on each side of the orbital corridor as it met the airlock, and a fifth blocking the path that ran deeper. Even knowing to expect them, the pair of them would be dead had the group wished it. Indeed, caught off guard they wouldn't have even had time to react before the five of them collapsed upon Wendy and Lucille.

But they weren't off guard.

Lucille stopped as they called out to her, their voices smashing into each other and dismantling the words. But that didn't matter, the tone was sufficient. When she complied, the rifles went down and flick-batons came up, and two of them approached her.

She let them get close, and then she took them down.

Lucille had lost some of her grace as a result of the last attack, but none of the ferocity. If anything, the limitations of her wounds had led her to be more brutal, more bestial. There was little redirection of their energy now, instead she took the blows, let the pain fuel her rage, and lashed back twice as hard. They were down in seconds, and she was already onto the third by the time the others could react.

The third went down just as fast, his head slammed hard into the wall, joined quickly by the fourth. While the fifth managed to snatch up his rifle and let off a few rounds, he either missed or Lucille shrugged them off. She took him by the throat and drove his face into her knee, sending his nose up and into his brain.

Wendy had been prepared for all this, had seen similar not too long ago at all, and still it scared the shit out of her.

But Lucille didn't slow down. She was running now, deeper into the Squib, one of the retrieved rifles in her hand, and moving at such a speed that Wendy could scarcely keep up. There was a lot of blood left in her wake, which didn't help. Wendy had to be careful not to slip on it as she pursued her.

With a roar, Lucille burst into the control room. The last man was waiting, gun in hand, and those bullets definitely hit her. Wendy saw her body jolt as each round struck home, saw the sprays of blood. And she also saw Lucille raise her own gun and put a single round through the man's head before she fell.

When Wendy reached her, barely a second later, Lucille looked even worse than before. Even without the bullet holes – three of which were oozing steadily high on the left side of her chest, it was clear all the exertion had taken its toll. Lucille had moved like a person who hadn't been wounded, and doing that mean ignoring key warning messages from the brain. That came at a cost.

'Don't look at me like that,' she said. 'Believe it or not, I've had worse.'

'Yep, I don't believe that,' Wendy said.

'I was drained, Wendy,' Lucille said. 'Had to do it quick or I couldn't do it at all.'

'You've made your wounds worse.'

'Quick, not clean. Needed to do it while I could. Think of it as another step on my road to atonement. Give me a hand?'

'Sure.'

She looked over to a far wall and Wendy helped her over to it. Lucille was very heavy now, and she did very little to help Wendy in moving her. Once in position she slumped against the wall and smiled.

'This'll do. Lesson two: if you're hurt, you need things to take your mind off of the injury.'

'And you'll get that here?'

'Good view of the whole room. Will be able to see everything you do to try and get us to the Roller. Better than nothing.'

Wendy patted her on the head and moved to a console, setting about finding the Roller on the sensors. 'Does talking help?'

'Sometimes,' Lucille said. 'Great for diagnosis. If someone can't talk, it's usually something bad.'

'So talk then.'

'About what?'

Wendy frowned. 'Anything.'

Lucille was silent for a while. 'This is going to get bad before it gets better.'

'I'm not an expert, but I think that's taken as read with bullet wounds.'

'Not this. This. All of it. The situation. Say we do expose these people, what then? Wars and witch hunts. Both necessary, but it won't be pretty.'

'And leaving them in the dark means more things like the Strider could happen. Even if they think they are doing what is necessary to save lives in the long run, at this rate there won't be anyone left.'

'I know,' Lucille said. 'That's what got me so disillusioned with the cause. But even knowing that, even knowing what I do about all of this, about what needs to be done, I don't have it in me to start a war. To pull that trigger? To be responsible for what comes next?'

'It's a lot to take on,' Wendy said. She let out a humourless laugh. 'But hey, maybe we'll get lucky and people will think we're a pair of crazies. No war. Yay.'

'Most likely outcome,' Lucille said. 'It's not like we're reputable. We weren't even there when it happened.'

Wendy nodded. Everything just had to be complicated, didn't it? Killing a single person was so unconscionable now that people had a hard time believing it when it happened, but a whole city? That would be a hard sell even if she had a reputation upon which to sell it, and she didn't.

She found the Roller on the sensors. A few hours walk it seemed, heading roughly in this direction. Gave her time to work out what she was going to say, if nothing else. Wendy punched in the co-ordinates and settled in for the journey.

Rostrum's device hung heavily in her pocket now. She had forgotten all about it as they made their escape, filed away into the not now part of her mind. But as everything was slowing down it pushed its way back to the front.

She took it out. A small, unassuming black cube with a universal connection on the base. A storage drive for his book, she expected.

Without thinking, she plugged the device into the console. A small green light started to blink in the centre, and she immediately chastised herself for doing something so rash. The damn thing could have been anything! But sure, let's just slot that right into the central computer of the one thing keeping either of them alive right now. Brilliant idea, especially to read some shit book by a dead man.

It wasn't a data drive, which just made her feel worse. It had a small amount of data memory contained inside, but those were drivers designed to ensure compatibility, it seemed. Instead, it was some sort of portable data receiver. A pirate link into the trunk network.

Well, he had said he'd hidden his book on the network. She should have seen this coming.

If you're hurt, you need to find things to take your mind off the injury.

Wendy wasn't physically hurt, not anymore, but she didn't really want to spend the next few hours trying to determine the best way to word all of this either. Or to think about it at all. She wanted to go back to the world she had been in before, where secret factions weren't murdering people and making it look like accidents, where her friends were still alive, and where her relationship with Lucille wasn't so weirdly twisted that she had no idea what was going on anymore.

That life didn't exist now, she knew that. Eyes forward, accept reality and carve a path, all that motivational bullshit. And she'd do her part. She'd live her life and deal with the world as it now was, not how it had been. She wasn't going to shy away from that.

But she had a few hours. A little escapism couldn't hurt.

The book – such as it was – wasn't hard to find. There were only so many places one could conceivably hide something on the fledgling network, and Wendy worked through them quickly. Once she'd found the first two chapters, she had a very good idea of where to find the third, the fourth and so on. Rostrum had wanted it found, so once she had the pattern down, accessing the chapters was easy.

Easier than reading them.

They were written with love and excitement, but not skill. Each was better than the last in terms of the craft, but she only managed to read two or three before she found herself skipping ahead randomly. She would read them all, she promised a dying man that much, but she just had to know how many chapters there were to read.

After a couple of overshoots, she found it, the final chapter as written, on the final node she and her crew had spiked. A nice bit of serendipity there.

This one was a departure – two chapters on one node. Weird to break his pattern now, of all times. It was enough of a curiosity that she couldn't help but open it. Skipping to the end of the story was the same as reading the whole thing, right?

Her brow furrowed as she read the first line, then she grinned and turned towards Lucille. 'Do you know when the last proper war was?'

'Over a century ago I think,' she replied sleepily. 'Maybe two. Why?'

'What started it?'

'I don't know. Mining rights? Why all the questions?'

'Was it worth it?'

'I don't know. I'm not a historian.'

'I hope it was.'

'Why?'

Wendy sighed and looked back at the screen. 'Because I'm pretty sure we are going to start a war.'

She read the words again, a third time, to make sure she had them right. She did.

My name is Vandal Morley, accredited clandestine agent of The Crawler, making this statement without coercion or duress.

The following is a detailed report of what happened to the Strider...

ABOUT THE AUTHOR

You're nosy, why do you want to know things about the author? He writes books, like this one, on a computer that overlooks a garden. It's nice – he can see a tree.

He lives with one, sometimes two, cats and from time to time family move in and get in the way.

Also, for what it's worth, he's very much in love with you because you actually took the time to read the book. Unless you didn't, and you just skipped to the end. If that is why you're on this page, well, tsk tsk.

Anyway, if you want to know more you can find the author knocking about on twitter **@stevetheblack** or on his website **stevekpeacock.com**

Go on, that's your lot.

Nosy.

MORE BOOKS BY STEVE K. PEACOCK

Diplomancer

Lore and Order (Book 1 of the Warlocks of Whitehall Series)

Ghosts on the Wind

Printed in Great Britain
by Amazon